ONE TOO MANY

USA TODAY BESTSELLING AUTHOR
JADE WEST

One Too Many

Copyright © 2018 Jade West

The moral rights of the author have been asserted.

All rights reserved. No part of this publication may be reproduced, distributed, or transmitted in any form or by any means, including photocopying, recording, or other electronic or mechanical methods, without the prior written permission of the publisher, except in the case of brief quotations embodied in critical reviews and certain other non-commercial uses permitted by copyright law. For permission requests, write to the publisher, addressed "Attention: Permissions Coordinator," at the email address below.

Cover design by Letitia Hasser of RBA Designs | www.designs.romanticbookaffairs.com
Edited by John Hudspith | www.johnhudspith.co.uk
Book design by Inkstain Design Studio
All enquiries to jadewestauthor@gmail.com

First published 2018

To Letitia. You are amazing.
Thank you not just for the cover, which I love.
But for the title and the seed of an idea it brought me, too.
I'm glad we've worked together on so many.
There'll never come a time when you've designed me One Too Many.
See what I did there? Yes it was cringe, but still. I love you.
You are an incredible talent, and it's an honour to work with you.

ONE

TOO

MANY

ONE

BRETT

It was one of those strange, outlandish moments that stick with you for a lifetime. A hyper awareness as I looked across at my wife and saw the cold, hard damage our failing hotel venture was doing to the woman I loved.

Our bar was almost empty that evening and so were our glasses, clinked with a token *happy anniversary* amidst the stress of another final demand letter in our to-pay pile. Our handful of residents had left with nods and smiles, all of them none the wiser as they thanked us for a *lovely* evening and headed upstairs, and my Grace had smiled right back at them, only not with her eyes.

She's never been a good liar, I'd just chosen not to see it that winter. Chosen not to hear the sadness in the silence in bed at night. Chosen not to feel the exhaustion in her sigh as the alarm went off every morning.

In that one strange moment on the evening of our tenth anniversary, I saw everything.

Her dark hair was curled at the bottom and sprung up from the nape of her neck, maybe for my benefit, even though I hadn't noticed, not that day. Her dress was a ruched, tight, navy blue, her knees crossed tightly on the barstool. Her eyes were smoky, lips darkened just a touch from their natural rosy-beige — as she liked to refer to it.

While the makeup would be good enough for the casual observer, it didn't hide the truth from me.

It didn't hide the tension in her jawline, or the way her eyelashes fluttered downcast. It didn't hide the way her fingers tapped the stem of her glass, or the swish of her foot below.

Her pale throat looked choked and vulnerable. Her shoulders braced against an invisible weight, elbows angled like spiked cordons on the bar top, protecting her heart.

My wife was a beautiful woman, but the moment her misery hit me with full unspoken force was the ugliest moment of my life.

I felt it in my gut. My spleen. My spine.

Anger, and guilt, and resentment. Disillusion.

Grief.

All of it.

Apathy and fervour competed for my soul as I swigged back the last of my wine.

I placed my empty glass on the bar top and leaned across just a touch, but it was enough. Enough that she flinched away from me, as though the tiny gesture of closeness would be enough to topple her.

"I can't believe this is happening to us," my wife told me, and her voice was barely more than a breath.

I gritted my teeth, not at her, but at myself, cursing the promise of the dream that had brought us grinning like fools to the back end of the Welsh coast for this *great new life*.

An easy life. A happy life. A meaningful life running a venue all of our own with the waves crashing out front and gulls cawing overhead. Without suits and bustling city commutes and corporate meeting rooms.

A place for sunset walks hand in hand along the coastal track, and laughter through the evenings with travellers from all over. *Paying* travellers.

A place for a couple of dogs maybe. A couple of kids, too, just as soon as our new life was worn in nice and steady.

Only nice and steady never found us.

It was only a whispered rumour that saw the previous Cliff House B&B owners sell up quick sharp and cite a craving for pastures new, but it didn't reach our ears until it was far too late. There was no hint of the budget hotel chain taking over one of the rambling spa resorts two miles down the road and pricing us clean out of business when we signed the contracts last spring and moved on in, but it didn't take long for word to sweep through the village and up to our door.

So, there we were on our tenth anniversary. Sipping cheap house red at the hotel bar, shackled to the property which had taken every scrap of the inheritance from my father and then some. We were mortgaged up to the hilt. In debt up to our eyeballs. Credit cards maxed out on Grace's expensive decor choices, but now wasn't the time for that.

She hadn't known.

We hadn't known.

"It'll be alright," I hiss-whispered, despising how gruff my voice sounded in the quiet. "We'll offer a discount on rooms, spring break with breakfast included. Take some more pictures of the front when the sea's up high. The bookings will come with the weather."

She was shaking her head before I was even finished, fingers to her temples as if my words were too much to bear.

"It opens in March, Brett. *March.*" She gestured to the emptiness behind her, the cleared tables so neat and orderly. *Vacant.* "We're fucked *now*, we'll be well and truly screwed when fifty budget rooms open a mile down the fucking road and you know it. You know it just as well as I do."

Her eyes spat fear and fury, but were only ignited for a heartbeat before she slumped back down on her stool.

"What, then?" I asked her. "We sell up and head back to Bristol with our tails between our legs? Like anyone's gonna buy this fucking place. Want to skulk back on the event hosting circuit, do you? I sure as hell don't want to go back to fucking recruitment. I'd rather stay down here and take a fucking bar job at the poxy new piece of shit hotel down the road."

I towelled down the side to illustrate, well aware that she was staring at my pitted brow as I scrubbed at an imaginary stain.

"We won't get through the month," she whispered. "Not even if we lose Elaine and do the laundry ourselves. I called the bank myself earlier, when you were doing the barrels, and they said…" Her voice trailed off and she took a breath, shunting her glass over for a refill.

I grabbed a fresh bottle of the cheap stuff from the rack. Like one paltry bottle was gonna make a difference to our finances.

"The bank said what?"

"They said we're fucked," she told me in a sing song voice that grated down my spine.

My fingers looked so big against hers as I handed her glass over. Hers were shaking as she took it, gripping tight to raise it to her lips and swig back a decent mouthful.

It was one of the things I always loved about Grace — her being so slender and delicate. Fragile and feminine and gorgeous enough to hitch my breath, even after all these years. She'd always made me feel so big. So strong. Such a protector.

Such a man.

But not anymore. Not for a while now.

I watched her swallow her drink down through the eyes of a man looking at a woman afresh.

Grace still looked like the girl I married in every way that meant something, even though she'd turned thirty a few months previous. Even through her misery, her lips beckoned mine and promised to fit just fine for kisses. Her cheekbones were high and pixie-like, her brows shaped with the same high arches and downward flicks. Her cleavage was pinched tight in the swathes of pretty fabric, hinting deliciously at the perky pair underneath.

I tried to recall when I'd last fucked her like I meant it. One month? Two? Three?

Five at least.

It had been five whole months since I'd fucked my wife like I really meant it.

I wasn't thinking lights-out-missionary after a few drinks when the bar had done for the night, or the cheeky number we'd done before breakfast in the shower when we were cutting it fine to get the tables downstairs laid out a few weeks back. I was thinking nights like we'd had in the city. Nights where there was only her body and mine, insatiable and needy. Craving skin on skin and sweat and whimpers. Seeking out heat and depth and the slam of flesh against flesh.

And now nothing. Just tiredness. Aches and gruelling days begging the bookings to chime through from the online booking system. A simmering of nerves below the surface every time we totalled up the profit and loss for the months just gone.

"What?" she asked me, her eyes narrow on mine. "What are you thinking?"

I couldn't tell her.

There's no way I could switch up the desolate mood by explaining my search for happier times. Hornier times.

I couldn't share my last memory of fucking her the way she deserved it, right there on that spot. Her back arching against the beer pumps as I slammed her in our brand new venue last spring. She'd laughed and screamed and begged for more. Told me this was *ours, all fucking ours, forever.*

Forever.

So many promises of forever seem to fall flat on their faces. Ours was one I couldn't face, not just the hotel, but *us*. We were bleeding down the drain with the capital investment, years of love and life dripping away with our failing dreams.

"We'll make it," I said out loud, not completely sure it was for her benefit more than mine. "We'll get through this month and we'll pick it up. We'll fucking pick it up, Grace, even if I have to grab the assholes from the beach and drag them in here myself." I felt the tick behind my eyes, full of desperation to relieve hers. "I'll borrow the money from that seedy lender in Tenby. The one who charges gross high interest. And if not him, I'll find someone, I'll find *anyone*. Fuck the fucking bank, we won't need them. We'll find someone else."

"Who else?!" she seethed. "Credit cards, bank loans, a few grand from my sister… who else is going to pitch into this sad mess, Brett?" Her eyes pierced mine, dark and wild. "No lender worth shit is going to bail us out of this. Not a single fucking one."

She was right.

I hated how right she was.

Hated the beautiful place we'd carved our dreams around, only to watch them rot and fester. Hated how the strain of this place was straining us, straining everything we'd ever stood for.

In that heartbeat I wondered if we were too late already. If the rot had worked its way too deep inside and we were all but fucked and done. If the rings on our fingers were circling nothing but the empty hope that we'd hold on tight for all time.

Did she still love me?

Were we really so fucked up that I needed to ask the question?

It was on my tongue even then as she shook her head and braced her palm flat on the bar top. Her wedding band was right there for the viewing as if answering my fears, its perfect circle still sitting snug where it belonged. At least for now.

"We need a way out of this," she whispered, and those fingers reached out for mine. "We can't carry on like this, Brett. It's killing us."

"I'll find a way out," I promised, even though I had no fucking clue where I'd go looking. No idea where we'd find the thousands we needed to make it through the imminent final demand pile, let alone set us up to make it through to the spring trade.

"Where?" she asked. "Who is ever going to give us a way out of this shit? What have we even got to offer besides a business that's draining us dead?"

And that's when he cleared his throat, the figure stepping up to the bar.

The figure I hadn't noticed in the room with us, and barely remembered serving the whisky to earlier.

The figure who'd clearly heard every word we'd said and still opted to venture closer.

That either made him an asshole or an alcoholic, and I knew which my money was on given that I'd served him three times that evening tops.

My wife's face drained to pale as I felt my own embarrassment flare, but his smile wasn't one of pity or apology, not even of sympathy at eavesdropped troubles.

He was confident, reeking of pride, shoulders tall and straight as he took a seat a few down from my wife like he owned the place and us along with it.

Yep, an asshole, and a slick one at that. Suited and styled like one of those rich city dicks, with geek-chic glasses which didn't hide his rugged jaw and his perfect features.

The guy knew he was a handsome bastard, and his smirk told me he knew I knew it too. And so did my wife.

My whole body despised him even before he'd said a word.

His gesture was strong and easy as he put down his empty glass and looked from Grace to me and back again.

I felt a twist deep in my gut when I saw the way his eyes fixed on hers.

"I've got a proposition for you," he said, and his eyes moved right across to mine.

TWO

GRACE

I'd been the one to check him into the best room in our hotel this morning — Mr Thomas Heath from some swanky address in North London — the man who sat himself down at our bar like he knew our whole life story and then some.

Brett was scowling and *sure*, I felt it too — exposed and embarrassed and mortified all at once. But, unlike my husband, I engaged my common sense and struggled on regardless to beam out a polite hostess smile.

I could've strangled Brett and the way his pride stood off our guest without so much as a move to offer him a refill, but the guy wasn't asking, only staring. Right at me.

My cheeks flushed as his eyes dug into mine. They were green flecked with hazel, just like my own, only a whole world more self-assured. They held for too long to be comfortable, but I didn't shift or break the contact.

I couldn't.

The guy was a paying customer, even if he had somehow managed to keep himself elusive enough to overhear a private conversation in a dead bar between two people who were far from at their best in life.

I didn't get it, where he'd appeared so quietly from. I'd wiped down the tables myself after the last small group finished up earlier, and the room had been empty. *Seemed* empty.

My skin prickled with more than a little suspicion this wasn't a chance appearance, which only made the humiliation worse.

"Bar's closed," Brett grunted as the stare simmered, ignoring whatever *proposition* we were about to be presented with.

I could've definitely strangled him then.

"Would you like another whisky?" I asked our guest, caring fuck-all for the way my contradiction undermined my bristling husband and his bruised pride.

We were desperate for every solid five-star review and recommendation we could get right now. Pride had no place here, not this season. Maybe never again.

Thomas Heath from North London gave me a smile that made his eyes sparkle behind his glasses. There was amusement there, and it smarted hard. A fresh bout of humiliation slammed me in the heart, but I kept my chin high and shoulders firm.

Fuck my husband's pride, but fuck this guy too.

Fuck him and the tailored shirt he was wearing on a Saturday night in a seaside bar. Fuck the heavy gold watch on his wrist that probably cost more than a whole year's salary for most of the population.

Fuck his judgy smirk, and his laughing eyes, and the way he thought he knew our business.

"Sure, why not, I'll take another," he answered in a beat, and his voice was clipped and curt, dripping with posh-boy school.

The amusement was still bright on his face as he moved his stare across to Brett.

I felt like an absolute shit when my husband bended to instruction, reaching up to grab a fresh shot from the optics. My heart dropped like a rock at the state of us.

It would never have happened in Bristol, Brett bowing so willingly to such a bitchy counteraction, not in a million years. I barely recognised the man whose desperation made him this compliant, even at my request.

His broad shoulders seemed stooped even though he was holding them firm, his frame smaller than I'd ever seen him, even though he was still easily big enough to make me feel tiny in his shadow. His dark brows looked beat and the dark eyes under them looked like they belonged to someone on their knees.

Someone I didn't know.

This wasn't the man I married. Wasn't the man who'd been so strong at my side before we boxed up our life and moved from city to seaside for ventures new.

Wasn't the man I fell in love with all those years ago, back in high school.

I had to hold back a hitch of breath as I realised I was hardly the woman he fell in love with either.

Thomas Heath took the whisky from Brett's outstretched hand and gestured a wordless *cheers* before taking a sip.

I wondered if he'd overheard our anniversary toast earlier. If he knew we were supposed to be celebrating a decade of married life together, even if these days were turning out to be a damn sight shittier than hoped. If he even cared a single toss for us and our troubles or simply wanted a nightcap.

My question was answered without delay.

"I heard you're in the shit," he remarked, and I wished the ground would open up. "I get it. Times are hard. Money's tight. Bigger hotel down the coast about to fuck you over."

"We'll be just fine," Brett grunted, but our guest laughed out loud.

I don't think I could have blamed my husband if he'd smashed the whisky glass over the asshole's head, but the grit of his jaw was his only immediate sign of aggression.

"How long do you think you can keep hold of this place?" our guest asked, and I cleared my throat loudly before Brett had the chance to answer.

"We'll keep it," I assured in a tone that sounded unusually blunt.

He pointed a finger in my direction as if he was acknowledging a joke, and in that moment I hated him easily as much as Brett did.

"One month," he said. "I bet you'll last a month tops."

"How much do you wanna fucking bet?" Brett shot back, and finally the gruff in his voice was at least a little bit familiar.

Thomas Heath took another sip of whisky as Brett leaned back against the beer fridge and folded his arms tight across his chest. His shirt strained with the tension in his biceps.

The two men were chalk and cheese. Brett was dark and broad where Thomas Heath was a dark dirty blonde and toned but lean. Brett was rugged where Thomas Heath was preened to perfection. His suit, his shirt, the neatness of his finely trimmed beard.

Two very attractive men from very different spheres. Both toned and ripped enough to present a fine specimen of male power, just in very different flavours.

I hoped I wouldn't watch their differences pitted against each other first-hand.

The thought gave me an edgy shudder tinged with something too intimate to be embraced. It must be the wine.

The wine and far too long without a decent fucking.

I hated myself for even noticing my own seedy reaction.

"Ten grand," our guest said without even flinching. "I'll give you ten grand quite happily. Only it's not for a bet. That's not quite what I had in mind."

It was my turn to laugh, but Brett didn't laugh along with me.

"Ten grand for a non-bet?" I asked. "I didn't think you'd had that many whiskies. Maybe it's time you got some sleep."

I was laughing on my own and it dried up in a heartbeat when I caught the fierceness of the stare between the two men in front of me.

I was missing something. Something unspoken. It made my belly flip and lurch.

"What do you mean?" I asked. "What's even going on here?"

Brett grabbed the towel back up and carried on wiping the bar. "Bar's fucking closed," he grunted again. "Drink up, pal. Enjoy the rest of your fucking stay and don't come back."

I didn't contradict his rudeness this time, but our guest made no move whatsoever to finish up his drink.

"Ten grand," he repeated. "Straight into your account."

"You heard me, fuck off," Brett barked, and I felt it again, that belly flip.

"What for?" I asked, feeling like a dumb idiot but unable to hold back the question.

I couldn't believe he'd give us 10k. The thought was insane. Ridiculous.

Surely he was joking? Surely? But he didn't look like he was joking, which begged the question all over again, even as Brett's jaw gritted tighter and the posh guy's eyes landed back on mine.

"What for?" I said again. "You want to buy something? From us?" I paused. "What the hell have we got here worth ten grand to you?"

And there it was, the thing that Brett must have been bristling over. I felt it even as the words left my mouth.

I saw them often, the looks men gave me at the bar after a few beers. The way their eyes scoped me up and down like a piece of meat they wanted to shunt their dick into. I barely gave it a thought other than flashing them a happy smile with the hope they'd spend more at the bar and book to come again.

Even so, despite all the stares and the nods and the over easy eyes on my ass every time I turned around, I hadn't been feeling all that desirable of late, not with this stressy shit hanging over our heads every single day.

I'd even had to talk myself round to dressing up and making the effort for our anniversary since Brett barely noticed me these past few months. I doubted he'd even observed I'd curled my hair the way he used to like, or picked out the dress he told me looked great on me at a friend's party last spring.

I doubted my husband noticed anything about me these days, especially not how I wriggled for his touch in the middle of long nights when I was lonely. I doubted he'd noticed how I picked my smokiest eye shadow out this evening so he couldn't see how I'd been crying over final demand letters.

I doubted he'd fuck me tonight, ten year anniversary and smoky eyes or not, not given the amount of crap picking at our bones under the surface.

But this other guy would.

His eyes were hungry and made my legs quiver even crossed. His smile was filthy and made me flutter inside. Deep. Places I most definitely shouldn't, especially not with my husband about ready to fly across the bar and smash his face in.

I shouldn't want it, and I didn't. *Mainly.*

I was in love with my husband, just like always. *He* was the man I wanted to grab me and hold me tight this evening. *He* was the one whose touch I craved.

So why did Thomas Heath's filthy gaze make me shudder and prickle?

I was no cheat. Not even in my head. Not ever.

And maybe I was wrong anyway. Maybe Thomas Heath didn't want a thing from me.

I'd barely even collected my thoughts when he spoke again.

It was Brett he spoke to, with a confidence that made my cheeks burn.

"Ten grand for one night with your wife," he said, and I felt my mouth drop open.

"What the—" Brett began, but the man's words carried on right over him.

"Ten grand for a night with your pretty wife. I'll fuck her until I'm done, nothing too crazy, just a good hard fucking until I've had my fill."

Brett's fist pounded the bar top so hard I jumped and shrieked. His fingers jabbed toward the other man's face and his grimace was like nothing I'd ever seen from him in my life.

Maybe my husband still had more fire in him than I'd given him credit for.

"You'd better fuck off before I lose my fucking shit," Brett boomed, and I got to my feet, gesturing the guy away before this really did spill over into two guys fist-fighting in our lobby.

Thomas Heath rose to standing slowly. Really slowly. His hands were up in some kind of half-assed apology as he took a step away.

"Think on it," he offered and I cursed under my breath. "Ten grand for one night, I'll be gone in the morning and you'll be a whole lot richer for your time."

"Fuck you!" Brett thundered and I closed my eyes against the craziness of all this.

I was grateful for the hulk of the bar between them, even as Brett threw himself towards the hatch.

I looked into our guest's face while Brett wrestled with the catch, and he was serious.

Oh my fucking God, he was serious.

"Nothing too fucked up," our guest told me. "Maybe you'll even enjoy it."

I couldn't swallow the weird lump in my throat at the thought.

And that's when my husband crashed on through to our side of the bar.

Brett shoved the guy backward with enough force that he stumbled, but Thomas Heath really was toned under that suit, because he didn't even come close to falling down.

"Ten fucking grand," he repeated, and I wondered if he had a death wish. "Don't be a a fool, man. Think what you could do with ten grand."

I was already thinking, even if Brett wasn't, even though it was utterly insane. Ten grand was enough to lessen our *pay now* pile and bring us back to some semblance of breathing space. Enough to help us through this godawful fucking month and then some.

Enough for us to try to hoist ourselves up from the floor.

"Brett," I said, and my husband's eyes were filled with terrible hurt and rage when they focused on mine.

He knew.

I hated how he knew I was thinking about the money. I just hoped he knew I was thinking about us. About *him*.

"No fucking way," he told me. "There's no way in a million fucking years I'd send you upstairs with this seedy fucking prick, not even for ten million fucking grand. Not ever."

The man with the suit and watch and ten grand to spend on some other man's wife didn't seem fazed. He didn't even flinch.

His smirk was still there as he took his room key from his inside pocket and gestured upstairs.

"You wouldn't have to send her up to me," he said. "Part of the proposition is that you come with her to watch. Non-negotiable."

How the guy ever made it out of that room in one piece I'll never know.

I was latched onto Brett's flailing arm and screeching *no* as he went for him, digging my heels into the carpet as he dragged me along to chase the other man down.

Ten grand we could do with, one of us serving time for assault, we could not.

"Leave it!" I yelled, hoping Brett still had some tiny scrap of restraint in his raging skull.

Thomas Heath from North London looked back at us from the doorway once I'd managed to get my flailing husband under some semblance of control.

Before making his way upstairs his words were clear and calm enough to reach us both.

"Let me make this easier for you," he said, "twenty grand. You know which room I'm in."

I felt the heat from Brett. Felt the heat from myself. Felt the adrenaline filling the air.

"Wait!" I said as Thomas Heath made for the stairs.

He turned to look at me, a satisfied smile on his face that I could have happily punched. I swallowed the hot lump of trepidation in my throat. "Thirty," I told him. "Thirty grand."

THREE

BRETT

I couldn't explain the heavy beating of my heart. I couldn't explain the surreal sense of pride I felt for Grace right then. Couldn't explain the strange heat in my balls as Thomas Heath took a step forward.

"No," I said, quite fucking simply.

"No?" He cocked his head at me.

The words stung my throat even as I coughed them up and out at him.

"Fifty grand. Fifty grand and I watch your every fucking move."

My wife's eyes were saucers, mouth open wide. For a horror-filled moment I wondered if my complicity to this fucked-up proposition was a stab in a very wrong direction, but her clutch on my arm stayed tight. I was staring right at her when the asshole's reply came.

"You want fifty grand for one single night with your pretty wife?" His face was bursting with the kind of amusement I could quite happily pound off with my fist. "That's quite an advertisement to how much you think I'll enjoy it. Unless you're trying to cheat me out of good money, that is."

Grace's fingers dug in so tight I felt her nails pinch through my shirt.

"You'll enjoy it," I grunted. "Fifty grand or go fuck yourself."

I could feel Grace's shallow breaths tickling above my collar, cool against my burning skin. I was barely breathing myself, eyes locked on the sonofabitch who'd slammed into our anniversary like a typhoon on the rocks, raining gold and shit in equal measure.

He had money, of that I was sure. Who the fuck knew from where, seeing as he looked younger than me by a couple of years. Inheritance from some crazy London trust fund, maybe. A rich lover somewhere, laying back on some plush chaise longue while he played obscene games for a seedy thrill.

Who really cared? Fifty grand was fifty grand, and in the scheme of things one night was one night. We'd pick up the pieces after, buy all the therapy a couple could need and then some.

I wish my gut didn't twist quite so bad at the thought.

His eyes were as sharp as his tongue as they checked me out, trying my already stretched patience. He was weighing me up along with Grace, and his scrutiny panged deep.

I wondered what he thought of me, man to man, offering up my beautiful wife for his sordid thrill. I wondered if he'd already long assigned me a loser status on hearing the heap of shit we'd found ourselves in.

Maybe it was only me who'd assigned myself the loser status. Maybe he was just an opportunist looking to get his dick wet inside someone who clearly didn't belong to him.

Grace would never belong to him.

"Fifty grand it is," he said finally, and I wasn't sure whether it was regret or relief or pure fucking terror that pulsed up my spine. "The scenario on offer will need some amendments, of course," he added.

"Go on," Grace said, before I had the chance.

He took a step forward, so cocksure with his swagger that my fists clenched on instinct.

"I'll have to extend my stay," he began. "Fifty grand demands more than an impromptu post-midnight fuck on a Saturday evening. I'll need to make preparations, enjoy the ambience of the place a little more fully before I… *indulge*."

"Preparations?" I challenged.

"Higher investment means a more *adventurous* experience, as I'm sure you'll appreciate."

I was about to say fuck off all over again, but Grace jumped right in.

"*Adventure* is fine," she told him. "Fifty grand gets you whatever you want." She paused as she caught the disgust on my face. "Within reason," she added too late.

Hell only knew what filthy shit was whirring through her head.

"Within reason," he repeated. "Here's how it's going to roll. I'll extend my stay until mid-week. You'll close the bar early on Tuesday and our evening will begin at nine p.m. sharp. You will be mine until sunrise. Fifty percent cash transferred up front, fifty percent on completion."

"And if we call time out?" I interrupted. "Besides smashing your fucking skull in if things turn sour, I mean."

He cracked a smile, but I didn't. "If you call time out before I've reached my first climax, the agreement is null and void. Past that point the fifty percent rule applies until sunrise. I can draw up a written contract if you'd prefer?"

I didn't need to answer that. Like fuck an agreement like this one would ever stand up in court, and like fuck we'd ever face the flames of public humiliation by taking it that far.

It was Grace who nodded her head to seal the deal. A simple gesture. Quiet but firm.

Honest.

It seared my fucking gut, the whole sorry fucking lot of it.

"Fifty grand," she confirmed, and I wondered if she was really buying into this crazy shit. "Bar closes at ten on a Tuesday, breakfast starts at seven. That's your full night, take it or leave it."

Nine hours.

With any luck he'd last nine fucking minutes and call off the rest himself.

Even nine minutes fucking my beautiful wife would be fuel enough for me to rip his spine out and not feel a scrap of remorse.

But the cash.

So much fucking cash.

Everyone has a price. *Everyone.* Ours was fifty fucking grand and a life without fearing the postman every bastard morning.

He knew it. Of course he knew it.

The smirk on his perfectly smug mouth told me he was no stranger to this kind of bartering.

"Done," the piece of shit said. "We'll need to iron out more of the detail, but I think a clear head will be considerably better for the fine print. No need to shake on it, I'll see you at breakfast." A pause. "Sleep well now. Sweet dreams, I hope."

He could laugh at us all he wanted. We'd be the ones fucking laughing when the prick was long gone and we had fifty grand in our bank account.

If.

If we had fifty grand in our account.

But somehow I knew the sonofabitch was telling the truth. Somehow I knew he'd walk this path as far as we'd follow.

Somehow I knew he was asshole enough to push through with whatever shitty offer he slapped on the table.

And we'd take it.

Desperate.

Pathetic.

Broke *and* broken.

I didn't watch him turn and head upstairs, but Grace did. She watched him all the way, fingers still so tight on my arm they'd likely leave bruises. I waited for her to speak, even as her eyes stared into the blank space he'd left behind.

"He's bluffing, right?" she asked when she was sure he was gone. "I mean it's fifty grand… that kind of money is crazy… it's…"

Her words may have stuttered, but her tone was flat and solid. She didn't believe he was bluffing any more than I did.

"And if he's not?" I said, not missing the sharp breath she drew as the thought slammed in hard.

"And if he's not, I guess we…" Her grip dropped away and she turned back to the bar. "I need another wine."

So did I.

I needed a whole fucking cellar full.

GRACE

Fifty thousand pounds.

Enough to pay every single creditor in our backlog and give us a few months' breathing space. And with enough left over to add some additional hotel features, just to set us apart a little from the bargain basement opening down the road.

A hot tub. A better bar maybe. Complimentary bathrobes and slippers.

Just about anything to add to our online listings would be a plus.

Brett poured a fresh round of drinks with a face like death. I'd seen plenty of foul expressions on his face these past few months. A grimace every morning at the mailbox, a gritted jaw as he totted up the takings of a lacklustre Saturday night. The way he stared at the ceiling in the darkness and I'd pretend I didn't notice.

I always noticed.

"We don't have to…" I began, but he shook his head.

"*You* don't have to, Grace. It's your call. You tell me you don't want to go near that seedy prick and I'll have him out of this place before morning, money be fucked."

I couldn't hold back the grit of my own jaw as I reached for my wine. This was it. Exactly this. One of the real damn problems between us these days.

It wasn't that his intentions weren't good and well meaning, or that he was taking even a single liberty and trying to push me into some shitty thing I didn't want to do.

It was the opposite. Always the opposite.

My call. Always my call. Hands off while I stewed over the decisions, and then the mistakes that followed.

Egyptian cotton bedding? Heavyweight curtains with blackout backing? Hand carved dining furniture?

Always my call.

This venue? Definitely this one? We're really cut out to up-end from our jobs and move out here into the back of beyond?

Your call, Grace. Whatever you want.

I knew he resented me for it, late at night with a churning gut, just like mine. I knew he blamed me for overspending and dashing us headlong into this whole new start, swirling him along in the whirlpool of my enthusiasm.

And that was the worry right then and there, right at the heart of it. Not that I'd fuck some posh asshole from London and maybe he'd get a little rough and dirty. Not that I'd be nervous as all living shit and terrified of taking another man while the one I'd pledged my life to stood and watched every seedy second of it. Not even that the guy would fuck us over and leave us up shit creek, one dirty fuck cheaper and without any more of a financial cushion than the bones of our ass we were currently sitting on.

The real worry squirmed in my gut like maggots on roadkill.

My call.

My fuck-up.

My mistake to hold against me for all time to come.

My choice to whore myself out to a random hotel guest who flashed the cash.

"What are you thinking?" he asked me, and I realised I'd been swirling my drink by the stem, my teeth still gritted tight.

Maybe I should've told him the truth. Slapped my fears right out there on the bar top and granted them life. But I didn't.

As per usual, I buried them for the sake of keeping the peace and making it through this crap without clawing at open wounds.

"I don't know," I lied. "I guess I'm wondering if he'll keep to his word."

Brett shrugged and took a long swig of red. "If he doesn't, he doesn't. We're in the same boat we were an hour ago."

"And if he does…"

Another shrug and I wanted to shake him. Shake him for a reaction, for an outburst, for his inner caveman to come out grunting and flailing and demanding that no other man would ever lay a filthy hand on me, hotel and money and our future be damned.

What I got instead was the gaze of a man who'd always wanted to do the best for me. A man who'd been there for me since I was still a slip of a girl with arms open wide.

"You don't have to do anything," he said again.

"And if I do?"

His eyes didn't falter, not for a second. "And if you do, I'll be right there. We'll work it out, together. Work through it, together."

"And afterwards? Nine hours is one thing, we've got a whole lifetime to cope with any jealousy shit."

He raised his lip in a smirk. "You think I can't cope with jealousy shit? Like I'm some kind of caveman warrior who'll never recover from one shitty meaningless night?"

Part of me wished he really was a man that could shrug this off as nothing. The other part worried he'd surprise himself in the aftermath when the horse had long bolted.

My heart was pounding and my throat was dry, even after another gulp of wine. My head was reeling and spinning and trying to work out how this insanity was going to pan out for the pair of us.

My voice came out much softer than I wanted it to, quaking a little around the edges. "We need this, Brett. The money."

Dreams I'd been terrified were withering away before our eyes jolted and gasped with a hint of life again. The beautiful building we'd longed to raise a family in. The promise of sunset on the waves. Everything.

I felt it all.

And I knew then I'd do anything to keep our dreams breathing, even for just a little bit longer.

Even if that *anything* was a tall, posh stranger as my husband looked on.

"Do you..." Brett began, and I had to hold his gaze to prompt him onward. "Do you... you know... *like* him?"

"*Like* him?"

His smile was nothing but thin bravado. "I mean, he's a good-looking guy, right? It could be worse."

My response was instant. "And I'm a married woman. There are plenty of good-looking guys out there. I don't *like* any of them. I *like* you."

Finally, my husband reached across the gulf of bar space and took my hand in his. I felt the strength in it. The solidarity in our shit pile as his fingers squeezed mine.

"Well, Mrs Foster, it's fair to say I *like* you too."

For the first time in months I saw the man I fell in love with. The warmth in his rich brown eyes, the roguish shadow on his jaw. The breadth of his shoulders, strong enough to carry a thousand fears.

And past those things to the beautiful imperfections I knew by heart.

The tiny ridge on his nose from a college football collision. The faint scar above his left brow from a biking accident after school.

The way one of his lower teeth stuck out just a fraction from the others, making him a little rough around the edges.

He was perfect.

Gorgeous.

Mine.

"It's just one night," I whispered. "What harm can one stupid little night do, hey?"

"And I'll be right there," he replied. "No matter what. All the way."

And he would be. Quite literally.

I dismissed the tiny little quiver between my legs as down to the wine.

FOUR

THOMAS

They didn't recognise me. Not even a cock of an eyebrow or a simple stare as they tried to place my face.

It shouldn't have surprised me. I barely recognised myself from the boy I was all those years ago.

I did, however, recognise them. My memory was true to the finest detail.

Grace's high cheekbones and pixie smile. The sparkle in her eyes as she raised one of her fine arched eyebrows, even tight-lipped and suspicious as I made my presence felt at the bar. Her voice, sultry yet sweet, all at once. The gentle slope of her hips under the tight wrap of fabric as she leaned back on her stool.

Nothing had changed on that front. Not about her.

And not about him, either.

The arrogance in Brett's shoulders was still standing strong these days, even if he wasn't. His bullish attitude, the low aggressive grunts as he faced off opposition like he could punch the whole world to the floor without even breaking a sweat.

I remembered him on the sports field, heading up team after team. Winning. Always winning. Bellowing war cries as he held up the team trophy like it gave him a status of a god amongst mere sad mortals. Parading himself through the streets like he owned the whole place and everyone in it. Those who were even worth his acknowledgement.

But he didn't own the world. Not now. The world was a lot bigger these days, and so was I.

My game was strong now. Strong and slick and well prepared.

They'd never see my true intentions coming. Neither of them. Not until it was far too late.

I smiled to myself as I walked straight past my door on the second floor. I took the back stairwell from the building, dropping down into the hotel's rear courtyard and slipping around to the front while the waves crashed loud on the beach below. I could see why they'd been so taken with this spot, such a marvellous little slice of the wilderness. Tranquil, yet wild. Peaceful, yet rugged. Enough of a dream to see them cast upon the rocks of financial ruin. An exposed vein right there for the pricking.

I took a seat on one of the few picnic benches in the beer garden out front, careful not to trigger the motion-sensitive light on the main porch. It was the perfect vantage point to watch the aftermath of my filthy unexpected proposition.

I'd have put another wad of healthy money on the fact they'd need a wine or twenty for the shock to settle down, and so they had. By the time I got out front they'd resumed their stations on opposite sides of the bar, Grace's foot tapping the air once she'd hoisted herself back up on her stool. Brett's expression didn't shift any, not at first. He looked like he'd happily snap my neck as soon as catch sight of me again.

It suited him. That kind of aggression always had.

It seemed funny now, in such close proximity to the guy after all this time. Funny how I'd always wanted to be that kind of man too, just as he was. Strong, brutish, rugged.

I'd been none of those things growing up. My aggression had always been more intellectual, more introverted. Harder to come by. My muscular form was sculpted through blood, sweat and the challenge of not ever being good enough, not through the easy win of blessed genetics.

I'd worked hard to present myself in just the right way, making the most of my limited assets and pushing them to their limits and beyond.

I was slim but toned, through a rigorous schedule at the gym. Groomed and well-kept with the benefit of tailored outfitting to make the most of my assets. My armour and arrogance were driven by money and mind, rather than muscle. Luckily, I had plenty of both.

I'd expected much more of a fight than the one I'd received on Brett and Grace's sweet home turf. I'd expected a punch or two to the mouth before they stewed with needy bellies enough to truly consider my offer. It meant only one thing — the pressure was higher than I'd anticipated.

The price was a bargain in my book.

I'd have gone higher to make it happen. Much higher.

I pulled a cigar from my pocket, being careful to angle the flame of the lighter away from the window as I lit up. It was overly cautious. They were still fully engrossed in conversation as I took my first puff.

I didn't need to hear their words. I could read their sentiments more than easily enough in their body language, tense but hopeful. Grace's hand went to her hair and scratched idly at the nape of her neck, and I wondered how her soft skin would feel against my mouth as I slammed that gorgeous little cunt from behind.

Maybe that's when I'd take a punch or ten to the mouth from the raging bull.

I'd take it gladly, just to see the rage in his eyes as I finally fucked the woman he'd claimed all those years ago.

I'd smirk like a sonofabitch when she wrapped her ringed wedding finger around my dick and worked me hard while her brute of a husband looked on.

I was both disgusted and excited at the thought, my dick hard in my pants as the waves kept on crashing behind me. I couldn't tear my eyes away from the pair of them, not even for a heartbeat as I toked on Cuban cigar excellence, enjoying every single moment of their muted discussion. Brett shrugged his shoulders, once, twice, and Grace pursed her pretty lips, choking back whatever words were on her tongue.

I loved how easy they were to read from this safe distance, without the distraction of language. They were a tight couple, certainly. In love, almost definitely, even up shit creek without a paddle.

Unbreakable. No.

They never were.

I'd fucked over twenty married women in the past three years. Twenty delicious bodies had writhed and squirmed and grunted under mine as their husbands watched on with jealous eyes.

Twenty grand had been the most I'd ever agreed to before this evening, to a couple in London who were about to be evicted from their friend's pad in Canary Wharf. The cheapest I'd ever negotiated was… considerably lower.

I brushed my palm over the swell in my pants as Grace took a swig of wine and shifted in her seat. I wondered if her body was betraying her, even at this early stage. I wondered if the wine made it easier for her belly to flip and lurch at the flattery of fifty grand for one short night with her stark naked body.

I'd seen it over and over. The bloom of pride as they registered how much they were wanted by a stranger, even with a wedding band on their finger.

Sometimes it was about the money, sometimes it was about far less. One woman had been so taken with the prospect of a night in my bed that she'd followed me right out of the bar when her husband had threatened to beat the shit out of me. She'd laid her sweet little body on a platter for free, no payment necessary, for whatever I wanted, and I'd laughed. How I'd fucking laughed.

And then I'd refused, pure and simple. Thanks but no thanks, offer withdrawn.

Her pretty face had been a pretty picture, but not as much of a picture as her husband's when he'd caught her up in the middle of her bargaining.

I heard they'd signed divorce papers less than three months later.

Brett closed the distance between him and his wife, and she took a deep breath before her tapping foot finally stilled. I held the cigar smoke in my mouth as they leant in close, wondering whether this would finally be the time a couple talked themselves down and threw me out of their lives unceremoniously.

But I doubted it.

They always agreed, festered in the aftermath and came calling for more.

Every morning after the event I'd left my business card behind, and every time I'd received the follow up call. Sometimes it took a week. Sometimes a month, or two, or three. But they'd always call me, always. All twenty women with shaky voices as they reminded me of their names and told me how much they'd enjoyed the experience.

Brett took his wife's hand across the bar top and it sparked a weird twitch in my gut. It passed in a beat, quickly, barely obvious, but I grabbed hold of its meaning before it sank out of trace.

It was hope. Something I rarely ever felt these past few years. Stupid, irrational hope that maybe this time they'd prove me wrong.

It was his smile as he stared into his beautiful wife's eyes and leaned in closer still. The tenderness under the rage as they talked about my offer and what it would mean for them, their life, their future. It was in the way she clutched his fingers in hers, the desperation for his strength as she whispered whatever quiet reservations she was feeling into the space between them.

I was considering walking away into the night without even grabbing my suitcase when my phone vibrated in my inside pocket.

Even though it could have been any lonely woman pinging my number at this time on a Saturday evening, I knew who it would be.

I knew it before I'd even turned my back on my pair of latest conquests and thumbed my handset into life.

Don't do it. Not this time.

The words cut me deep, even in the heart of nowhere with my ultimate challenge framed and snared, almost ready to go. My thumbs were like lumps of concrete, my cigar tight between my lips as I tried to form a response to the request on screen.

She'd sent another before I'd even finished typing.

Please, Tom. Hold onto hope. You're nothing without it. Walk away.

It sealed the deal for me.

Tom.

Nobody called me Tom. It was *Thomas*. Thomas fucking Heath. Head of Heath fucking Global and early crypto-currency tycoon.

Mr Thomas Heath. Twenty-nine year old entrepreneur with every scrap of his shit together, living it up in central London, shaking business leaders' hands across the whole fucking world.

And I was done with hope. Hope meant shit to me.

I deleted the words I'd typed out on screen and powered down, cursing under my breath that she was even trying to piss on my parade during a conquest this big.

Grace Anne Whitley, now Grace Anne Foster.

The woman I'd wanted for years.

Beautiful. Playful. Sweet and pretty and tight-lipped and shimmering with temptation.

Everything I'd thought of through long nights as a gawky teenager.

Nothing I could ever have, not even in dreams.

Until now.

In three days' time she'd be mine, in body if not in soul. Soul would come later.

It was an angry smirk on my lips as I shoved the handset back in my pocket and shifted back around to resume my viewing.

What greeted me was nothing I was expecting, a surprise even under the circumstances.

His fists in her soft dark hair, her body tense and tight as he kissed her deep. Hard. Raw.

A man possessed. *Possessive*.

A man claiming what was his. Staking his ownership. Proving whose ring was on her finger, and which man belonged inside that sweet little cunt.

He should make the most of it, because he wouldn't belong there much longer.

FIVE

BRETT

It was the way she looked at me. Nervous but needy.

The way her fingers trembled in mine, even as I held them tight. The way her eyelashes fluttered as she looked up at me across the bar, seeking reassurance, strong words. Strong *everything*.

And it was about more than that. About more than her. About more than the hope of a big, fat payout to see us through our troubles. About more than the most fucked-up ray of light in the darkness of our shitty venture.

It was about him.

That smug asshole Thomas Heath and the way he wanted my fucking wife.

My. Fucking. Wife.

Mine.

Grace was mine. My ring on her finger. My name at the end of hers.

My heart in her hands, for all fucking time.

And *my* fucking cock that belonged in that tight little pussy, for now and for fucking always.

She let out a gasp as I took her pretty curls in my hands and guided my mouth to hers. My lips pressed hard and my tongue pressed harder, hunting hers down before she'd even managed to compose herself. Her hands took a moment to find my arms and squeeze, sliding up to my shoulders and along to my collar where her fingers fizzed and fumbled at buttons.

It had been too long coming.

This.

Us.

The wine glasses went tumbling and wine spilled without care as I tugged her body with mine along the bar top to the hatch at the side.

She'd dipped underneath and into my arms before I'd even sprung the catch, pressing her body tight to mine as I tugged her pretty dress up from the hem.

"We should go to our room," she whispered, but there was no way we were going anywhere.

No lights off. No hiding. No sensibility of love under the covers.

She was mine.

Anytime. Any place. Any-fucking-how.

Not least in our own fucking bar in the middle of the night.

Not least where *he'd* been.

It was unspoken between us, but it was there, loud and clear as our bodies clashed and ground and sought out the familiarity of her curves against my ridges. Her thighs were clammy and her knickers were soaked, and in one vile flash of jealousy I wondered if that was all for me.

"You're wet," I grunted, my eyes on fire as they found hers. My fingers were fierce as they curled inside the lace between her legs and found her wanting.

Her mouth was open as she parted her legs for me, but the flush was there on her cheeks, more guilty than any words could have made her.

I was rough, my thumb balling her clit until she gasped, two fingers plunging deep as she rocked for more.

"I want you," she rasped. "Only you."

She believed her own words, but her body didn't. Her body didn't believe a scrap of it, shuddery and ragged at the thought of another man wanting her enough to throw an obscene amount of cash at her.

Natural.

I told myself it was natural.

But fuck, how I raged in the pit of me.

My grip on her hair was harder than she was used to, her eyes opening wide as I tugged her head back to feast on the pale skin of her throat.

They were barely kisses I planted there, sucking and nipping with a ferocity I hadn't known in years, not since the opposing team wolf-whistled and jeered obscenities at her from the side of the football field back in high school every Wednesday evening. I'd felt it then.

I'd felt it at one of her early work Christmas parties when her letch of a boss ran his hand down her back and landed it on her ass during a load of mindless office chatter.

She shivered as I sucked a mouthful of flesh between my teeth and nipped hard.

"Ow, Brett," she whispered, but her hand hooked behind my neck and held me close, her breaths short and wanting more.

It was primal, this crazy need to mark her all over. I could've bitten my name across her tits and it still wouldn't have been enough.

Her flesh bloomed pink as I pulled away, my lips tingling from the pressure. My dick pulsed as I pulled my fingers from her sopping pussy and forced them into her mouth.

"This better be for me," I grunted as she sucked them clean. She nodded as she slurped, eyes honest and desperate as she hitched against my thigh.

My fingers were wet with her spit as I trailed them down her throat and down further to the tight neckline of her dress.

I heard a tear as I tugged it down to free her tits, caring little for the fabric as I forced it to a gathered ruffle at her hips. She arched her back, trusting my steadying arm to take her weight as she offered herself up to me.

Her nipples were pebbled tight, dusky pink and ripe under the bar lights. I forced her back further still as I took one in my palm and pressed hard, rolling her flesh against her ribs as she whimpered.

"You'll always be mine," I told her.

"Always," she breathed.

"No matter what."

"No matter what," she confirmed.

I flicked my tongue across her nipple and she squirmed like the girl I knew way back when.

Nervous. Desperate.

All for me.

"Fuck me, Brett," she breathed, and my own breath hitched.

Her eyes were dark and hungry, driven by a wildness at odds with the memory of sweet girlish Grace from way back when.

This Grace was all woman. Her body demanded all of mine, and all the years between us.

I'd give it to her gladly. All of it. All of me.

We moved on instinct, her body yielding without question as I spun her in my arms and shunted her forward over the bar top. I pushed her flat, her bare tits tight to the wood as I bunched her dress up around her waist and tore her wet knickers clean off at the hips.

I kicked her legs nice and wide at the ankles, loving how taut her muscles were in heels.

My breath was in my throat as I admired the view of my beautiful wife splayed out for me. I freed my dick and worked it hard in my hand as she waited, wide, wet, and wanting.

The look she shot me over her shoulder was needy enough to tense my balls.

"Fuck me, Brett," she hissed, and I'd stepped up and thrust my cock inside her before she'd even grabbed a breath.

Her moan was frayed and mine was deep. I slammed hard. Deep. Brutal enough that her whole body thumped against the bar.

"Happy anniversary, darling," I groaned, and she pushed right back at me, wanting rough on top of rough.

"I've missed this so much," she whimpered, and I knew it. I'd missed it too.

"Every night," I promised. "I'll fuck you every fucking night until you beg me to stop."

She shook her head hard enough that her curls rippled against her bare shoulders. "Never. I'll never beg you to stop. I'll never get enough."

And then I said it.

"When he fucks you, you'll be thinking of *me*. Wanting *me*."

Her intake of breath was sharp and loud. Her pussy clenched tight enough around my dick that I almost shot my load right then and there.

"It's only you I want," she hissed.

"You're mine," I said, loud in the quiet of the room. "You'll always be mine. Only mine."

"Yours," she moaned. "I'm yours."

I spread her ass cheeks wide and my hands looked so big against her tiny curves. I soaked in the sight of my dick buried to the hilt in that gorgeous cunt of hers, craving more depth than in any way fucking rational. I wanted to be all the way inside her. Filling her up more than she'd ever known.

I spat on my thumb before I sank it deep in her puckered asshole, loving how she gasped and squirmed, clenching that dirty little hole so tight it sucked me in deeper.

I wondered if he'd take her there, balls deep from behind.

I wondered if she'd like it.

"Please," she called, and her voice was louder this time. "It's been too long…"

And it had been. It'd been months since I'd slammed my way into that tight little ass the way I should. Months since she'd turned feral and clawed my skin and begged for more.

I usually took my time, opening her nice and slow with a couple of fingers to loosen the blow. But not tonight.

My dick was slick with her juices as I pulled out of her pussy, but her ass was still tight enough that I gritted my teeth as the head popped past her clenched little ring. Her hiss was pained but still she begged for more.

"Yes, Brett, yes! Please!"

Sinking deep was pleasure enough to roll my eyes back in my head, my whole body thrumming with the need to consume every fucking part of her.

My thrusts were deep and savage, but slow enough that I savoured every inch of that delicious fucking hole. She snaked her hand down between her thighs and rubbed at her clit as she took me. I watched her shiver, listened to the beautiful fucking sounds of her body.

"You're gonna take another man's cock," I said out loud, and she twisted a glance back at me.

"Only if you say so."

I should have said it, then and there.

You'll never take another man's dick. Not now. Not fucking ever. Not for all the money in the fucking world.

I should have drawn a line under this craziness and let this whole sorry place tumble into the sea.

But there was something there in her eyes, behind the fear and the love and the way she needed my cock.

A thrill.

A want.

An excitement that sizzled deep, kept under wraps by her desire to keep me happy until she was sure I wanted the same thing.

I'd seen it often, but never like this. Never reined so tight.

Viewing this place, moving cities for another job, seeking out a wedding venue she loved but I thought was too pomp and circumstance.

And now.

Wanting another man's dick for fifty grand while I watched.

"Brett," she urged, pushing back against my dick so hard I groaned. "Tell me no. Say we won't do it. We won't do it, not if you say no."

But I didn't. I didn't say no.

"I won't..." she began again, but my body silenced her, my weight pressing hard on her back as my lips found her ear.

"You will," I snarled, and brushed her fingers aside to circle her clit with my own. "You'll take his dick for one fucking night, and I'll watch every fucking second. We'll take his money and we'll make this place everything you ever wanted. Better than that shithole down the road. Good enough that people will say fuck it to the budget basement and pay over the odds to come to us."

I knew then that I had her.

Her knees gave in, her body quivering in climax as I pinned her hard and kept those fingers fucking circling.

"You'll take his dick," I barked. "And you'll be watching me every fucking second while you do it. And then, when he's done and gone, I'm gonna pound your pussy every fucking night until you don't even remember his fucking name."

I closed my eyes as my balls unloaded deep, spasming in her asshole as her ripples of climax sent me over the edge right along with her.

We grunted. Squirmed. Sweaty bodies shuddering in the quiet as we came down, knowing full well the deal had been sealed.

We were really doing it.

He would really fuck my wife.

And I'd let him.

SIX

GRACE

I fell in love with my husband all over again as his cock still twitched inside me, pinned hard by his weight as I struggled to catch my breath. My legs were like jelly and my clit was still flying high, my ass feeling every inch of the pounding I'd just taken, and I loved it. I loved all of it.

Even his dirty words.

Especially his dirty words.

Forbidden. Unexpected. Never contemplated once in all the years we'd been together, not even for a moment.

My belly twisted in knots, my adrenaline spiking in spite of the endorphins of climax.

You'll take his dick. And you'll be watching me every fucking second while you do it.

I wondered if that was really true. If this insanity tonight was really happening and wouldn't just disappear into a ridiculous cloud of crazy nothingness in the cold light of day.

As nervous as I was in the quiet of the room with my naked tits pressed to the bar top and my spread thighs slick with wetness, I wasn't even sure I wanted it to. Not with the money looming, not with Brett so...

Different.

My husband was different.

His lips were fierce even as he kissed my temple and sighed in the afterglow. I had so much to ask him. So many things to clarify. So many worries. So many hopes and fears, and more. Dirty little ghosts in the back of my mind I didn't want to acknowledge, let alone voice aloud. The dirty parts I found at night when Brett was asleep beside me and I couldn't stop imagining... things...

Filthy things.

Things I'd never done with my husband. Not in all these years.

Things I usually told myself I wouldn't want in real life. Not if it came to it. Yet still they were always there, waiting. Lurking. Sending me to orgasm with my fingers down my knickers and my teeth clenched tight to stop myself making a sound.

The people were always faceless when they weren't my husband. I'd never thought about another man clearly, not someone identifiable. I only hoped it wouldn't be Thomas Heath's chiselled face in my fantasies from this night on.

It couldn't be.

Just couldn't be.

I loved my husband too much to want that. Too much to enjoy sex with our strange money-splashing guest.

"You're thinking about him," Brett grunted in my ear, and I shook my head before I'd even realised I was lying.

"I was just..." I began, but his breath rasped loud.

"You can think about him. I mean it's normal. Natural. Whatever."

I flashed him a look over my shoulder, eyebrow raised. *"Normal?"* It was a relief to let out a laugh. "Brett, sweetheart, this is anything but *normal*."

It was a relief to see him smile back. I winced as he pulled his dick free.

"We're solid though, right?" he asked, as though the question was the most rhetorical statement on earth. I nodded without even a second's hesitation. He raised an amused eyebrow right back at me. "Solid enough to survive one night of some random asshole's seedy proposal. Maybe you'll even enjoy it."

It was too soon for that. I flipped onto my back to face him as soon as he lifted free, holding a hand up between us.

"I'm not doing it for fun, Brett. Not even close. I never could."

"Sorry," he said. "Too much. Line crossed."

"He's not you," I said again. "Having sex with random men is hardly a staple part of my regular interests."

His smirk was still confident from the fucking he'd just given me. "Just as well, Mrs Foster. Don't be getting any ideas now. This is strictly one time only."

He shoved his dick back in his pants and zipped up. He always had that advantage over me, being back to passable in a flash. He looked barely dishevelled, where I was still raw and naked with my tits on display and my poor anniversary gown nothing but a crumpled mess around my waist.

I tugged it down enough to cover my throbbing pussy at least while he picked up our toppled wine glasses and wiped down the side. I had red wine stains on my elbows, but now wasn't the time to worry about it. I yanked my dress up the other way to cover my tits, but it didn't sit properly, torn at the underarm seam. He really had been on a mission.

"This place will be amazing with all that money to spend on it," I said, and his eyes were still alive with horny humour when they met mine.

"What you thinking? Spa and sauna? Horse riding centre in the back yard? Fairy tale themed rooms with actual gold leaf wallpaper?"

I bit my lip and leaned in to fasten his open collar. "I'm thinking of greeting the mail guy with a smile in the morning. Gold leaf can wait a while."

"Amen to that," he said and wrapped an arm around my shoulders.

He'd always been strong, Brett. Always been muscular, his body firm and sturdy against mine. His arms had always felt warm. Safe.

Even in our misery I'd known he was in it with me. His hand in mine for the long haul. But there it was again, that *difference*. In him. Something primal behind his smile, the sense of ownership in his touch.

I hadn't felt it for a long, long time. Probably not since I'd said *I do* and we'd settled into married life like we'd levelled up to maximum in the relationship game. I guess he felt safe too. My hand in his for the long haul, squeezing his fingers just as tight right back at him.

I felt a shiver of something deep, and it wasn't bad. Alien, maybe, but definitely not bad.

I couldn't deny it. The offer of so much money, being worth so much to a stranger. And more than that. The way my husband's desire was so angry, so powerful.

I felt attractive. Wanted. *Needed*, even.

I felt like more of a woman than I'd felt in years, at the suddenly greedy hands of the man who'd called me his own for well over a decade.

I swilled the bar towel in cold water and wrung out the dregs of wine he'd wiped, and once again he approached from behind and pressed in tight. My ass clenched and fluttered at the ridge of him, nervous of a rerun so quickly, but his kiss was for my hair, not for my mouth.

"We really should sleep," he said, and I nodded.

"Early start. He said fine print at breakfast, right?"

"There'll be plenty to negotiate," Brett told me, and I was grateful for the confidence in his tone.

He flicked off the lights behind me and kept my hand in his as he led us through the darkened bar. Our living quarters were ground floor, further on back past the kitchen, and I was relieved when we were firmly back in the familiarity of private space.

Any hopes I had of a repeat performance disappeared when Brett set the alarm for the morning and I saw our remaining sleep time flash up on his phone screen.

Shit.

I'd be needing an intravenous caffeine drip to make it through the breakfast shift, let alone handle any… negotiations.

Still, that didn't stop me staring at the ceiling when I slipped into bed in my soft cotton nightdress, all washed up clean for the night. Brett's arm draped easily across my waist, his breath hot on my shoulder, slowing down with its regular steadiness until I knew he was dead to the world.

I always admired how he could sleep so easily, even in the midst of all kinds of shit.

Me, not so much.

I must have made it nearly thirty full minutes by the time my nerves were jangling too loud to ignore. My legs were twitchy, restless, more than happy to launch me to my feet once I'd slipped from Brett's sleepy grip.

It was the window I went to first, hoping the darkness of the waves outside would be enough to relax me back to bed and sleep along with it. But no.

A walk. I needed a walk. Me and the sea air out front, and some space to get my murky mess of thoughts in some kind of order.

Brett didn't even stir as I pulled on some flannel PJ bottoms and a huge fluffy cardigan and slipped outside our patio doors.

✦ ✦ ✦ ✦ ✦ ✦

I'd smoked a pack of ten cigarettes as a teenager, too inexperienced to even hold them in the right fingers. I'd coughed through every single one and never bought another pack since.

Stepping out into the dark front garden outside our hotel that night was the closest I'd ever come to wanting to try the habit again.

I pulled my cardigan tighter around me, being careful to tread carefully in my comfy pumps as I made it down a couple of steps to the main patio area. The waves were loud, the moon low over them, shimmering a path into the blackness that reminded me all over again why I'd been so consumed with the need to buy this place last year.

And reminded me all over again why fifty grand would be worth doing all kinds of crazy shit for.

I didn't take a seat on any of the picnic benches, my legs on a mission of their own to reach the railings on the front so I could stare down onto the beach I loved so much. I came out here often in the middle of the night, unconcerned for any passers-by in such a small village, especially in winter. I guess that's why it took me so long to register his presence along to my right, leaning on the iron fencing, staring out to sea just as I was.

He was smoking. It was the glow I saw first, before the rest of him. My eyes had to adjust before his tall figure came into focus. My heart jumped and ran, my belly flipping hard as the man who wanted to buy my body for 50k edged a little closer and held up a hand in greeting.

I considered rushing back inside and safe into Brett's arms without so much as a wave in return, but the legs that had been so restless just a few moments back turned into solid lumps of lead and held me rooted to the spot. I sucked in a breath as he stepped closer still. I could taste the smoke on the breeze, and the shape of the cigar in his fingers became obvious.

"A beautiful night," he commented and toked a fresh mouthful.

"Always," I said, relieved when my voice came out steadier than I felt.

"It's always beautiful out here, that's why we moved."

"And why you're so keen to stay," he added.

I blinked a few times in his direction and my eyes adjusted well enough to see the lighter tones of his hair. I took a step in his direction, sliding along the railings like I wasn't concerned for proximity in the slightest, even though every inch of my skin was prickling.

"Finding it hard to sleep?" I asked him. "Guilty conscience, maybe?"

He laughed, then paused long enough for a particularly loud wave to crash below. "Guilty for what? Offering a fair business proposition to two people in need of the money? Tell me, why should I feel guilty for that?"

I laughed myself, a snippy little giggle that didn't sound quite like me. "I dunno. How about trying to be a marriage wrecker? Offering dirty propositions that would make most people blush. Or run a mile."

Another side step and his elbow was less than an arm's length from mine. "I don't see you running. Blushing, maybe. It's too dark to tell. But running, definitely not."

"If you think you're going to wreck our marriage–" I began, but the burn of his eyes, even in the dark, dried the words up in my throat.

"What happens in your marriage is no concern of mine. I pay for one night, for my own amusement. No strings. No emotional importance. Nothing but your body doing my bidding for ten hours straight."

"Nine," I corrected. "Nine hours straight."

His teeth were bright in the moonlight as he cracked a grin.

The man was beautiful.

I felt guilty for even thinking it.

"I was testing you," he laughed. "Nine hours. Yes." He gestured back over his shoulder to the hulk of the hotel behind us. "I imagine your husband is sleeping soundly after his exertions. Maybe he should've given you round two to tire you out enough to join him in slumber. I'll be sure to leave you ready for sleep when I'm done, that's a promise."

It took me a long second to understand his meaning. The cock of his brow. The dirtiness of his smile.

No.

But yes.

He laughed again, and this one made me shiver. "I was enjoying the quiet of your patio. The windows are big in the bar. They gave me quite a vantage point."

Oh how my cheeks burned, scorching against the cool wind as I wished the waves would swallow me up.

"You watched us."

"A very satisfactory product demonstration. I enjoyed it very much."

I wanted to tell him he was an asshole, but he'd been a customer on our grounds, every bit entitled to enjoy the gardens. I wanted to tell him manners cost nothing, and personal space invaders were nothing but pricks, but I knew we'd been asking for it, hungry for flesh on flesh in the bright lights of a hotel bar.

My question came out unexpectedly, unfiltered.

"Why me?"

He didn't ask me to repeat the question, just angled his body to face mine, his eyes heavy, brooding dark as the moonlight graced his perfectly chiselled face with milky white highlights.

"Is that a request for flattery?" He tipped his head. "Do you want me to indulge your ego by reeling off a list of your finer attributes?"

My mouth flapped open, struggling with a comeback. It was absurd. This whole thing was absurd.

My ego was tenuous at best, given the threat of ruin these past few months. My face felt plain and vulnerable without the armour of makeup. My hair felt windswept and ragged in the salty breeze. My PJ bottoms were dotted with puppy dogs and my cardigan was far from at its best.

He stubbed out his cigar on the top of the railings. "You don't believe you are beautiful enough to warrant a fifty grand price tag."

It was a statement, not a question. I didn't have a response, so I didn't offer one. Instead I shuddered at his closeness, at the oriental spice scent of him. At his pristine appearance even at fuck-knows-what o'clock in the morning.

"Your smile," he said. "I love how hard you force it, even when your eyes don't match. Your hair frames your face, just so. It's beautiful." I closed my eyes as the very tip of his index finger grazed my forehead. "You're vivacious, even when you're suffering under the weight of the world. You have a magic in your eyes that even your dismay can't snuff out. Your laugh is..." His smile was glorious. "Intoxicating. Heady."

"You don't have to–" I whispered, but his words didn't stop coming.

"You carry yourself with pride and poise, unaware of your own prowess, your own beauty." I flinched as he reached for my hand and took my fingers in his. But I didn't pull away. Couldn't bring myself to pull away. "Your hands are delicate. Your fingers dance absentmindedly." He ran his thumb over my knuckles. "Your foot taps, you know that? It's like a jittery little window into the frenzy of your brain. You're a thinker. I can tell. A worrier, too."

"With good reason," I said, and finally managed to tug my hand away.

"You'll be a treasure around my cock," he told me, and I sucked in a breath. "Easily worth fifty grand, though please don't think that is open to further negotiation."

My laugh in the night sounded bitter but empty. "I don't get it... I mean, there are plenty of women... plenty of young, pretty women who'd love to spend the night for free. I don't see..."

"Why I'd want you?"

I shrugged. "It seems ridiculous. Crazy."

His face was so stern when he cleared his throat that it hitched the breath in mine. "I want you," he told me. "One full night where I sample everything you have to give. I'll appreciate every part of you, every hidden crevice, every nervous shiver, every little fantasy I uncover in that busy mind of yours."

And he did.

Want me.

I could see it.

Obvious. Blatant.

Real.

More real than this one crazy night. More real than some random offer in a hotel bar.

It was deeper. Darker.

I thrummed with it.

I hated how much I thrummed with it.

"I have to go," I whispered. Ragged. "Sleep. I need to sleep."

I was backing away without even a goodbye, retreating into the safety of my regular life, even though I knew it was shaking on its foundations.

"Goodnight, Grace," he said and I managed to turn my back on him with only the vagueness of a wave, unsure if he could even see it in the moonlight.

Unsure if I even cared.

Unsure if I ever wanted to see him again. Or worse.

If I did.

I kicked off my pumps by the patio doors and ditched my cardigan over our cosy armchair, casting it off like it was dirty, like me. Tainted, like me.

Brett shivered at my coldness as I slipped between the sheets at his side, but clutched me tight despite the chill, his breath still even in his sleep.

And I held him.

Oh fuck, how I held him.

SEVEN

THOMAS

I loved it when negotiations took their time. Transferring a sum of money on a couple's split-second decision and taking my fill of the wife's pussy just a few minutes later was one thing. Discussing the intimate conditions of the proposal in the hard light of day and drawing out the suspense for days on end was quite another.

I was very much looking forward to it as I made my way down to breakfast. I'd held back as long as possible after my short, sharp power nap, taking my time to shower and dress in another finely presentable outfit, suited and booted in a freshly pressed shirt and fine cashmere sweater under a pale grey day jacket. I made sure my hair was groomed to perfection, my glasses crystal clear and positioned just so before I took the stairs down to the Foster's breakfast room.

An elderly couple were finishing up their poached eggs as I picked up a broadsheet newspaper from the rack at the front and took a seat by the window. I barely acknowledged Grace's presence as she loaded her arms with empty plates from a vacated table near the condiments bar. It took her a few moments to notice me sitting there. When she did, she contained her reaction well. Her back straightened just a little as she balanced the stack of plates on her forearm, her throat bobbing just a touch from a nervous swallow. She tipped her head in acknowledgement, caring little to offer the beaming hostess smile she flashed at the other guests on her way back through to the kitchen.

I scoured the stock listings in the back of the newspaper, happy to observe that one of my recent well-tipped acquisitions had already made me back the cash I'd be spending on Grace's sweet pussy with some to spare.

Getting to this level of self-generating wealth had been a long, hard battle, but the rewards were well worth the exertion. I loved money nearly as much as I loved the power it granted me. The man it made me in the eyes of outsiders looking on. The freedom it offered me to do whatever the hell I wanted in this world.

And yet it meant so much more still to the boy who'd gone without for all those years. I still felt him deep inside sometimes during long quiet nights, remembering so vividly what it felt like to be an invisible nobody with chilled toes where the rain came through my tattered school shoes. During dark moments at far reaches of the globe, sometimes I even heard my sad, lonely tears, echoing from those times gone.

But not today.

She avoided my eyes as she approached with her notepad, making sure to stand at a healthy distance with the bulk of the table between us as she tipped her head for my order.

I said nothing, keeping my attention firmly on my newspaper until she was forced to speak aloud. Her voice was edged with the nerves she'd been trying so hard to hide.

"What can I get you?"

I folded the pages of the broadsheet closed and placed it neatly on the table top before answering.

"Coffee, black. Full English. Toast, not fried bread."

She pinned her tongue between her teeth as she scribbled. My dick twitched at the thought of pinning it between mine.

"Help yourself to cereals from the front. Yoghurt, too."

I didn't hold back my stare, letting it eat her up until her pale cheeks flushed with a tell-tale bloom. She'd brushed up well on no sleep. A tight white camisole under an open floral blouse showed the swell of her tits nicely without being obvious. She was still scribbling away on the notepad as she cleared her throat.

"I didn't think you were coming," she said softly.

"Breakfast ends at ten today, no?"

I glanced at the clock on the wall behind her back. Two minutes still remained until the serving deadline.

"No, it's not that. You're in time, I just thought…"

I shifted in my seat before answering her unspoken question.

"I haven't changed my mind. I'm more than ready to negotiate the fine print when I'm done with my breakfast."

I wasn't sure if her short exhale of breath was relief or apprehension, it could have swung either way.

I smirked up at her before she retreated. "Please ensure your husband doesn't spit in my breakfast, or worse. Believe me, I'll notice. I have a fine palate."

Her glare was like fire. "We're professional here. Your food will be exactly as it should be."

I picked the newspaper back up and opened it at a random page. "Good. I hate it when my eggs are overdone, please ensure they're not."

I watched her from the corner of my eye as she headed for the kitchen. She only looked back once over her shoulder before pushing her way through the door and out of sight.

The other guests had disappeared during our exchange. The room was just me and the rumble of the fridge under the condiments bar. I took a deep breath and turned my attention to the view out front.

It really was a beautiful spot, and it was easy to see why they were so attached to it. Gulls circled over dull blue waves, muted by the cloudy sky overhead. The sea was at high tide, swallowing up the sand with foamy jaws and spitting out straggles of seaweed amongst the dunes.

Staying on an extra few days really wouldn't be a hardship.

I was watching a gull hop along the iron railings I'd conversed with Grace at when she landed my coffee down with a clank. It looked an adequate beverage, but far from quality. I had to fight the urge to tell her cheap sachets were beneath this establishment as I tossed the cruddy little packets of sugar to the side.

"Food will be up soon," she told me, and I offered a curt nod.

The bird had flown away by the time I looked back. Grace's presence stayed firm at my side. I wondered if she was quietly surveying the sea or the stranger she'd soon be spreading her legs for.

"I haven't told my husband about last night," she whispered, and the confession amused me so much I spun hard in my seat to face her.

"You make it sound as though there was something to tell." My laugh was low. "Believe me, last night was far from eventful in light of what is to come, but if it makes you rest any easier I won't bring it up if you don't." I leaned into her a little. She smelled of orchids with a hint of blackcurrant. "It can be our little secret." I raised a finger to my lips.

I loved how her teeth gritted in response. "We don't have any *little secrets*," she hissed. "I just don't want him to think I had trouble sleeping. He'll worry."

"I kept you awake, did I, sweetheart?" I couldn't hold back the grin.

She leaned down until her mouth was level with mine, close enough that her breath tickled my lips. Her eyes were fierce and fiery, tightening my balls deliciously. "I'm not your sweetheart," she told me. "And I have plenty of things to keep me awake at night. You'll be a distant memory this time next week."

I held her stare with a fire of my own. "So why is your sweet little cunt already wet for me?"

The flash of whites around those pretty irises told me more than words ever could.

"While we're talking of secrets," I continued, "if you have any special requests you'd like to share out of earshot of your husband, now would be a good time."

"I have no special requests," she claimed. "This is all about the money, don't flatter yourself for a single heartbeat by thinking it's not."

I folded my arms. "Your customer service is very poor. No wonder your bookings are low."

She stayed in position, folded at the waist in such close proximity I could feel the heat from her. "With all due respect, *sir*, not many of our customers tell me my *sweet little cunt* is wet for them over Sunday breakfast."

"Not many customers would be telling the truth."

"What makes you think you are?" she challenged and I broke the standoff with a smile.

"Only one way to settle the dispute."

"Put that cash into our bank account and I'll settle whatever dispute you want," she said. "Until then, my *sweet little cunt* is none of your business."

She picked up the discarded sachets as she left me to my coffee, swaying her hips angrily with every step.

I loved a girl with flames in her belly. Breaking them apart in the bedroom was all the more satisfying when they spat and sparkled.

She didn't say another word when she returned with my breakfast. I offered her nothing in return other than a thanks and a nod as I got stuck into a hearty meal. It was a decent tick in the service box, considerably more impressive than their barely passable coffee. The eggs were cooked just fine and the toast was nicely golden, not burned.

It was Brett who came for my empty plate just as soon as I'd patted my lips with a napkin, scooping up my leftovers with his trademark pitted brow.

"We need to talk," he said, and I flashed him a smile before tossing my napkin atop the plate he carried.

"I'm ready whenever you are," I responded, glancing beyond him to where his wife hovered by the doorway.

He whispered something in her ear as he passed her on the way back to the kitchen, and she slipped into the seat opposite me without meeting my eyes.

We waited in silence, her eyes on the horizon and my eyes on her. I wondered what she'd been thinking, in those dark recesses of her mind that twirled with fantasies of the unknown. I wondered if she'd already been pinning her deepest fantasies on the shadowy prospect of a night doing my bidding.

I wondered if she had any idea how she'd squirt like a wanton little slut from that hungry pussy of hers and beg me for more. I wondered if she knew how her asshole would wink from its wide open mouth when I'd finished stretching her holes to my liking.

Brett wasted no time with niceties when he joined his wife opposite me. His hands were firm as they landed in loose fists on the table top, subconsciously staking his authority in the proceedings as he cleared his throat and got straight down to business.

I appreciate no-nonsense communication. In a parallel dimension, I may have even liked the guy.

"Fifty grand," he said. "Nine hours on Tuesday night. We need some ground rules."

"You will watch," I reiterated. "From beginning to end, no interruptions or outbursts."

"Agreed," he grunted. "Now, you'd better tell me what seedy shit you want to do to my wife, and I'll tell you what'll get your head kicked in."

I relaxed into my chair, my shoulders sloped easily, at odds to the tension bristling right through his. His biceps were bulging in his dark shirt, the stubble on his jaw adding to the inherent masculinity he'd been wearing like team colours his whole life long.

"Ass, pussy, mouth," I said. "I'll take all three as hard as I like without protest. I like to push limits, so there may well be some tenderness for a few days afterward, but no medical intervention will be necessary."

Grace pulled her seat closer and leaned in to join the discussion.

"If you think for a second you're going to double fist me to the elbow like you're inseminating a cow, and I'm just going to take it like a good little whore, you're very mistaken," she told me. "My body doesn't work that way, sorry."

I raised an eyebrow. "I'm fully aware how your body will and won't work, Mrs Foster. Most likely more aware than you are."

"You hurt her, your body will be the one not fucking working," Brett grunted, and this time I wanted to roll my eyes at his same old bully boy shit.

"As I said, no medical intervention will be necessary. Bondage, spanking, stretching and verbal degradation, however, are most certainly on the table."

"You want to insult me?" she asked, and I straightened my back.

"You'll enjoy the way I speak to you, I can assure you."

She shook her head, laughing an incredulous little giggle. "Don't count on it. I won't be enjoying any of it."

And there was my moment. Pure and proud and perfect.

They both looked up at me open-mouthed as I got to my feet and stepped away from the table.

"Let's forget it," I said, thrusting my hands in my trouser pockets like it was the easiest thing in the world to walk away. "I can see we're not on the same page, and clearly you're not invested in providing the quality of service I'm looking for. Thank you for a delicious breakfast and good luck with the coming months."

I'd turned my back on them and made it halfway to the exit before Grace's voice called my name. I pretended I didn't hear her, walking on with brisk steps until she was forced to call out again, this time with a desperation that made my dick harden.

I turned back slowly, knowing full well I had her.

The fear in her husband's eyes at my potential departure made it perfectly clear I had him, too.

"Please," she said. "I didn't…"

I stood statue still while she stumbled over her next words.

"I *am* invested in providing the service you want, I swear. I'm just…"

"We're just on edge," he offered right after her, raising his hands and shunting a little way back from the table. "We'll make sure you get what you're looking for. Both of us."

His sliver of submission to my upper hand was a bolt of pure fucking brilliance up my spine.

EIGHT

BRETT

I wasn't sure whether I wanted to pat him on the back for his steel balls, or rip them clean off him as he launched into a polished monologue detailing exactly what he wanted to do to my Grace.

The prick had the upper hand and we both knew it. Hated it, but knew it all the same.

If we wanted fifty grand of his dirty cash to save our hotel, we'd have to keep our mouths shut and give him enough to keep him satisfied. As much as I wanted to let him walk away, I couldn't. Not with Grace so desperate to make this place our home. Not with so many sleepless nights where she cried body-wracking sobs into her pillow and hoped I wouldn't hear her.

I clenched my fists hard under the table as we listened to his filth, loosening them only slightly as Grace's hand slipped under the table and folded over mine.

I couldn't let myself picture the reality of the things he had in mind. Dare not imagine the guy opposite with his dick thrust balls deep down my wife's throat while she retched and choked with tears streaming down her pretty face. Shouldn't even contemplate the prospect of him stretching her tight little asshole wide open and filling the soft pink gape with his filthy cum. That and his tongue, his dick, his whole fucking fist if he had his fucking way.

We shouldn't be doing this, not for all the dreams in the world, not at the cost of even a scrap of her self-respect.

I tore my glare from him as he took a breath, chancing a look at my wife to gauge her reaction before stepping in and casting off this craziness for good, but the sight of her knocked me sideways.

Her eyes were wide and her lips were parted just enough for me to know she was fighting her ragged breaths for calm. But it wasn't fear or disgust that had her senses reeling. It wasn't even nerves.

I knew my wife plenty well enough to know when she was trying to subdue her excitement at something she was worried I wouldn't approve of.

Expensive curtains on the credit card, a great deal on a five star holiday during a time we shouldn't be taking leave from work, a pair of shoes she didn't have room for in her closet but wanted all the same.

Multiply that exasperated silence tenfold and you still wouldn't be close to the way she was staring dumbstruck at the man opposite.

I knew it then, in that terrible heartbeat, that on some level she wanted to spend the night with him. She'd never admit it, not in this lifetime. I doubted she'd even admit it to herself, maybe not even late at night when she played with herself thinking I was deep asleep at her side.

She didn't need to admit it, I could feel the truth with every bone in my body.

What was most concerning of all was that I could feel it in my fucking boner as well.

Of all the things I'd ever expected to get a hard on over, this was scraping the dregs of the unimaginable. A pompous prick, with an ocean more cash than decency, talking about fucking my wife on my own fucking property while I watched should have been enough for me to kick the dickhead out on his posh boy ass before hearing another word of it.

But it was there regardless, the unapologetic biological truth throbbing in my pants under my clenched fists. My balls tight and angry and begging to fucking blow as he asked us if we'd ever explored bondage and submission.

It was like he was asking how we liked our red wine. The guy didn't blanche for even a second at the intrusion.

Grace answered before I had the chance.

"No," she said. "At least, not really. Not seriously."

I remembered back to our early days when I'd once tied her wrists with my tie and given her ass a slap for the fun of it. I hadn't thought she'd wanted more, not in all the years since. Hadn't considered repeating the experience with a little more clout than I had after a couple too many beers after a work night out.

"We've done plenty of things," I grunted, hating how defensive I sounded.

Grace shrunk back in her seat a little, her fingers squeezing mine under the table in some weird unnecessary apology.

The prick flashed another of those cocky grins I wanted to smash from his face. "I'm hardly a relationship counsellor. Your intimate dynamics are of no interest to me. I'm simply trying to gauge your experience level."

"She's had plenty of practice," I told him.

"I'm sure," he said, clearly not believing it.

I hoped he'd last ten minutes in bed before shooting his load in a miserable dribble and failing to get it up for a repeat. I hoped he was all mouth and no bollocks to go along with it, but I knew I wouldn't be holding my breath.

You don't find self-assurance of that calibre in someone struggling with staying power.

Nor in someone with a small dick.

My gut twisted at the thought I'd see it in glorious fucking detail, threatening to bring up the food I'd grabbed during my breakfast chef run, yet still my cock throbbed down below, at odds with everything I thought I stood for.

I didn't want another man to fuck my wife. I'd never in the whole time I'd known her wanted to see her with someone else. Never even thought about it.

"I won't make you take my fist unless you ask me for it," he said, grabbing my attention right back again.

"I won't be asking for it," she said in a beat. "I'll be taking what you insist and nothing more."

I'd have believed her before breakfast. I still wanted to believe her now.

I hated that I didn't.

I hated the shy smile she flashed me, seeking reassurance.

She really did have no idea that she wanted this.

"My wife won't be taking your fist," I told him. "You'll realise that soon enough when Tuesday night comes. She isn't like the cheap whores you probably pick up in the city."

He laughed as though the idea was ridiculous. "I don't use whores, Mr Foster."

"I don't give a shit what you do," I responded. "I'm just telling you that my wife isn't some kind of cheap slut who could take a horse and ask for more. She's not that kind of woman."

He leaned across at me. "With all due respect," he said, "I'll gauge for myself what kind of woman your wife is. I think she may surprise you."

"Don't fucking count on it," I growled, and he shrugged as though I was a fucking moron.

I knew then that I'd break his jaw if there wasn't fifty grand on the table.

"Does that conclude the fine print?" he asked, and I met his gaze deadpan.

"Get your rocks off however you want," I warned, "but the minute Grace calls my name and says she's changed her mind, it'll be game over. Push her too far and it's all out the fucking window."

"And what about you, Grace?" His attention landed on my wife's wide eyes and I felt a fresh bout of desire to wring his neck, fifty grand be fucked. "How do you feel about the conditions?"

Her shrug was barely visible. "I'll take whatever you want," she said. "As long as I physically can and it's within the allotted hours. It's a service, you're paying well for it."

I wasn't expecting his outstretched hand across the table, ready to shake on this fucked up deal. Mine were so clammy in fists that I had to wipe them down before making a move to accept the handshake, but Grace had reached hers out between us before I had the opportunity.

"Just one more thing," she said, and her voice was breathy with the nerves she'd done so well to keep close to her chest. "Why Tuesday? Why not tonight? The sooner the better, in my opinion. No point keeping it hanging over our heads, right?"

She had a point. The sooner this was done and the asshole was gone, the better, but the shake of his head put paid to that concept.

"No good, I'm afraid," he said. "I'm expecting some deliveries." He tipped his perfectly preened head in her direction. "Plus, I'm very much enjoying my stay here. You really do have a corner of paradise. I'm glad you opted to keep hold of it."

"Deliveries?" she quizzed, caring shit for the compliment.

"Of the private kind," he elaborated. "You'll be able to admire my purchases up close on Tuesday evening."

He offered his hand afresh, this time directly to her.

I watched her dainty fingers grip his with hate spitting in my gut.

"Oh, one final thing," he added, still holding tight. "I insist on no protection. I trust you are on the pill? I assure you I'm clean, I can get my latest medical emailed over if required."

I don't know why the thought of him riding her bareback was the final straw that broke my back, but I got up from my seat with a face like death, grunting that we were done with the fucking small print before heading back to the kitchen, angling myself to make sure that neither of them caught sight of the swell of my dick as I went.

I didn't wait for Grace to join me before I headed further on through to the back bathroom.

I couldn't stand her seeing me like this. Couldn't bear the thought of admitting that something about this fucked up filth made me hard. It left me one option, and one option only.

It was the angriest fucking hand job of my life.

NINE

GRACE

I hated my body for betraying me.

I couldn't deny it, even though I wanted to with every scrap of decency in me. I was fluttering like the horny little teenager who'd first crushed on Brett back in high school, but it wasn't about my husband, and it wasn't about kisses and hand holding and the thought of his big strong arms holding me tight.

It was over this arrogant asshole of a guy in front of me, and the filthy words from his mouth. It was over all the dirty things he was planning to do to me, and the way he'd listed them off like they were nothing more than a grocery list.

Maybe they were nothing to him, but they were everything to me. Far beyond anything I'd ever done with Brett, even in all these years.

I guess that's why I stayed in my seat while Brett made his exit like an angry bull. I needed to. I needed to tell this stranger exactly what he was dealing with and hope he had enough of a heart to bear it in mind with his crazy plans.

"I've only ever been with my husband," I said quietly. "I just thought you should know."

If he was in any way surprised he didn't show it. It made me wonder if it was that obvious. If I was so painfully monogamous that the whole universe could see it a mile off.

"Every cloud has a silver lining," he said back with a smile on his face. "Take it as another benefit. An unexpected broadening of your horizons."

"You make it sound like that's a good thing."

"Isn't it? Curiosity must have presented itself over the years, no?"

I raised an eyebrow. "Curiosity killed the cat."

"Or made her come harder than she's come in her life."

I swallowed down the urge to flash him the finger and tell him to get out of our lives.

"Don't hold your breath," I muttered.

He laughed, but it wasn't an unkind one. It was confident and honest, like he really believed this shit.

Maybe he did.

Maybe he really would know my body better than I knew it myself.

I dismissed the thought as soon as I felt the shitty little traitor in my brain. My husband knew me. My husband knew how to make me come. My husband was more than everything I'd ever wanted.

The man in front of me linked his fingers on the table top. "With all due respect, sweetheart, you've been with one man your whole life. I don't think your benchmark of prowess is all that objective."

"My husband is a great lover. As I'm sure you saw well enough for yourself through the window last night."

"I saw plenty," he replied. "I saw indeed that you were enjoying yourself, but my opinion still stands. Your benchmark isn't objective."

"I'll let you know if you've changed my parameters when Tuesday night is done."

"Please do," he said and offered his hand for another handshake.

I gripped hard. "One thing's for sure. I'm flattered you think such an inexperienced little idiot is worth so much money."

"Inexperienced doesn't equal idiot, and I'm confident you'll be worth every penny."

I was the one to drop the handshake, managing just a flash of a smile before pulling away. "I'm going to spend time with my husband. Enjoy the rest of your day, Mr Heath."

"You'll find him with his dick in his hand," he said as I stood from my seat.

I laughed out loud. "That's the most ridiculous thing I've ever heard."

He shrugged with a smirk on his face. "Go and find him if you don't believe me. Hurry though, or he'll be done and you'll be none the wiser."

I rolled my eyes as I walked away but he didn't see me. His attention was fixed through the window at the sea I loved so much. He didn't even give me another glance.

The idea that my husband was pleasuring himself was the most ridiculous thing I'd ever heard, but it didn't stop the weird little rumble in my belly. It was Thomas Heath's unfaltering confidence, in everything. The way he stared so easily as he spoke, as though his words were absolute truth and nothing else. As though he could see right into the heart of me, of us, of everyone.

And what would he see in mine?

I pushed through to the kitchen and called Brett's name, but there was no answer and no sight of him either. I poked my head around the pantry doorway, but he wasn't in there, which left only one place remaining. The bathroom at the back past the fridges.

I don't know why I approached so quietly. I don't know why I pressed my ear to the door and held my breath to listen.

And I don't know why my whole body chilled to the bone when I heard the familiar grunts and slick slaps of hand motions as my husband worked his dick on the other side.

"Brett," I said, and knocked once, loudly. "Brett, let me in."

I heard him stumble and curse and flush the toilet, no doubt struggling for composure before letting me in like everything was normal.

But things were anything but normal.

"Just a sec," he grunted, but I knocked on the door again.

"Let me in, Brett. Now," I ordered with a voice strangely on edge.

The bolt clicked on the other side and he pulled the door open with a fake smile, his face still flushed from his exertions and his zipper still flying low.

I pushed my way inside and closed the door behind me, just him and I standing in the small space, eye to eye as the toilet gurgled and refilled behind him.

"What were you doing?" I asked.

His smile and shrug were fake to the core. "Taking a piss. That's what people usually do in the bathroom, no?"

I don't know why I felt the tears coming. My whole world felt flipped upside down and shaken raw. Everything was topsy turvy and unbalanced.

Scary.

Horny.

Fluttery and sad and guilty.

I didn't even know anymore.

"Hey," he said, landing a firm hand on my shoulder. "What is it? If you don't want to go through with this shit, we'll call it off. Just say the word."

I sniffed back the crazy hulk of emotion and shook my head. "It's not that."

"What then?"

His eyes were so warm. So familiar. But his stance wasn't. The way his dick was still a thick ridge in his pants and his breath was still short was anything but familiar under the circumstances.

"I heard you," I whispered.

"Heard what?"

I rolled my eyes even as they filled with tears. "What's happening to us, Brett? What's going on here?"

"You tell me," he said. "Back there, the way you were looking at him. You want him, don't you?"

"No!" I spat. "Fuck, no!"

"I'm not criticising," he told me, his hand still gripping tight. "Fuck, Grace, I hate his fucking guts. Hate his fucking face. Hate everything about this fucked-up situation."

"So do I!" I told him, but he shook his head.

"But you don't. I saw it in your eyes. You want to, but you don't." He took a breath. "And neither do I. I walked out of there with the equal desire to smash the cunt's teeth in and jerk one off before I jizzed in my fucking pants."

"I'm glad you opted for the latter," I said, managing a weedy laugh at the absurdity of all this.

"I don't know what the fuck is going on," he admitted. "But I do know one thing. We're in it together, all the way."

I took a breath and nodded, relieved that he was still a constant in the chaos.

"Fifty grand," I whispered. "It's really going to be fifty grand."

"And it's really going to be you going through with all this shit," he said. "But I'll be right there with you."

I cast a look at the ridge at his crotch. "What were you thinking about?"

He shrugged. "The things he said, I guess. You with your throat full of cock. Your ass open wide."

The words took me aback a little coming from him. I guess it was obvious, because his brows pitted a little as his eyes ate mine up.

"You liked it too," he told me. "The things he suggested."

It was my turn to shrug and fake smile. "I don't know, Brett. I guess it intrigued me. It doesn't mean anything."

"It can mean whatever you want it to mean," he grunted, and his eyes darkened in a heartbeat.

That one moment changed everything.

His grip on my shoulder tightened and he pushed me to my knees with a force I wasn't expecting. My breath caught as I dropped, eyes widening up at his as he glared down at me with a ferocity I didn't know.

"On some fucked-up wavelength somewhere the guy might be doing us some good," he growled, and I couldn't hold back a gasp as he tugged his cock back free.

He was still swollen, dark and veiny and huge in front of my face.

"I can do everything he can do," he grunted and pressed the wet tip of his cock to my bottom lip. It was the most natural thing in the world to open wide and suck him deep.

I slavered like a hungry little slut, losing myself in the comfort of his rough hand in my hair as he shunted himself forward.

This wasn't us, not even close.

My husband didn't manhandle me to my knees in our tiny back kitchen bathroom and fuck my face like he wanted to choke me to tears.

But he did today.

All because of the man who'd be doing it in two days' time.

I stared up at him like the girl who'd crushed on him back in high school, realising all over again how magnificent the man was that I'd pledged my life to, and realising along with it how much more of each other there was still to explore beyond the smooth channels of routine and years in bed together.

"Be a good girl and take it," he growled, and I shivered at his words. He tugged my cami top down until my tits spilled free, pinching a nipple between his thumb and forefinger while I spluttered around his cock.

I didn't know this Brett, not like this, but I liked him.

"You'll suck him to the fucking balls, but you'll be thinking of me," he barked, and I nodded my head as much as I could manage. "You're mine, don't you ever fucking forget it. He's a nobody. Just one fucking night in a lifetime."

I loved the jealousy in his words. Loved the possessiveness with which he tugged at my hair.

His.

I was his.

My fingers slipped between my legs and I murmured around his dick as my clit sparked like a needy little slut.

"This was why I was hard," he grunted from above. "Thinking of you, doing this to me."

He was convincing himself, not me, but he was welcome to. I hoped I was equally as committed to self-delusion.

I feared we'd both need it, just as we both needed this, right here, right now.

When Brett shot his cum over my tear-streaked face in long thick streams while he cursed and groaned and swore I was all fucking his it was the most raw I'd ever seen him.

And when he hauled me to my feet and buried his face between my sopping thighs, bringing me to climax with his seed still dripping from my filthy cheeks, my screams were all for him.

TEN

THOMAS

Over the well-worn course of paying for sex with other men's wives, I'd become accustomed to expecting the unexpected.

Still, it had been a surprise to see the glowing flare of excitement behind Brett's disgusted eyes as he'd glared at me across the breakfast table.

I didn't expect any less of the rage from him. The simmering gutful of hatred clearly straining to unleash across the space between us was as satisfying as I'd ever dreamed it would be. I didn't even expect any less of the nervous but heady anticipation fluttering across from Grace and her big wide eyes, either. I mean, I wouldn't. Monogamous and committed or not, the prospect of a well-groomed stranger offering you a vast sum of money to take his dick was enough to make even the most frigid of women wet their knickers.

No. Nothing much surprised me, not these days. But seeing Brett storm away from the table, angled in a pitiful effort to hide the tent in his pants as he struggled with his demons, was enough to bring a smile to my face.

I do enjoy unexpected turns in the road.

I remembered with delight Grace's utter bemusement at my words.

Hurry though, or he'll be done and you'll be none the wiser.

I wondered if she'd scurried along quickly enough to have found him with his fist clenched tight around his dick, or if he'd managed to evade her scrutiny a little better than he'd evaded mine.

Maybe he was pounding that pretty little pussy deep as I drank up the rest of my average coffee and vacated my table. The question would be – if either of them were truly honest with themselves – were they thinking purely about the animalistic desire to consume one another amidst the chaos, or were they thinking about the filth to come.

I knew where my money would be.

I grabbed my thick woollen overcoat from my room upstairs and ventured out along the front for a closer look at nature's beautiful canvas. The tide had shifted, pulling back in flat, shallow sweeps of magnificence. It seemed a good time to venture down the sandy stone steps and onto the beach itself, so I did. I took off my brogues and winter socks in favour of sinking my bare toes into the sand. It was dusty at first, and then wet, hard under my feet even as the waterlogged ground squelched around my toes. I breathed in deep and long, enjoying the gusts of wind around my ears as my lungs drank in the tranquillity of the wide open space.

I kept walking, slowly, my eyes up ahead to the rocky crags and the sloping incline back up to civilisation. I had no urge to venture amongst humanity, not today, so I kept well away, daring to skirt the edges of the waves and caring little for how they swallowed up my trouser cuffs and left my skin raw and cold underneath.

I'd climbed an outcrop of rock amongst the ebbing tide before those text messages from the previous evening came back into my consciousness.

I picked at some barnacles on the rock face and considered denying her an answer entirely, but the sad little boy inside scratched at my poor dead heart until it jolted into some semblance of emotion.

It was a shiver of regret. Barely more than a guilty nip in an ocean of oblivion. I pulled my phone from my inside pocket and the text was still there, still glaring, taunting the weakness inside me and begging for more.

Please, Tom. Hold onto hope. You're nothing without it. Walk away.

My response was curt and cold, just as it should be.

Hope is dead. Tuesday night she'll be mine. Signed, sealed. And truly delivered.

A particularly large wave crashed up around me, fighting the death throes of its inevitable retreat. Its foam misted my glasses as I smiled at the horizon.

Even nature fights its course, just as people do. Struggling to cling onto ground that's no longer theirs as it pulls from their grip. They could spit and foam and snarl, like the waves around the rocks this morning. They could burst forth in one final moment of rage and madness, marking the scene with one final spark before burnout, but it was always the same.

The tide would wane and retreat, and the bond between sand and sea would sever until the water was just a glint in the distance and the beach was shivering naked out of reach.

Brett and Grace would fall, just as the others before them. Their bond of a lifetime severed with a blade so sharp and practised they'd never even feel it coming.

I ignored the vibration of the new message until the waves really had given up their bid to hold onto the outcrop. There was only the stillness of rock pools around me as I pressed the button to call up the text.

You're better than this.

It made me laugh out loud in the stillness.

She was wrong.

My distant Polly's beautiful notions of the humanity inside me were sweet in their idiocy, coloured by her foolish optimism that love was anything more than the pitiful illusion of human closeness amongst the chaos.

Love was selfish. Fragile. Temporary.

Grace and Brett would find that out for themselves soon enough, and so would the sweet girl back home when I told her of the final jewel in my crown of spite.

I scrolled through my online purchases to distract myself, checking again the priority delivery dates. Everything would be in place by Tuesday. Packages of toys and tools to turn pretty Grace into a whimpering little slut as I took her body to places she'd never known.

I found myself pondering if Brett's filthy fascination would extend to a hard on while he watched his wife take my cock all night long.

One guy some months back had taken his dick out halfway through and attempted to join in proceedings. He'd taken the rebuttal like a slap in the face, flailing like a clumsy teenager in his objections until I'd threatened to halve their payment.

I really couldn't imagine a bull like Brett doing the same. He'd keep it under wraps, of that I was certain.

My phone vibrated again as I considered lighting up a cigar for the walk back. The words flashed at the top of the screen before I had the chance to ignore them.

Please, Tom, talk to me. Don't shut me out.

How I wished I had something to say.

I missed the naive kindness in her voice, untainted by years of bitter inferiority. I missed her sweet laugh as she told me about her day, the same old shit from the same old customers at the bakery she'd been working at for ten years straight. She amazed me with her ability to find reward in the same static routine on loop. Never tiring, never growing jaded. Always seeing the best in everything and everyone around her.

Leaving her alone for pastures new had been the greatest decision I'd ever made. For her, not for me.

I may have been selfish, but I'd never scraped the depths enough to take her down with me. I thought too much of her for that.

It was just a shame she'd never know, and more of a shame that I'd never feel that kind smile of hers against my lips.

My cigar was a struggle to light but its deep plumes were like satin in my throat. I dropped back to the wet sand with feet so cold they were burning. The familiarity of the discomfort was a welcome reminder of all that had been, and all that would be.

I was smiling all the way back across the beach.

Soon it would be done, and finally, for once in my life, that little boy in me would find his peace. Even if just for a triumphant heartbeat.

ELEVEN

BRETT

We busied ourselves that afternoon, smiles fake but bright as we went about our everyday business, checking out the bulk of our handful of residents and pretending as best we could that Thomas Heath didn't exist. I scrubbed the kitchen after we'd waved them off, while Grace took stock of our supplies. You'd never know there was anything afoot from the outside when I kissed her cheek and she disappeared upstairs to sort out the bedrooms for tomorrow morning.

It was while I was changing kegs in the cellar that I opted to do a bit of research on the guy promising us fifty grand. My fingers were shaking as I scrolled through the internet search, my pride smarting at the full extent of this guy's successes in the city.

He was loaded. Really fucking loaded. He had directorships listed in so many companies I lost count. Profiles listed on Britain's most wealthy sites with grainy pictures of him grinning that smug smile of his like he was lord of fucking everything.

He was one of those weird virtual currency winners, investing early and cashing out with what one site estimated was over fifty million a year or so back.

Fifty fucking million.

No wonder he could cough up 50k for a night with Grace. He could fuck her every night for a month and not even break a sweat.

It was a strange feeling, being up against a guy like that. All smirk and cockiness and a bloated bank balance. I wished he was a balding, fat guy in his sixties with inch thick glasses, not the suave geek chic things he wore like some kind of genius professor.

Genius professor with a six pack and perfect teeth.

I wished I could take those off him with my fist at least.

I'd never suffered with confidence. I wasn't the kind of guy who got intimidated by other men, or people in general. I'd been born lucky on that front, doing just fine and dandy through those formative school years that fucked some kids up so bad they went into adult life with more issues than sense. I'd been proud of my career, proud of my marriage, and proud of buying this place at thirty-two.

So why did I feel like such a loser against this prick who'd showed up in our bar?

I poured myself an early evening beer when I was done in the cellar, figuring it might steady out the twisted pile of dread in my gut. It didn't.

I'd been hard at the thought of that cunt with my wife. Hard enough that I'd had to take my dick in hand in my own fucking bathroom.

What did that even mean?

I'd knock his teeth out as soon as share a drink with him. I had less than zero interest in seeing what he was packing under that stuck up suit shit he had going on, and the thought of Grace seeing it was enough to drive my hands into fists.

But there it was again. That throb in my fucking pants. The tightness in my balls at the thought of him pushing hard into her tight little ass and making me watch.

Fucked. I was fucked.

I swore under my breath as the sack of shit himself came through the doorway at just gone five and sat himself down on a barstool. He took off his coat and draped it over the seat at his side, smirking over at me like this was just a regular Sunday drink in a regular seaside hotel.

"What do you want?" I grunted, and he gestured to the optics behind me.

"Surprise me. Your finest."

I grabbed him a double of our finest rum and resisted the urge to spit in it.

"Not my usual tipple," he commented and took a sniff. "Get one for yourself… on me."

I flashed him a glare as I grabbed a glass, wondering just what the fuck he was planning with this man to man shit.

"I asked your wife if she had any special requests," he told me. "I thought I'd offer you the same courtesy."

"Keep away from my fucking wife," I snapped back in a breath, holding back a curse as I realised the cunt was still calling all the shots here.

"I was being amiable," he told me and held up a hand. "Simply trying to make the experience as pleasurable as possible for all parties involved."

"And what did she say?" I asked and he smirked that shitty fucking smirk of his all over again.

"A gentleman never tells."

My fingers were under his chin, hooking his collar and pulling tight before I could stop myself. His eyes were cold and unflinching against mine, but he made no move to shake me off. "You're no gentleman."

"Says the man acting like a thug."

"You think this is acting like a thug?" My breath was hot and heavy on his face, but I didn't give a shit. "You have no fucking idea."

"I'm offering you a lifeline and you repay me with disdain. That's poor manners on your part. Very poor."

"You're buying my wife's pussy for your cheap kicks. That's not a lifeline, that's a dick move."

He turned his face away with a grin, only to clear his throat and come right back at me. "Don't tell me it doesn't make you hard."

I hated how my eyes widened. "Of course it fucking doesn't."

"It makes your wife wet, you know that, yes? Please tell me you aren't so deluded that you can't see how much she wants me."

"She wants the fucking money. Nothing else."

His laugh was filth. "She wants more than that. You both do. I'm simply offering the opportunity for expression."

"You're the one who's fucking deluded," I said, and forced myself to laugh right back at him. I dropped his collar and spun my fingers against my temple. "You're fucking insane. A fucked up crazy cunt."

"What excites you more? The thought of me taking which hole?"

I shook my head and took a breath. "Nah, fuck you. I'm not playing this stupid game. Talk about the weather or fuck right off. You're paying for Tuesday night, not to get in our faces the rest of your fucking stay."

I turned my back and took a decent swig of rum, hoping with any luck he'd down his drink and piss off somewhere else, but he was still right there as I resumed emptying the dishwasher.

"How will it feel to know you aren't the only one who's been inside her?" he called over, but I ignored him. "Something that will keep you awake at night?"

His laugh was so easy I figured he must be some kind of sociopath, revelling in people's misery.

"Something that will keep *her* awake at night, probably. I wonder who she'll enjoy most."

I flashed him the band on my finger. "No contest. We're worth a lifetime, not one seedy little night with a stuck-up cunt."

He nodded like this whole thing was just chitchat over dinner, and in that moment I wondered whether this was his stupid idea of humour. Maybe this whole thing was a crazy game to him, some joke to regale his friends back in the city after a couple of beers on a Friday night.

I looked at him afresh, beyond the stupid tailoring of his suit and the prissy styling of his hair. Beyond the way he held himself so composed, like he was untouchable, unreachable.

"What are you trying to prove with all this?" I spoke aloud, realising I was as genuinely curious as I sounded.

"Prove?"

I got to my feet and closed the distance back up, taking his almost empty glass and refilling it with another measure.

"This city slick act you have going on. Rolling in from the big smoke and paying a shit ton of money for a random guy's wife. What's the fucking point?"

His eyes were like lasers on mine. Too steady. "Because I can."

I shrugged. "One night in a lifetime for enough money to change people's worlds. Of course you can. Anyone would say yes."

"Your point being?"

"My point being that it doesn't make you a bigshot." I refilled my own glass. "Curing some godawful fucking disease or opening an animal sanctuary, that makes you somebody. Risking your life to save someone from a burning building, that makes you someone. Investing in some climate saving technology or using your cash to reduce homelessness on the streets, that's worth something." I paused and still his eyes stayed firm on mine. "Fucking someone's wife for fifty grand, that just makes you a jerk with more money than sense."

"Be careful you don't talk me out of it," he said, deadpan, but I was already onto him.

It was nothing more than a hunch in the pit of me. An inkling of something lying deep behind his calm. Maybe he was a sex addict, or a guy who got his kicks from flashing the cash. Maybe he was someone fucked up by adultery, or suffering from some weird mental health condition that made him a dirty cunt to random strangers.

I didn't know. Couldn't know.

But there was something.

I knew right then and there he wouldn't walk away from this. Not before Tuesday night. Maybe not even if I really did knock his teeth out.

"Drop the bullshit," I said, and for the first time since meeting him I raised my glass across the bar in some fucked-up guy to guy toast. "Here's to a fucked-up Tuesday night, and for an exchange that sees all of us get what we need from this fucked-up situation."

"I don't need anything," he said. "This is all for my amusement."

"Whatever you say, mate," I laughed and his laser eyes lost their firmness for the tiniest flash.

I clinked his glass before he could refute me, knocking the drink back in one, and his stare was right back at full intensity by the time he'd knocked his back along with me.

It didn't matter.

I'd already seen enough.

The sonofabitch needed to fuck my wife while I watched, just as much as we needed the money he was offering for doing it.

It put us strangely on a par.

And made me feel strangely proud of the power my wife had over the prick as she headed down the stairs to join us.

TWELVE

GRACE

I wasn't expecting to find them like old chums, toasting on shots like they were school buddies catching up on a winning sports streak.

It was strange, disorienting as I dropped down the final few stairs and made my way over to the bar. Brett's eyes were twinkling weirdly, with the kind of pride I remembered back at college when he'd paraded me in front of his rival rugby team after winning the trophy.

My whole face felt flushed as I closed the distance, even my neck was burning at the scrutiny from both guys at once. I wished I was better dressed for it, not still clad in jeans and the same boring cami from my exertions with the bedding changes upstairs.

Thomas Heath's eyes were hungry. Dirty. Eating me up with the kind of confidence that made my pussy flutter along with my belly. There was no denying it. I was excited.

Scared shitless, but excited.

I hated myself for it. Maybe I always would.

I blew a stray wisp of hair from my eyes as I made to hoist up onto one of the vacant barstools, but the guy with the perfect blonde hair gestured me closer with a nod, moving his folded coat from the stool nearest him to the bar top at his side. I flashed Brett a look before I accepted the seat, but he didn't give me any indication that I should keep my distance. I daren't even look at the man who wanted my body for a high price, keeping my eyes on my fingers as I tapped them in a rhythm in front of me. It didn't matter. I could smell him, his fine musky scent mixed with cigar smoke and the sea. I could feel him, the electric heat of his body so close.

I jumped in my seat as his knee eased out and rested against my thigh, a flash of embarrassment breaking into a smile as I settled back into some kind of composure. Nothing. It was nothing. Just a knee through denim.

I cast a glance down at our legs to make sure the contact was just that, and couldn't hold back the surprise as I noticed his feet were bare, his shoes and socks cast underneath his stool. The bottoms of his trousers were damp and stuck tight to his calves, and I couldn't tear my eyes away. It felt invasive. A sliver of humanity behind the perfect shell of his appearance.

Maybe he was just a guy after all.

Brett poured me a wine and I took it gladly, swigging back half of it before wiping my lips with the back of my hand.

"I needed that," I said and he smiled, his eyes conveying his empathy as he raised his own glass to his mouth.

"That's on me," Thomas said, and I wondered what was with the generosity. Showing off to excess on top of the insane money he was throwing our way? Trying to build bridges in places there was only spit and fury?

"We should be buying your drinks," I told him. "You being the well-paying customer and all."

"Maybe you can get the next round." His smirk was smug but not antagonistic. I was getting weirdly used to his expressions, and weirdly used to the way they sparked the tingles in my belly.

"There's going to be another round, is there?" I asked, and he raised an eyebrow.

"Unless you're planning to close the bar early. I notice it's quiet."

I didn't want to tell him he was the only guest left in the hotel, and it was obvious Brett didn't either as he took the other man's glass back up to the optics for a refill before I could say a word.

"We don't close the bar early," my husband said. "Service is everything."

They were so different, these two men. Brett was broad and heavyset, his hair short and his stubble heavy enough to give him a foreboding seriousness. Thomas was lean and lighter, his eyes light and sparkling, confident with an edge of amusement that never seemed to leave him, not even when he was angry.

It was that cockiness. It never waned.

I wondered if it would be like that in the bedroom.

I hated myself for hoping so.

I changed the topic of conversation, even though there wasn't one.

"You've been out," I commented, gesturing to his bare feet on the rung of the stool.

"It was windy," he told me. "Brisk. I liked it."

"A bit cold for bare feet, no?" I asked, and he smiled a guarded smile, as though I'd touched on some private humour.

"I'm used to a chill in my bones," he said. "I enjoy the sensation, reminds me where I came from."

The question came so easily. "Where did you come from?"

He hesitated just a moment before answering. "I came from a mother who didn't have enough sense or stability to take care of a growing boy. The stones would come into my shoes, the rain too. I got used to it."

Brett blanched along with me, but the guy knocked back another swig of drink as though it was no grand revelation. He caught our expressions and let out a sigh.

"Please, no pity. I can't tolerate people's misguided sympathies."

I was aware that my foot was tapping and he could feel the movement against his knee, but I couldn't stop. "Sorry," I said. "I just didn't expect… you seem so…"

"Rich?" he finished. "Polished? Upper class?"

I shrugged. "Self-assured was what I was thinking, but all of the other statements apply."

If he was offended he didn't show it. "My success was earned not granted. I built a life for myself, success for myself. That's really all that matters when the night draws in."

"I'm sorry," I said, because it seemed the only good thing to say. "I was lucky, my family were good. Kind."

Brett leaned across the bar and took my hand. "We had it lucky," he said. "A rough start is hard, doesn't give you an excuse for being a royal cunt, though, no offense."

I couldn't believe my ears, my mouth dropping open even as my eyes found his and saw them sparkle.

He was joking.

Actually joking.

"None taken," Thomas said and smirked his trademark smirk. "In the end, everyone gets what's owed to them."

"Money doesn't matter shit," Brett grunted. "Not really. People are what matter."

His fingers gripped mine tighter, showing off the gesture to the man at my side.

He laughed at us. "If that's so, why are you so keen to risk your marriage for fifty grand?"

Brett laughed loudly back at him, right from his stomach. "I wouldn't risk my marriage for fifty grand."

"It's not at risk," I said after him.

Thomas tipped his head at both of us. "I can't decide if you are naive or purposefully ignorant."

Brett finished up his drink and gestured for the other man to do the same. I wondered if any of us would be walking in a straight line out of here this evening. Maybe we would get drunk and dive into the whole crazy spectacle ahead of time, right here in the deserted bar.

Part of me wanted that. Part of me despaired at the prospect I wouldn't remember the details in the aftermath.

I watched Thomas Heath's throat bob as he downed the rest of his shot. I wondered how his lips would feel on mine. If he would kiss me at all. How his tongue would taste. If he'd be fierce.

"*You* can't decide if we are naive or ignorant," Brett said. "*I* can't decide if you're a sex addict or a man struggling with far too much money and time on his hands."

"Neither," he said. "I just like what I like, and I like your pretty wife. I think she'll be a delight around my cock."

I dropped my eyes from him, staring at my fingernails. Too much. The flattery was too close and personal.

"I like my pretty wife too," my husband said. "I'm not surprised you'll pay fifty grand for her, I'm just proud as fucking punch she'll be mine on the other side of it. You'll be kicking yourself for sampling her and having to walk away. The knowledge of what isn't yours to keep will taunt you for a lifetime."

And I couldn't. Couldn't take it. Not the weirdness, or the over inflated notions of my body's brilliance.

"Stop," I said, holding a hand up to both of them. "I'm not some kind of supermodel the world's going crazy over. I don't have Models Weekly magazine knocking at my door. I'm just a girl with cellulite on her thighs and fingernails torn from changing bedsheets. Stop the cockerels at dawn thing, even if it is over a couple of drinks and an attempt at some fucked-up camaraderie."

I chugged back the rest of my drink and slipped from my stool.

"I'll let you fuck me," I said to the guy staring at me without even a hint of awkwardness. "But you can't think I'm some kind of superwoman. I'm not. There won't be any refunds when I don't match up to whatever crazy vision you've dreamed up in that filthy head of yours. There won't be any grunts of disappointment when my thighs are flabbier than you're hoping for and my tits don't bounce like a porn star's."

I hated how his eyes burned.

"What makes you think I want that?"

"How am I supposed to know shit about what you want?" I snapped, and the whole sorry guise of friendliness smashed at my feet. "You're just a stranger at a bar. We've had hundreds of them through here. None of them have offered a shit ton of money for a night in bed with me."

"Grace," Brett said, but I didn't break the stare with the guy with bare feet and sorry stories of how they were cold as a kid. "Grace, sweetheart," he said again, and I wrenched my eyes away with a groan.

"What?" I asked, but the love in his eyes knocked the wind right out of my sails.

"You're worth every penny," he told me. "More than every penny. I'm not even vaguely surprised there's a random guy at our bar wanting to buy a night with you. He'll be sorry when it's done, and we'll be glad he's gone and left us all the richer."

There was that unsettled feeling again, swirling deep. I felt it rise to my throat and threaten to spill. My nerves jittery as I registered the reality of taking another man for real.

I wouldn't even know what I was doing with another guy's body.

Brett gestured me back to the bar and picked up the bottle of red for a refill. "Relax," he said. "We all need to relax around here before someone ends up losing their shit ahead of schedule. Two more nights and we'll be done. Finished. Let's make it through with as few theatrics as possible."

I don't know how he was managing to be so calm tonight, but I was grateful. Right then, I was grateful.

My Brett was strong, just like always. On my side, just like always.

My eyes were all for him as I gathered myself together enough to slip back onto my seat.

I jumped another mile as the guy at my side landed his fingers on my thigh out of view of my husband, but there was no seediness in his touch, only a squeeze of reassurance that shocked me to my core.

I remembered what he'd said to me on the sea front. The kind words that had seemed so real.

And I hated it. All of it.

Hated how much I wanted them to be true.

"You'll be more than enough," he whispered as Brett put the wine away on the far side of the bar. "I meant every word I said last night. I'd have said a lot more if you'd let me. Maybe if I had you'd have even believed me."

His breath tickled my ear, and his fingers squeezed harder before they pulled away.

It was official, we were all going insane. All three of us.

I was grateful for the next chug of red that went down my throat.

If we were going insane, at least the alcohol would ease the ride to crazy town.

THIRTEEN

THOMAS

I shouldn't have drank so much rum with Brett Foster and his sweet wife. My legs were uncharacteristically unsteady as I made my way up to my room, my vision swirling uncomfortably as my heart pounded and my drunken belly rolled with the kind of emotional crud I usually kept at bay.

I'd spent my entire adult life hating the sonofabitch and his bully boy swagger. Years plotting that they'd be the ultimate couple to tear apart and leave broken in my wake.

Countless nights thinking about her monogamous little cunt sucking me dry, the ultimate gift to the wimpy little teenager who'd jerked one out over her enough times to smart for a fucking lifetime.

I'd grown too blasé in my memory of him, imagining him as an ignorant grunt of popularity and nothing more. I hadn't anticipated he'd be more than that. More astute, more perceptive. Smarter. Determined.

Proud.

Not proud like I was proud, with ice at the edges of every sentence.

Proud like a guy who loved his wife and shrugged off his lot in life as more than enough.

Maybe it was more than enough.

I threw my shoes and socks to the floor and braced myself before dropping to the edge of the bed. I steadied my breaths and ran my fingers through my hair. My scalp tingled. Scratchy. A glance in the full-length mirror opposite showed me looking exactly as I'd cultivated for years, swaying and looping in my blurred vision, but still preened and polished all the same. It should have been a relief, but it didn't stop me feeling the things I spent my days hammering flat inside.

I felt like a fraud. An imposter in a nice suit. My bare feet still had a dusting of sand between the toes, I could feel it as I scrunched them against the carpet.

I'd nearly told them after a few more shots. Nearly told them how I knew them and spilled the sorry beans of our rancid history.

I wondered if they even knew the finer details. Maybe my tale would come as a surprise enough to leave them open-mouthed, dredging through their own memory in crazed confusion as they put the pieces together.

But I hadn't told them. Even through the rum, I'd bitten my tongue when it mattered.

Conversation had flowed far too easily in spite of all that was looming. Questions, so many questions. Questions about London and my life in the city. Questions about my business, about my apartment, my tastes in food. Questions like I was just a regular guest at the bar and the guy didn't want to punch my throat at the prospect of me stretching his wife's asshole wide open.

It had been a long time since I'd talked about my life. *Actually* talked.

Drunken fingers stumbled for my phone, calling up Polly's text message and considering an impromptu reply, even though it was approaching one a.m.

I wanted to tell her how close I was to victory. How I could almost taste sweet Grace Foster's cunt on my lips. How I'd fuck the woman so hard she'd never recover, not in a lifetime. How I'd be the man on her mind for all time, fuck her fucking husband and his school sports trophies and his bullish pride.

I wanted to tell her I was lonely. Lost. Drunk.

How I was still me. The kid she'd walked along the scraggy path after school and skimmed stones in the brook with. The kid whose glasses she'd repaired with tape after Brett's bully boy athletics friends threw me on my face for colliding with him on the sports field. The boy whose lip she'd dabbed with a cold flannel to ease the swelling and kindly ignored his teary eyes to save him the embarrassment of his weakness.

I almost typed out a message.

My thumb made it to the text box and hovered for a full minute before I came to my senses and cast the phone on the floor.

I threw myself flat on the bed and stared up at the ceiling, trying in vain to focus on the light as it swung across my vision like the pendulum of death.

It was just drink. One too many. It's always that one that sends you over the edge.

Maybe Grace Foster would be the one to send me over mine.

Maybe the drink was nothing more than a smart ploy on his part, plying me with easy shots and lulling me into a false sense of camaraderie. Maybe he was laughing with Grace right there and then a few floors down, laughing about how I wasn't such a cold fish after all, just a sad fucking loser who'd probably only manage to get it up once and leave her be.

Even through the drunkenness I felt the rage brewing. I remembered him in senior year, shouldering past me every morning in the corridor without even noticing how I'd shrink from him. I remembered how he'd jump into his mother's sporty convertible after practice and speed off to his cushioned life while I'd cower in the bus shelter with no coat, missing the bus on purpose just to avoid going home to my own mother and whichever brute she'd be shacked up with that month.

I hated the piece of shit.

Always had. Always would.

I hated this place he owned with its quaint old beams and its pretty picnic benches out front. I hated that he'd been given it on a platter and still couldn't manage to hold onto it.

How he'd sell out the one thing worth *anything*.

It was like this every time I offered cash for a woman with a ring on her finger. They'd always talk themselves into it as though it was no big deal. Cheapening their union to whatever monetary value I'd placed on them.

What they'd never found out, not a single one of them, was that I'd give them the money regardless if they'd just say no.

If they could stand shoulder to shoulder, composed and confident and committed to each other above a strange man's cash enough to tell me *no, thanks, never, no fucking way*, I'd shake their hands and deposit the money into their account and walk away with a smile.

Sad but true.

I'd hoped this would be the time. Another case of sad but true.

No matter how much I hated the cunt, or how many times I'd jerked off to his wife when she was just a girl at the same school, I still hoped he'd be able to prove me wrong about life, love and the idiots who believed in any kind of romantic permanence.

I'd hoped maybe it would even make me hate him less. Enough to go on my merry way and find whatever shred of peace was out there waiting one day.

Maybe even with Polly.

I rolled onto my side and retched into my mouth. Definitely too much drink.

One thing I hated even more than Brett Foster was feeling a lack of control.

I'd be in control when it mattered though. Cold, hard and calculated as

I took my fill of his wife and everything she had to give.

I'd take her to places she'd never imagine, never even hoped for. I'd imprint myself so deep inside her that she'd never be able to let me go. Show her a whole other world in that one filthy night, one at odds with her sweet little picture of paradise in this quaint little cove on the edge of nowhere.

I'd hurt her so bad she'd beg me for more.

Love it all better with enough skill that she'd cry for the ache all over again.

I'd snake my way inside her, through her slick wet pussy and the butterflies in her belly, right the way to her pounding heart, where I'd take it. Take her. Own her. Steal her.

And then leave her behind to pick up the pieces.

She'd call. They always did.

Only maybe this time I'd come back for her.

BRETT

I was surprised I could get it up after so much rum, but I could. My dick was throbbing proud as I stepped into the shower after my sweet Grace. She was still smiling from the wine, giggling as she soaped up her hair, leaning back against the tiles as my bulk filled the cubicle alongside her.

"I'm drunk," she laughed, like I didn't know.

"We're all a little drunk this evening," I said back, my dick in my hand as I let the jet of hot water slam against my shoulders.

She pressed her body to mine, pinning my cock between us as I wrapped her in my arms and held her tight.

"Maybe we should tell him no," I whispered aloud. "Tell him to stick his money and fuck off. If I didn't know better, I'd even say maybe he wasn't such a cunt after all. Maybe he could recommend us to his rich city friends and come back for more rum. Maybe we'd even like the guy one day."

Her eyes were wide as they stared up at mine, her tipsy grin still bright. "Maybe."

Her belly ground against the ridge of me. I hissed out a groan.

"Fifty grand," she said. "It's a lot of money to turn down." She ground harder against my dick. "Clearly the prospect of a healthy bank balance is exciting you."

But that wasn't the reason I was hard. It wasn't about the money.

It wasn't about the guy's seedy cash from some weird ass currency investment, or how many posh towels Grace could fill our hotel with on the back of it.

It wasn't even about the to-pay pile, or sleeping easily at night.

It was about how much another guy wanted my woman. How hungry his eyes were for what was mine.

How the jealousy was addictive, raw, more intoxicating than the gutful of rum I'd downed with the asshole as he'd sat across from me.

How she'd still be mine afterward. How I'd see the pain in his eyes at walking away from the woman he'd find was everything and more.

We'd had rum and a conversation that made the guy vaguely palatable. That didn't mean I wouldn't enjoy watching him craving my woman when his fill was long spent.

Maybe I was a cunt, too.

Maybe Grace liked cunts.

Fuck, I was drunk.

"You won't fall in love with him, right?" I asked aloud and her face crumpled up with laughter.

"Are you fucking crazy?" She tapped my forehead. "I love *you*, Brett Foster."

I grabbed her ass and hitched her up on me, loving the way her shampoo slid over my fingers as she tipped her head back and rinsed it clean.

"He's hot though. Rich. Cocky," I goaded.

"And you're you. No contest."

She moaned as I shifted her high enough to take my cock. She was ready for me, nicely wet as I dropped her onto my full length. Her arms wrapped around my neck, her whole body rippling as she squirmed for rhythm.

"I'll hold back," she told me. "When you're watching, I mean. He's just a guy who's paying. I won't want it. He won't make me come, not like you do."

She was definitely fucking drunk.

"And what if he does?" I grunted. "What if he makes you scream for him?"

The way her pussy clenched told me everything.

Strangely, I didn't fucking care.

"You can come for him," I added. "If I'm watching, I'd rather be watching you having a good fucking time."

Her lips found mine, her tongue pushing deep as she whimpered.

"You don't mean that," she hissed as she pulled away.

I did mean that. A combination of hard on and rum and her tight wet pussy milking me dry.

"Come for him," I grunted. "It's once in a lifetime. Enjoy it."

"You were suggesting we tell him no a few minutes ago," she giggled, bouncing deeper to take her fill. "I can't keep up with the crazy of all this."

It was crazy.

I was feeling it right through me, my brain spinning, trying to straighten out twisting senses that wouldn't fall into order.

I'd given up trying by the time my sweet, horny wife came for me, riding my dick like a woman possessed, grunting and humping and grinding for more.

I shot my load inside her with a grin on my rum-drunk face.

FOURTEEN

GRACE

Thomas Heath wasn't at breakfast next morning. Brett and I hovered around the dining room, nursing hangovers right the way through the allotted time, but he didn't show.

I took it more personally than I wanted to, as though he was taking a step back from us somehow, offsetting the easiness we'd grudgingly reached in each other's company after a drink or ten.

He may not have shown that morning, but his parcels did. The couriers started arriving just after breakfast, dropping them off in one long troop at our reception desk.

It felt strange signing for the things he'd be using so filthily on my body.

All of them were in plain packaging and their discretion made me nervous, wondering just what was waiting for me inside. Whips, chains, donkey-sized dildos? A rainbow-tailed butt plug that plays music in your asshole?

I had no idea.

When we were kids, my sister rescued a canary from some family down the street who weren't taking proper care of him. He would have these crazy moments in his cage when he first arrived, hopping from perch to perch so fast he was a bouncing pinball of feathers and squawks just busting to get free.

My heart felt just like that.

My pussy, well that felt like something entirely different.

Brett shook one of the smaller parcels when he passed by with a load of flattened cardboard for the recycling bin. He pulled a face at the thump of whatever solid item was inside.

"Maybe he wants to dress up as a rubber chicken," he told me, with an easy laugh at odds with his hangover. "Maybe he's been getting farmyard fantasy props. You can be the farmer, he can be a dirty little piggy boy."

He snorted and raised his fists as flailing trotters until I rolled my eyes.

"As if," I snapped, taking my hangover a whole lot worse than he was.

"Relax," he said. "Anything too crazy and I'll shove the whole fucking truck load up his ass before I kick him out on it."

I don't think he was even joking.

Late afternoon came and the deliveries eased off. Still there was no sign of our only remaining guest. I took the time to call my sister back home in Gloucestershire, reminiscing about the little yellow bird before letting her know the tides may well be turning on our quiet beach. It was exactly the call I needed to refocus my scattered senses, savouring the prospect of being able to return the couple of grand she'd lent us through sheer desperation a few months back.

The interaction did me some good. Enough that I made myself a tall latte and took a window seat in the empty bar while Brett busied himself in the cellar. I pinged a few of my old school friends on social media, no longer fearing the moment I'd have to tell them we were bailing on the dream we'd thrown everything into. I browsed other hotels on our online booking portal, seeking inspiration for some choice purchases once the cash was in our account.

And I stared.

Up at the stairs he may appear down at any time. Out at the rough white waves through the window as the sun sank beyond, hoping to catch sight of him enjoying the same view with a cigar and flyaway hair. But there wasn't a sign of him. Nothing.

I considered calling his extension from the front desk and letting him know about his deliveries, but there was no way he wouldn't be well aware what was due. I even considered rapping on his bedroom door and offering him them across the threshold as an ice-breaking gesture for the day, but I was too scared of his cold stare frying my heart alive.

Thomas Heath from North London was a very slippery fish indeed. The rum had opened him up enough to tell us about his flash apartment in the city, with its floor to ceiling windows and its twinkling urban skyline. Even now, I couldn't imagine him with holes in his shoes back at whatever school he trudged along to every morning. London must have been a shitty place to grow up on the breadline. No wonder he'd made it his life's mission to step up the financial ladder.

I typed his name into social media, seeing as I was still back and forth trawling my own timeline. I was expecting nothing, just a sea of Thomas Heaths from all over the world, but there he was, right at the top of the listings. One mutual friend.

I had to blink hard a few times over to make sure I wasn't losing my mind, but no. It was him. The same cold stare behind his expensive glasses, the same perfect clip of his dark sandy beard.

I couldn't believe for the life of me that we had even a single friend in common, but there it was, the name in tiny italics.

Polly Piper.

I had to click on her name before I remembered her, and even then the recollection was hazy at best. She'd been a friend of my sister's once upon a time way back when. In the same school year, the year below mine. A quiet girl with curly red hair and freckles. That's the only real reason I remembered her. I scrolled through her profile to find she was still living in Gloucester, working at the bakery we used to grab a sneaky doughnut from on the way back home some days.

How the fuck did Polly Piper know Thomas Heath?

She had other friends in common with me, but nobody I'd really spoken to in years, just the same sorry batch of school mates you add out of courtesy when their requests come through.

I pinged through a message to my sister, but she wasn't showing as online. She rarely was these days. Two kids and a full-time nursing job put paid to that.

Do you still speak to Polly Piper?

I switched back to Thomas Heath's profile but it was a fortress of privacy. I could only flick through his profile pictures, of which there were just three. The original preened shot of him staring stoic at the camera. One of him in a suit with a couple of other guys also in suits, still with the same stern glare I'd seen so many times these past few days.

It was the third shot that took me aback, listed as three years previous. He was smiling on that one, his grin so much more natural than I could have pictured. His glasses were thicker and his hair was messy enough to give him an air of *hipster on a Sunday morning*. He was wearing a t-shirt, his toned arms tanned and rippled with fit-guy veins. The t-shirt wasn't anything I'd have placed him in in a billion years.

People disappoint, pizza is eternal.

Just no. No way.

I was staring dumbstruck when Brett slid into the seat next to me and landed a big sloppy kiss on my cheek. I didn't speak a single word, just angled the phone in his direction with my eyebrows up high.

He squinted, his own surprise registering obvious when he caught up with the plot.

"Got to be an old pic," he said. "Teenage or some shit. No way that's this past century, you don't turn into that much of a prickly cunt overnight."

I zoomed out so he could see the date and he squinted again.

His shrug was more throwaway than concerned.

"Something must have happened to him to make him change so much," I said. "It's just too weird."

"Maybe he can relax in his free time."

I pulled a face. "This *is* his free time."

"Life, work, the pressures of being a mega millionaire. I guess they take it out of him. Poor asshole."

I tipped my head toward him as I weighed it up, but it still felt weird. *Pizza is eternal.* I couldn't even imagine him eating the stuff.

"I didn't look him up on social media," Brett told me. "Didn't even think about it. Did check him out on Google though. He's got more businesses than you can shake a stick at, loaded on top by some weird shit currency investment. He's every ounce the lord of cash he makes himself out to be, don't you worry."

I laughed a little to myself, loving how Brett had done his research without saying a word.

"What?" he asked, and I laughed again.

"You didn't say you were playing detective."

"Didn't want to talk about the cunt any more than necessary. Just wanted to know he could cough up the cash when the time came."

"There's much more than that," I said, clicking away from his profile picture and back to the mutual friends screen. "We have a friend in common,

Polly Piper."

He jabbed a thumb at her image. "Who the fuck is Polly Piper?"

"A girl from the year below at school, my sister knew her. She works in the bakery on Church Row, just behind the main square. Red hair, remember her?"

His eyebrows knotted in the way I knew so well. "Not a clue. Small fucking world, though."

"Too small?"

He shrugged. "Seven degrees of separation. Maybe he bought a donut from her once and she sent him a request. I expect he gets a few."

"Feels close to home."

He wrapped an arm around my shoulder and pulled me closer. "We don't know Thomas fucking Heath. Believe me, we'd remember. A guy like that's not exactly easy to forget." I let out a sigh as he nuzzled close enough to breathe in my hair. "I don't know Polly Piper and it sounds like she's not exactly high up your contacts list. If you think a guy like Heath is gonna go chow down on an iced bun and tell the world he fucked sweet Grace Foster from Churchdown High School up the ass while her husband watched, I think you're barking up the wrong tree."

I hated how he did that. Put things in such a way that I sounded like a crazy.

He'd always done it, laughing at my interest in murder mystery serials on TV and shrugging off my finger pointing as I yelled out the potential culprits five seconds into episode one.

"Ping her if you want to dig for info," he offered, too little too late.

It was my turn to shrug. "I don't even know her, must have accepted her request years ago. I don't think I've ever even hung out with her, she was friends with Sarah, but not good enough friends to ever come over."

"Ping her anyway," he said, but I shook my head.

"Hey, Polly. I'm about to fuck a guy I think you know. Thomas Heath? Anything I should know about him? He's good for fifty grand, right?" My tone was sarcastic

enough that Brett jabbed my ribs with his fingers and tickled hard.

"Smart ass. You're the one who's playing private investigator."

"Says he who can list Thomas Heath's directorships from memory."

"You don't know I can do that… I may have just been browsing…"

But I did know that. I knew everything about him. Including how much he liked my fingers to sweep up the sensitive skin on the nape of his neck. He shivered as I did it, eyes closing.

"I'm going to ask him," I whispered, and his eyes opened.

"Don't ask him. Don't tell him anything about us. Not who's on your friends list, not which school you came from, not how you know Polly Piper on his friends list. We want the asshole to disappear into the ether and never come back."

He had a point.

I sighed and nodded as I clicked away from Polly's picture, casting the handset on the table.

"Fine," I said, and snuggled tight into my gorgeous husband's side.

Just where I belonged.

FIFTEEN

THOMAS

I kept my distance from the Fosters. I needed nerves, the wonder of surprise in pretty Grace's eyes as I took my fill of her perfect little body. I needed disdain, hate, maybe a flash of insecurity in Brett's as he watched me take his wife to places she'd never dreamed of.

Friendly drunk conversation had crossed some barriers. I wouldn't be crossing them again.

I avoided breakfast and easy walks along the beach. I avoided the bar entirely that evening, slipping out through the rear exit and heading further into the village for a steak at one of the few small pubs I'd seen in passing.

It went down a treat in light of the cruddy hangover symptoms. Thick cut and rare, with a healthy side portion of greasy fries and onion rings. I opted for a cold pint of bitter, sipping it down steadily by the warmth of a crackling fire, my feet kicked out as though this was a regular holiday and I was a regular passer-by.

I moved to the bar after declining dessert, dropping onto a stool and ordering a refill of local beer. The place was quiet, but not empty like the Fosters'. Locals, I guessed, laughed in a small huddle, tossing darts at an old battered board at the back.

I kept a smile on my face as I watched them over my shoulder, waiting for the barman to strike up the inevitable conversation. It didn't take long.

"You staying round these parts?" he asked, with a smile to match my own.

I made sure my expression was easy. "The hotel on the front."

"Cliff House?"

I nodded. "Nice place. Seems quiet though. Heard there's another hotel opening a few miles down."

The guy grunted out a sigh. "Budget shit hole. Whole place will feel it. All of us."

"The Fosters said they haven't owned the place long, bad timing on their part, it seems."

He nodded, his bushy eyebrows furrowing. "Poor sods. Between you and me, I think the Keswicks shafted them royally last springtime. They knew about the new place coming, just wanted out before it took them down. New guys didn't stand a chance."

"Guess you'll all be hoping for a miracle. Maybe the ground will open up and swallow the place before it gets going."

"We can pray," he said, and pulled himself a beer from the nearest pump. "New place will bring crappy supermarkets and all the other bigger town dross, most likely. Seen it happen further down the coast. Once one of them comes it opens the doors to all the rest."

"Sorry to hear that," I told him, and I was, in a distant part of me.

Not just for the confirmation that the Fosters were screwed by hoteliers dashing for an easy escape, but for these other people, about to see their small-time coastal haven swallowed up by the first of the incoming corporates.

I'd seen it happening all over the country, in one way or another. I'd been involved in some of it myself.

It wasn't the most satisfying aspect of business, even if I did enjoy seeing small-time assholes coming unstuck along the way.

I thanked the barman for an excellent meal soon after and headed back slowly through the quiet lanes, approaching the hotel from the rear where I could sneak easily back up to the top floor unseen. It was a good time to think. An easy time to think, even though I should've probably steered well clear of the introspection.

I lit up a cigar and pondered as I strolled, staring up at the stars in the cold sky overhead.

I knew well enough what was coming, from that poor sad barman's expression regardless of his words alongside. Fifty grand would go some way towards keeping those guests checking in Cliff House hotel, in spite of the bargain budget prices down the road. Fifty grand might well limp them along a little further in their dreams, but fast forward a few years, to the influx of opportunists and chain stores and those looking to make a quick buck off the transformation of a quaint little bolthole, and what you'd have is more of the same as they have now.

A dead business. Debts racking up overhead. Tired dreams and weary legs.

And a shattered marriage along with them.

But that needn't concern me. They'd have a shattered marriage long before that. Maybe I'd even be doing them a favour, a split in a few months' time might ensure they had at least the dregs of my cash remaining to set them up anew.

They should be thanking me in the aftermath.

The telephone extension started ringing a few minutes after I arrived back in my room. I picked it up with a grunt of *hello*, halfway undressed for the shower.

Grace's voice was gloriously uncertain as she greeted me on the line.

"Mr Heath? I saw the light in your window. There are um… parcels…" I heard the nervous smile on her face. "Many parcels."

"Keep them for me," I told her, preparing to hang up sharp.

"We didn't see you... today..." she added, and it made me smirk to myself.

"What did you expect? A timetable of my bathroom visits? A request for your signature on a permission slip to allow me to venture elsewhere?"

"No, of course not," she hissed, and I laughed aloud at how swift her hackles were to rise.

"Goodnight, Grace. Please sleep well, you'll be needing all of your energy tomorrow evening."

"Tomorrow," she said. "Yes. Will you be at breakfast?"

I wanted to say it was none of her business and to be standing pretty in the dining room just in case I made an appearance, but the local ambience of the village must have softened up my mood.

"I'll be at breakfast," I told her. "Now, if you'll excuse me. I have an evening to get on with."

Her apologies were delicious. Her goodbye was feeble enough to make my cock twitch.

I pressed to end the call with my fingers already casting aside my trouser buttons.

She wanted me. The stubborn little minx might still be denying the obvious, but it was there, as plain to see as the dead-end future of this quaint little bud of paradise.

She wanted to know our deal was still on, that the filthy items in those parcels were really going to be used on her tomorrow evening. She wanted to know I still wanted her, was still willing to pay for her, was still busy thinking about all the filthy things I'd be doing to her.

And I was still busy thinking about the filthy things I'd be doing to her.

My dick was swollen hard, throbbing with a dull ache even as I gripped hard and worked fast. Tomorrow evening she'd be right before me, on all fours with that tight little ass stretched wide open, a pink tunnel of dirty flesh winking as I dribbled a healthy gob full of spit down into its depths from my hungry mouth.

She had no idea how badly I'd hurt her in the name of ploughing her deep. No idea how the ache in that tender cunt could pain her good enough to beg for more.

But she would.

And that's when I decided to have some fun, my dick still rigid in my grip as I picked that phone extension back up and pressed for reception.

Her voice was just as needy as she answered my return call.

"I've changed my mind," I told her. "Bring them upstairs. Alone."

"Alone?" she asked, and I grunted my exasperation.

"Yes, Mrs Foster. Alone. Call it room service. The customer is always right."

"But Brett…" she began.

"I'm perfectly aware what our agreement is," I barked. "Are you bringing them or not?"

I counted to three before she answered.

"I'm bringing them."

"Good girl," I told her, and hung up the phone all over again.

GRACE

Brett was watching a rerun of the football in our living room when I gathered up those parcels and headed upstairs. My arms were filled to the brim, packages on top of packages. I only hoped my balance was good enough not to set them all tumbling back downstairs as my shaky legs made the climb.

I told myself my ragged breath was from exertion and not from nerves.

I told myself I'd have let Brett know where I was headed if he'd have been closer, and I would have. It was no big deal, just delivering items to a paying customer. Nothing more.

I felt clammy all over as I approached his bedroom door, my heart pounding so loud I could feel its thump against the boxes pressed to my chest.

I managed just the sharpest tap to announce my presence, being sure to hold on tight to his precious purchases when the door swung open and revealed him in nothing more than one of our Egyptian cotton bath sheets.

I couldn't stop the way my eyes widened. Didn't have a single hope in hell of delivering even the most clipped of words through my gaping mouth.

He saw it all, of course he did. His eyes twinkled as he stood so easily, his weight on one hip and arm up high on the doorframe as he beckoned me inside.

I looked anywhere but at him as I stepped over the threshold. His suitcase was standing neatly in the corner, his coat folded over the back of the armchair by the dresser. His sheets were rumpled and I struggled not to picture him in them, his naked body tossing in his sleep and his perfect hair a mess on the pure white pillows.

"You can drop them on the bed," he said, but approached close behind all the same and took the majority from me, hoisting them easily over my head and carrying them the rest of the distance himself.

I didn't say a word as I followed him and positioned the remainder gently on the bottom of the bed.

I couldn't avoid looking at him from that proximity. The towel was slung low around his hips, showcasing that he was every bit as toned as I imagined.

His chest was smooth and hairless, his nipples dark against his golden torso. His abs were ridges of muscle under rippling skin, the V of his hips proud, with the most tempting of happy trails down beneath the white of the towel.

He was nothing like my husband.

Brett was broad and toned, but paler. His chest was dusted with dark hair and his happy trail was far more prominent. His hips were wider, his bulk meatier and less professionally sculpted, the glorious tone of his body all natural and good genetics.

My husband was gorgeous beyond words, more than enough for my wildest dreams, but this other man, this handsome stranger with a million dirty parcels and a bank account rammed full of cash to back up his cocky smirk was a whole different ballgame.

Different.

That's the only word for it.

I hated myself for wondering what his cock looked like behind the swathes of white. I hated myself more for realising my pussy was tingling at the thought I'd find out soon enough.

"Curious, no?" he asked, and there it was again. That damned smirk. Always that damned smirk.

"None of my business," I managed, flinching at how he laughed out loud.

I was getting used to that, too. That laugh. Always with that edge of something nasty, something dirty. Always at my expense, even when it wasn't.

"Oh, Grace. It's plenty of your business." He dropped to sitting on the edge of the bed, the towel straining across his thighs almost enough to grant me sight of his precious assets. I froze as he patted the mattress beside him and picked up one of parcels. "Relieve at least some of the curiosity. Come on. Open one. Don't tell me you haven't been wondering."

"Curiosity killed the cat," I repeated, just like the last time around, but my body moved of its own accord, sitting a safe distance along from him and taking the parcel from his hands.

One wouldn't hurt. If anything it would relieve me, just to know. Just to see there was nothing too insane about his filthy collection.

If there was nothing too insane about his filthy collection.

"Go on," he prompted. "Tear into it. I'm as curious as you are."

My fingers were dithery as they dug inside the tape at the top end of the package. I held my breath as I first peered inside, my heart in my throat as I realised what I was looking at.

"Show me," he said, but I couldn't. I handed it over still half-wrapped, knowing my face would be beetroot as he tore the rest free.

The dildo was huge. A thick length of rubber in glossy black. It would never fit. Not in a million years.

He held it up and raised a fist up alongside it. "Excited?"

"No fucking way," I told him. "Never in a million years."

His cocked brow made me shiver. "Don't be so quick to say that, sweetheart. You'll be begging me for this monster by this time tomorrow night."

"Don't hold your breath."

He offered another parcel and this time I tore into it with less restraint.

A set of cuffs. Not the sweet ones from the cute sex shops with leopard print fur and safety catches. These were the real deal, stainless steel and glinting with menace even in their packaging.

He tore into a third parcel. I watched mute as he revealed a set of leather paddles. One of them had holes cut out in a pattern like a cheese grater.

"Less air resistance," he explained like I'd asked. "Should give your pretty ass quite a thwack."

"I'll be a wimp," I blustered. "There's no way I'll–"

"We'll see," he interrupted. "We'll see on everything."

I picked up another box without being encouraged. This one was big and tearing into it revealed a huge waterproof sheet with loops to fit it over a mattress.

"Worried about wetting the bed?" I asked and wished I hadn't.

"Not worried," he said. "Maybe you should be though."

I managed a bitter laugh. "I'm not wetting the bed, Mr Heath. I haven't wet the bed since I was a toddler."

"You're mine for nine hours straight. You'll be doing whatever I tell you to do."

It was enough. I got to my feet and brushed my prickly arms down as though I could brush his filth right the way off me.

"Open the rest yourself," I said. "I'm done with this."

"You wish you were." He wasn't smirking this time, and that made it worse somehow. His face was entirely serious. "Except you don't wish you were, pretty Mrs Foster. You're lying to yourself, even now. Pretending you want out of here when all you'll be thinking about in bed tonight is all the ways I'll be using these things on your tight little body."

I cleared a couple of paces before I dared to cough up a comeback.

"You're deluded," I told him. "You think this is about you."

His stare was hard. "I know it's about me. Long after the money is in your account, it'll still be about me."

I forced another laugh. This time it sounded nasty. Cold enough to be evil.

"Goodnight, Mr Heath," I told him, shooting only the shortest glance back over my shoulder before I escaped to the safety of the corridor.

It wasn't short enough to miss the tent under the bath sheet, or the size of it.

I made it around the corner and down one flight of stairs before I came to a standstill and pressed myself back against the wall.

I needed a moment. Just one long moment to compose myself before heading back down to my husband.

But I didn't.

I needed more than that.

I pulled the skeleton key from my back pocket and let myself into the nearest vacant bedroom.

And I hated every second it took to rub myself to a frantic orgasm in the crisp white bedding.

SIXTEEN

BRETT

I woke up with a start on the big day. It was well before the alarm, the sky still dark outside. Grace was snuggled into my side, her breaths steady against my shoulder as she adjusted herself to my movement.

Dread. That's all I felt. The kind of sickness you feel as a kid when you've got a dentist appointment looming and know they're going to use the drill on you.

Only worse.

Ten times worse.

A hundred times fucking worse.

I told myself I had a hard on because that shit is hardwired first thing, regardless of the circumstances. Regardless of the fact Grace had wanted my dick until the early hours, craving more, more and more on top, even when she was flopping limp from exertion with sweat glistening on her forehead.

I stayed put under the covers, trying to keep myself still so I didn't wake her, staring up at the ceiling and wondering just what the fuck that sonofabitch really had planned for her. Wondering if I'd be able to watch without losing my shit halfway through and saying balls to the wall to the whole sorry lot of it. Wondering if I'd shame myself beyond all reason by getting another hard on while he was shunting his way inside the pussy I'd called mine since before she'd even let me have it.

I was still staring up at the ceiling when the alarm finally did go off and my beautiful wife stirred at my side. She stretched, yawning wide before it dawned on her too, just as it had me.

Her eyes found mine in the half light and they were petrified.

"Shit," she whispered. "It's really today."

"Only if you want it to be," I said for the millionth time. "We can say no."

"And say goodbye to our dreams for this place along with it."

She rolled away from me and gulped a load of water from the glass on her bedside table. I admired the slope of her naked back, wondering if I should use the opportunity to distract her once more before getting up.

She made the decision for me, swinging her legs from under the covers and rising in a beat. She grabbed her dressing gown from the hook behind the door and stepped up to the window, pulling back the curtains to stare at the morning sea.

"We have to do this," she said. "I love this place too much to leave."

"And I love you too much to see you do anything you don't want to."

She didn't answer, and there was that gut curl again. The one that told me she wanted this in the same sordid way I wanted to see her do it. That vile ghost of perversion baying down deep.

"He'd better transfer half the cash this morning, or I'm ruling game over," I told her and she nodded.

"We should cut down on the to-pay list, spend some of it before I crap myself and shy away from his door later."

My frown felt etched into my skin and her eyes widened as she caught sight of it.

"That was supposed to be a joke," she said, but she wasn't laughing.

I showered quickly, then brushed my teeth and watched her through the steamed glass as she took one after me. I couldn't believe I'd be sharing her, the woman who'd only ever known my touch.

Maybe it was the biggest mistake of my life. Maybe he would be better than me.

Maybe she'd like him more.

I was grimacing at my own stupid paranoia when I swilled my mouth out. She wrapped a towel around her head as she stepped out. I watched her in the mirror as she pressed herself up behind me and wrapped her arm around my waist.

"What are you scowling at?"

"I'm being paranoid. It's ridiculous."

"Paranoid about the guy upstairs? Yeah, it is ridiculous," she assured me.

"If he does anything amazing you'll have to teach me the tricks. Anything *he* can do and all that."

Her smile was real and full of love. "You know plenty of tricks already."

I made sure I was dressed well, even for the kitchen. I wanted to feel as much of a man as another guy fucking your wife for cash allows you to feel.

Fine jeans and a decent black shirt would do the job.

Grace took her time in front of her wardrobe, clearly weighing up her own clothes choices.

"What do you think he'll want me to wear later?" she asked and I shrugged it off as barely worth a thought.

"You'll be wearing whatever you want to wear, fuck what he thinks about it."

She pulled out a tight purple blouse with pretty white spots on it. "I guess he's interested in me out of clothes, not in them."

I took her hand before we headed through to the dining room, being sure to keep her close as we waited for the asshole to show his face.

He was earlier today, suited and booted as per usual with a broadsheet paper on his lap before nine a.m.

I gave him a nod and headed through to the kitchen as Grace went to take his order, wondering if I should try to engage him a little, man to man, on the run up to the seedy spectacle later. He wanted a full English, again. Eggs not overdone, again.

I cooked it up quickly and peered out through the doorway as Grace ferried it over to him. The way he looked at her was ravenous, and it wasn't for bacon.

That's about when I figured the cash transfer was due, breakfast in peace be fucked for him.

I took a seat opposite as he folded up his newspaper and picked up his cutlery, and if he was surprised he didn't show it, cutting up his mushrooms like it was any other weekday morning.

"You want the money," he said, and I hated how the guy seemed to know all this stuff. He pulled his phone from his pocket and pressed his thumb to the fingerprint thing. "I'll need your details."

I recited them by heart, the wind taken out of my sails a bit to find him so amicable.

"Done," he said, just like that, and sure enough there was twenty-five grand sitting in our account when I logged into mobile banking from my own handset.

"Thanks," I grunted, still struggling to believe the figures in front of me were really real and there for the taking.

"The pleasure will be all mine," he said. "Now fuck off and leave me to my breakfast."

Fucking off away from the prick was my fucking pleasure.

Making it through the day was a whole lot easier with a whole load of cash to spend, too.

Grace spent most of the afternoon on the phone paying bills, and I spent it sifting through paperwork.

It was when she called her sister to transfer back the couple of grand we'd borrowed that I overheard her asking a question out of the blue.

"Do you still speak to Polly Piper?"

My ears pricked up at the name. I shook my head across the table at her, but she waved me aside with a scowl.

"From school, yeah. She's friends with a guy called Thomas Heath, have you ever heard of him?"

The sag of her shoulders told me she was onto a dead end.

"No, definitely not Thomas Browning. Thomas Heath. Tall, fit, super gorgeous, from London. Rich."

I raised an eyebrow as she said her goodbyes and hung up.

"She hadn't heard of him, then?" I prompted.

"No, never. Polly Piper was friends with a kid called Thomas at school, but it wasn't that one. She didn't think Polly had ever even been to London, said she's been glued to the bakery since forever."

"I guess it will be one of life's mysteries then," I commiserated, then wished I'd picked my words better. Grace hates an unsolved mystery.

"When we head back to visit maybe I'll call in for an apple turnover, see what I can get out of her."

Over my dead fucking body. Thomas Heath would be the last thing on her mind by then.

I only just managed to bite my tongue, and had to bite it again when he joined us in the bar at just before seven.

I didn't even get the chance to ask him what he was drinking before he held a hand up and placed a coat hanger draped in black satin across the bar top. His words were all for Grace.

"For you, later. Please wear this," he told her. "I'll be back for a quick drink before time."

I made to tear into the assortment before he was even out through the door, but Grace's hand slapped on mine before I'd even taken a look.

"No," she said. "Let me see first. I might be embarrassed."

My grunt was loud and more than a little obnoxious. "We can be embarrassed together, open it up."

But she wouldn't.

Her eyes were fierce, burning with a whole pit of nerves as she snatched the hanger from my reach.

I guess it was the first sign of the troubles in the water.

I should have heeded the warning.

SEVENTEEN

GRACE

I guess that's when it hit me, absolutely for real.

The twenty-five grand landing in our account in concrete figures on Brett's mobile banking app was cold, hard reality, as were the voices of our creditors when I called and paid off our outstanding balances. But this. This bundle of whatever outfit Thomas Heath had conjured up for me to wear for him was another level of *oh fuck, this is really happening* altogether.

My cheeks were scalding under my foundation, even before he'd draped it on the bar top and left me staring dumb as he retreated. Brett's curiosity was almost childlike in his enthusiasm to check out what was waiting within the satin shroud, and that's the first time my nerves really shot away beyond all control.

My slap to his outstretched hand was hard and fast, his recoil one of shock, eyes wide as they met mine and found my defensiveness burning off the scale.

"No," I snapped. "Let me see first. I might be embarrassed."

His grunt had a sulky quality that set my hackles up even higher. "We can be embarrassed together. Open it up."

But no.

No way in hell.

I scooped the bundle up in my arms before he could protest any further, crushing the fabric tight to my side as I backed up to a safe distance.

"I mean it," I told him. "I need to do this on my own."

Need.

I hated how desperate the word sounded.

He didn't understand, and I didn't blame him. He couldn't disguise the hurt as it flashed across his face, even if he followed it up straight after with a shrug. I knew I was being a bitch, but I couldn't stop. Barely able to function enough to breathe and keep my shit together, let alone apologise.

"Please yourself," he offered. "If you don't like it, don't wear it."

My heart was in my throat, so all I did was nod, my lips pressed tight together in what must have looked like a mean little line.

I wanted to say I was sorry. That I was just scared. For me, for us. For this night of craziness and what it would mean tomorrow and the day after, and all the days from then on.

For the humiliation of wearing something picked out by a stranger with filthy designs on my body, despite never actually seeing it in the flesh. For the potential horror of having to tell him it didn't fit. That my thighs were too flabby, or my tits weren't big enough, or I couldn't get the buttons done up at the waist.

For seeing myself in the mirror and feeling like a has-been rack of mutton trying to dress up like a fifty-grand lamb.

I wanted to tell Brett I loved him. That I was scared of him seeing me like this, whatever *like this* might be. That I didn't want him to keep this vision of me for the rest of our married life, remembering how I trussed myself up in some other guy's seedy clothes choice and performed like a circus clown with my holes spread wide.

"Go have a look," Brett said, and I realised I was hovering there like an iron scarecrow, the muscles in my arms straining tight at my sides, doing nothing useful and wanting nothing more than to wrap around my husband's big safe shoulders and tell him this was a mistake.

But no.

It wasn't a mistake.

Paying the creditors hadn't been a mistake, nor had the joyous surprise in my sister's voice when I'd called to pay her back the monies owed.

Looking out of the window at our treasured beach this morning and knowing I was safeguarding a thousand more mornings of doing the same, that wasn't a mistake either.

I managed a nod and the faintest of smiles.

My voice was raspy when it came out. "I'll be back soon."

I turned away before he could reply, forcing my legs to carry me out the back through the kitchen and on to the safety of our own private bathroom.

I wriggled the bolt closed behind me and it grumbled out a rusty screech I'd never heard, having never used the thing in all the time we'd been here. I sat on the toilet lid, trying to calm my erratic breathing as I braced myself to confront the first fantasy of the man upstairs.

I was picturing leather. Latex. Something I'd need a sack full of talcum powder and a vat full of baby oil to get into, if it was even possible.

Maybe he'd dress me up as one of those tacky farmyard animals after all. Maybe I'd be wearing a horsey harness all ripe for the ponytail butt plug up my ass later. Maybe I'd be one of those naughty nurses, or a thirty-year-old schoolgirl, or even worse.

An adult baby in a frilly pair of panties.

Maybe he'd make me call him stupid names on my knees, trussed up like some stupid idiot with my muffin top sagging over ridiculously tight latex panties. *Daddy*, or *Master*, or some other pompous title that would make me cringe forever and never be able to meet my own eyes in the mirror without bursting with shame.

I could have cried, so nervous that my hands were shaking at the thought of looking inside the satin and facing the inevitable.

I knew it was ridiculous. An outfit was the least of my concerns under the circumstances. It just felt so… invasive. So… humiliating.

And more than that.

Even under all the nerves and the raspy breath and the burning cheeks, there was something more.

My damn thighs were quaking, edgy enough to tremble along with the flutter of what was between them. I'd been clammy all day, in places I shouldn't be. Places I didn't want to be.

I had no idea that it was possible to be so utterly petrified and turned on at the same time.

I was nauseous as I dared to hitch the black satin cover up and off the hanger, but what greeted me was enough to take my breath in one gulp.

It was beautiful.

Not leather or latex or farmyard fancy dress.

Black lace and ribbon, beautifully stitched and presented on the hanger. The cups of the bodice were low, no doubt cut off under the nipple, but the fabric was quality and the shape would be flattering, even if my curves weren't as toned as they would have been a decade ago.

The panties were a thong with satin tie ribbons at the hips and a slit in the gusset. I wondered if he really was planning to slam his dick inside me with those pretty knickers still in position. I almost hoped so, and this time I didn't fight it, because what was the point?

I liked it, or didn't. Wanted to run upstairs into Thomas Heath's dirty hands and out the front door and far away all at the same time. It would be heaven, or hell, or both. My pussy clenched at the thought, even as my belly churned with the horror.

I turned my attention back to the outfit, taking a breath and forcing myself to focus.

There were suspender belt attachments hanging from the ruffle at the hips, and a pair of lace top stockings hooked onto the hanger on the back.

He'd picked well, both in choice and in size. The selection was perfect, both in overall sizing and cup size, much better than Brett would have ever managed, even after all these years.

I wondered how a stranger gauged my measurements with such accuracy, prickling at how closely he must have been examining me all those times in his company.

I realised what a paranoid bitch I'd been, sitting there and fighting back tears of relief along with giggles as I let my guard come down. Brett could have easily looked along with me without any fallout. He could have even got a happy advanced preview. The hand slap was entirely overkill and so were the bristling nerves.

I was losing the plot. Absolutely, entirely, without any doubt.

But still, as I held that outfit up once more to the overhead light and examined the gorgeous pattern in the lace, I was glad I'd taken this moment as my own.

I remembered *the night* all those years ago when I was barely legal and had whispered to Brett after college one day that I was *ready*. We'd been fumbling for months through that summer, edging closer and closer, but that night was a world away from all the other impromptu make out sessions. I'd gotten myself ready with a long hot bath, preparing myself like some kind of sacrificial offering before he'd arrived with a big grin on his face for a night at mine. Soaping and shaving, preening and prepping, curling my hair in the perfect wave and using what felt like every single item in my makeup box.

I'd forgotten how the nerves had danced up my spine as I dressed in my favourite underwear, all ready for him to make me his for the first time. I'd forgotten how my heart had raced at the thought of the ultimate sensation, him claiming my body in a way that could never be undone.

I felt that way all over again as I hung Thomas Heath's chosen outfit on the back of the door and turned the shower jet on full. I cast off my everyday blouse and jeans like I was shedding my skin, stepping under the faucet as though I'd step back out a whole new woman.

No, not a woman. A nervous girl with a fluttering belly, worried about a strange man's hands on her body for nine hours straight.

I soaped and shaved with as much care as I had for my husband when he was just a fumbling teenager. I let the magic of being seen, exposed and vulnerable through a stranger's hungry eyes, wash over me with the body scrub.

It didn't need to be hell.

It could be anything but a nightmare.

It could be an awakening. A night of experimentation in a lifetime of stability. It wasn't cheating, or adultery, not even close. The stranger upstairs could hurt me, drag my body screaming to places from his twisted imagination, but I'd be doing it for my life with the man I loved.

I was exhausted with my own frayed emotions, tired of see-sawing through the crazy reactions of the past few days. It already felt like an age since our loaded guest had stepped up to the bar and made his filthy offer.

Letting the emotional crud wash away was easier than I expected when push finally came to shove. Call me a realist, a pragmatist, a rationalist accepting her fate, but I let it all go and forced my chin up to face whatever perversion was coming my way.

I towelled off my freshly shaved body with gentle hands, moisturising every single inch of skin when I was done. I brushed my teeth with the vigour of someone on a first date, drying my hair in the waves I'd practiced so well for my husband. I applied my makeup carefully, steadying my shaking fingers with a nervous smile on my face.

And then, finally, I slipped on the beautiful bedroom outfit.

The full length mirror told me everything I needed to know, and so did the tears pricking my eyes as I twisted to give myself a better view.

They weren't sad tears threatening to fall, or even nervous ones.

They were the tears of a woman taken aback by how good she felt in her own skin.

I couldn't wait for Thomas Heath to see me like this, there was no denying it.

But more importantly, I couldn't wait for my husband to see me like this either.

EIGHTEEN

THOMAS

A text message buzzed in my pocket as I made the final room preparations.

I finished lining up the impressive array of props on the dressing table before I took a look at it, my excitement tingling deep through my balls.

Don't. Please don't do this to yourself.

Her good intentions pained me, but not nearly enough to make a difference.

My poor sweet Polly was missing the point entirely. For every ounce of dead hope I was bringing down on myself through this endeavour, I was bringing a world of pain to the guy I'd hated right the way through living memory.

And beautiful Grace, the girl I'd lusted after since before I really knew what the word meant. She'd be mine.

I'm certain Polly was missing the true meaning laced within my plans, assuming my infatuation with Grace would lead me down a treacherous path, veering between self-hatred and some strange semblance of romantic love turned bad. But she was wrong.

Grace Foster would be mine, but there would be no hearts and roses. No long evenings laughing over shared jokes, the way she'd been doing with her husband for years.

Grace Foster would be mine in soul. Shackled by the tainted memory of the way I'd played her body, and her spirit along with it. Her skin would crave my contact, even as her bruised heart bled from all the fallout.

She'd want what she could never have. A soul-felt connection like the one she'd believed she'd been blessed with as a married woman. Only more.

More lust. More sweat and shivers and the crazed ripples of a body driven over the edge.

Maybe I'd give her the latter all over again, once or twice to seal the deal. Maybe even once too many, beyond all reason, her siren's call tempting even a stone-hearted sonofabitch like me.

Or maybe I'd abandon her to her shattered memories and never return her calls.

I tightened the waterproof sheet over the bare mattress, stretching it taut before stuffing the covers and pillows out of sight in the big double wardrobe.

I shifted the hulk of furniture along the carpet slightly, ensuring the full length mirror was positioned just so, prime for all parties to see all glorious angles of the action.

Brett's chair was already in place, mid-way along the bed and close enough to see the dirty display, despite being just out of arm's reach. If he broke with jealousy enough to spring to his feet and assault me halfway through proceedings it would be the biggest mistake he'd make in his life.

I'd already set up the camera and app with its infrared mapping light on the bedside table. One move across the trigger line and their remaining twenty-five grand would retreat from its holding account and rush safely back into mine.

It wouldn't be the first time money had slipped from a couple's grip in such a manner.

Part of me hoped it would pan out that way, just so I could witness him at maximum pain in his jealous rage. It was one of the unfortunate side effects of leaving in the morning with only a business card in my wake — never getting to witness the ensuing relationship meltdown first-hand.

I could only imagine. As luck would have it, I'm a very imaginative guy.

My shower was short but thorough, my spritz of classic scent generous as it clung to my still-damp skin. My suit was my finest, crisp in its stark black and white lines, so perfectly monochrome. My brogues were polished and my teeth were brushed and flossed. My hair was swept back from my face and my beard freshly clipped and smoothed neat.

I'd never been more ready for a pretty woman's cunt as I was for Grace Foster's inexperienced little treasure trove, I just wished I had ninety hours to explore her rather than nine.

I took the stairs down slowly to the bar, arriving at just after nine for an hour of careful drinking before proceedings began. The room was empty of outsiders, which was somewhat of a disappointment. I'd hoped for at least a few oblivious guests thrumming around the place, forcing my hosts into easy smiles at odds with their rattling nerves.

Instead it was only Brett, propped at the bar with a beer half drunk, scrolling through his phone and feigning ignorance of my presence.

He knew I was there, just as I knew he knew it. His surly pretence of superiority did nothing but encourage my inner bastard, my smirk at full smugness as I took a stool opposite him.

"A scotch," I told him. "Single shot this time. I want my senses… *alert*."

He made sure to leave me waiting a few seconds before switching his handset to sleep mode and grabbing a full bottle of scotch from beneath the counter, slamming it in front of me along with an empty glass.

"Knock yourself out," he grunted. "It's on the house. Piss your pants in a drunken stupor and be my guest."

My laugh was full of malice. "I wouldn't hold your breath."

He stood me off, eyes burning and shoulders high as he took another long swig of his own beverage, and then he laughed a bitter laugh of his own.

I poured a single shot, and he scoffed at my measure.

"You really think this means something, don't you?" he said. "You're really so puffed up with ego you think we're gonna be fucked up proper by one sad fuck on a January Tuesday." He took another swig of beer, but his eyes held mine. "We won't be holding a toast to your memory every twelve months, if that's what you're thinking."

I enjoyed the smoky fragrance of the scotch before I took a sip.

"*You're* really so bloated in ego that you believe your own sorry bravado," I retorted, making sure my shoulders were as relaxed as ever.

"This ain't bravado, pal–" he began, but his words dried up in a flash as his eyes widened at the doorway behind me.

Spinning to face the object of his distraction was instinctive, as was the way my own throat dried up at the sight of the beautiful woman walking through to join us.

She was Grace Foster, but she wasn't. Her tight red dress was divine on her curves, finishing high enough on her thighs that the lace tops of the stockings I'd picked out for her were visible for a flash with every step. Her heels were high enough that her calves were straining tight, black gloss stilettos with a hint of hooker that her classic beauty offset so perfectly my dick was pulsing in seconds.

Her makeup was smoky and her lips were deep red to match her dress, her hair shining dark with a side parting that highlighted her high cheekbones.

There wasn't a price tag in the world that could do justice to the hunger she drew from me. If her brute of a husband had slapped me on the shoulder and called off our deal in favour of sweeping her to bed himself I'd have risen my glass to him gladly.

But he didn't.

He was uncharacteristically dumbstruck as his beautiful other half arrived alongside me, his eyes full of the sappy kind of adoration I'd devoted the past few years to proving impermanent.

"Did I polish up alright?" Grace asked, but she was playing. I loved the confident twinkle in those hazel-green eyes as she smiled first at him and then at me.

She knew she looked incredible. She maybe didn't appreciate quite how incredible, but she was well on her way.

Being the catalyst for such a confident transformation of the poor, broken woman I'd seen at the bar a few days earlier was a strange, heartfelt pleasure.

"You look beautiful," Brett told her across the bar, and his words bubbled with the kind of honesty that brought many a man to his knees.

I gave them a moment, sitting silent as the look of adoration simmered between them, well prepared to back away if they came to their senses enough to realise fifty grand was worth nothing more than a drop in the ocean of their commitment to each other.

But no.

Grace's eyes were still sparkling bright when they turned their attention back to mine.

"Are you satisfied with your investment so far?" she asked me with a flutter of those falsely thickened lashes.

"Very," I told her. "It'll be almost a shame to strip you of those gorgeous adornments."

"Almost?" she prompted and I smiled.

"Come on, dearest Mrs Foster, fishing for flattery doesn't become you.

You know how magical you look this evening. You could Pied Piper every male in a hundred mile radius with one flash of that siren smile."

I'd have believed her nerves had vanished if it hadn't been for the way her fingers trembled as they took a glass of wine from her husband.

"Just the one," she commented, clearly for my benefit. "I want to be in control of my bodily functions, after all."

"I want, doesn't get," I responded drily. "I'll be the one in control of your bodily functions this evening."

Her eyes were all on me as she took her first sip, and there, behind the glossy confidence of a sexy set of lingerie and the fried nerves of a woman giving herself to another man for the very first time, in the quiet shadows, in the core of her very being, was the palpable flutter of desire. I felt it. All of it. Every breathy quiver. Every clench of that curious pussy in the black lace I knew was kissing the soft pink lips between her legs.

And tonight, without a doubt — despite the husband across from her with puppy dog eyes and the steady grip of his ring on her finger — that pussy's wetness was all for me.

NINETEEN

GRACE

Seeing the way two pairs of eyes ate me up was enough to set me alight. It was far more potent than the glass of red in my hand, far more affirming than even the gross amount of money Thomas Heath would pay for the pleasure.

He couldn't stop looking at me, even though he tried to disguise his constant stare with an arrogant nonchalance. I knew his dick was already hard for me under the fine suit he'd virtually ironed onto his body. I knew he was clammy at the thought of what was to come, even through his cucumber cool veneer. Just as I was.

And just as my husband was, too.

Brett was keeping a tight lid on it, but I could read the way he shifted his weight from one hip to another and scratched a nervous itch on his jawline. I could see the tiniest hint of sweat at his temples, even though he kept his smile firm and bright.

No sooner than I was settled on a barstool and enjoying my drink, I blinked and the hour was ending.

I watched the big hand on the clock on the far wall make its final click onto the hour, and despite it being out of his eyeline, Thomas Heath got to his feet on cue.

"And so it begins," he said. "Drink up."

I could barely swallow my final gulp of wine, my throat tightening as the nerves slammed back hard. *Bye bye, confidence. Hello, I don't know what the hell I'm supposed to do now.*

Brett got the lights from behind the bar and plunged us into a shady darkness that made the light of the beckoning staircase beam all the brighter. He dropped under the hatch and appeared at my side, slipping his hand into mine with a comforting squeeze.

"Let's get this show on the road," he commented, and I squeezed his fingers right back.

Heath beckoned us on ahead of him and I flashed him a glance over my shoulder as we walked on by. I could feel him there all the way, his warmth scorching the back of me, even though he was two steps behind.

My feet felt slippery in my heels, my thighs awkwardly tight as I climbed the stairs mute alongside my silent husband, wondering if we were really going to do this at the final hour. If this was really, really going down.

We arrived at the top suite and the man who'd paid to use my body slipped his key into the lock and pushed open the door. I stepped across the threshold first, fighting back a gasp at the scene before me.

It looked barely anything like the room I'd changed countless times. The mattress was stripped bare and cloaked in the thick waterproof sheet I'd seen in a box the night before. It looked seedy. Dark and foreboding in its purpose.

The dresser was covered in every filthy toy imaginable. Towering dildos and curvy vibrators. Plugs and clamps and shapes I couldn't even comprehend. Floggers, whips, and cuffs were hung over the knobs of the chest of drawers, resting within easy reach of the far side of the bed. Two chairs were positioned with purpose, one at the side of the bed facing across to the window, and the other at the bottom of the bed facing the top.

"For you," the man with the plan said to Brett and tapped the back of the chair facing the window. Only it wasn't facing the window, not really. It was facing the mattress, close enough that he'd see everything, smell everything, *feel* everything.

Our dirty blonde guest tapped the top of what looked like a black box on the bedside table nearest us. A thin line of red light presented itself on the carpet.

"This is the boundary," he said as I struggled to fathom what he was talking about. "Cross this line and the money in the holding account reverts to mine. Agreement null and void."

I could hear the pride in Brett's growled response. "I won't be crossing the fucking line. A deal is a deal. Just make sure you stick to your end of it."

The other man raised his hands with a laugh. "I think I've already demonstrated how serious I am. I trust you enjoyed spending the first instalment."

Neither of us said a word, Brett simply squeezing my fingers in one final gesture of support before taking his seat as instructed.

He was tense, his legs rigid and spread wide, foot tapping as he braced his elbows on the armrests. I didn't blame him.

"And what about me?" I dared to whisper. "Where do you want me?"

I'd grown used to his smirk, but this time it came with a filthy glint in his eyes that set my spine tingling. I could have bolted for the door quite happily, even as my pussy tingled behind my fancy lace panties.

He gestured to the side of the bed, between Brett and the mattress, and I shifted slowly on my heels, tiny steps edging me in his direction. I wondered if this was the moment. If he'd grab me in those solid toned arms and manhandle me every which way he wanted me, but no sooner had I reached his appointed spot than he took the other chair for himself, stretching out his long legs and crossing them at the ankles.

I was dithering in the open space, two pairs of eyes scorching me from different directions.

"What now?" I asked, despising how uncertain my voice sounded.

Where was the diva from my bathroom that could take on the world? Where was the woman who'd pictured riding Thomas Heath like a filthy slut while Brett stared on, proud of the seductress blooming strong in his lovely wife?

"Nothing," Heath said with a smile. "Let me look at you."

I shrugged like a petulant teenager, catching my own ridiculousness before beginning a slow turn for him. I felt like a fool, and a clumsy one at that, regretting my hooker heel choice in a heartbeat.

"Like this?" I prompted after one full spin.

"Like however you want it to be," he said, and I forced myself to take a breath.

No big deal. The more time I spent entertaining him with my poses, the less time he could spend double fisting my asshole.

I stopped twirling, instead sucking in a deep lungful of air and settling into my own skin. I parted my legs a little to gain more balance, sliding my hands down my waist to rest on my hips, checking out my reflection in the mirror behind him.

I looked considerably more composed than I felt inside.

I didn't want to face looking at my husband while I was still wrestling my nerves, so I didn't. I kept my eyes on my reflection, shifting smoothly from hip to hip as my bare arms goose-pimpled at the scrutiny. I tipped my chin up high and pulled my shoulders back enough to showcase the swell of cleavage his bodice gift was helping with so beautifully.

And then I looked at him. Thomas Heath from North London with his piercing eyes that matched mine in colour behind his geek chic glasses.

There was no smirk on his face. Not even a trace of amusement as his gaze roved up and down the length of me. I couldn't fight the way my heart fluttered, couldn't fight the thumping pulse that pounded hard throughout my entire body.

"That's good," he said, and his voice was quiet yet commanding. "Relax."

I took a long breath in through my nose and out through my mouth, wetting my lips — which were drying out even under glossy lipstick — with a quick sweep of my tongue.

"Now take off the dress," he told me.

My fingers were trembling as I slipped them behind my back to pull down the zipper. The fabric peeled loose from my cleavage and I watched my exposed nipples appear in view, hard little bullets poking over the low cut lace cups underneath.

I shimmied my way out of the red dress, letting it fall to the floor before stepping out. It was one step closer to the man who'd be slamming his way inside me before the night was done and I felt every inch like it was a mile.

The mirror told me I still looked every bit as good in the lingerie as I had getting ready, but my beating heart found it hard to accept.

"A perfect fit," Heath commented, and I could tell from his tone that he'd known it would be.

"A perfect choice," I admitted. "It's beautiful."

"As is the woman wearing it."

I sensed Brett shift in his chair and wished, for the first time since agreeing to this madness, that he wasn't here to watch. My self-consciousness at being so dirty in front of the man who loved me with all his soul was enough to make me rattle.

"Climb onto the bed," Heath told me. "Kneel up high, thighs spread nicely."

I did as he wanted, positioning myself in the middle of the mattress, my eyes still firmly on the me in the mirror.

He made no move to join me. No move at all.

"I want you to touch yourself," he said. "Not for my benefit. No shows or theatrics or fake porn moans, just you, touching yourself however you like to be touched."

I dared to hiss out a laugh. "I'm hardly one for fake porn moans."

Even Brett let out a low laugh at the thought. It was strangely comforting.

I looked rigid in my reflection as my fingers swept down between my legs. It was a pathetic attempt at pleasure, my motions barely stimulating the right spot in my awkwardness to do his bidding.

He said nothing, just watched. And so did I. First myself in the mirror, and then his back in the reflection, only daring to look right at him when the glass of wine from earlier settled in my veins.

It was enough. Just enough.

His eyes were sharp and bright. His stance was easy and relaxed, even though he was switched on enough that I could feel the sizzle.

He sizzled.

His suit was glorious on his perfect body. The angles in his face arranged flawlessly.

In other circumstances… in another world… maybe, just maybe I could fall for a man like Thomas Heath.

Or at least have a schoolgirl crush on him.

Definitely a schoolgirl crush on him.

I abandoned the efforts on my clit and snaked my hands up over the gorgeous black lace of my bodice, my palms brushing my tender nipples and rippling the first wave of genuine pleasure back through me.

I tugged at them, pinching in just the way I did in bed at night when the fantasies came calling. I flicked them with tiny flutters of my fingers, breathing long and low as the sensations danced in my belly. And lower.

I shifted my thighs further apart and rocked my hips forward enough that the lace of the knickers gripped me tight. I rolled my lower half in wide circles, sinking into the rhythm as my fingers kept on dancing over my prickling nipples.

And I felt it.

For real, I felt it.

When my fingers slipped back down there was no staged performance this time around. My clit was grateful for the sweep of my hand, my knickers wet with genuine need for more.

I closed my eyes, blocking out the reflection and the room and everyone in it, focusing on the thrum between my legs and the way my clit sparked against my touch. It was slow, torturous, much more sensual than the way I usually strummed one off in a ragged heartbeat with Brett asleep at my side.

I tipped my head back as my breaths turned shallow, one hand still palming my exposed tits as my fingers circled the sweet spot through sopping lace. I didn't speed up, not even when my body demanded it, setting myself up for an orgasm that rippled right through me, regardless of the witnesses.

I was too far gone to hold back when I finally opened my eyes and met those of the man in front of me. My squirms were all real as I worked my clit into a natural frenzy, the mattress rippling under my knees as I braced for the waves.

My mouth was open when I reached my climax, and so was his, his breaths mirroring mine as I shuddered and came for him.

And then it was done.

I couldn't hold back the heady grin as I sank to the bed and let my breath calm along with my thumping heart.

TWENTY

BRETT

Seeing my wife like that, exposed for another man's eyes with her fingers playing with the pretty little pussy I knew so well, was enough to boil the blood in my veins. My forehead was tight and tense, my hair slick with sweat gathering from the pressure of staying still, but still I was swollen hard as a fucking bullock.

She was stunning. Breath-taking in the dirty black lace that sonofabitch had chosen for her.

Her nervousness was spellbinding and her excitement was all real. I knew the raspy pattern of her breath as she peaked, the tightness in her shoulders as her fingers worked their magic.

It took everything in me not to charge across that shitty red line and take her as my own, the way I should do, the way we were born to do.

I gripped the armrests with white knuckles as she relaxed in the aftermath, dreading what was coming when the prick decided to make his move. But he didn't. He didn't move a fucking muscle, just sat there as though he owned the fucking place, which I guess he did tonight, watching my wife unfurl with a clipped smile on that smug bastard face of his.

"Shit," my wife breathed, laughing with a ghost of a giggle, her chest rising and falling as she leaned back on her arms, her stiff nipples on show, her legs still folded underneath her and those crazy high heels jutting out like lethal spikes against the mattress.

She should be looking at me, but I was almost glad she wasn't. I was scared of the unspoken words that would pass between us, of her realising that I was seething in my seat and filling up with a torrent of regret that would steal her ease for the rest of the night.

And it would be a long fucking night.

Even more than I wanted peace for myself, I wanted peace for her.

I chanced a glance at the asshole a few feet away. His eyes were fixed on Grace's. His attention all for her.

I could have stormed him with enough of a surprise to break his neck before he'd even got his guard up. It was tempting.

So was the hard on in my pants, begging me to thrust my seedy hand down deep and jerk myself into a frenzy.

"A beautiful performance," the cunt said, and I could almost imagine him giving her a round of applause.

It brought her to her senses enough for her shoulders to tense, the colour in her cheeks blooming.

I expected that would be the moment he made his move, but still nothing. His legs stayed easy, his body relaxed, like he had all the time in the world. Still, the night was young. Maybe his stamina wasn't up to a full nine hours. I could fucking hope.

I could see Grace contemplating what was next, knowing well the way she pinned her lip between her teeth, pondering not slutty. Still, it was horny as fuck.

In those moments I'd usually brush her pretty mouth with my thumb and pull her in for a kiss. But not tonight.

"What next?" she asked him, breaking the silence with nothing short of cute awkwardness.

He made her wait before he answered, and I felt the pause just as hard.

"You keep going," he told her. "Relax. Lay back. Find your magic all over again."

Her smile was as natural as her orgasm, bracing for another giggle as she stared straight over at him.

"I can't, um… not right away…"

"So take your time," he said, and he meant it.

She kicked off her heels and dumped them on the far side of the bed as she adjusted herself to a more comfortable position. I could see how clammy her thighs were as she dropped onto her back and closed her eyes, her legs spread gently open and bent at the knee.

Her hands lay flat on her stomach at first, moving with her breaths before she ventured to slip them down lower. I knew her body almost as well as I knew mine. Knew how she shuddered when her clit was tender, holding back from more until she could take it, but tonight was different. It had to be.

I watched her eyes tighten at the intensity as she dared to brush her fingers over the lace of her thong. Her other hand was gentle as she grazed her exposed tits, perky nipples pointing at the ceiling and craving round two, even if her pussy protested.

"I can't believe you're seeing me like this," she whispered, and it smarted that her words were all for him.

"Show me what feels good," he said in that satin fucking voice, urging her on with such calm fucking purpose that I wanted to wrap my hands around his throat and squeeze the life out of him.

We must have made it through the best part of a full hour by the time she found her groove for a second time round. It irked me to realise that we never usually left it this long, moving straight from her breathy climax onto different games, games involving her pretty mouth around my dick, or me slamming balls deep inside her, or grinding flesh on flesh, mouth on mouth, more, more, fucking more.

The cunt was skilled and practiced, just as I'd feared in that pit of paranoia in the back of my mind. He knew what he was doing, barely breaking a sweat as he watched her find another frantic rhythm.

I hated how this part of Grace was unfamiliar to me, even after years at her side. Her body movements were known to me, but the tender rapture on her sweet face at the forced patience imposed by a stranger was edged with something I didn't know so well.

My wife wasn't a screamer. She didn't wail and hiss and curse in the bedroom, not even when I ploughed her hard enough to hiss myself. She was reserved in her outbursts, a gentle flower blooming and bursting, all natural in her whimpers and rasps, just understated.

But not now. Not on round two.

Her body couldn't hold back the shudders as she sought skin on skin and plunged her needy fingers inside her knickers. I could hear the wetness above breaths that turned to low rasping moans, her thighs falling open to give that dirty cunt a better view of his purchase.

"This is… oh fuck…" she whimpered, and my balls tightened like volcanic rocks threatening to fucking explode.

"That's good," he said right back at her. "Show me."

I knew her fingers were dipping inside her pussy without looking. My eyes were firmly on her open mouth as she tipped her head back and spread those thighs even wider, her heels gripping the plastic sheeting underneath her and angling her higher.

Both hands were between her legs, one pushing fingers in deep while the other circled that clit in a blur of motion that made my mouth water. I couldn't resist looking at him, his eyes greedy on the lace stretched tight across her knuckles.

"*Oh fuck,*" she whimpered again, and her whole body shunted back and forth, teeth gritting tight as she grunted low.

My Grace fucking grunted, like she was taking hard fucking cock, only she wasn't. She was taking two fingers at best, lapping up the thrill of two pairs of ravenous eyes on that gorgeous fucking body of hers.

"Good girl," he told her, and her reaction was explosive. Her body was rigid, back arched as she buckled under her frantic fingers, squelching in wetness as she reached the edge of a second orgasm, so much fucking harder than the first.

She liked it.

She fucking liked it.

And worse than that, so did I.

I couldn't stop staring, couldn't stop my throbbing dick threatening to blow in my fucking pants.

I was transfixed as she murmured and wriggled, and she was lost to both of us, lost to everything but the sensation of those sweet fingers down her knickers.

Until he moved.

Oh fuck, how he fucking moved. Like a cat, stealthy and slick with perfect fucking timing.

I couldn't have timed it better my fucking self.

He was fully clothed as he climbed up onto the mattress alongside her, positioning himself at her side, his long fucking legs draping down next to hers as she tipped her face to stare up at him.

She couldn't have stopped if she'd wanted to, her body was long gone to nerves or reason. Her whimpers were right at him, her mouth open as his lowered to press against her bare shoulder. His fingers were big against her pretty pale tits as he pinched one of those hard nubs and flicked his wrist in the same way she'd done earlier.

And it was enough.

Fuck, how it was enough.

One single touch had her reeling senseless, her fingers bucking in her knickers as his hand slid down and pressed on top.

"Beautiful," he whispered. "Now kiss me like you want me."

She shuddered, holding her breath as the shock of the second wave ripped through her body. It was brutal in its perfection, her feet scrabbling as she reached her peak.

Even in her madness she managed to look across at me before she acknowledged his request.

Her eyes were hungry and wide, and she wanted him.

Fuck, she fucking wanted him, she just wanted me to say it was okay.

A nod was all it took, barely more than a tip of my head was all that I could manage. Her face turned to his in a heartbeat, mouth parting as he came in for the kiss.

She kissed him like she wanted him, because she fucking did. I watched my wife kiss another man with a pain like I'd never felt, right in my gut as my fucking cock kept on throbbing.

And I couldn't blame her, not for a moment in the madness. Not for one single breath as I dared to palm my dick through my own trousers.

Because as much as I hated the man on the bed with my woman, part of me wanted it too.

TWENTY ONE

THOMAS

She was glorious. A delicious wonder writhing under her greedy fingers as they pumped her to her peak.

The boy in me was air punching, swept away from his usual melancholy to something far more exciting.

It was a victory, beyond all doubt, one that exploded in one brilliant flash as Grace Foster's mouth welcomed my tongue and sucked me in.

This wasn't like the slow, steady victories of my professional career, granted after long, concerted and physically draining bouts of effort for years on end. This was an another beast, a rousing beast, a beast that burst forth in me with a strength that took me aback.

She was more than I'd ever dared to imagine as a teenager. Her tongue was a paradox in its movements, both eager and shy in equal measure. Her lips were soft, meeting mine with a gentleness at odds with the force with which I claimed them. My kiss was violent and deep, perfectly timed to meet her own crest of pleasure. She couldn't fight the shudder of breath against my open mouth, her throat rumbling low enough that I could feel the vibration against my fingertips as they swept down her neck and onto the sensitive swell of her gorgeous tits. I shifted against her, pressing the hardness of my dick against her hip, throbbing even through the thick fabric of my suit trousers.

I loved the contrast of our attire. Pretty Grace Foster dressed for my pleasure, exposed in unfamiliar garments with her dainty fingers frantic in her wetness. Me, still suited for a day playing hardball in the boardroom.

It was more than the simple divide of the clothing. There was a psychological resonance echoing through our differing appearances, undeniable in its vibrancy, and it was making my dick as hard as all hell.

I was in control.

Firmly in my comfort zone just as far as she was outside of hers.

I loved it that way. *Needed* it that way.

But it was more than the selfish power play of the teenage ghost inside me. The dynamic was as essential for her pleasure that evening as it was for mine.

I needed Grace to yield to my natural authority with every fibre of her being. It was only through basking in my strength that she would ever allow herself to fully embrace her vulnerabilities, and therein lay the ultimate revelation, waiting quietly for exposure.

As her defences crumbled and opened her up to my touch, so the quiet desires of her deepest filthy soul would be there for the taking. Claiming that shadowy side of her blossoming sexuality would be the ultimate prize, and the one that would leave her raw and desperate in the aftermath, an addict craving more.

And that, ultimately, was why I was really here.

Not to get my dick wet in some other man's woman. Not to prove a passing point that another man's cock could feel as good as her husband's. Not even to prove that cash was king in a world stuffed full of valentine's trinkets and grandiose statements of forever.

This was about the man bracing in his seat as I lowered my mouth to his beautiful wife's nipple and sucked hard enough that she cried out for me. This was about the history between us, the rivalry that spanned a lifetime, even if he was too sheltered by his ignorance to feel it.

This was about me proving that I could shake his marriage to its foundation in nine short hours.

Proving I was the better man. The more skilled man, more worthy man, the more powerful, gifted, sensual, fucking *everything* man.

That *I* fucking mattered.

That *I* was fucking somebody.

I pulled away from Grace's body as the fire inside roared too deep to contain. I calmed myself with steel will, staring down at her open, puffy lips as her body strained for her second climax.

"Good girl," I said again, loving the way the thrill flashed across her pretty face.

I watched her orgasm through cold eyes, detached from her squirming groans as she unravelled before me. It was something truly special, the surprise in her dilated pupils a treasure to behold.

The groans were all natural as she buckled and lashed out with her feet, her body betraying her shyness with every jerky motion as she cried out and rode the waves. She tensed in the throes for long blissful moments, head tipped back and mouth wide before the inevitable collapse that followed.

Her breaths were heavy as she recovered, her fingers recoiling from her sensitive cunt and coming to rest on her belly. I could smell her wetness, musky enough to make my mouth water and every bit as appetising as I anticipated.

Her eyes were closed as she gathered herself, only fluttering back onto mine as I raised two of her wet fingers to my lips and sucked them clean.

She shivered but didn't look away, making no effort to fight me as I took her other hand in mine and stretched both of them high above her head.

The cuffs were already waiting, on chains that stretched under the mattress, waiting like coiled snakes out of sight.

She murmured as I clicked the first steel restraint around her slender wrist, but didn't argue. It was Brett that shunted in his seat, but I didn't grant him even a sliver of acknowledgement.

I knew he was a proud fool enough to stay seated, an angry bull stomping at the glowing red line on the carpet, but impotent all the same.

All for the sake of a paltry, pitiful fifty fucking grand.

I clasped the second cuff closed around Grace's raised wrists, smiling just a fraction as I slipped back down the bed to her side. Her face was tipped in my direction, her endorphins still spiking as her breathing steadied.

"Relax," I told her, and she kept her eyes on mine as she tested her restraints.

"Please…" she whispered. "Please just… wait… I'm so…" She rippled against me as she struggled to find the words.

But I knew.

Of course I knew.

Her body was prickling all over, her pussy aching from the crest of her second wave. Her dark hair was a nest on the sheet underneath her, her hairline glistening with sweat as she swept her tongue over her swollen lower lip.

She flinched as I placed a firm hand on her belly and slipped lower, whimpering as my strong fingers cupped her sopping wet mound through her knickers.

"Please, I'm so sensitive…" she said again, but I shushed her.

My mouth pressed to her ear, exhaling deep before I spoke. "I'm going to give you what you need, you just don't know it yet."

My fingers were brutal as they dug inside the slit in her thong and ploughed hard into that tender cunt. She flinched, her thighs clamping tight around my hand, but I knew exactly what I was doing.

The hook in my gesture was precise, pressing fierce on the bundle of nerves that pulsed behind her engorged clit. I located the spot in moments, angling my wrist for optimum pressure, and she moaned. Fuck, how she moaned, straining against the cuffs that held her wrists, buckling even as I set her alight.

"That dirty little pussy needs filling," I hissed. "You'll be crying out for less even as it begs me for more. Trust me."

She didn't trust me, her eyes were wide on mine as I stared down at her, the chains rattling at her wrists as she squirmed. It didn't matter.

She may not trust me, but her body did. That tight wet hole gurgled its pleasure and strained for more. Her grunts were primal, expression full of confusion as I worked her from the inside.

And then she said it, barely more than a breath. *"Yes..."*

I stretched her wider with a third thick finger and her thighs dropped open.

"Yes..."

I kept my fingers sweeping slow enough to drive her crazy, rippling for more until she was panting like a bitch on heat.

"Yes... please..."

"Please, what?" I grunted, letting my tongue taste her clammy cheek as she tugged at her chains for more leverage.

"Please..."

"Tell me," I pushed, and rubbed that swollen clit from behind, hard enough to hurt if she wasn't so fucking gone for me.

"Please give it to me," she whimpered and her eyes were full of pretty

shame as they begged mine. "Fuck me, please fuck me."

And there we had it. Fifty grand be fucked.

This wasn't about the money, not for her, not anymore.

"With pleasure, sweetheart," I whispered.

My smile was victorious as I finally met her husband's raging stare.

My eyes stayed fixed on his as I freed my swollen cock and his expression said it all, just as hers did.

This wasn't about the money for him either.

It was about the fucking hard on that pulsed underneath his fucking palm.

And hate. It was about hate.

Hate and shame and humiliation in the face of his own sordid desires.

I wished I could taste the pain in his eyes as I slammed my cock inside his pretty wife's pussy and made her mine.

TWENTY TWO

GRACE

It shouldn't have felt so good. Shouldn't have had my whole body burning with need to take Thomas Heath's cock inside me.

I couldn't bring myself to look at my husband, petrified of seeing the disappointment in his eyes. The betrayal.

Because that's how it felt, even as I whimpered and begged the man paying for my body for more. A betrayal. Of my husband, and of myself. Of the younger me who'd pledged a lifelong commitment to Brett Foster a decade ago. Of the girl who knew he'd be her everything, forever, the only man she'd ever want.

And I did want him.

I wanted him there alongside me, his familiar hands on my prickling body along with the stranger's. His hard on grinding against my clit even as

Thomas Heath sank his dick into me from behind.

He was hot, even through his suit, his firm lines pressing tight to my back as he flipped me onto my side and thrust his dick in hard.

My pussy wasn't used to this, already thrumming so raw it was bordering painful. Brett's fingers were skilled and fierce, but not nearly so brutal as the other man's had been when they'd fucked me hard. He was something else, something different, something alien but addictive.

And he was big. Thick. Enough that my breath caught as his balls slammed against my ass.

I was used to big. Brett was big. Impressive.

But Thomas Heath was… different.

Fuck, everything was different.

The chains rattling above my head as I stretched and strained were different. The grip of metal on my wrists was different. Even the grip of lace panties against my clit while that cock took me in long, slow thrusts was different.

My cheek was still slick from where he'd licked me, his breath tickling my ear with a heat that set me alight, and there was sweat, so much sweat that the plastic sheeting under me felt glossy. It was in my hair, my scalp damp enough that I could feel it gathering at my hairline. It was clammy between the lace of the bodice and my tingling skin.

I felt dirty, nothing but a filthy little slut. I felt like every bit the whore the fifty grand had turned me into as I hooked my leg back over Thomas Heath's thigh to take him deeper.

My clit was exhausted, fluttering so hard that the press of the thong against me was a beautiful torment. My pussy was groaning even as it ached for more, my hips rocking on instinct, out of all control as I took what I was given.

"I knew you'd be a dirty bitch," he breathed, and I hated him for speaking the truth aloud.

I didn't want to be a dirty bitch, not for him. I didn't want to be anything for him. But even though the thoughts kept piling in at the guilt inside me, I knew I was lying to myself.

The saddest thing of all was that I'd been lying to myself since the moment he'd first offered his seedy proposition. He'd seen truth in me, in both of us, that I'd been blind to even after years in my husband's arms.

I tipped my head back as his fingers snaked around my throat and held me firm, shivering as his mouth pressed to my temple and breathed in my sweat-slick hair. There was no denying the thrill of the restraint. The forced obedience of the chains made submission to his needs so natural it was like sinking underwater, swallowed up by forces outside of me.

My stomach panged underneath the pleasure as his next words reached my ear, and this time they were louder. So much louder.

Because they weren't for my benefit.

"Look at your husband," he told me. "Show him how good my cock feels inside that tight little cunt."

I was caught. Snared between a rock and a hard place. My cheeks burning up with embarrassment even as I dared meet the eyes of the man who loved me.

It was every bit as painful as I feared.

Brett's face was as pale as mine was burning, his brows heavy and eyes dark as they glared back at me. His mouth was pressed tight, even though his chest was heaving.

My mouth dropped open in horror, my whole soul reeling in protest as I struggled to come to my senses.

And then I saw it. The thing that changed everything.

His palm was rubbing at his crotch as his glare swallowed me whole. His hips were circling in tight little rounds, grinding his swollen dick against his hand as he fought the excitement.

He was as torn as I was; split in two between the filthy need for more and the pain of another man coming between us.

"Tell him," that other man ordered. "Tell him how fucking good it feels."

Oh fuck, how I groaned as he shifted upwards on the mattress. His dick changed angle, grating so hard on the tender nerves behind my clit that I hissed like a whore.

"Tell him," he repeated, and his voice sounded so in control, so ice calm that it made me feel disgusting in my wantonness.

"Good," I whimpered. "It feels good."

His laugh was a low rumble. "You can do better than that, pretty thing."

His fingers slipped down from my neck to tug at my hard nipple, and I knew then that he was so much more than I'd anticipated. He saw everything, understood everything. Every impulsive reaction of my body, every dirty truth behind my clipped words, every brazen whimper of need as his touch claimed me as his.

Knowing my clothes size was the very tip of the iceberg. This man was a poker player with laser vision, cutting through us both.

"Tell your husband you want me," he goaded, and my shiver said it all.

Another tug at my nipple had me squirming. A sweep of his lips against my clammy shoulder was more than I could take.

"Tell your fucking husband that you want me in your dirty little cunt," he rasped, and I couldn't help but screw my eyes closed.

"I want you…" I whispered.

"More," he snapped. "Tell him how fucking wet you are for me, or I'll show him myself up close."

I tightened at the thought, the pulse of wanting them both at once enough to knock me senseless.

"I want you…" I said again, too petrified to risk it. "I want you inside me."

I knew his exact smirk as he pressed it to my cheek. "Now open your eyes and tell him to his face."

I looked at my husband quickly enough that I couldn't hide from the impact. "It feels good," I told him. "He feels good."

Brett's face was a scowl, even as he grunted out his own low expletives. His palm was jerking fast between his legs, rubbing his length through the thick denim of his jeans.

And then it all stopped.

I cried out in protest as Thomas Heath's glorious big dick pulled out of my pussy and he rolled away. I spun my head to face him, watching him rise to his feet and shove his cock back in his suit trousers, even as my chains rattled hard overhead, and my pussy… Lord help me, my pussy screamed for more, clenching on nothing and aching in despair.

I rolled onto my back with my legs spread wide, rocking myself in the same echo of a rhythm and whimpering for more.

"Relax," the smug voice called over as he stepped up to the dresser to the side of the wardrobe. "There's plenty more to come."

I raised my head to watch his back as he surveyed the toys in front of him, wondering what the hell the ice cold stranger was planning next. I would've been scared if I wasn't so lost to the pleasure, and again I didn't understand it. Not how this felt so different to the years of amazing sex I'd shared with my husband.

Brett knew all of me, every inch enough to drive me crazy.

Just not this kind of crazy.

This, with *him*, was crazier than crazy. So fucked up I wondered if I'd ever be able to walk straight again.

I used Thomas Heath's turned back to shoot the first vaguely human look at my husband since this sorry night started. His own desperate palm had slowed to almost still, his breath calming, even as his eyes still burned.

I hoped he could read my expression, even though I was still craving more. I hoped he knew I was there for him, even as another man played my body like some kind of universal master.

I knew Brett's smile was forced as it flashed for me, but it was relief enough that I took a breath and closed my eyes back up again.

He'd be ok. *We'd* be okay. And we'd be fifty grand richer to soothe the trauma.

I didn't register Thomas Heath's reappearance at the foot of the bed until I started at the warmth of his hands on my thighs. He was positioned at a crouch, staring up into my clenching pussy like this was some kind of personal examination. I flinched as he tugged the ribbon sides of my thong loose and ripped the scrap of fabric out from under me, suddenly blooming afresh with self-consciousness as my most intimate parts were bared naked for his viewing.

He hooked his hands around my thighs and yanked me further down the mattress, until the cuffs bit into my skin and my arms were well and truly stretched tight. My heels left the bed, finding natural purchase against his back as I hooked them over his shoulders, and even then my body betrayed me by coaxing him closer.

His fingers didn't touch the sensitive nub of my clit. They landed either side and splayed me wide, so close to his face that I was sure he could feel the damp heat.

"You truly have a gorgeous little cunt, Mrs Foster," he told me, and his tongue slipped inside for a taste.

It was electric.

The cuffs pained as my back arched, my breath too ragged to even moan.

His tuts were so patronising I could have happily slapped his perfect face as he pulled away and smirked up at me.

"Now, now, pretty Grace. We're just getting started," he said, and this time his words were all for me. "Let's see just how much this tender little pussy can take, shall we?"

TWENTY THREE

BRETT

The asshole was everything I'd feared. He'd pulled out of my beautiful wife with barely a wince, shoving his dick back in his pants like this was a day at his swanky office and nothing more.

He was a slippery fish, a cold-faced cunt without any hint of emotion as my Grace whimpered and squirmed.

I guess that's when it hit me for sure, the nasty reality that this was something more for him. Fuck knows what, or why, but this wasn't about taking another man's woman. It wasn't even about taking my beautiful Grace.

Whatever he was spending fifty grand of his cash on was beyond cheap thrill-seeking. It felt personal somehow. About something I should fucking know about but didn't. About *me*.

But that was crazy. Batshit. Crazier even than this bizarre sex show.

I shoved the insanity aside as I caught my breath and forced my hand away from my straining dick.

The last thing I wanted to give the prick was the glory of seeing me jizz in my fucking pants while he fucked my woman. Fuck that for a fucking laugh.

I knew she was as fucked-up as I was when he turned his back and she looked right over. I knew she could see the grim hate on my face, even with my dick still swollen. I wanted to tell her it was alright, that we'd be alright. That the prick was a nobody, even if he was playing her like a dirty fucking professional. That he'd be gone in the morning and she'd be back in our own bed where she belonged.

But I didn't want to say a word in front of that smug asshole.

I managed a smile, and it was enough. I relaxed as she did, taking a breath along with hers as she let herself calm down.

I'd have gladly strangled the motherfucker ten times over before kneeing him in his big brass bollocks for the thrill, but it would be playing into his hands somehow.

Not only was he a slippery fish, but he'd done this before. It was obvious. His composure was obvious. As was the fact he'd fucked a whole shit ton of pussy before hers.

I guess that's what irked me as much as the rest of it. Sure, I knew how to get my wife off. I knew what she liked, what she didn't and what drove her out of her pretty mind. But this... whatever this crazy shit was, was well out of my remit.

We sucked, fucked and came. Many times over some nights. Enough that we'd last a lifetime through and still never tire of it.

We didn't have a whole fucking truck full of dirty sex toys waiting in line on a nightstand. I didn't truss steel chains under our bed ready to clamp my wife in position whenever I wanted to fuck her brains out. I didn't make her scrabble against a plastic sheet with crotchless fucking knickers on.

Maybe I should have.

Maybe I would from this night forward.

Who the fuck even knew what we'd be doing in bed after this shit show.

My balls ached with the horrible notion that I'd be thinking about another man's cock in Grace's pussy when I was buried deep inside her forever more. Because it was shit but true that I liked it. It was fucked-up beyond all reason, from some random dimension that made no sense whatsoever, but I couldn't argue with the straining hard fact in my jeans.

I liked watching her whimper and grunt as her pussy took someone else in front of me. I liked the thought of her stretching around someone else's meat, even if they were a sad sorry cunt with more money than fucking sense.

She didn't see him approach her and drop to his knees at the bottom of the bed. She jolted like a fish on a line as he tugged her down the bed, draping her legs over his shoulders as the prick ripped those fancy knickers right off her.

My own mouth watered as he took a taste of her, knowing full well how delicious that puffy pink pussy would be against his tongue.

She hadn't seen the big purple dildo he'd stuffed down by his knees ready to go. Her eyes widened blankly as the dirty prick spoke up at her.

"Now, now, pretty Grace. We're just getting started," he told her, smug as shit. "Let's see just how much this tender little pussy can take, shall we?"

He was quick with it, thumping the toy against her clit three times over before he jammed the head inside. She couldn't move, not with the chains stretched tight, but I could. I was halfway to my feet before I grabbed a hold of myself, slamming back into the chair with my fists clenched tight.

He hadn't fucking shot his load yet. Wasn't even close. As much as I hated the asshole, I wasn't a man to go back on my word, and Grace wasn't a woman who'd go back on hers either. No spunk, no cash. Not even the twenty-five we'd already dug deep into.

She was wet enough to take the toy, even if she hissed out her breath as he pushed it all the way. It was bigger than his dick, bigger than mine too. I hated how much I hated not being able to see the way her pussy stretched up close.

But I could see enough to set my balls off again. Her perky nipples jutting up at the ceiling. The excitement in her eyes as she stared down at the man fucking her with plastic. The base of that purple dick straining her hungry slit open wide.

He circled it deep, still jammed in all the way. Slow and smooth, knowing the right fucking motions to make her moan all over again.

Maybe I should pay him back some of the fifty fucking grand for some lessons in how to be a filthy cunt. If there wasn't such undeniable hate sizzling between us, I may have shaken the prick's hand and congratulated him on a job well done.

He took an age over fucking her with the big purple dong, teasing her slow, even as she started rocking for more.

I didn't touch my dick, even though it hurt with the strain. I kept my hands clenched tight on the armrests, counting down the minutes like I wanted them to end.

I did, and I didn't. I'd lost track of everything but hate and hard on by the time that wanker was working her back up to frantic whimpers.

He left the toy inside her when he got back to his feet and went for another. She saw him this time, and saw the monster in black he was carrying back to her.

"I can't..." she protested. "I can't take that..."

"You can," he told her, and he was so confident she believed him, parting her legs nice and wide as he pulled out the purple and rubbed the big fat head of black around her swollen pussy lips.

Her grunt was loud enough that I gritted my teeth when he eased it inside her. His thumb brushed her clit as he pushed deep, and even though her thighs narrowed on the bed before him, she didn't balk at the strain.

"I'll never go back to normal..." she whimpered, and he laughed that low bastard laugh of his.

"I promise you, you will, sweetheart," he said. "You might not want to, but you will."

And there it was. That asshole edge I'd known was there since that very first night. The asshole edge in him that knew he'd change my wife forever with his crazy fucking pussy mastery.

"Lift your legs up," he told her, and she did it without question, pulling them up to her chest and dropping them wide. His angle was brutal but she took it all, her wetness squelching loud enough for her cheeks to blush a whole new shade of pink.

"I can't wait to show you how pretty your cunt looks when it's gaping," he said, and even though it brought the bile up in the back of my throat, my dick pulsed so hard I thought I was gonna fucking blow.

I looked away at the bathroom door, just to keep myself together, only daring to look back over when the sack of shit groaned along with her.

The toy plopped free of her pussy with a squelch, and she really was open wide, stretched raw as he angled her shaking body to the mirror to give me a clear fucking view.

His dirty fingers hooked inside and splayed her, his eyes on mine as he forced that hole to its full stretch.

I'd never seen her like that.

I hated how much my mouth watered as I stared at the gaping tunnel another man had drilled wide.

"Beautiful," he said. "A little more play and she'd take two in one. You'd like that, wouldn't you, Mrs Foster?"

His eyes were still brimming with spite as he cracked me a grin.

"Only *I* don't share," he added. "Only fools share such precious things."

I could have pounded him into a bloody pulp, but still my dick twitched in my pants as he slammed that black monster back inside.

TWENTY FOUR

THOMAS

Grace's sweet cunt was hungry enough to gulp in whatever I offered. Her stretch was glorious, enough to make my balls pain as I stared into glistening pink.

I was merely taunting her husband with the prospect of two inside her at once. His wife was far from up to taking that kind of strain, even if the spread of that tight little hole looked mighty impressive for a few hours of careful effort. I think the idiot had actually believed me, flinching at his own pathetic desires.

I would never have shared a beauty like his wife, especially not with a man like me. Not for fifty million, nor the finest hotel on the planet.

If only I could be lucky enough to see how much he'd regret it in the coming weeks. Basking in his pain would be a pleasure I'd appreciate far more in close proximity, but alas, it wasn't to be.

Nevertheless, the night was still relatively young as I pushed that thick toy back inside his pretty wife's tender hole and teased her clit with a brush of my tongue. Her excitement was a tightrope, taut between the heady rush of want and the pain of over-stimulation.

Luckily for her, I was a fucking master.

People may be quick to say it was a foolish endeavour to pay so much money to thrill another man's wife for hours on end, but they'd be wrong.

It's in controlling someone else's pleasure that the real man finds his own. My own throbbing dick was demoted to the outskirts of my awareness, my focus razor-sharp on that beautiful woman's enjoyment as she confronted sides of herself she'd barely known existed.

It was always like this for me in these situations, but this time more so than ever. This time more so than everything.

My instinctive awareness of the minutes passing dulled to a blur as I ploughed that slick, wet cunt with whatever toy took my fancy. Her juices were pooling under her ass on the plastic sheeting as I worked her into frenzy after frenzy, stopping at the most sadistic point of her crest time after time. Fingers, mouth, the sharp slap of my palm against that soft smooth mound whenever I knew her body could take it. The strain of a hooked toy against her sweet spot, the stretch of a dildo circled wide, more, more, always more, and she took it with the acceptance of a woman awakening to her deepest self.

Grace was a submissive who'd been slumbering through a lifetime of vanilla, ready to unfurl in just the right hands. Not a submissive in the sense of hard spankings and a red paddled ass, not even of *sir* as a means of address. The tools hanging on the drawer handles would be largely redundant, but it had taken intimate experience of her body to make that call.

She was submissive in the sense of naturally yielding to another's instruction, soaking up the guidance of experienced hands and a sharp tongue with a delightful revelry. Her wide eyes became ever more eager in seeking mine out as the night drew on, her body switched on to mine as I took her in hand and pushed her to heights she'd have balked at a few hours earlier.

It was a delicious massage to my already proud ego to witness how her husband watched everything. Saw everything. No doubt *felt* everything.

I knew his dick was easily as hard as mine was, his balls just as tense with the urge to shoot their creamy load inside his wife's sweet wet cunt as she stared up with rapture.

I guess there were more similarities between us than I'd ever dared to acknowledge — both of us transfixed by the delicious creature he'd claimed before I'd ever had the most basic of attributes required to snare such a wonder.

Her breaths were a dry rasp as she came down from another whimpering climax, her whole body collapsing flat to the mattress as she rippled in the aftermath.

It was time.

She didn't move a muscle as I got to my feet, too caught up in the endorphins for even a shudder of nervousness as I presented myself at her side. She moaned in gratitude as I took the key to the cuffs from my inside pocket and freed her sore wrists from their shackles. Her arms pulled back to her chest in a flash, fingers rubbing frantically at the marks the restraints had pressed into her skin as I stepped away and sought out the minibar by the far bedside table.

Any suspicions she had as to my intentions had long dried up in the face of her body's obedience to my will. She took the bottled water from me with a genuine smile, her eyes full of thanks as she unscrewed the top and took a swig.

"I needed that," she told me, downing the rest of the measure and handing me back the empty bottle.

Then came the moment that tested the true reach of my inner cunt. I was surprised when my own bitterness came up short enough to offer a friendly lifeline where none was warranted.

Brett looked as surprised as I felt when I headed over and deactivated the infrared sensor in order to hand him a bottled water over the line. He offered a nod, if not a thanks, swigging back a decent mouthful with the same fervour as his wife.

"Don't think my hospitality grants you any liberties," I told him as I reset the device, and his eyes flashed with offense at the implication.

"Would take a shitload more than a bottled fucking water to make us pals," he said. "And I know full fucking well what I agreed to and where your pissy little red line is."

I was coming to grudgingly admit that he was a man of greater moral compass than I'd given him credit for, even in the most perverse of circumstances. If I wasn't such a careful guy I'd have even considered turning the thing off again and trusting our gentleman's agreement.

But I am a careful guy.

I took a water for myself and stared out at the dark night through the window as I drank my fill. I could see him in the reflection of the pane to my left, his gaze seeking out his wife's as she rolled onto her side to face him with her thighs clamped tight.

I had to give them credit. Usually by this point in proceedings the communication between the couple was already stretched thin, both of them knocked sideways by the realisation that things would never return to normal.

But not here. Not yet.

I dropped my empty bottle on the windowsill and turned to the pair with a smile bright with cockiness.

"Enjoying yourself considerably more than you expected," I goaded. "Both of you, nonetheless. If I'd have known this was going to be such a pleasure for all parties involved, I'd have negotiated the terms a lot harder."

Brett's voice was every bit as bullish as I predicted. "Like fuck you would have. Cut the crap, Heath. This shit ain't new for you. You've got plenty of fucking experience at this game, and paying for it."

"Astute," I said with a tip of the head. "Who'd have ever thought there was such a brain behind your macho sports field grunts?"

It was my first slip up.

I saw my words rattle loud behind his eyes, the venom in my question far too alive to be spoken by a passing stranger in this backward slice of paradise.

"You seem that type," I added in a breath, but it didn't undo the damage.

"Who the fuck are you?" he asked me, ever blunt in his communication.

"Nobody you know," I responded. "Just a man who's paying handsomely to fuck your pretty wife while you watch."

"I call bullshit, you weird ass sonofabitch," he snapped back, and it made me smile with genuine amusement.

"Call whatever you like, Mr Foster, but do it on your own time. This is mine, bought and paid for, so quit with the caveman speculation."

The unspoken standoff lasted almost a full minute as I forced myself to relax back against the window, inwardly cursing my poor grip on the situation. There was no red line in the world that could hold him back from storming over and demanding the truth with a pummel of fists. Not if he was so motivated. There was also no smooth mask of cool disinterest that could gloss over the crack in my polished veneer.

"This isn't over," he told me as he dropped his empty bottle at his side and adjusted himself in his seat. "Whatever fucking beef you've got with me, you can spit it out when we're done or forget about it. I don't fucking know you, and I don't fucking want to. Believe me, however our paths have crossed in the past, I don't fucking remember it."

"Paranoid as well as possessive," I goaded, but he shrugged me off without a blink of self-doubt in his suspicions.

It was Grace whose eyes were flickering with some dull half-light of speculation as they stared up at me. I hated the twist of concern in my stomach, hated the way the ground felt set to crumble underneath my backtracking steps.

"Any false move from either of you and this whole deal is off," I told them both, making sure my voice was bristling full of the confidence I feared crumbling under me. "No cash, no financial lifeline in this shitty hole you've wound up in, bye bye, sweet hotel dreams."

It was Grace who held up her hand this time, shaking her head as though I was preaching to the converted. Maybe I was.

"You can ease up with all this," she told me. "We know the deal here. Both of us."

I settled grudgingly back into my stride, discomfort appeased for the short term at least. Grace reclined back on the mattress, her eyes still fixed on mine as she struggled to keep up with the choppy sea of interactions in this one tiny hotel room.

There was only one way to truly ensure she didn't blurt out any unwelcome questions, and her distraction would be my pleasure, quite literally.

"I think it's about time you returned my very generous favours, don't you?" I asked her, and finally shrugged my suit jacket from my shoulders.

Thank fuck for endorphins and the consuming lust of a pussy driven wild.

Her thoughts were right where they should be as my fingers went for my shirt buttons.

TWENTY FIVE

GRACE

I was done with lying to myself. I wanted the enigmatic stranger who'd flipped our whole life on its axis. His brutal fingers, skilled enough to drive me crazy. His mouth, so consuming. His devilish smirk, his arrogance, his cutting words.

He was magnificent under his suit, tight abs rippling as he cast his shirt aside and unbuckled his belt. His cock was standing proud as he dropped his pants to the floor, his happy trail paving the way to the beast of flesh I'd felt so deep inside me.

My whole body was a victim to the sensations running wild as he dropped onto the mattress at my feet.

"Come," he said, his voice firm, even though quiet.

My limbs felt weak and bandy, my thighs protesting as I scuttled down to join him. It felt strangely natural to drop down under him as he positioned himself on top, his ridges welcomed by my curves as he lowered his weight onto mine.

He didn't have to ask me to kiss him this time. My lips were already parted as his came in hard. My calves wrapped around his thighs and pulled him close, my whore of a pussy seeking out his cock as his tongue hunted mine and found me wanting.

This was more like I was accustomed to. Flesh on flesh, mouth to mouth, my fingers instinctive as they swept up his tight muscled back to tangle in his hair. I knew this place where two bodies met and moved as one. I knew the warmth of a firm chest pressed hard against my tits. I knew the strain of male thighs as his full length ground against mine.

I was ready to take him inside me, hitching hard and aching for more. I held back the words, even as they gathered on my tongue. The ridge of him was a promise against my tender clit, his hips circling to set me hissing.

This was me. I knew it. I felt it. I wanted it.

What I didn't know so well was the ease with which he pulled away at his whim and left me hanging like a needy slut. I fought the urge to protest as he got back to his feet and left me panting breathless, but he didn't leave me yearning long before his strong hands slipped under my arms and tugged me to the edge of the bed right after him. I flopped like a fish as he let my head drop over the side of the mattress, and my instincts were on point again as the swollen head of his dick slapped my cheek. My mouth opened wide in a heartbeat, welcoming the length of him as he pushed his way in.

I spluttered at the intrusion but he didn't ease up. He shifted his hips to dig deeper, burrowing into my throat until I retched on him, and even then he kept on thrusting, stretching my gullet just as he'd stretched my pussy.

"Spread your legs and show your husband what he's missing," he ordered, and I didn't even think about it, letting my thighs loll open so Brett could see the wet mess the other man had made of me.

Clearly it wasn't enough for Thomas Heath. His grip was brutal as he yanked my knees up high and rolled my hips for more exposure.

I wondered what was so appealing about showing my husband the result of his filthy touches. Why it was so important to show off the guilty arousal of a woman driven insane.

The wondering didn't stop me sucking in the best way I knew how, struggling to lap at the length of him with a noisy mouth as he swept across my tongue and plunged in deeper. I knew how to suck dick. I *liked* sucking dick. As it turned out, it wasn't just my husband's either.

What I didn't like so much was how Thomas Heath seemed oblivious to my greatest efforts, driving me to a slobbering wreck of slurps and slavers as I struggled to bring him off. Nothing I did made any difference. His dick was solid and steadfast, fucking my face without so much as a hint that he was losing control.

I couldn't imagine him ever losing control. Not in bed and not in life. Not ever.

Not even when I reached up to grip his thighs and coax him harder did he show any signs of losing his cool. He kept hold of my legs, raising them so high that I felt my pussy splutter along with my throat every time I jerked with effort. I was a pot on the boil, spitting and dribbling down the sides, and he kept on stirring without so much as breaking a sweat.

"She's got a fine dirty mouth, your pretty wife," he told my husband, and I despised myself for the burst of pride in my chest at such seedy praise.

I despised myself equally for the desperation in my whimpers as I practically begged for a mouthful of his cum. I don't know how a paying customer's salty seed was reward enough to drive a girl wild, but I'd have run a naked mile with my tits bouncing high just to taste him.

My eyes were streaming with tears from retching, and I'm sure my smoky eyes had bled makeup across my wet state of a face. My slobber was dangling in thick streams from his dick to my open mouth before landing foamy against my upturned cheeks and dribbling down into my sweaty hair, one slimy retch at a time.

This wasn't me. Wasn't sex I knew. Wasn't anything I'd ever imagined, loving the way he made a whore out of me.

He was laughing as he tugged his dick all the way clear and took a handful of my curls to tip my face up toward Brett. I'm glad my eyes were too blurry with spit, tears and makeup to focus clearly, and glad any expression of pain on his face escaped me enough that I didn't have to feel like an adulterous bitch as I snaked my fingers down to my still humming clit.

"Delicious," Heath growled and folded over at the waist to lick my hacked up spit clean off me. His tongue was hot and flat against my cheek, sweeping across my open mouth where he sucked up all my filthy drool and smacked his lips with a grunt of approval.

I felt sick. Actually nauseous as my flickering fingers picked up a notch between my legs.

I'd never get over this. Not ever. Not with the whole fifty grand ploughed into sex therapy for the next ten years. Not even if Brett washed me clean and told me I'd lost my mind under pressure. Not even if I believed it myself.

"Beautiful like this, isn't she?" the filthy guy said to my poor husband, and I felt anything but. "I love a woman who knows how to worship cock. Is she ever so enthusiastic with yours down her throat?"

My cheeks scorched so hard I wanted the ground to open up underneath me. I did try hard with Brett, always. But Brett was so much easier to try with. I knew how to suck Brett's dick. Knew the flicks of my tongue he liked the best. Knew how to work my mouth along the length of him with a smile on my face. Knew how to cup his balls just so with my hand to push him over the edge.

I didn't need to slaver like a dirty slut for just a hint of a reaction, but I would. If he needed it, I would. But that didn't matter, not in that moment burning between us, not with the evidence of my efforts for Thomas Heath smeared dirty across my face.

"Tell me," the filthy guy continued, and I didn't know if he was talking to Brett or me this time. "Does she enjoy having her ass stretched as much as the other holes?"

I could barely even breathe as my fingers kept on strumming, real tears joining the ones coaxed by Thomas Heath's dick and rolling down my humiliated cheeks.

It should never have been like this.

I should never want anything as much as I wanted Thomas Heath to tear me open.

Looking up at him was enough to mash my love and hate into one pile of confusion. I'd need untwisting in the aftermath, my whole body scrubbed clean with bleach and reason.

And then he spoke. My poor husband spoke.

"She likes it," he grunted. "Just don't fucking hurt her."

"Give me some fucking credit," the other man laughed. "Your wife is begging for my touch. She'll miss me when I'm gone, so I'd suggest you pay attention. Maybe you'll learn something."

My eyes were still closed, brimming with bursting tears as his strong hands twisted me again, this time back onto the bed, where he flipped me onto my front with enough strength that I squeaked out loud.

My tits pressed to the slippery plastic under me, reminding me of a grimy bouncy castle I'd fallen onto my front on back at a kid's birthday party long ago. My neck was straining as he kept hold of my clammy curls and tugged my head back to face my husband at close distance.

And Thomas Heath's voice was as commanding as ever when he barked out instructions that my body obeyed without question.

"Show me that tight asshole of yours, Mrs Foster," he told me. "Spread those cheeks nice and wide and beg me to stretch that dirty little hole."

I still couldn't bring myself to open my eyes and meet the glare of my husband. My lip was trembling with the heartache of wanting another man so bad. My fingers were slow as they swept back behind me and took hold of my sweaty ass cheeks, trembling as they parted them wide.

I felt the dribble of spit land right on target from his mouth above, warm as his thumb used the wetness to slide through my tight little ring and squirm around.

"This might hurt a little," he hissed, and pressed the head of his dick in hard.

TWENTY SIX

BRETT

I'd have been well and truly fucking mortified if the whole experience wasn't so surreal. This wasn't my wife inside the hotel we'd made our home in these past twelve months. This wasn't the woman who'd spent her whole adult life in my arms, laughing as we shared a bottle of wine after a hard day's work, cooking a Sunday roast after a sleepy morning in bed with her legs tangled in mine as we argued who was going to get up to make coffee.

This woman was a wanton wreck of desire for another man, a man who'd paid us for every scrap of his sordid pleasure. A man who hated me. Hated whatever he saw in me. Whatever he thought I stood for.

Hated what we had, here, between us.

But he didn't hate Grace. Even through his slick asshole composure I could see the glint in his eyes as he watched her. Touched her. Teased her to the edge of fucking insanity and drove her beyond any sane limit she'd ever known.

I watched them with a sickness to my stomach I didn't think I'd ever heave up and out, even though my dick kept on throbbing. My hands gripped those armrests tight, fighting back the urge to pull my own hard on free and give in to my own fucked-up temptations, but I couldn't for the life of me shake off the suspicion there was more to this cunt's offer than one night with my wife. He knew me, from fuck knows where, I had no idea. But watching the way he ravaged my Grace like a dam bursting after a whole fucking lifetime, I knew in the pit of me he knew her too.

He still hadn't shot his load, not in all these hours. We were still in total refund territory, which was a joke in itself, and one I had no doubt he'd been well aware of when he set up the terms.

The guy was inhuman. Some fucking porn star with balls made of steel. He wasn't even flustered. Barely a sweat, grunt or gritted teeth as he worked his dick into whichever of my wife's needy holes he wanted.

She was anything but a porn star. She looked broken, lip trembling with shame and hurt as her body begged him for more.

I'd never have signed up for this. Not for five hundred grand. Not for a million. Or ten million, or all the hotels in the fucking world. And yet my knuckles stayed white as they gripped my seat, my dick straining as I cursed my own sonofabitch body for wanting more. And I did want more. My eyes were open wide as the cunt in front of me lined up my Grace to fuck her tight little asshole, my mouth watering at the thought of her taking him deep and whimpering for more.

The most painful thing about the whole sorry experience?

Not that I hated wanting more, or that Grace was hot for another guy, even through tears. The most painful thing about the whole experience was that he'd known the whole thing was coming. Like a chess master playing with other people's lives, always one step ahead, shunting the pawns along with checkmate in mind. And that's what worried me, right now, in the pit of me.

Checkmate.

I didn't even know what it looked like, but I knew we were heading right there, slipping down the path of his construction, ending unknown.

My wife wouldn't look at me, eyes shut tight against the shame as she reached around and spread her pretty ass cheeks wide. He spat right down on the puckered ring I knew so well, even if I couldn't see it, warning her it was gonna hurt as he lined his dick up for entry.

He wasn't fucking lying.

She grunted and grimaced, tits jiggling free underneath her as she squirmed forward. He had her by the hair, grip firm enough that she wasn't going anywhere.

I knew this bit at least — the moment where her body protested the invasion. Her motions were like watching behind the scenes footage of one of your favourite childhood movies, your best loved characters living out your best loved scenes from a whole other angle. A far less fucking magical one, but still it got you fired up, like you were peeking in on some secret world you'd been missing out on your whole life.

That's what this was.

Seeing my Grace's mouth drop open as his cock stretched her asshole and slammed in to the balls. Seeing the way she rippled as she clenched and loosened, clenched and loosened, adjusting to the girth with a wide open mouth.

I'd seen it, felt it, lived it a thousand times over, but not as he lived it, so detached from the fucking show as he stared down at her with a smile on his face.

He wasn't fighting, not straining against the urge to unload deep in that dirty hole. Even as Grace fell into her regular rhythm of humping back and demanding more, demanding longer, demanding hard, hard, deep fucking deep, he wasn't struggling to hold back long enough to give her what she needed.

His eyes met mine over her panting head, and they weren't even close to the edge.

I was closer to jizzing in my pants than the guy was to spurting his cum in Grace's gorgeous asshole.

Her pleasure as she realised he could go on forever was a real fucking wonder to behold.

The smile crept slowly on her face, at odds with the state of the rest of her. It was wild, free, lost to everything but the joy of bouncing back on another guy's dick without time restraint. She bobbed back against him like a fucking trooper, knees shunting and sliding on the plastic sheet underneath, nipples like bullets as those tits bobbed along with her.

And then she came.

Feral, like a wild cat roaring, spitting, cursing. Wailing to him, *us*, how good it felt, how good *he* felt, how she was fucking destroyed by the perfect thrusts of a perfect dick inside her asshole.

I'm sure my face was as grim as his was grinning when he pulled himself free and let her fall flat to the mattress. His cock was still as hard as ever. Thick in his grip as he tugged it a few extra times for good measure.

It had to be medication. A whole fucking handful of those little blue pills to see him through the evening. I knew that was macho bullshit reasoning even as it occurred to me. The guy didn't seem the type to lean on props like that, his smug smirk was all real, and I guessed that's why it was on his face so often. The kind of bulletproof arrogance that comes with knowing you really are the dog's bollocks in life.

He leaned back against the windowsill, catching breath he didn't need to catch as he stared across at us like we were filthy spinning tops waiting to tumble and fall, and it was then that I wondered again where the holy fuck I could know this guy from. He wasn't the kind you'd miss in passing, even if he was across a bustling street during rush hour commute.

"I think you need a minute," he told my wife, and she nodded her head gladly. She'd rolled onto her back, limbs spread wide as she gathered her ragged breathing. She was fucked. Beyond fucked. I counted our blessings as I noticed the faint glow of morning light behind Heath's shoulders in the window.

Seven o'clock couldn't come fast enough.

I didn't move a muscle as he headed around the bed and strolled nude in my direction. He shot me a glare before he switched off the sensor, firing it up again right after him as he stepped past me toward the bathroom.

"Piss break," he said. "Talk amongst yourselves to relieve the boredom."

I didn't even acknowledge him. My eyes were all on Grace as he stepped into the en-suite. The door creaked closed behind him but didn't click shut.

Her eyes were all on me when the first splash of piss in the toilet bowl sounded out, and this time she didn't close them as the tears came down.

TWENTY SEVEN

GRACE

"Hey," he said, as I fought back the sobs. "I hope that's not on my behalf. Worse things in life than enjoying a dick in your ass, Grace."

His voice was low and the humour was forced, but it didn't matter. I blinked the tears away and managed a smile back.

"This is so fucked up," I whispered. "I don't even know…"

He tipped his head toward the bathroom. "*He's* fucked up. We're just people living our lives, trying to save our dreams on the coast."

I wished I could reach my hand out for his just to feel his fingers squeeze mine. Just to squeeze his right back and say I was his, just as much as he was mine.

"This isn't who I am," I told him, hoping that would cover some of the head-fuck of the last however many hours.

"This isn't who either of us are," he said back. "Baby, I have a hard on in my pants from watching a freakish porn star asshole fuck my wife all night long. It isn't gonna go on my gravestone."

I loved my husband's voice so much, thanking God for Thomas Heath's bladder break and the moments it granted us.

"Maybe he could do a reading at our funerals if he outlives us. *The night I fucked Grace Foster into insanity and paid her fifty grand for the pleasure.*" My laugh wasn't more than a breath, but my smile was a ride of endorphins.

"Maybe I'll have to pound his face into oblivion before he gets the chance." He flashed me a half smile back and I rolled close enough to mouth *I love you,* knowing he would see it.

His eyes were still warm for me when he mouthed it back. A stolen moment in the silence while the man who'd made me come a billion times this evening flushed the toilet and turned on the basin tap.

We didn't have long and I knew it. Seizing the moment and making it count was my only option, my heart racing under the pressure of making this as right as it could be. Whatever that even meant.

"I can't make him come," I whispered, speaking the truth out loud. "Whatever he's used to, I'm not enough. Not good enough, hot enough, tight enough, *crazy* enough. Whatever, I can't."

His face was a picture as he stared back at me, and I struggled to believe he hadn't seen my failings as clearly as I'd been feeling them for the past few hours.

"Grace—" he began, but I shook my head.

"I can't make him come," I continued. "But I can make *you* come. So do it. Stop fighting it and take your dick out. At least get some pathetic little scrap of fun from this shit storm we're caught up in."

"I'm not jerking off in front of that cunt," he protested, but it was empty man-pride and nothing else. Even as he said it his knuckles whitened back up on the armrests.

"You wouldn't be," I argued. "You'd be jerking off in front of me. At least give me that. Surely I can get one guy off this evening, hey?"

I flinched as he slid forward in his seat, scared shitless that he was going to cross that crappy red line and this whole sorry affair would be all for nothing. But he didn't.

His eyes were burning serious as he leaned in as close to the border as he dared.

"Grace, listen to me," he said, knowing as well as I did that we were likely moments away from Thomas Heath's cocky reappearance.

I inched toward him to show he had my attention, and his expression was deadpan as he continued.

"You could get *any* fucking guy off you put your mind to. You're beautiful, horny as all living fuck, and your efforts are more than enough to drive any man crazy, even a cold ass sonofabitch like Heath."

I was shaking my head but he didn't stop talking.

"He paid fifty grand for a night with you, I'm sure as fuck you're capable of wiping that smug porn star smirk off his face. Just be yourself. Show him who you are. He won't be able to resist."

I couldn't believe what he was saying. "You think I should–"

"I think you should do whatever you want to get the most out of this fucking night. You think you can't make him come, I think you're selling yourself seriously fucking short. Don't sell yourself short, Grace. Not for anyone, especially not that smug-faced prick."

I forced myself up onto all fours as the sound of running water dried up in the bathroom.

"I'll make him come for me," I hiss-whispered to the husband I loved more than I'd ever loved him in my life. "But you'd better come for me too. I can't do this without you, Brett. We're in this together, right? You said so."

"Always together," he whispered back, and I wished I could reach out and tug his cock out of his straining jeans for him.

"So *you* enjoy it too," I said. "Please. I can't do my best to make him come for me unless you're going to come for me too. And I can't… I'd rather walk away from this right now than know all you felt was pain when I lost my fucking mind for a stranger."

"That's not how this is," he breathed. "Grace, that's never how I'd see this, not in a million years."

"I know," I told him. "Or I hope I do. But please, Brett, I need you right by me."

Hell only knows what kind of fucked-up place we were headed after all this, or how much toxic fallout we'd need to wade through over the rest of our lifetime, but right then, right there, I needed him to lose himself to the same crazy I was, even just a fraction. Even just one cruddy hand-job's worth.

"I love you," I told him, not giving a shit anymore for how Thomas Heath would hear my outpouring from the room next door. "More than anything. Always."

"I love you too," he told me back. "Fuck this fucking shit, Grace, let's just go with it for all it's worth. Tomorrow's another day, and ours will be just fine, I swear."

And then *he* appeared, the cold ass sonofabitch my husband was convinced I could drive crazy, even if I didn't share his confidence.

He was just as cold as ever as he stepped back into the room with us, his cock still hard as he finished towelling it dry from whatever wash down he'd just given it. He tossed the towel to the floor as he turned off his silly little sensor, and his smile was nothing more than a dead mask underneath burning eyes as he crossed the line back over to me.

I stared at him all the while he fired it back up again and approached for a brand new round, and this time I didn't scuttle away with spiralling nerves and a traitorous pussy screaming wild.

This time was all for me. All for the woman my Brett believed could win over a man like Heath and drive him just a little way toward crazy.

Even if I didn't believe in her myself.

TWENTY EIGHT

THOMAS

I'd caught enough of their exchange to know my plan for the Fosters wasn't nearly as on point as I'd anticipated. Their words weren't the bitter grunts of a woman reeling and a bull-brained husband racked with rage.

Grace and Brett weren't stumbling through awkward silence, nor choking on a useless spiel of words to make sense of the situation. Their expressions were still glowing bright with some delusional semblance of commitment as I stepped back into the bedroom — clinging to irrational optimism and a conventional shit-shaped illusion of forever.

Pathetic.

It was pathetic.

And along with it *I* felt pathetic, ears straining for more as I'd glared at myself in the bathroom mirror.

So, pretty Grace wanted to please me. Coax me to my own shuddering climax as my self-control took a back seat and her husband watched on proud. She thought I'd leave this place desperate and shocked into silence, dumbstruck at her prowess in the bedroom as her husband congratulated her for seizing the day.

But no.

I was always one step ahead of other people's foolish ideas of success.

I wouldn't be shooting my load into her gaping pink holes, not any single one of them. Her failure to get me off would eat at her slowly, scratching her insides in bed at night as her pussy dreamed up ways she could've done better.

She'd never have done better, not without me fully behind her efforts.

Mastering my own bodily urges was something I'd given attention to for years. Mastering *myself* was something I'd given attention to for years. That's what happens when you're born a pathetic excuse for a human being with a face that doesn't fit and a father that doesn't give a shit. You either crumble to dust or you rise tall enough to take a stand on your own two feet. To *prove* something, both to yourself and to those who fucked you over.

And if those people aren't still around, you go for the closest living survivor.

I hated Brett Foster more in that moment than I had in years. The fact that he didn't recognise me, didn't know me, hadn't given me enough respect back then to even acknowledge my existence and the shit he'd inadvertently helped bring down on me simply made it worse.

An apology would never come from a mouth like his, not one that really meant something. The only respect I'd ever get from a guy like him was the grudging, hate-filled acknowledgement that I'd taken what was his without even really wanting it. Taken his self-respect, his overblown confidence from a life lived on the easy side of the street, his natural belief that he'd always come up smelling of roses.

Their stupid plan for the rest of the evening tightened and razor-sharpened my own, an even greater victory presenting itself ripe on the platter.

I'd take Brett Foster's wife from him, just as I'd planned. I'd destroy their marriage from the inside out, sitting back patiently while it crumbled around their ears until finally, she came calling after me. The man who'd opened her eyes so wide to greater pleasures.

Only this time she'd be leaving a loyal husband to run after a man who hadn't even wanted her enough to shoot his load once this evening.

Brett wouldn't know humiliation quite like it. Not in ten lifetimes.

His pretty Grace was more confident than I'd seen her as she waited on all fours for me to join her back on the bed. There was a twinkle in her eyes, the siren within her calling loud at the prospect of driving me wild.

Her admission of feeling like a failure these past few hours was a lethal weapon in my grip as I climbed onto the mattress with a wider smile than I'd previously allowed myself.

Failure always hurts so much more when you give your all and come up lacking.

She'd shrug it off at first, I was sure of it. Brett would tell her it didn't matter that I didn't shoot my load for her, that I was just an idiot, that she was more than good enough in the bedroom for him, where it mattered, but it wouldn't be enough. Not for long.

Not when the memory of her failed efforts came back to haunt her at night.

I'd been planning to leave her pussy dribbling slick with a parting gift as generous as the load I'd planned to leave in her asshole.

Now she'd get nothing.

Not one fucking thing for her efforts. Not one fucking smile at my expense as she reminisced fondly back to how I'd lost control.

I wouldn't be losing control. Not ever, and certainly not tonight.

"I think it's time that tight little cunt of yours took my cum," I told her, and her eyes lit up like the greedy slut I'd been hoping for. I wrapped my hand around her neck and held her firm as I pressed my mouth to hers, and she was more aggressive with her kisses this time around, slipping her tongue against mine like a minx on a mission. I let her guide me backwards as she made a move to climb on top, relaxing as she straddled me and rubbed that sopping wet slit along the length of me.

"Fuck me," she breathed. "I want to feel you come for me."

"Work for it," I grunted. "Show me you deserve it."

I felt like a cunt, even under the gutful of self-righteousness I carried like a shield through every aspect of my world. I knew I was a selfish bastard as her sly little smile made her whole pretty face light up.

What I didn't expect was for her to ride me so fucking tenderly. Her fingers so genuine in their needy exploration of my body.

I didn't expect her to move on me in understated motions, soaking me up like she really did want to understand what would make me harder. Hotter. Desperate to lose control in that sore little pussy of hers.

This wasn't the writhing, moaning dance of a woman purely on a mission to milk the cum from my balls. These were the intimate gestures of a woman really finding her footing between us, struggling for a connection.

The kind of connection that scared the shit out of me where nothing else in this world still had power to.

"I want you to feel like I did when you pushed my body to the limits," she whispered, and dropped her tits to my chest. "I want you to feel as crazy as me in all of this."

Her mouth brushed my cheek so softly, her exhale deep and natural as she relaxed her body onto mine.

"Hold me," she whispered, and I felt a terrible thump in my gut. "Hold me like this means something. Believe me, it's the only way you ever really feel someone else."

And I didn't get it.

Couldn't get it.

Didn't want to get it.

The soft lust in her eyes as she sought out affection in a stranger's arms was enough to set my heart racing in panic. In revulsion.

Disbelief.

Want.

And there, in the quiet voice deep inside, was that sad little teenager again, causing yet more havoc on top of the lifetime he'd caused me already.

I told him it was false. Fake. A stupid game on her part that meant nothing.

That just because she wasn't riding me like some kind of wannabe porno queen, didn't mean this was any less of a cheap illusion.

But she held me like it wasn't, her fingers working magic patterns against my skin as she stared with such eager eyes into mine.

And for just a heartbeat I was certain she saw that little boy crying there, wanting every little bit of love he'd been denied back when it mattered.

I expected her to close down every flutter of kindness in her bones as I grabbed her with angry hands and slammed her down hard on her back.

"I'll fucking *hold you*," I grunted and threw her legs up onto my shoulders, ploughing so fucking deep into that tender pussy of hers that she cried out in hurt. "Take this, you dirty little bitch. Take this like it really fucking *means something.*"

Her eyes were full of pain as they held onto mine, her whimpers all from the heart as I slammed her with enough force that it left me grunting.

"Ow, fuck," she breathed. "I'm so sore…"

"Show me how much you want my fucking cum now, Grace Foster. Work for it. Beg for it."

I lowered my face to hers, my breath fierce against her open mouth as she struggled to take me. "I want it…" she whispered. "Please… if this is what it takes, I don't care…"

I'd make her fucking care.

Her eyes were wide as I shifted my weight onto just one straining arm and slipped my other hand down between us. Her legs thrashed against my shoulders as I pushed two thick fingers in that poor little pussy along with my dick. I fucked her with venom. Pure fucking venom.

"It's never hurt like this..." she squeaked.

I heard Brett rise from his seat but she held a hand up to him.

"No," she said in his direction. "It's alright, Brett, I want this. I *need* this."

"Only good girls get my fucking cum," I hissed. "I don't think you're such a good girl, Grace Foster. I think you're a wanton little slut who's playing with fire."

I ground my hips until she bucked for me, that tender cunt clenching around my filthy fucking dick-plus-fingers combination.

"I might not be a good girl," she whispered, and her expression was so real in her hurt, in her wavering self-confidence, in her splayed fucking soul. "But I want to be... I want to be..."

Her fingers were shaking as they swept up my raised shoulders and traced a path up my throat. They came to rest on my face, a palm pressed gently to each cheek like she truly cared a shit for me.

I should've pulled away. But I didn't.

"Give it to me," she breathed. "Please, Tom, give it to me."

And I couldn't...

Oh fuck, how I couldn't...

"Nobody calls me that," I snarled, but it was too late. Her smile was all real.

"Because you don't let them," she said. "Because you try so hard to be in control that you'd rather hurt people than let them feel you. I'm right, aren't I?"

I didn't say a word, just kept on fucking her. Kept on hissing. Breathing. Thrusting.

She looked like a filthy little angel underneath me, the dawn light glowing in through the window to mix with the dull yellow overhead light on her sweet face.

And then she groaned. Genuinely groaned. Bucking that clit against my thumb as my fingers squelched along with my dick.

"Please," she said and urged my face down onto hers. "Kiss me like you mean it."

Kissing her right then was the dumbest mistake I'd made by far that evening. Her tongue was all for mine as I slipped it in her waiting mouth, tasting me like someone who really wanted it. Wanted *me*.

It was then that I noticed the slap of flesh on flesh to my left — the undeniable low grunting rhythm of a guy working his own meat as his pretty wife worked her magic on a filthy dirty stranger.

I couldn't look. Didn't want to look. Didn't want to flash him even the smuggest smirk in my repertoire.

My eyes were all for his wife. The woman I'd dreamed of back when I still had such dreams to hang onto.

And then my balls tightened. Hard.

My dick started tensing inside her as my breathing turned ragged.

I'd have pulled out if her touch wasn't so fucking magnetic.

"That's it, Tom," she breathed. "Fill me up."

I heard Brett grunting in his seat, cursing out expletives as his wife came one final time.

I was with her. So close. So close to breaking and giving her what I'd sworn against in the fucking bathroom with fire in my eyes.

And then the alarm sounded.

TWENTY NINE

GRACE

My fingers jumped from his face as the alarm started screeching. It took me a frazzled second to realise what the bone-grating bleeps meant.

Seven.

It was seven a.m. and we were done.

But I didn't want to be. Not then. Not so close.

I felt like Cinderella at midnight, pained and reeling as the magic ran out and the ugly truth of reality came crashing back in.

The magic disappeared the second my fingers left his face, like I'd been the one to break the spell by pulling away, not the damn alarm clock bleeping and buzzing from the dresser. I didn't even know he'd set one.

I cried out in horror as he stilled his breath and pulled out of me with one sharp jerk of his hips. My eyes were fixed on the length of him as he retreated, still hard as steel with his balls still filled to bursting.

I'd failed.

I shouldn't care. It wasn't an accomplishment worth having, not now or ever. Whether Thomas Heath came for me should have been so far down my list of priorities that I'd shrug it off with a smile as I waved him goodbye forever, but it wasn't.

In that moment it felt like everything. And I felt like nothing.

Endorphins. Stress. Exhaustion. A body played by a master all night through.

I tried to tell myself my own feelings weren't reliable. That I was all twisted up and emotional. That I'd get over it by breakfast.

But I was lying to myself.

Again.

"Time's up," he said, like it wasn't already obvious. He was on his feet in a flash, pulling his pants back up his perfect toned legs from the heap on the floor.

I was a quivering jellyfish with straggly limbs spread wide as I watched him, my pussy still throbbing with the weird mix of pleasure and pain he'd drummed in hard.

"But you didn't…" I began.

His shrug hurt more than his fingers stretching me to breaking. "As I said, good girls get my cum, Grace Foster. At least you tried."

I hated him. Hated the way tears of embarrassment sprung up in my eyes before I could swat them away. I swung my legs off the edge of the mattress, struggling to get to my feet and find my discarded dress.

"Turn this fucking red line off," Brett barked out, and I daren't look at him. Couldn't bear to look at him. I'd rather hide under the bed than have him see my disappointment at failing another man.

Thomas took his time heading over to his stupid sensor, his shirt already half buttoned as he keyed in his ridiculous code. The line blinked off and

Brett charged across the divide in a breath, taking hold of my flailing arms as I scrabbled under the bed frame for my hiding clothes.

"I need to get dressed," I snapped, hating the way my voice sounded so fragile.

"Shh," he told me and hugged me close, warm arms wrapping me tight and holding my shivering body to his.

He smelled like him. Felt like him. Moved like him as he rocked me in the tiniest sways from side to side.

I peeked out at the mirror behind his shoulder, eyes still following the other man as he fastened up his top button like this was any other morning. He caught my eyes in the reflection and his smirk was still right there. His mask was so real. So impenetrable.

At least for me.

I took a breath against Brett and thanked my stars I still had the love of a man who would show it.

It was Thomas who dropped to his knees and pulled my evasive dress out from under the bed. My eyes were still on the mirror as he handed it to Brett behind my back. The voice inside losing her shit over my ridiculous failure lapped up the gesture, my stomach lurching at the notion he wanted me clothed as soon as possible. It was crazy. Crazier than the rest of this stupid night.

I didn't want to let go of my port in the storm, still clutching tight to my husband as he tried to help slip the fabric over my head. My arms were clumsy as I finally raised them and Brett fastened me into the gown. It felt scratchy, uncomfortable, and so did I.

I knew I'd never wear it again. My confidence last night in the safety of my own bathroom was a joke now. My sexy girl bravado long since dead and buried, maybe forever.

"The rest of your payment should be in your account anytime now," our dirty blonde guest told us as he shrugged on his jacket. "I'm satisfied with the evening."

Satisfied.

Even as he said it, I knew he was disappointed in me. His smirk said nothing more than he was a man who knew he was winning in life, just like always, but it was there. Under his words. Under the way he threw his clothes on like the whole night had been a passable distraction.

I hadn't been good enough.

But I'd had him there. Almost.

So close.

If I'd only had a few more minutes.

"You don't need to rush off," were the words that left my sorry mouth. "Not if you want to… finish up…" I couldn't believe what I was saying.

Brett's whole torso tensed against me at my blurted invitation. Thomas didn't meet my eyes in surprise, nor in want either.

"Nine hours was nine hours," he commented as he picked up his shoes from the far side of the bed. "I appreciate the offer though."

He didn't want to carry on. Not even for free.

Brett was as stiff as a board as he pulled his phone from his trouser pocket. A few seconds of thumbing the screen and he slipped it back out of sight.

"Money's in," he told me. "We should go. I'm sure we'll be catching up with our lovely fucking guest a bit later."

"Check out is at eleven, yes?" Thomas asked, and I nodded.

"There's no rush," I told him. "We have guests arriving, but this room isn't booked."

"The city is calling," he replied.

Brett's hands were firm on my shoulders as he pushed me back far enough to meet my eyes. His were digging, confused, more worried than offended by my kind gestures toward the guy who'd just fucked my brains out for money.

Maybe he really had fucked my brains out.

"Let's go," he said. "Get you cleaned up."

I nodded but didn't say a word, scouting the floor for the hooker heels that had helped me feel some of the way toward a fifty-grand seductress. They were by the nightstand. My whole body was aching as I dropped to grab them.

"I guess you'll be wanting breakfast?" Brett asked the man behind us.

"I need a good walk first," he replied. "How about we all take a break and call it nine sharp in the dining room?"

"Fine," Brett said. "See you at nine."

He tugged me along with his hand in mine, wrapping an arm around my shoulders for stability as soon as the bedroom door closed behind us and we were out in the corridor.

"It's done," he said, his breath in my hair as we began the descent to our own turf. "Done, gone, finished. Fare-fucking-well."

But it wasn't done. Not for me. My whole body was still humming with another man's touch. My exhaustion was more than physical, more than a strained body needing a hot shower and a cosy warm bed.

"Talk to me," Brett said as we reached the lower floor, but I didn't. Couldn't.

It was all I could do to cling on. To him, as well as myself.

THIRTY

BRETT

All I felt was relief. Pure fucking relief that that asshole's night with my wife was over.

My jizz was squelching like cold custard in my pants after buckling myself up at the bleep of the alarm. I felt dirty as sin as I led my Grace back downstairs, but that didn't matter. None of it mattered except the fresh chunk of cash in our joint account and making sure my trooper of a wife was back on her feet.

She was dazed to all hell, not that I blamed her — pressing tight to my side as I opened the door through to our own quarters and led us on through. It was only as I took a proper look at her face under the harsh lighting of the bathroom that I realised how fucking mortified she looked.

My gut spat with a truckload of regret. That and fear. The nasty chill of something I didn't want to face yet. Something grimy and unwanted, sickly smug like that asshole upstairs.

"Hey," I said. "It's over. We wave him off after breakfast and enjoy the rest of our lives together." She closed her eyes as I kissed her forehead. "You did it. You did so fucking well, Grace. So well. I'm so fucking proud of you."

"But I didn't..." she whispered. "I didn't *do it*..."

There was a heavy pause as I fathomed her meaning. She was shaking her head as it fully dawned on me.

"Fuck it," she said. "It doesn't matter. Who cares, right? He got his nine hours, that's all he paid for."

I did. I cared a fucking lot. Not that the sonofabitch didn't get to shoot his load as part of his investment, but that she was feeling like some kind of fuck-up for not giving it to him.

My thumb brushed her cheek hard enough that it dug into her soft skin. "Grace, you did more than enough. That shit stain got more than he deserved. You gave him fucking everything."

I didn't believe her shrug. Didn't believe the smile she shot as though she believed me.

"Done," she said. "Good fucking riddance. Amen."

"Good fucking riddance," I repeated. "Now let's get you in a nice hot shower."

I turned on the water and stripped her bare with hands that struggled for calm. Her body looked different this morning, reddened and stretched and pawed by the prick upstairs. But that wasn't it. The difference was in the blaze of memory, seeing her so fucking different on that bed earlier. Different to the woman I knew well enough to call her the other half of me. Different to the woman I'd spent every single minute that meant anything with over the past ten years.

"Steady," I said with a smile as I helped her step under the flow. She flinched as the jets landed hard on her shoulders, then tipped her head back to take it all over.

I was out of my own clothes in a tangle of madness, kicking my jeans so hard they landed on the toilet seat and flopped down onto the tiles. Her arms were waiting as I stepped in to join her, her face pressing tight to the nook of my neck as I held her close.

"Soap," she whispered. "I need soap. I need to clean myself…"

I didn't let her go. Didn't want to let her go. Not now, not ever.

"Give yourself a break," I said. "Just breathe, Grace."

Her body sagged against me, as though every single inch of her needed the support of mine. She could take it. Take everything. Take my beating heart from my chest if it would help her stand tall.

"I got you," I whispered. "He's nothing. Just a sad fucking memory."

"I'm just tired," she lied. "I'll be fine in a few hours."

I massaged her shoulders and forced a grin. "I'm thinking a full English when that asshole's gone. American pancakes with syrup to follow. Maybe even a chocolate milkshake. Maybe even two."

"Chocolate milkshake sounds good."

I kept rolling with the promises.

"I'll check in today's guests and we'll spend the afternoon watching shitty TV in the lounge. You and me, that fluffy throw from the armchair, and reruns of that crappy sitcom you like so much."

"You hate those shows." She whispered a laugh against my skin. The thought of a cosy Wednesday afternoon seemed to bring her a little closer to her senses. She managed a smile up at me, pushing herself away just enough to meet my eyes. "I don't deserve you, Brett Foster."

"Oh, you do." I laughed. "You deserve the moon after that performance you just gave for this little piece of paradise."

It was her thumb that brushed hard against my cheek this time around. "It was worth it, for us," she told me. "For my sister, too. For the money we owed her and the rest of the world. For our dreams. For our cute little picnic benches out the front and the kids we're going to bring up here."

I nodded, but didn't break her flow.

"We're going to have dogs." She grinned. "And maybe a hot tub. Maybe even a four poster in the suite upstairs. And a chef."

I raised an eyebrow. "A chef?"

Her smile was beautiful. "Evening meals. The whole works. That crap hole down the road won't have shit on us."

"We'll put an ad in the paper this afternoon," I told her. "We'll get the best chef this side of the border. They'll be coming for miles to sample our menu."

She sighed as she pressed her cheek to my chest. "We really did it. The money is really ours."

"Really ours."

"I don't even know how to say goodbye to him after breakfast," she whispered, and I felt it too.

How the fuck do you say goodbye to an asshole like that?

As much as I hated the cunt, he'd been true to his word. All fifty fucking grand's worth of it.

"Fuck knows," I said. "Maybe I'll give him an extra slice of bacon for saving ours, no matter how much I still want to kick his fucking head in."

"He did everything he said he would," she commented, voicing my own grudging thoughts out loud.

"And so did we. We're evens. Worth a handshake at least before I tell him to never show his smug fucking face around here again."

Her arms squeezed me tight. "Maybe we should eat with him, a token gesture before he goes. I mean the bad feeling's over now, right? We delivered, he paid."

I'd squirted shampoo onto her hair before I had an answer for her, lathering up her curls with fingers determined to wash that asshole away.

The bad feeling would never be over, but I didn't want to trash her optimism by pointing it out. It wasn't even *my* bad feeling I was talking about, even though I'd still happily bust his nose across his perfect fucking face just for the hell of it.

It was *his* bad feeling that wouldn't die off with a generous breakfast and token handshake. That spite was rancid, inhuman. Fucked up beyond measure. The nasty chill crept back up my spine as my memory blurred its way through faces, names, connections.

Nothing. I found nothing.

Thomas Heath.

Who the fuck was Thomas Heath?

I soaped Grace slowly, fingers gentle as they scrubbed his prints from her skin. She lapped it up with her eyes closed tight, sighing with relief as I coaxed the knots from her tense shoulders. She tipped them back as my palms brushed the tits he'd slavered over, but I didn't linger there, uncharacteristically fleeting with my touch as her nipples hardened for me.

She didn't say anything, not until my hands were between her legs, lathering her up as quickly as I could then sweeping down lower to the tops of her thighs.

"You can touch me," she told me. "I'm not too sore." Her smile was bright, even though her eyes were nervous. "I mean I'm *sore*, but not too sore. Not too sore to touch."

Her fingers snaked around my dick and it hardened on instinct as my belly tightened. "Breakfast," I said. "We've got to get to breakfast."

She didn't nod, nor move her hand away, raising up on tiptoes and aiming her wet lips right for mine.

And I couldn't. I fucking couldn't. Not knowing how that asshole fucked her throat like a fucking demon.

Shying away from her kiss was the biggest mistake I'd made this whole fucking affair. Her eyes were so hurt as she dropped back away from me that I'd have punched myself in the face along with him.

"It's him," I grunted, feeling like a piece of shit. "Where he's been."

She nodded, but her eyes still hurt raw. I knew they were welling as she tipped her face under the cascade and bared me a weak smile.

"Grace," I said. "It's just a stupid guy thing. I'll be over it by the time we're done with bacon."

"I get it," she told me. "He's been there, all over me. I just…" She shook her head. "It doesn't matter. Let's just get dressed."

She was away from my body and washing hers off before I could protest, head down as she stepped right by me and grabbed a towel from the rail.

"Wait," I said, but she didn't. I soaped my own privates even quicker than I'd soaped hers, barely even washing off the suds before I was out and after her.

The towel was wrapped tight around her as she pulled out clean underwear from the drawer. I stared mute as she tugged on knickers over her still-wet legs, cursing my own idiot clumsiness as she turned away from me to put her bra on.

"I'm a dick," I told her. "I'm fucking things up before I've even managed to make them better."

She shook her head. "You're not. It's just weird. This whole thing is weird."

"Nothing milkshake won't fix," I said, but my stupid goofball humour didn't even touch her.

She'd pulled on a top and jeans before I'd so much as wrapped a towel around my waist. I was fumbling around for a clean pair of boxers when she headed back for the bathroom, trying to shove my foot through the leg hole as I hopped back over there.

And then I heard it, the screech of a bolt on the other side.

My hand was firm as I slapped at the door. "Grace. Let me in, I promise I'll be less of a dick this time around."

But she didn't. I pressed my ear to the wood in time to hear the basin start up. The sound of her toothbrush was frantic, ragged, as were her heaves as she spat into the sink.

She brushed her teeth for a full five minutes as I stood helpless in my boxers on the other side. I started as the bolt screeched back again, ready to grab her tight when she stepped right out at me.

It was her who shied away this time, turning her cheek to my mouth as I came in hard for her. I was a dripping fool with a dripping ego, hating the caveman part of me that ran loose with paranoia as the woman in my arms pushed right off me.

"Let's just get breakfast," she said and I nodded.

"Sure."

She didn't wait for me to finish getting dressed before she headed out there.

This time it wasn't the door I slapped but the wall. More of a thump than a slap, three times over as I cursed myself for not having the slick-sure moves of a slippery sonofabitch like Heath.

He'd know what to say. How to fucking smirk. How to do fucking everything, just like he'd known how to make my wife come like I'd never seen her fucking come in her life.

And me?

I was just a fucking fool. A fool who'd cared more about bricks and sand and fucking sea than the woman who'd been my life since it meant anything.

I brushed my own teeth with the same vigour she'd brushed hers, spitting the taste of shame right out of me. I got dressed with a face like death, the relief I'd felt at seven just a hazy memory as I spritzed myself with aftershave and tried to pull my shit together enough to serve up breakfast and shake the motherfucker's hand.

But it turned out I didn't need to.

Grace's face was pale as I joined her in the dining room, her mouth open slack as she stared at her palm.

A business card. I couldn't see the lettering before I was right on top of her, but it didn't matter, I already knew what it would say.

Mr Thomas Heath.

CEO Heath Global.

And his telephone numbers. Three of them. Office, direct line and mobile.

"He's gone," she said, and I wished there was more relief in her tone. "This was at reception. His car's gone from outside."

"Good," I said. "Good fucking riddance."

I plucked the card from her fingers while she was still staring, storming right to the nearest trash bin and tossing it in while she watched.

"Won't be needing that," I told her. "Now, let's get that fucking milkshake."

THIRTY ONE

THOMAS

I'd packed up my regular suitcase before the night started. An empty case had been waiting ready in the wardrobe for my new selection of Grace Foster's pussy-scented toys.

I'd tossed them in with less of a sense of victory than I'd been hoping for. I felt ragged, uncharacteristically disjointed as I switched the hotel room lights off and took the rear stairs down to my car.

It had barely been seven twenty a.m. by the time I'd done loading up and headed back through to reception. There was no sign of life, which was a tiny blessing in the madness at least.

Leaving a business card was a signature move of mine, always bailing long before the couple could ever see me leaving. I had no time for clipped goodbyes or frosty handshakes. No time to see the reined-in lust staring out from the woman whose body I'd ravaged all night long. Only this time it felt different. *I* felt different. I doubt I'd have been able to keep my smirk at full force if I'd wanted to, which was another gross revelation I'd rather not have been faced with.

I had limits. My control had limits. And she'd pushed them.

Pretty Grace Foster had pushed them.

I didn't even know where I was headed as I sped away on dead country roads. I didn't bother with satnav, caring for nothing more than putting distance between this sorry place and my tattered hopes of what it would mean to claim the pussy I'd been denied back when it mattered.

I was halfway back across Wales when I pulled into a shitty little service station in the middle of nowhere.

I grabbed a coffee, black and cheap. It almost burned my lips off when I took a swig, my fingers shaking as I hissed out a curse and tossed the Styrofoam cup of rancid crap in the outdoor bin.

My phone was still flashing with the alarm I hadn't properly silenced when I pulled it from my pocket. I dismissed it with a swipe of my thumb before Polly's messages pinged up.

Please say you didn't.

You did, didn't you?

It won't solve anything.

Tom, please say you haven't done this.

Did you tell them?? Please at least say you told them who you really are.

You have to tell them, Tom. Put this stuff to bed once and for all. Maybe he'll be nice when he knows?

I guess you're still with them. I hope she was worth it.

Congratulations. I hope it feels every bit as good as you hoped.

I could barely focus on her messages, my temples thumping as I scrolled. The last one was from ten minutes earlier.

I can't do this anymore. I'm sorry, Tom. You're on your own.

I blurted out a laugh but it sounded like death. *On my own.* Like I hadn't been on my own for a fucking lifetime already.

I was back in my car when I fully contemplated a response, my fingers still shaking like a fucking weakling's as I dithered over the letters.

Tell me something new, my words said, but they were a lie. It *was* new. Polly being like this was new, because in spite of the way I'd kept her at a country's distance for the past few years and at arm's length for the years leading up to it, she'd always been there.

A quiet part of me hoped she always would be. That maybe the Fosters really would be the ones who proved me wrong and opened the doorway just a sliver on my belief in a love that really meant something.

But no. They hadn't proved me wrong. Not about that. Not about the fact that two people's love couldn't be undone in one single sorry evening.

Not even about the fact that two people could really, truly know each other after a lifetime in each other's arms.

Her jerk of a husband hadn't even touched the sides of his beautiful wife's potential, as oblivious to her deep, dark fantasies as he was to my existence, even though I'd rocked up bold as brass onto his doorstep and smirked right over at him.

Polly would never be my forever. Her messages were just a sorry confirmation of what I'd long known.

I tossed the handset onto the passenger seat without sending my response over to her. There was no point.

I couldn't do this anymore, even if she'd been willing. I couldn't cling onto a friendly face in the ether in the hope that one day I'd have her at my side all over again. Those days were gone, finished. They'd been numbered right from the start, since she'd sent me the barely disguised Valentine's Day card on my fifteenth birthday and prompted me to uncover the truth about who'd really sent it.

I knew who'd sent it. The writing was hers but slightly more squiggly, the envelope sealed with the heart-patterned tape she'd carried in her pencil case since the first year of high school.

I hadn't been good enough for her back then, even if she hadn't realised it. I wasn't good enough to have a girl in my arms. Too weak and weaselly to have someone else's fingers on my pale nerd body.

And when I was good enough? Finally?

I didn't believe in *I love you* by that point. Didn't believe in the strength of the line of hearts she'd drawn under the question mark on that Valentine's card. Didn't believe in anything but money, pride, and my ability to destroy people before they ever came close to destroying me.

My relationship with Polly had had numbered days from way back when, and now the countdown was over.

But Brett and Grace's countdown had only just begun.

I grabbed my handset back up to click on my calendar app. I set the date for two months' time, then remembered the horror on her pretty face when the alarm sounded out and I'd pulled away.

One month.

I set the date for one month.

My predictions up until now had never been more than a week out, not even the ones I'd set early enough that I'd been barely back at my desk before the woman's call came through on my mobile.

Grace Foster would call me in one month's time, or near enough as dammit.

And I'd be waiting.

Breaking her apart all over again was all I had left to look forward to. Destroying Brett Foster's marriage was the only victory left to claim in my damnation.

I unfriended Polly on social media before I called up satnav and keyed in my London address.

I didn't even let myself feel the pain as her profile picture disappeared from my messenger list. I slapped the sad boy inside me before he could cry his tears, forcing him down in the depths so deep that I swore I'd never hear from him again.

And then I thought about Grace Foster's needy pink cunt all the way back to the city.

THIRTY TWO

GRACE

We put a face on it, welcoming our new guests with our usual wide smiles and friendly handshakes. We showed them to their rooms, gushed about the beautiful beach and told them all about breakfast times, acting like life was all peachy here in our little slice of heaven.

I almost believed it myself.

We spent that afternoon in the lounge, just as Brett promised, holding each other tight through the unspoken tension while my favourite sitcoms blared on screen.

We served our fresh handful of guests in the bar that evening and asked all our usual friendly questions about their lives and loves. We talked about tennis, countryside living and the state of the economy, only this time financial topics didn't fill me with the same dread as they had just a week ago.

We shared a few bottles of house white with a particularly nice couple who enjoyed a healthy friendship with alcohol, and finally, at the end of the night, we wiped down the sides and switched off the lights, filing on through to the quiet of our own private space.

And there I lay, in my baggiest PJs, staring up the ceiling in bed while Brett finished in the bathroom, trying not to think about the man who'd flipped all my switches and left me a mess in his wake.

My pussy was still sore, and my ass still felt fresh from a battering, my belly tumbling at the horror of all the dirty things I'd done. But still my clit pulsed and tingled at the thought of being stretched open wide by the man who'd known my everything, despite being a total stranger.

I rolled into Brett as he slipped between the covers, hooking a leg over his and resting my cheek on his shoulder. His arms were welcoming, but his dick was not.

"You must be sore," he told me, kissing my head as though his lack of desire was all with me in mind.

"It's going to be like this, is it?" I asked him.

"Like what?" he grunted, still holding me tight.

"Like I'm soiled goods now I've been used by a man for money."

My words were overly harsh and I knew it, but I couldn't take them back. Didn't want to take them back.

His eyes were fierce enough to burn in the darkness as he turned towards me. "You aren't soiled fucking goods," he said. "You aren't soiled anything. You're just sore and I'm just tired, and this is night fucking one after that cunt's departure. Give it a fucking minute, Grace."

It wasn't enough. Not for me. Not now.

My hands were persistent as they snaked down to his boxers and slipped inside. His breath was a hiss as my fingers gripped and tugged, coaxing him to put this filthy mess behind us and make it right again.

"Fuck, Grace," he said, and thrust into my grip. I was on autopilot as I pulled the covers back and peppered his body with kisses, trailing down his belly as I freed his cock and positioned him ripe for my mouth.

I knew this game. Knew how to suck, lick and tease. Knew how to slide my fingers down his thighs and bring his skin to horny goosebumps as he fought the urge to buck into my mouth and leave me retching.

But no. Not tonight.

His fingers were rough as he took my hair and made me suck him deep, thrusting up from the mattress and into my throat in a blatant imitation of the other man's violent moves.

It was brutal. Desperate. Filled with fake fire as he groaned and snarled and aimed for maximum impact.

But it wasn't the force which had my excitement flatlining. It wasn't even the drastic change from all our years of learned compatibility.

This wasn't him. Wasn't us. Wasn't love in the way I'd known it from him my entire adult life.

I took it gladly regardless, with a thumping heart and churning gut, hoping this was just a stupid blip and we'd be right as rain in the blink of an eye. But even as I took it all, staring up at him with warm eyes as he jammed in hard, I knew he was thinking of him. Of Thomas Heath. Of me with spit streaming down my face as I thrashed and spluttered and begged for more.

I'd have given the same to Brett if I knew how. I'd have given the same to Brett if he'd seized it from me the way Heath had.

But he didn't.

Couldn't, maybe. Floating on the same sea of uncertainty as I was as we jammed to some alien groove.

The halfway house of fucking me hard but not hard enough was a sickly no man's land where nothing felt genuine. Not my effort nor his pleasure.

My eyes watered, and it wasn't just from my gag reflex. The sadness was a tarnished penny I'd swallowed down deep, metallic and bitter and enough to put me in the foetal position, knees up high to my chest once I'd swallowed down his cum and retreated. Having him curled around the back of me made no difference. His steady breathing did little to lull me into my sweet little bubble of security.

It wasn't regret that haunted me that night. Not the disgusting reflections on a man who'd used me like a cheap slut while I'd begged for more, or my desperate efforts to make him come for me. It wasn't my swimming thoughts which drove me to the edge of the bed and away from Brett's warm arms, nor the promise of the soothing sea through the window.

It was Thomas Heath's business card in the dining room rubbish bin.

I wasn't going to call him, not in the rest of this lifetime, but still I fished it out from the depths with my breath held tight, rubbing a grease stain with my finger to make sure the contact numbers were still readable.

I slipped it into the reception desk drawer with other guests' contact details for upcoming bookings, uncertain quite why I was rescuing it as I closed that drawer up tight.

And then I went back to bed with my husband, praying to everything on this earth that it was still where I belonged.

THIRTY THREE

BRETT

I wanted to fuck my wife like he had, but I didn't know where to fucking start.

I could slap and grind with an edge of roughness, calling her my dirty little bitch as she grinned back at me over her shoulder. But it wasn't like he did it. Wasn't even close.

Maybe I didn't have it in me. Maybe that kind of inhuman prowess was the result of some tantric guru sex teachings – that and the boulder-weight chip on his shoulder. Maybe he really was on little blue pills, or had some medical condition making jizzing impossible. Maybe that's why he paid for it with such fucking delight, just so his conquests would think him a God.

Fuck really knows, but still I kept pushing Grace to give me the same slutty doe-eyed rapture she'd given that sonofabitch, and still she kept on seeking what I wasn't able to give her.

I slammed her body every night that week once her tight little holes were up to it. I fucked her ass like a man possessed, holding her face down into the pillow as I called her my dirty little slut. I fingered her sweet pussy with four fingers instead of my usual two, and all she did was hiss and spit and say it hurt too much to take it.

She took it for him though. Begged him fucking for it, in fact.

I started jerking myself off in the shower every morning to ease the spitting tension in my gut. I'd slip that rusty bolt into place and work my dick hard, thoughts jammed full of the Grace I'd seen open wide for him.

That Grace wasn't my Grace, but I wanted her. *Needed* her. Craved her with every drop of cum in my balls.

My Grace still smiled sweetly and helped me on the breakfast run. She still laughed with guests every evening and snuggled up to me in bed at night. She still took every pounding on offer, whimpering for more in a voice that almost rang true. Almost.

The first real grin I got from my wife was when the advert for the chef position I'd phoned into the local paper appeared in print and I opened up the job page in front of her.

"You really think we should do it?" she said, eyes bright at the thought of a new hotel adventure.

I didn't think we should do it. Not even close. Not with a looming competitor opening in two short months, able to staff their place with ten chefs for every one of ours if they so wanted.

"I think we should do whatever you want for this place," I told her, and I wasn't lying.

"It could be great for us," she said. "A reputation for good food can spread for miles. We could be rammed to the ceiling with bookings on the back of a perfect steak."

And so they came calling. Chefs and trainees and people applying for any old job they thought they could get their hands on. Spotty teens and grumpy old men. Women whose experience didn't exceed their weekly Sunday roast and packed lunches but had always fancied making a good trifle.

Grace sighed after the tenth shitty interview in a row, opening a bottle of house red at just past lunchtime and cursing the pool of wannabes in our ten-mile radius.

"Maybe we should sell up and go back to the city," she said after taking a glug. "Maybe we really are doomed in running this place."

I shook my head. "We'll do alright. It only takes one person walking in through that door with the right set of skills, and this whole venture could flip on its head."

Her eyes widened on mine as I said it, and I knew she was thinking about him. Heath. The sonofabitch with his *set of skills* who'd flipped our whole fucking *life* on its head.

"Forget about him," I barked, and she dropped her mouth open in feigned ignorance.

"Jesus, Brett, I wasn't. I've barely given him a second thought since he left."

How I fucking glared at her as she dropped her eyes and dicked about with some glasses from the dishwasher. I could see the bloom on her cheeks, smarting hard at my observation. I'd felt her in bed at night, rubbing that horny little clit after I'd fucked her senseless, no doubt thinking of that prick and his superior skillset every time she thought I was out for the count in dreamland.

"You need to stop this," she told me with a voice full of prickles. "Every time I think for a single fucking second, you think I'm thinking about him."

"Because you are," I snapped.

"Because *you* are," she snapped back. "You're the one who has the fucking problem with him, Brett, not me."

It was her choice of words that got me going, more than the flash of guilt in her eyes.

"No," I grunted. "You haven't got a problem with him, have you? You fucking loved it, Grace. You'd have him back all over again in a heartbeat, only next time you wouldn't need fucking paying."

It was when she launched the wine bottle across the bar top that I knew I'd pushed it way too fucking hard. It crashed into the nearest table, glugging red all over the upholstered seats underneath as the shards glittered like ice on the woodwork.

It looked like blood. Arterial bleeding as we both stood staring, dumbstruck at the veins of disgust still pulsing dark between us.

She went for it first, but I headed her off at the hatch, taking the dustpan and cloth from her before she'd got the chance to dive under.

"I'll do it," I told her. "It was my dick move that set you off."

She joined me anyway, picking up the big shards with careful fingers as I dabbed up the worst of the spill.

"I know you jerk off in the bathroom," she whispered. "I hear the bolt click every morning and press my ear to the door. You think about him, don't you?"

"No more than you think about him when you think I'm asleep," I countered, but she sighed out loud.

"We're both guilty of thinking about that night," she said. "Maybe we should be talking about it rather than brushing it under the carpet and hoping life has a chance of returning to normal."

I hated the twist of fear as it sliced my insides. "We are returning to normal," I argued. "It's just a little slower a process than I was hoping for."

"We need to experiment," she said. "You and me, and whatever crazy shit we conjure up with our dirty money. If we can't beat him, join him, hey?"

I didn't follow at first, not until she bit her lip and spelled it out for me.

"He had a whole arsenal, Brett. Toys and gadgets and goddamn sheeting. Surely we can spice it up like he did? Make some memories of our own?"

It was a thread of hope, and one I grabbed hold of with everything I was worth.

My smile was eager, just as hers was relieved when I nodded my head. "Alright," I said. "Let's place an order. If it's good enough for that sonofabitch, it'll be good enough for us."

And so it started.

Me, Grace and a tablet full of sex store browser tabs that evening in the bedroom. Racking up a cartful of purchases that asshole paid for with his dirty money.

I was grinning as we clicked confirm on the checkout, pulling my pretty wife close and landing a hungry kiss on her sweet mouth. She was waiting, squirming out of her nightdress before we'd even had the ping of the confirmation email, begging me to fuck her in some semblance of similarity to how she'd asked him to do the same.

This time I fucked her like me. Brett Foster, the man who'd loved her forever.

And she was my Grace, the woman who'd cracked apart for another man but still loved me in the aftermath.

But there, in the heavy breaths of two people dreaming of a dirty future, I caught my first glimpse of the minx he'd shown me inside her, bucking for dick and straining for more, eyes glinting with need as I jammed my fingers in her hungry asshole with her pussy plugged tight with my dick.

"Two at once," I grunted. "I'm gonna give you two at once when those big fucking dildos arrive."

Her climax was enough to milk me dry to the fucking bone, spurting cum into that sopping wet pussy until my balls were aching with the strain.

"That's what you think about?" I grunted as I flopped down beside her, but this time there was no anger in it, just a genuine curiosity.

Her shrug was a pathetic excuse for an answer, so I kept quiet until she granted me more.

"I think about what would have happened without that stupid red line being there," she admitted. "I think about what would have happened if he'd been serious about me taking both of you in one."

I fought my initial revulsion at the thought of his balls slapping mine.

"You'd have liked that? To have me there along with him?"

Her laugh was genuine, even through the endorphins. "Is that a serious question? Of course I'd have liked you there along with him. You're the one I want, he was just a bonus."

A bonus, not an unfortunate requirement. Her natural choice of words said it all.

"We'll start with toys," I said, reeling at my own natural choice of words.

"Start with?" she asked, her voice full of shock as she shifted to stare at me eye to eye. "You really think we'll ever do something with another person?"

I should've said no, fuck that. Fuck Thomas Heath and other guys and sharing that pretty cunt with anyone else in the next hundred years.

But I didn't.

Of course I didn't.

Seeing my wife looking like she had on that bed while that prick worked her ragged was all I'd ever dreamed of, even if I hadn't known it. I couldn't undo what I'd seen, what I felt. What *she'd* felt.

Pretending it was nothing was going nowhere.

Ignoring the repercussions of one crazy evening was heading towards certain doom.

"I don't know," I said. "What I do know is that there's a whole world of weird kinky sex we've never explored. I think it's time we broadened our horizons. It's not just that smug-faced cunt Heath that can get his wacko groove on, you know. Some of us just haven't shown it yet."

"I love you, Brett Foster," she said. "Always."

As I did her, only I didn't get chance to tell her so that evening.

Her mouth was already pressed to mine as she climbed aboard for round two.

THIRTY FOUR

GRACE

The parcels came in discreet packaging, just like Thomas Heath's had. It was like deja vu as they mounted up behind reception, only this time I had much more than an inkling of what dirty treasures were hiding in each package.

I wondered if this really was the beginning of a whole new era for our marriage, hoping in every tingling part of me that my husband would push me to the same horny limits the other man had that night. Hoping that I'd be able to drive him to a whole other level of excitement in return, succeeding where I'd failed with Thomas Heath.

My shortcomings from that evening still pained deep — my heart still fluttering with embarrassment at the memory of disappointing the man who'd paid so much for my body.

I felt like a fraud no matter which way I looked at it, taking all that money for services lacking in… *quality*, but I couldn't voice it, not to Brett. I couldn't tell him about the rescued business card hidden amongst the paperwork in the reception drawer. Daren't tell him how I still thought about him and Thomas Heath doubling up for a night beyond my filthiest dreams. How it kept me awake in the early hours, even when he'd fucked me to exhaustion.

Brett could skirt the idea of us bringing in another man all he liked, I'd believe the reality of it when it was right there in front of me. He teased, dangling the prospect of two at once so temptingly during my most exposed moments, but I wasn't sure he really meant it, not enough to carry it through.

Even if he *was* considering it, one day far off in the future, there's no way it would be Thomas Heath he'd be calling. His eyes darkened at the mention of his name, despite the way he still jerked himself off so regularly out of my sight in the bathroom.

I knew it was happening, bolt closed or not. He probably knew I was rubbing my clit to my own tune just as frequently.

As far as blind eyes go, this was one I figured we'd live with. The *Thomas Heath effect*. Neither of us mentioned his name as we unwrapped our purchases and surveyed the range of items so inspired by his night with us.

Big rubbery dongs and strings of beads. A set of cuffs with the same absence of safety locks, and a length of chain to thread under the bed, just like he'd had. Crotchless lingerie and nipple tassels, a fresh pair of hooker heels for me to repeat the striptease I'd so nervously done for both seated men, and a feather tickler for lighter games of bondage and submission.

I could hardly wait to get the guests out of the bar that night, glancing over at my husband with hungry eyes during every lull in the conversation across the bar top.

I loved seeing the way he looked back at me, his eyes dancing with sparks of his own. I wondered if he'd take me to that wild place Heath had, driving me to the edges of reason with hands that pushed every physical boundary my body could bear.

I wiped the bar down in a frenzy when the last of our customers said goodnight, flashing the dirtiest grin I could muster over my shoulder as Brett loaded the dishwasher behind me.

"We've got our own nine hours tonight," he told me. "Maybe your pussy will still be dripping at breakfast tomorrow morning."

"Maybe," I said with a smile. "Maybe my ass will be dripping too. Maybe I'll still be spluttering with a mouthful of cum as I'm taking the food orders."

He got to his feet and pressed me into the counter, words dripping with promise as he hissed them at my ear.

"You're getting a filthy mouth on you, Mrs Foster. Any more trash talk like that and I may have to punish you."

"Spank me," I giggled and poked my tongue out. He gripped it in his fingers and I wiggled it hard, coaxing him tighter as his body came at mine.

"You don't want to be spanked," he growled. "You want to be fucked. Stretched. Gaped fucking wide from all those plastic dicks with your name on them."

"Show me," I pleaded, linking my fingers in his as my nerves tightened.

I wanted this. Needed this. Needed more of the filthy wonders Thomas Heath had blessed me with.

If Brett could give them to me, I'd be the happiest woman on the planet, regardless of my own failings when it came to giving the thrills right back.

I shut the thought down, just like always, trying hard to ignore the consistent pang of uselessness that popped its head up high at the most inopportune moments.

"Come on, dirty girl," Brett hissed. "Let's get you in that bedroom."

I followed him gladly, bouncing on killer heels all the way through the kitchen and into ours. He kicked the door closed behind us, hoisting me up before we'd made it anywhere close to the bedroom. I wrapped my legs around his solid waist and pressed my mouth to his, conveying in that kiss just how much I was his for the taking, if only he knew how to take it.

The new toys were all unboxed and ready, lined up on the dressing table in an imitation of Heath's arrangement. We'd done it together in an afternoon lull, both of us handling the products with dopey grins on our faces as we'd weighed up the order of play.

I wished now that we hadn't, that this was as much of a surprise as it'd been that night. That he ploughed me with plugs beyond my dreams, forcing them into me in a routine of his choosing, his pleasure.

Just so long as he got more pleasure in return than Heath did.

"I want you to come inside me," I whispered as we crossed the bedroom threshold, and Brett quirked an eyebrow as though I was saying the sky was blue in summer.

"Is the Pope Catholic?" he asked and dropped me from a height down onto the bed.

I bounced, tits still jiggling as I stilled, and his dick was out in seconds, veined and thick as he presented it to my open mouth.

"Gonna take you to all the places he did," he snarled, and I flinched at the sentiment, even though I was hoping for the same.

He forced his dick all the way to the back of my throat, another imitation of the natural filth in the other man's moves.

I said nothing, just took it, praying that he'd find his own personal groove and rule it hard, like Heath, just in original Brett Foster flavours. But he didn't.

I knew it as he pulled me backward and fastened the cuffs around my wrists in the very same way Heath had. I pushed aside the cynicism as he tore my flimsy dress from my ribs. yanking my skimpy bra down over my tits and palming them hard.

"Gonna fuck you so fucking deep," he told me, dick in his hand as he looked me up and down.

I didn't tug on my cuffs. Not when he tore my knickers from me and not when he slammed three fingers all the way inside. I wanted it to feel good, and it did. It felt really good. But his eyes kept on searching mine for some kind of bubbling sexual bliss, as though I should be unravelling right then and there as he worked me with frantic pumps of his wrist.

I shifted so he hooked the right spot, but he shifted his wrist right back again for greater leverage. I whimpered louder than I needed to, and the performance made me cringe. I gave him the sultriest stare I should manage, belly lurching as he picked up pace down below.

"That's nice," I told him.

"Nice?" he barked. "I want more than nice. I want fucking wonderful."

So did I.

I bucked against his movements and closed my eyes, seeking out the same gorgeous strain that Heath had forced on me, telling myself this was it, the moment we found that epic groove of deviancy amongst the host of crazy toys. I told myself he'd be better than Heath, just as I'd be better for him than I was that night. That we were on the edge of a whole new awakening, just ripe for the plucking.

It was when the first thick dong pushed in deep that I knew we were far from a whole new awakening.

My pussy protested by clamping tight, thighs tense with the urge to slam shut and say this was a no go.

"Take it," he growled, and I did. I arched my back and stretched my legs open wide, convincing myself the ache inside me was a prelude to ecstasy and orgasms running wild.

"My clit," I whispered. "Touch me."

His fingers were rough and heavy, like Heath's but missing the moment and falling short. I tried to make my grunts sound horny, not pained, but through gritted teeth they were anything but.

"You want to be my dirty little slut," Brett told me, and I did, my nod was all genuine. "Come for me," he ordered. "Show me how much you want it."

And there we had it. That age old chasm of a decision to be made in the heat of the moment. One I'd thankfully never had to make until this night.

To fake it, or not.

He deserved better than that, and I knew it. He'd never asked for anything other than my genuine reaction to his touch, nor pushed me for volume or porn-star outbursts.

I'd never considered being anything other than my natural self until that one desperate expression was on his face, seeking reassurance under his filthy stare.

So I gave it to him.

I moaned and murmured, thrashing my feet against the bed like a woman gone wild.

I hated it. Every single second of the stupid playacting. Every false moan insulted both my integrity and his, but more than that, it insulted the way his body knew mine.

I didn't notice he'd stopped thrusting that big fat toy until too late, so lost to my writhing outburst that I'd lost track of his efforts, my pussy allegedly losing all control.

I was begging for *harder, like that* when he tugged the plastic dick free of my aching insides and tossed it aside. It seemed too much of a contrast to shut up my whimpers after being so absorbed in my pleasure, so I didn't, face burning as I kept up my silly fake moans.

"Don't stop," I hissed. "Please, Brett, don't stop."

"Quit it," he said, and his voice was as flat as a pancake.

The chains jangled as I hauled myself as close to sitting as I could manage. "Quit what?" I asked, another dumb move on my part.

He was on his feet and stomping away before I could call after him, my fingers wrestling with those cursed fucking cuffs despite knowing full well there was no safety catch.

"Brett!" I shouted, but he was long out of sight. "Jesus, Brett, let me out of these fucking things!"

I'd read about this in a horror novel years ago. A woman getting trapped in handcuffs in some remote log cabin somewhere and having to peel her skin from her wrists like an orange. I remembered thinking, even back then, that I was lucky Brett and I were so compatible. Would never suffer the kind of shitty miscommunication that lead to sex games gone bad.

Yet, here I was, pussy cursing my dumb decisions along with the rest of me.

When Brett came back through to the bedroom his eyes were on fire and his jaw was hard. He unlocked the cuffs with a hiss of breath that stopped my own, barely staying around to see me on my feet before he was off on the move again.

I grabbed my dressing gown and pulled it tight around me, only venturing out into the living room when I'd calmed myself in the bathroom enough not to sick up everywhere.

I went on the attack as soon as he came into view, arms gesturing at nothing as I launched into a stupid tirade about him dumping me when I was flying high.

"What the fuck?!" I insisted. "What was that?! Pulling away in the moment like some kind of fucking sadist!"

His laugh was bitter enough to cut. "Cut the fucking crap," he snapped. "Jesus, Grace, just fucking listen to yourself."

His arms were folded as he pressed himself against the far wall, the bad feeling so palpable I could feel its stench between us.

"What?" I said. "What's all this about?"

"I can't believe you're even asking me that."

I dropped to the sofa with my head in my hands, wishing I had one of Thomas Heath's swanky cigars to light up on the front. "This is supposed to be a good night for us," I said. "We're supposed to be experimenting."

"Experimenting, yeah. Not fucking lying through our teeth."

I shook my head. "I wasn't lying. It felt good."

"Not that fucking good, it didn't. I was fucking there, Grace. I know what you fucking looked like when he was hitting the mark. I know what the real wanton Grace Foster sounds like when she's begging for more and means it."

"You told me to show you how much I wanted it…" I started, but he shook his head. I carried on regardless. "I wanted it. I wanted to want it more than anything. I wanted to lose myself the way I should do. The way I want to lose it. With you like I did with him. *Better* than I did with him."

"But it wasn't happening, was it?"

I shrugged. "I don't know, Brett. I don't know what's happening anymore."

"You and me both," he snapped, and stared outside.

The tears pricked, so pathetic. Guilt on top of guilt. For lying, for faking stupid moans just to please him. For feeling such a ridiculously vulnerable need to please him in the first place.

I got up quietly and slipped away, leaving him staring out to sea as I sought the same solace for myself.

My pumps weren't even laced as I stepped out onto the terrace from the side door. I didn't give a shit for the lack of lighting overhead as I stumbled down the patio steps and out toward the front.

I cried at the sea. Big, racking sobs with only the ocean and sky as witnesses, cursing Thomas Heath and his shitty fucking cash for walking into our life and ripping the good right out from under us.

I hated my body for wanting the other man's touch enough to unravel.

Hated my self-conscious need to please in the aftermath of being such a failure.

Hated Brett for letting this happen just as much as I hated myself.

I'd cried myself cold by the time I calmed enough to breathe in the salt breeze and stare out at the horizon with clear vision. My cheeks were puffy as I patted them dry with the sleeve of my robe, sniffing back the grotty snuffles as I turned on my heel and headed back to the warmth inside.

He was already in bed, his body stiff as a board as I slipped in next to him with my dressing gown still wrapped tight. I'd have cried all over again if it hadn't been for the simple touch of his foot reaching back for mine.

I knew it was all he could manage, and that was ok.

Reaching mine back to meet his was all I could manage too.

THIRTY FIVE

THOMAS

It was usually a pleasant affair, waiting for the fallout. I'd be able to relax comfortably behind my London office desk, staring out at the skyline and imagining the sweet, dirty thoughts of me the poor woman was plagued with in her husband's arms at night. If she was still there, that is.

Sometimes the relationship didn't make it that long.

I'd been expecting the weeks following my night with the Fosters to be the most thrilling of all, my fantasies of Grace struggling with the memories of me the most victorious I'd ever been blessed with.

But no. The weeks following were anything but victorious.

I kept my business engagements clipped and curt, and my gym sessions isolated with earphones blaring my favourite songs. It didn't matter. None of it mattered.

I couldn't stop thinking about her. *Them.* Couldn't stop imagining another night pushing her body to her limits. Only this time, unlike all the others, I was imagining him — *Brett* — being there too.

I'd have booked myself into a therapist if I thought they'd achieve anything whatsoever with a cynical bastard like me.

I didn't even have the kind words of my distant best friend to help ease my discomfort. I'd been the one to delete Polly from social media, but she'd made no move to contact me through other channels.

I found myself staring at my phone whenever my workload had moments of calm, wondering if she was missing my virtual presence as strongly as I was missing hers.

I *was* missing hers.

She'd be on my mind late at night, just as soon as I'd finished shooting my load over fantasies of Grace Foster's hungry pink pussy stretched wide. I'd find myself smiling sadly at childhood memories of her laughing at stupid jokes and pulling silly faces. Of scrabbling to finish her homework on the school bus, digging for answers from my nerd brain when hers was lacking.

Polly Piper had been a constant in a life without basic constants. My only source of stability through my bitter quests of destruction.

And she was gone.

Without all doubt, she was gone.

No calls, texts, or friend requests. No emails to my work address. Nothing but radio silence after telling me she was done.

That little boy in me who'd hoped for more from our lifetime of closeness hated me enough to keep his distance. He was quiet, weeping in the far shadows where I couldn't hear his cries. I was glad of it, even if my detachment from life wasn't holding up as well as it should have.

I knew his mind well enough to know how he'd interpret Polly's silence during his fleeting moments of optimism.

He'd say she was hurt beyond repair by my relentless pursuit of another woman, even if I did mean her no good whatsoever. That her drawing such a concrete line in the sand after all these years was testament to the strength of her emotions for such a fucked-up asshole as me.

I'd never been an optimist, not in ways it mattered. My belief was in my own talent for wreaking havoc in other people's lives. In my cold, hard intelligence and my application of strategies to everyday life. In business, in money, in cynical endeavours.

Not in people. Not in love. Not in the ability of two people to weather the storms that came tumbling in around them, their fingers linked through the chaos tightly enough to stand shoulder to shoulder through it all.

I didn't believe in Polly Piper being the woman for me.

I didn't believe in Grace Foster being that woman, either — I just believed I'd enjoy my limited time destroying her marriage.

Maybe it was already done.

I checked up on Cliff House B&B through the online booking portal and found it functioning as normal. I discovered an advert for a chef position in their local newspaper and laughed to myself at their efforts.

It would take more than an evening meal restaurant to bridge the gulf I'd left between them, but regardless, if that was indeed their hope for a brighter business future they'd be struggling all the same.

That same advert was in the job section three weeks running, which can only mean one thing in recruitment.

Nobody fucking suitable. Not in a hundred mile radius of that backwater backyard.

It was that observation that piqued my interest enough to look at the state of the venture down the road from them. The budget hotel opening along the coast was bleating loud from their website, as well as having advertisements in the same job section of the newspaper crying out for staff for all roles within the hotel space. Maids, waitresses, bar staff. Cooks and gardeners and someone to maintain a swimming pool.

Interesting.

Navigating their online booking portal showed them full to bursting for three months straight after opening, but I'd been in business long enough to know the strength of illusion in corporate appearances.

I called a contact in my property subsidiary, asking them to do some digging on my behalf in the hotel trade. They reported back their findings that same afternoon after a stint at the golf course nearest the hotel chain head office.

The bookings were void. Faked to disguise the issues they were experiencing in opening such a small town venture. They'd refunded the initial rush of paying guests and moved them to alternative locations as a gesture of goodwill.

There would be no hotel opening in March, nor April, either.

The new date scheduled was mid-June, and even that allegedly had the management contact groaning at how they'd potentially have to pay agency staff to get the place up on its feet.

I wondered if the Fosters knew about the change in their rival's opening schedule. If it allowed them to sleep a little more easily at night, despite the more pressing issue of another man coming between them.

I doubted it.

They hadn't done enough research to know about the looming rival in the first place when they went double or bust and invested the entire sum of Brett's inheritance on the mortgage deposit.

One hundred and seventy five thousand pounds handed over in its entirety, less than two years after his *daddy's* death.

I hoped he would be turning in his grave at the fuck-up they were making with his hard earned cash, realising in the afterlife just how much of a bull-headed loser his precious boy was after all.

Brett was worth nothing. A failure with a face that fit, hurtling through life on the back of an unfounded ego.

Soon he'd fall, and I'd be waiting, just as I had been for years.

Smiling.

Laughing.

Bathing myself in delight after years of hate and spite.

But not today. Today I'd be shutting down another cruddy little family business and swallowing up their life's work with my gnashing corporate jaws.

Today I'd be Thomas Heath Global, master of his whole sorry fucking universe.

And today, most importantly of all, I'd be the man who waited. Patiently.

THIRTY SIX

BRETT

I buried those toys deep in the dresser for the time being, fuck Heath and his stupid props. The days were easier than the nights, but we did alright, slipping back into the same routines we'd been in before he ever landed in our space. We were patching up a wound with a useless excuse for a bandage, throwing ourselves into making the hotel the place to be for our straggling guests and dreaming up plans for the future, but it was the best we knew.

Maybe we'd have got somewhere if a chef of any actual calibre had shown up for an interview. Grace remained smiling through the whole sorry process, shrugging off yet another fast food chicken applicant as a temporary blip in our recruitment plans.

"They've got to be out there," she told me, even as her shoulders sagged at his exit. "We just need to find them."

I nodded my agreement, wishing I shared even a scrap of her forced optimism.

"Maybe we should try a newspaper further afield to run the advert?" she asked. "I mean it's commutable, for the right person. Maybe we should even advertise in the city and offer accommodation as part of the salary package?"

It was there that I drew the line. No random asshole was moving into our tense little chicken coop alongside us. No brooding city chef with an ego to match his superior palate, waltzing in to shove the cat amongst the pigeons when we were struggling to keep our shit together as it was.

She rolled her eyes as I grunted my aversion to having a member of staff under our roof.

"It's standard, Brett. We work in hospitality. Loads of hotels have live-in staff."

"Not this one," I argued. "No fucking way."

She'd folded her arms as I hoisted boxes of breakfast supplies up on our kitchen shelves, leaning her hip against the worktop as her eyes scorched my every move.

"Maybe she'll be a girl chef," she said. "Maybe it'll be you I'll have to be mindful of the next time someone enigmatic walks through the door."

"It isn't me you'll have to be worried about," I snapped. "My come face is my fucking come face. Don't expect you'll find me morphing into some kind of fucking porn star in some other woman's pussy."

Her lip trembled before she bit it, and I cursed myself under my breath.

"Jesus, Grace, I'm sorry," I said, realising how often I had to say it these days. "I'm just feeling the fucking pressure, that's all."

It was true as well. I was feeling the pressure. Not of cash nowadays with Thomas Heath's dirty reward safely stacked up in our bank account, but the rest of it. The new hotel opening down the road. The prospect of never being as good with my wife as that sack of shit was that night. The thought that we'd trashed a decade of closeness by letting a slimy cunt like him come between us and leave his mark.

It was an ugly mark. Slippery when wet and hard to pick up and cast away, blooming its disgusting pock-filled face in bed at night, goading from the sidelines as we attempted to find the same old groove we gelled in before.

We were having sex every night when the bar closed as standard, throwing ourselves into each other's arms as if a token bump and grind could recapture the magic. I would have believed it if I hadn't been burned by the full potential of Grace losing her mind for the right man.

For the first time in forever I was plagued by the notion that I *wasn't* the right man.

I was also plagued by the never-ending desire to jerk myself off at the thought of her with Thomas Heath's smug cunt fingers stretching her wide. It wasn't a guilty pleasure, it was a revolting one, but it was an addiction I couldn't shake off for the life of me. My early morning wood would throb at the memory of seeing her bucking on his dick, but over the weeks it switched from a memory into a full-blown fantasy.

No red line. No stupid rules from Heath's cunt of a mouth.

Just us, and her — two men competing to drive her wild, only this time I'd come out on top. I'd learn from his deviant ways and forge a path of my own, pushing her further with me alongside him than he ever could alone.

Taunts of two in one were the sure-fire way to get her whimpering over these past weeks — the only real taste of her newly revealed inner slut I'd seen a glimpse of since his departure.

She wanted it.

I wanted it.

But there was no way I'd fucking suggest it for real. Not now.

It was in bed that night after the chef argument that she flopped down beside me after riding hard on top. She caught her breath and stared at the ceiling, uncharacteristically quiet as we let our exertion settle.

"You think about it, don't you?" she said. "About me and him."

"I wish I could stop fucking thinking about it," I replied. "I wish we'd never done it in the first place."

"You're not alone in that," she told me, and her voice was stretched thin with pain. "Fuck the fifty grand, it was never worth it."

It brought a smirk to my face to rival his, remembering loud and clear how the sack of shit had goaded us with the same hard truth before we'd gone through with the dirty deed. Cunt.

I wondered if he was thinking about us, far away in his swanky London pad. Maybe he was onto his tenth married couple since us by now, barely even remembering our names.

But I knew that was bullshit as soon as I thought it.

I still didn't know how he knew us, either of us. I'd done some more digging online and found nothing other than that mutual friend from Grace's sister's school year. I didn't even know the girl myself.

It was a mystery, but one that was still bugging me weeks later. I imagined it was bugging my beautiful wife just as bad.

"He'd have offered us more," I said to her. "Whatever it would have taken to get your knickers off in front of me."

She scoffed at the suggestion, and I knew in her head she was weighing up his cash investment against her worth and finding herself lacking. That was another load of utter bullshit about this whole shit storm — that she didn't think she'd earned the money.

"I mean it," I told her. "He'd have given us whatever it took. He wasn't some random seeking out a few days of quiet on the coast. He was after us. Specifically us."

She didn't argue with that, wrapping her legs in mine as she snuggled into me. I put my hand on hers and squeezed, solid in sentiment if not in the finer daily details.

"But why? What did we ever do to him to bring him calling?" she asked after a pause.

"Good question," I said.

But was it a good question? Was it even worth thinking about?

"We should sleep," she commented as if dismissing my unspoken query, and then she sighed. "Sarah wants to head down with the kids next week, just for the one night. Maybe I could ask her about Polly Piper. She might know something."

My gut lurched at the thought of digging into a sandbox full of shit, but our ostrich stance was getting us nowhere. Nowhere good.

"She'll think you're crazy, asking after some random guy from London and some girl she knew from high school."

"I am crazy," she whispered. "We're both crazy, and he's the guy who's driving us mad."

I didn't have anything useful to add to that reasoning, so I didn't.

Maybe Grace's sister would be able to shine a light on the slick city dickhead. And if not, at least Grace could get some of the bullshit off her chest by trying.

Hell knows, we needed all the relief we could get.

THIRTY SEVEN

GRACE

I greeted my sister with open arms and a screeching heart as her car pulled into the car park, needing the sibling companionship right then like I needed air. I hugged her tight enough as she stepped out of the driver's seat that she made a joke of it, patting my back like I'd lost my mind as her girls ran on to Brett and told him how many sandcastles they were going to build.

"Are you alright, sis?" she asked, pulling away with a smile like mine and quizzing me with eyes that knew all too well how to read my secrets.

I hoped she wouldn't manage it this time.

"I'm alright," I told Sarah and she raised an eyebrow.

"We need some sisterly one on one time, I think," she said. "And maybe a nice chilled bottle of white."

I laughed, nodding like a lunatic as I slung an arm around her shoulder and grabbed one of her overnight cases with the other. "Wine and time sound divine."

Brett had already set the girls up with lemonades and neon straws when we dropped the cases in the bar and took a seat on stools right next to them. Their happy chatter was a blissful relief, exactly the tension reliever we needed. I could see it beaming in Brett's eyes just as bright as I felt it in mine.

Family. There was nothing like it.

We could do well to remember that when the spikes started prickling from the shadows.

Sarah was just a bit younger than me, an accident of our parents by all accounts, but the best possible one. Her hair hung in waves like mine, her eyes a bit darker but twinkling with the same little glint of life mine did when I was on form.

I knew she'd have a million questions I'd avoided by phone. Questions about our hotel neighbour dilemma and how the hell we got our hands on enough cash to pay her back in one lump sum.

I'd been contemplating how much to tell her, but as she took a sip of her own lemonade through a neon straw to match the girls, I knew it was a redundant line of thought.

She'd know everything by the time she left in the morning, maybe bar the grosser details of the filth our deviant guest had put me through.

"How's Doug?" Brett asked as he grabbed himself a bottled water from the fridge. "Off on some techy course somewhere?"

Sarah nodded. "Tech and male bonding, I think. All the guys from his office have gone."

I liked Doug, we both did. He was stable and kind and everything you'd ever want in a brother-in-law with two young kids and a mortgage to take care of.

"Dad said he'd come next time and build a sand dragon," Amy chirped up from two stools along.

"Oh yeah?" Brett asked. "Well in that case maybe we'll have to build a sand dragon in the meantime, set a high bar for your dad's sand sculpting skills to live up to. He likes a challenge."

I laughed at the girls' frantic nodding, falling in love with my husband all over again in that one beautiful heartbeat.

We weren't dead. Not even close. He was still everything to me, just as I knew I was everything to him when he smiled right back at me.

This was just… a rough day at sea. Maybe a rough few weeks of it. The clouds would clear and the water would calm and we'd be right back on deck enjoying the sunshine, we just needed to believe it.

I did believe it, with all my heart. It was just sometimes the grey of the storm seemed too threatening to pass by and leave us unscathed.

Sarah must have caught the look passing between us, letting out a happy sigh as she shook her head.

"You guys. Always so *in love*. Just wait til you've got kids to steal all your time from the lovey dovey stuff."

"Ewww," the girls groaned, whispering how gross *lovey dovey* stuff was.

They were growing up, too fast. Eight and six on their last birthdays, proper little girls now, even though they fancied themselves more like teens.

Being around them transported me back to a forgotten world of our own, kids living life in a small town like it was the whole universe and we were orbiting planets colliding in school-yard chaos. Always so much school-yard chaos.

Polly Piper came to my mind in a flash. I couldn't ask Sarah about her, not with Brett and the girls in earshot, so I choked it back for later, focusing instead on the cool-uncle grin my husband had always been a natural with.

"How about the beach?" I said. "Elaine is here on laundry duty for the next few hours so we can all make a break for it."

The kids didn't need much encouragement, dropping from their seats and diving in the cases for supplies before I'd even finished speaking. I was glad they were a distraction as Sarah dropped down after them to load them up with warm layers. I was all too aware how our staff was still barely skeletal in this place. Just a part-time housekeeper and nobody but Brett in the kitchen.

You didn't need the glowing lights of a huge new hotel complex down the road to let you know we were in trouble. This place screamed it loud in its quiet. Without Heath's money in our account our quest for a perfect coastal life would be in the dirt already, bills too chunky to manage with two of us working the beast of this to the bone, plucking off scraps of flesh with every passing week the *vacancies* sign hung bold on the front porch.

I called up to Elaine before we left for the front, letting her know to keep an ear out for the reception bell before grabbing a coat of my own. The wind was brisk and breezy, inflating my lungs with a cool breath of life as I braced myself for the descent to the sand.

Brett was already out there, barefoot as he chased the girls down with buckets and spades. They set themselves up on the perfect belt of damp sand, well out of earshot of two sisters gossiping, and Sarah wasted no time as she unrolled her bamboo beach mat and planted her ass on one side of it.

It felt the most natural thing in creation to drop down alongside her and stare at her girls enjoying themselves with a glistening sea backdrop.

"You'd better start talking," she said. "You've been more evasive than I've ever known you these past few weeks."

I couldn't hold back the smile. "Doug's not on a course, is he?"

She laughed the laugh I knew so well. "He's back this evening. It's a day thing. I just thought it was a good excuse to pay a visit."

"I'm alright," I lied, shooting her a look that tried to convince her. "Things are just…"

"Weird as all hell?" she asked as I paused. "Are you pregnant or something?"

That really did make me laugh out loud. "Fuck, sis, I hope not."

She raised an eyebrow. "But you and Brett–"

"Definitely don't want kids at the moment," I finished. "Things are a little up in the air for that kind of pressure."

My heart did a flip even as I said it, eyes soaking up the way he called the girls so close and helped them with their spades. He was born to be a dad. Much better cut out for it than his dad ever was.

"Please tell me you didn't get the cash from that dodgy lender in Tenby Brett told Doug about when he was pissed at Christmas."

I shook my head. "No, nothing like that."

"Then what?" she asked, and I knew it was now or never.

"You wouldn't believe me if I told you."

"Try me," she insisted. "Did you sell a kidney, or agree to be a surrogate for money? Maybe you won it from some criminal gambling ring, or pimped out Brett for dirty cash."

She was joking, but I wasn't as my eyes met hers.

"Not Brett," I said, and her grin dried up as she clocked my meaning.

"Are you for fudging real?!"

I loved her responsible parent substitutes for curse words, and my amusement eased the tension a little as I nodded.

"The guy I asked you about a few weeks ago, from London. Thomas Heath. He was a guest who rolled on up here and offered us fifty grand for a night with me."

She started so hard she left the mat, spinning to her side to face me with her mouth open wide. "Holy shit, Grace. You took the money?"

I guessed the shock was too much for curse substitutes this time.

The smile on my face felt weird as I shrugged. "How could I not?"

It took her a full minute of staring dumb before she spoke again. "I can't believe it. It's like that dirty film where the guy pays a million dollars for a night with that architect's wife."

"Yeah," I said. "Didn't think it would be us actually doing it one day. Who the hell ever comes along and offers you a stupid sum of money for something like that?"

"Thomas Heath from London, it seems." Her face was still one of utter shock. "He didn't splash out a cool million though, unfortunately."

I laughed at the comparison. "And I don't look like Demi Moore, unfortunately."

"What the hell did Brett say? I'm surprised he didn't knock the asshole's front teeth out."

"He almost did," I admitted. "It was close."

I knew she was struggling to digest all this, but I carried on regardless, outlining the whole sorry story and the negotiations. What he looked like, what he smelled like, and how he kept that smug smirk on his face for days on end.

I left the finer details of the arrangement itself to a point where she seemed immune to any more shock, picking my moment carefully with my eyebrows braced high.

"He demanded Brett watch," I revealed. "Behind some crappy red-line sensor like something from a sci-fi movie. It was quite ridiculous."

"I can't even…" she started. "I'd have wanted a red-line sensor too if I was him, I'd have expected Brett to snap my neck the moment I went anywhere near you, fifty grand or not."

I stared over at his easy smile as he shaped out a big curved dragon tail in the sand. He didn't look like he'd snap anyone's neck, not right then.

My sister scooted a little closer, leaning in tight like she used to in my bedroom as teens when she had gossip to drag out of me.

"So, what was it like? The other guy, I mean. Was he good?"

I opted for honesty. "Too good. Better than good. So fucking good that Brett's now got an inferiority complex and I feel like a useless piece of shit."

I laid out my own crappy performance as well as I could without overloading her with a pile of gross, and she listened with the concentration of a zen master.

"That's crazy," she said when I'd finished, and it twanged my heart that she really meant it.

"I couldn't get him to shoot his load once in nine hours. He got me off about five million times straight," I reiterated. "I didn't even know what my name was by the end of it."

"Lucky cow. I've got it good if Doug remembers where my clit is after a long week at the office. I wonder if Thomas Heath would pay me fifty grand for a night having orgasms? Maybe I could pay him instead…"

"Brett thinks he knows us," I told her. "Fuck knows how."

She pulled a face as she weighed it up. "Some guy from London with fifty grand to throw at one wild night at the seaside? Doesn't sound like someone we've ever known."

"Polly Piper," I said. "Remember I asked you about her? She's a mutual friend on his social media account."

"He's got a profile, has he? How about a profile picture?" she asked, and I rolled my eyes.

It'd taken every ounce of my self-restraint not to revisit his social media account since the moment he'd driven away. In truth, I was scared of Brett seeing my search history and losing his shit all over again.

My fingers were shaking as I keyed Heath's name into the search bar on my phone. His face pinged up like before, but this time it was several profiles down the page. No mutual friends listed at all.

"Holy living shit," she said. "He's gorgeous. Only you would land a hooker deal with a guy from *Men's Monthly*."

"She was here," I told Sarah, jabbing my thumb at the screen. "Polly Piper, she was right here."

"Sure you weren't imagining it?" she quizzed with an eyebrow raised. "He doesn't look the type to be friends with Polly. She's been in that bakery since forever."

But I was sure. Of course I was sure. I'd never been more sure.

"I don't get it," I said aloud. "They were friends."

I looked up Polly's profile instead and her friends were all visible to me. I tapped his name into her contact listings and it came back *no matches*.

Sarah snatched the handset from my grip with greedy fingers, scrolling through the names on some quest I wasn't fully aware of.

"Polly didn't have many friends at school," she told me. "I was a say hello in the corridor type of pal, that's all. She was friends with Thomas Browning, that gawky kid from the south end."

It didn't ring any bells, not until she clicked her fingers and coughed up another memory.

"His mum was that woman from Alvington Plastics, the slutty one who used to work with Brett's folks. Tina something. She went on to work at the grimy café in the square."

My cheeks chilled and it wasn't from the wind. "Not Tina Hadley? With the bleached blonde hair and pink lipstick?"

She nodded. "Yeah, that one. She fucked Kelly Brigston's dad in senior year, remember? Nearly got him a divorce."

I didn't remember that little saga, most likely after my time there, but I did remember the history with Brett's dad. Or rather the lack of it. His parents wouldn't talk about Tina Hadley, wouldn't even hear her name.

But that was all beside the point, we weren't talking about Tom Browning and his friendship with Polly Piper, we were talking about a whole other beast of Thomas. A London typhoon of gut-wrenching ego clothed in perfection itself.

"I can't see how Polly Piper would know Thomas Heath," I said. "They don't seem likely friends."

"You can say that again," my sister agreed. "I don't think Polly's ever been outside the county."

I forced another shrug and took my phone back from her. "I guess they aren't now, anyway. Looks like a dead end."

But I'd forgotten my sister was as into murder mystery shows as I'd been growing up. Her eyes were sparkling with enthusiasm as the smile lit up her face.

"Never a dead end," she said and raised her index finger to her temple. "Leave it to me. I'll get to the bottom of it."

There was no point shaking my head or telling her to keep her mouth shut, it would never work, not now she was on a mission.

"Be careful," I said and she raised her hands in feigned offence.

"Would I be anything but?"

I didn't have an answer for that so I didn't give one and it was just as well.

Amy and Amber were upon us with barely a breath's worth of footstep warning, jumping around the place and demanding we go check out their awesome dragon.

Their grins were too damned cute to say no.

THIRTY EIGHT

THOMAS

I had a meeting on the outskirts of Bristol, which was a perfect excuse to swing by home turf for some self-torture.

I forced myself back into the heart of my previous life every time I was in the vicinity, just for the up close and personal reminder as to why I was so committed to making the hard ass decisions I'd grown used to. Our small-time town was on the outskirts of Gloucestershire, a quaint little place that looked *lovely* on the drive through, but was hell on earth for a kid like me growing up in it.

Small town, small minds.

I parked up well off the beaten track, behind the old butchers down at the bottom of the High Street. I made sure to keep myself concealed behind the main thoroughfares, well accustomed to blending into the shadows from my experience as a boy. Polly's bakery was in the centre square, opposite a scabby little coffee shop that brought me out in dirty shivers. I went in there just to experience the disgust afresh.

My mother worked in this place for a while when I was still in primary school, scrabbling to claw her life back to some semblance of financial security after the blow out which cost her everything. Cost *us* everything.

I wondered where she was these days and if she'd remarried yet again. Sometimes I sent her an anonymous payment to her same old bank account, just to be sure she still had the bones to keep her alive.

Some parts of me at least still passed as vaguely human.

I saw Polly slipping out through the main bakery doors at lunchtime, my heart lurching for just a moment at the prospect she might call in for a mug of the cheap shit stuff they served here. She didn't.

She looked right, left, then right again at the traffic lights like a good girl, brushing a stray red curl behind her ear as she crossed the street further down with her head down low.

She was thinner, her face more gaunt than I remembered from last checking in on her. Her shoes were flat and entirely practical, her trouser legs baggy on slender thighs.

In another world I'd have loved to run up to her and take her face in my hands, telling her just how much I missed her in the city. Maybe she'd listen and greet me with a smile, or maybe she'd tell me to go fuck myself the way I deserved her to. Either way, it didn't matter. I wouldn't be running up to anyone, not in this lifetime.

The town bus pulled into the stop opposite, the same bright yellow as the one I used when I was a kid. I remembered the smell of it, the walkway so narrow as I stepped on board, praying that there'd be a seat free near the front so that I wouldn't be near the bullies who always crowded at the back and made me the target of their asshole ridicule.

I imagined many of them were still around these parts, hanging out in the same old pubs with the same old people, rattling off tales about their adolescence like it was a whole barrel of fun. For them I guess it was.

Brett and Grace used to parade through these streets like they owned the place, hand in hand as the other kids looked on with jealous stares. I'd watched them too, only not so obviously. I was much more covert in my malice, my jealousy far more potent and far more justified than any of the other onlookers, pulsing deep through my veins every single day of my childhood worth remembering.

Polly was long out of sight by the time I forced down the rest of my putrid coffee. I slipped out of the building with my head as low as hers had been, cursing this place and its memories with as much venom as ever as I decided to punish that sad little boy inside a little bit harder.

I took a right turn at the memorial cross, pacing fast out of town and down to the churchyard on the outskirts, stepping into the grounds through the wrought iron gates with a feeling of dread pulsing deep.

The flowers were withering in the steel vase in front of the gravestone, no doubt feeling the neglect that a couple of years in the ground brings your rotting body. I lit up a cigar as I faced off those cursed letters, a whole lot more malice springing up in light of recent events.

FOSTER.

"He's not all that, your precious boy," I said to the headstone. "His pretty hotel is destined for bankruptcy, I'm sure you're turning down there at the thought of it. I hope it pains you to know I fucked his sweet little Grace in front of him. She liked it. Loved it, in fact. At least someone worthwhile will finally be able to pass the judgement that I'm better than him in every way that matters. She'll see it soon enough, if she hasn't already, don't you worry. Bankrupt, desolate, unloved. Your boy has it all to look forward to. Let's see if he picks himself up from the floor even a sliver as well as I did. I'm sure you'll be smiling down proud when he's on his knees." I laughed at the sky. "Except you won't, will you? You'll be just as much of a dismissive cunt to him as you were back then to me."

I knew I was insane for talking to nothing, but it didn't matter. This was as close as I'd ever get to the utter bastard who'd destroyed my world.

A couple walked by with grief-stricken faces, frowning in disapproval of the bitter smile on my face and the cigar in my fingers.

I flicked the butt onto the bastard's grave as I finished up and walked away, hating how the defeat still chased me afresh after all this time.

It was when I reached the safety of my car I decided that the end of the Foster's marriage would finally be the end of my torture.

I only hoped it would come soon, so I'd never have to visit this godforsaken little shit hole ever again.

THIRTY NINE

GRACE

We had sandwiches for lunch and an afternoon in the lounge, the doors open onto the patio and cartoons blaring for the girls. It was nice. Peaceful. A good chance to breathe and remember life as it was when we didn't have this pile of crud festering around our every move.

Brett was more at ease than I'd seen him in months, chattering away with his nieces while I made small talk with Sarah. No matter what the topic was, I knew her brain was churning with my bombshell of a revelation. I'd catch her looking at Brett during every pause in the conversation and wonder just what she was thinking after my crazy beach confession.

She let me know after a fish and chip supper on the terrace, once the girls were finally tucked up in bed and our bar was empty enough of guests that Brett made some considerate excuses about paperwork, leaving us alone at the counter to enjoy a bottle of house white.

"I still can't imagine it," she said with a grin. "Brett watching you have sex with another man, I mean. He's always been so competitive. I can't believe he didn't rugby tackle the guy and throw him out through the window."

She had a point, and it reinforced just how much the financial pressures of this place had deviated us both away from our usual selves.

"I think it was a challenge to his self-restraint," I assured her as I took a decent swig from my glass.

"No shit. I can't even fathom it. Was holding onto this place really worth it? For him, I mean, as well as you."

I met her eyes as she voiced her question, flinching at the implication — the guilt from a long-past decision momentarily overriding my more recent blunders.

"He wanted this place too. He loves it here as much as I do."

I wish I believed the statement as strongly as I conveyed it, but it was tinged with enough defensiveness that she picked up on it in a heartbeat.

"I'm sure he does love it here," she said, without even a hint of backtracking. "But you know as well as I do that this place was your call when push came to shove."

I shrugged. "We were both tired of the same old corporate crap every day of the week."

"I guess," she relented. "It just always surprised me that he was so quick to up and leave the rat race. He loves that competitive stuff, always has. I can't imagine him walking away without a whole raft of reservations."

"What can I say? We're both full of surprises."

She tipped her head and flashed a smile. "You are today."

We'd had this conversation several times over already, going over the same ground with the same taken aback look on her face every time.

I found my foot was tapping against my stool leg, the same old nerves flaring up at the thought I'd pushed him along with me during one of his weaker moments in life. Since today was a day for open confessions I opted to push the chat to new uncharted regions — ones I'd avoided like the plague through the earlier reruns.

"It was his dad," I voiced aloud. "I think he was still reeling from his death. I don't know if he'd have ever made the leap if he'd still been alive, even if we'd had the finances."

"His stepdad?" she clarified, and I hated how she always did that, like that differentiation meant shit. Brett's dad had been his dad since he was five years old, no less committed to his upbringing than our dad was to ours, even if he did have his asshole ways running through the whole fatherly process.

"His dad," I argued. "The blood thing means nothing. His dad was his dad."

"His *dad* was a dick," she said, and I cast a glance at the bottle of wine between us. She'd had two glasses already, clearly more than enough to dull her sensitivities. "Don't tell me you think he's a saint just because he's gone. That's not your style."

"His dad left him enough money in his will to set us up in a whole new life. Dick or not, we've got a lot to thank him for." I downed the rest of my drink and poured the dregs of the bottle into my glass in an effort to catch her up. "He won't hear a word of it anyway, so keep your blurting mouth shut if he comes back in here."

She held up her hands. "As if I'd say anything."

She wouldn't, I was being a paranoid bitch, like so much of the time these days. I took a breath and forced a smile since the last thing I needed right now was to push my only welcoming ear away to arm's length.

"It wasn't just me," I argued with a kinder tone to my voice. "Brett wanted the move too, no matter how it looks from the outside. His dad was…" I tried to find the words without compounding her earlier insult. "Forceful. Demanding. I think Brett realised the pressure was finally off without him breathing down his neck. God rest his soul, but George was always keen to voice his opinion."

"Judging," she said. "That's what you mean. Judging."

I did mean that, but it didn't feel right to say it that way. "He paved the way for a whole new life, like I said. The deposit for this place was intense."

She nodded, eyes focusing on mine as though a lightbulb had just gone on in her head. "That's it," she announced. "The reason he was so keen to take the cash from the London guy."

I pulled a blank, tipping my head to encourage her to continue.

"The investment," she said as though my brain was mush today. "Just think about it. He spent his whole life living up to his dad's judgy standards, you don't think he'd want to let the old guy's money go down the pan with your venture, do you? He'd probably sell his own body if it meant his dad's precious investment was safe."

"That's not it," I said, but no sooner had the words left my mouth than I knew she had a point. I was shaking my head as I carried on all the same. "He did it to save our future here, not safeguard his inheritance. We could be cast out on the street and we'd still be together, holding tight. It's not about the money."

"Not about the money, no," she persisted. "About the shame of fucking up with his dad's money. Of being a loser. Of not winning. He'd rather cut his own dick off than lose a game on the sports field, and you know it. Hell knows what he'd rather do with stakes so high." Her smile was definitely on the drunk side. "Sell your pussy, it seems."

"That's ridiculous," I argued. "We made the decision together, both of us."

I was scrabbling for further coherent thoughts when she raised a finger in the air. I knew then that her speculations were getting serious.

"How many trophies did his dad push him to win back in high school?"

I shrugged. "A few, but Brett was always into the sports stuff. He was competitive, like you said."

"How many summer jobs did he juggle to impress his dad with his savings?"

Another shrug and I had to really think about it to remember. "A few. He liked being responsible."

"Liked living up to his dad's standards more like it."

I let out a sigh. "So what if he did? What difference does it make?"

Her smile was a beauty of shrewdness, reminding me afresh why we were both murder mystery addicts.

"It's all tied up in one crazy web of ramifications. All of this. You, this place, the struggles you're under to find your groove again after spending the night with a random guy."

"It is?" I asked, trying to piece together the same puzzle as her. "You sound like Agatha Christie on acid."

Her nod was one of the most self-assured expressions I'd ever seen. "It's confidence," she said. "He's losing his *winner takes all and that winner is Brett Foster* mentality. The change doesn't suit him, you should probably help him pick up his competition game."

"Neither of us are feeling like winners over here," I told her. "We were barely unpacked in this place when the rumour mill brought the bargain basement hotel crap to our door."

"And he's probably never known facing a scrum he couldn't win. When has he ever lost at anything? Name me one time?"

She was quiet as I struggled to find an instance. There wasn't one I could recall easily, not outside of these past twelve months.

"Okay, Sherlock," I said with a smirk. "Tell me what I do to fix this crap. A volleyball league on the beach this summer? A breakfast chef fry off with all the hotel chefs on the Welsh coast?"

"You make him face this shit head on," she said. "If he thinks this other man was better in bed, make him prove that's bullshit."

I raised my eyebrows. "Make him prove that's bullshit? How exactly? Our own explorations in the bedroom aren't exactly a pinup of success."

Her grin was definitely the result of too much wine. "I dunno, maybe call the guy back up again. Round two, no holds barred."

I laughed out loud and pushed her wine glass away from her. She grabbed it back with a roll of her eyes. "I'm not drunk," she said. "Not really."

But she was drunk, clearly a lot less familiar with a sweet glug of alcohol on a weekday evening.

"You're crazy," I giggled, even as my belly flipped.

"Oh, come on!" she giggled along with me. "You say the guy made you come five million times in a row, don't tell me you wouldn't like to get him back here if Brett could handle it."

I hated how perceptive she was, barely willing to admit to myself I rubbed my clit every opportunity I could as I imagined a rerun.

"There's no shame in it," she added. "You're bound to be hot for him now, even if you're still in love with your husband. It's natural."

It didn't feel natural.

"There's no way I'd get Thomas Heath back here," I told her. "Even if the idea wasn't insane, there's no way Brett would go for it. They hate each other. Fuck knows why the guy has a shitty thing going for Brett, but there's no way they'd ever double up and come out friends at the end of it."

"They wouldn't need to," she said. "Just as long as Brett came out on top."

I laughed afresh, shaking my head at the absurdity. "You're crazy," I announced again, like she didn't know it already.

"With all due respect," she told me with a grin. "I'm not the one who fucked a random stranger for fifty grand when I'm happily married."

"Touché," I said, and clinked my glass to hers.

FORTY

BRETT

Seeing Grace enjoying time with her sister did something to me. I felt it deep, the tug back toward the true heart of our lifetime together. Family, friends, the real connections that mean something in this world.

I left them alone for some chat time, hoping it would help Grace to find herself again in this chaos. That maybe an ear from someone who knew her both at her best and her worst would be enough to drag her out of this bullshit insecurity I felt from her but couldn't reach.

I really did plan to throw myself into pending paperwork, but behind the quiet of the reception desk I found myself brewing with bullshit insecurities of my own.

That's when it really hit me — the truth of all this. How deep our issues were already running before Heath ever stepped through this door. This stuff in us was already festering there in the half light, running riot through our days long before he'd ever offered us a financial lifeline.

It's always so easy to pin the blame on someone outside and hate them for your own shortcomings. That's one of the things my dad taught me young. One of the things he believed in.

It's always you, son. People can be shit bags and assholes, but our failures are always our own. Own them, change them, demand more from yourself than a pat on the back and a better luck next time.

I missed him. Missed both his praise and his criticism, even if I'd never have believed the latter while he was still around.

Had he really been gone so long that I'd forgotten the mindset he'd drummed into me since the the very first day he'd joined Mum and me at our dining table?

I found it hard to believe that a couple of years could be enough of a turning point, but it was true. I had forgotten the wisdom I'd lived by when I was a boy. I wouldn't be in this mess if I hadn't.

Heath had been such a beacon of hate for me, right from the first moment he'd slapped his filthy offer on our bar top. Not so very long ago I'd have laughed him off as a joker and not given a toss for his dirty cash.

Desperation had made me a weaker man than the one I expected to face me in the mirror each morning, but that didn't mean desperation was the only road ahead.

I gave myself a moment, wishing I could pick up the phone and call my dad just to hear his voice and ask him to drum his solid words right into me.

My mum was the next best choice.

I'd been avoiding calling her for way too long, holding back the point I'd finally have to admit my host of fucking failures over here. She greeted me with a *hello* that sounded half in shock, and the weirdest lump was in my throat as I forced out the words.

"Mum, sorry I haven't called. I've been busy."

I couldn't lie, not to her. When she asked about the hotel, I told her we were still on our knees. When she asked about Grace, I told her I was worried I was down on my knees there too.

And she did it, right when it was needed. She stepped into my old man's shoes and said it right how it needed saying.

"This isn't you, Brett. Isn't who you are. Isn't who you were raised to be."

I nodded as that lump in my throat notched up a gear.

"What if it is?" I asked her. "What if I'm not up to fighting all this shit and coming out on top?"

"Then you dig down deep and give your all until you don't have another breath left to fight it."

"It's not like that," I said. "This isn't crap I can face down and take on head to head. It's bigger than that, harder than that."

"It's *always* like that," she said right back, and I heard him there. Heard the soul of him right through hers. "You're making excuses for putting off the inevitable. You fight, you win, or you give your all trying."

It felt good to choke down my sadness and set my jaw the way I'd always set it.

She couldn't see me nod, but I knew she felt it. I needed to make my way over to see her, living up north in a nice plush pad with her sister. I hoped she was happy. That maybe she'd even met someone new after all those years with my dad at her side. Now wasn't the time to ask, so I didn't. Just as it had never been the time to ask her for a bail out like Grace had with her sister.

I'd be washed up on the streets before I ever plunged the depths enough to crawl to my mum for a hand out. My dad would turn in his grave at the thought.

"You let me know how you're doing," she said, and I grunted an affirmation.

"I'll let you know when I'm winning."

"Or when you've given your all, Brett. I'm your mum. My door's always open."

I knew she meant well, but her words fired me up deep. She'd never said that before, that she was ready and waiting to pick me up from failure. My gut spat at the thought she was expecting me to come up short this time. That the pressures of a shitty business down the road and some smarmy cunt from London were too much for me to take.

She didn't know about the details. Didn't even know Heath existed, but that didn't matter. She'd heard enough of it in my voice to paint a picture.

And that picture was mine.

Our failures are always our own. Own them, change them, demand more from yourself than a pat on the back and a better luck next time.

If Mum was hearing my own insecurities that loud from a hundred-mile distance after months of silence, how loud was Grace hearing them every day at my side?

No wonder that prick had taken her to places I never had. He was bristling with his own fight, battling my festering insecurities with a confidence way beyond anyone's I'd ever seen.

He'd owned her, just like he'd owned me, charging me down on a field I hadn't even known we were playing on. I barely even knew there was a ball in his hands until it was already in the net behind me.

Fuck him, but fuck me more.

None of it was too fucking much to take. Not a shitty rival down the coast, and not a shitty rival from the city.

If only I knew how to contact the fucker I'd face him right down for a rematch. Summon him back onto my turf and this time I'd own it.

I knew I was flaring like a bull-headed bastard, well beyond all fucking rational reason as I contemplated coming up trumps against Thomas Heath and whatever pathetic beef he had to grind out with me. I knew it likely had as much to do with the hard on in my pants every morning as it did the jockish call to slam his face in the dirt and call touchdown with my head held high.

But I knew it now. Knew a rematch was on the cards and always had been.

He'd always wanted back here, even if the cunt was as ignorant as I'd been, which I doubted. From that very moment he rocked on up with his proposal, it was always about something more.

The business card on the counter was every bit of a testament to his true fucking intentions, and fighter Brett would never have tossed that fancy-fonted little card in the kitchen trash.

Fighter Brett would have called him right up and told him to bring his game to an even playing field. No dirty cash, no stupid red lines, no shitty fucking nine-hour window.

Maybe I'd look him up.

It didn't take long to decide that I would do, just as soon as I was done with the pile of crappy customer registration forms I'd need for the morning.

It was when I tugged the desk drawer open with more force than necessary that that same pathetic fancy-fonted little business card slipped out from its jammed in place between the parking receipts.

I didn't know whether to smile or frown as I turned it over and over in my outstretched palm and goosebumps prickled my skin.

Maybe Dad really was up there, watching over me and demanding I dive back into the game, no matter how fucking sordid the game was.

But there was no doubt about it, not after the business card's miraculous sneaky rescue from the trash, not even for a fucking heartbeat.

My pretty little wife was demanding I dive back into the game too.

FORTY ONE

GRACE

Something happened that night. I don't know if it was with me and my slightly too much wine, or with Brett, or both of us combined, but things were very different once I'd waved Sarah off to her room and cleared our wine glasses away.

My husband was waiting in the doorway to reception when I got the lights. I started as I realised he was there, clutching my hand to my chest as I cussed him out for scaring me shitless.

He didn't laugh, nor apologise, nor make any move to ease my tension. And that's when I saw it. *Felt* it. Those brooding flames in his dark gaze I hadn't even known had been missing for so long.

My belly fluttered, my heartrate picking up pace well beyond the jolt of fear, but my body's reaction was so much more than that, instinctive to every cell inside me as I shifted on a hip, my pussy doing a needy little clench as Brett folded his strong arms tight across his chest and tipped his head.

"Did you sisters have fun?" he asked, his voice low and loud in the quiet.

I nodded like a fool, smiling like one too, not quite understanding why there was a strange zing up my spine out of nowhere.

"We did, thanks. Sisterly gossip is always the best."

He exhaled as he smirked. "I'm sure you girls had a lot to talk about."

I didn't know whether I should be self-conscious about sharing the details, so I gave a little shrug and changed the subject. "Paperwork done?"

He nodded, just once. "Everything's been taken care of, Grace."

The space between us ate me up and spat me out, all chewed and exposed, a mess in the openness as he held back and kept his distance.

"You coming to bed?" I asked, and he shook his head.

"No," he told me. "You're coming with me."

I managed a weak laugh as my brain raced ragged in its bid to interpret the weirdness, but my body was already there. Thrumming. Burning. Prickling with hungry little needles right across my skin.

"Where are we going?" I asked with a breathy voice.

He finally took a step forward, but just the one. "Remember when we first came to view this place?"

I nodded, everything well assigned to memory. "I do, yeah."

"Remember when the agent led the owners away and left us to talk over there by the terrace doors?" Another step and his head was held high, shoulders still big and strong as his arms stayed tight across his chest.

That particular memory tickled before it dawned, and I felt my eyes narrow on his. "You mean–"

"What I said to you."

The smile crept across my lips slowly. Really slowly. But not as slowly as his next long step toward me. The space contracted with the pressure, heavy like opposing magnets circling.

"You said you'd fuck me," I said. "Everywhere."

"And what happened?"

I laughed but it sounded stupid in the quiet. "You fucked me plenty, Brett, when we first moved in."

"I don't think I've been keeping my word these past few months, Grace," he told me. "I think your mind's been wandering, where I've been lacking."

I shook my head, so defensive at the *mind wandering* that it made me shiver. "No. Not wandering."

"Oh, yes," he insisted, and his next step brought him closer. So much closer. "I think you've been hiding secrets. Dirty little secrets, sweetheart. Dirty secrets about what you'd like me to do to that body of yours. How you'd like me to make you feel. How hard you'd like me to push you. We've both been hiding ourselves, forgetting ourselves, holding our breath when we should be speaking out loud."

We had a whole drawer jammed full of Heath inspired sex toys, but I could tell they weren't on his mind in the slightest as he closed the distance between us. His hand swept up my bare arm and across my shoulder to my neck, where his fingers hooked and pulled me tight, gripping with such strength that I figured he'd been overhearing Sarah and me.

I struggled to recall what we'd said exactly, sifting blindly through the wine in an attempt to fathom how condemning her observations about him losing his confidence had been from his position. So I asked him. Blurted it out with nervous eyes and an apology all set to blurt out behind it.

"If you heard anything–" I began, but he silenced me with a finger on my lips.

"I assume that means you girls have been gossiping plenty about my prowess," he said. "What did you tell her about Heath?"

My prickling skin made me shudder as my cheeks burned up. "Not much."

"Stop lying to me, Grace," he told me, but there was no real malice in his words.

This Brett was bristling with form, eyes alive with some simmering darkness I couldn't quite place, but I liked it.

I squeaked out loud as his arm snaked around my waist and hoisted me from my feet. I scrabbled in his grip as he dragged me with him back through the doorway into reception, but I was half-giggling, nervous all the way. We were under the hard lights of the main entrance hall when his body wrestled mine behind the counter and slammed me forward onto the desk. The guest comment book went tumbling as my palms fought for purchase, back arching with a mind of its own as his hot mouth ravaged the nape of my neck.

Tingles. So many tingles.

"What is this?" I asked, even as my ass shimmied back at his crotch.

I wasn't expecting the nip of his teeth on my shoulder.

"Remember that time Hanley School sent their rugby team over for the pre-season warm up match and we couldn't get it together enough to beat their asses that game? They goaded the ever-living fuck out of us before they got their bus home that night. And we took it in silence like a team of losers, because that's what we felt like. Losers."

I nodded, not having a clue what relevance that had to the way his fingers flicked my jeans button loose and slammed down inside my knickers. "I remember," I told him, "You looked like death when they pulled away. I thought you were going to kill someone."

"And what happened next?" he asked me.

I smiled at the memory. "The rematch. I'd never seen you so psyched in my life."

"Winners don't quit over one little loss, Grace. They come back stronger. They fight until they're done. Until the victory is theirs or they lose the battle so hard they lay down dead. We forgot it that game, but we never forgot it for another."

His fingers were so firm between my legs. Rough but skilled. This wasn't aimless lust gone mad. It was focused. Determined. I squirmed against the contact, hips begging him to push inside.

"You won," I whispered. "Fuck, Brett, you always won. I don't think I ever saw you lose a game after that. Not all the way through final year."

"Not until we arrived here," he hissed, breath panting hard against my ear as he ground the ridge of his dick against my ass. "Not until I fell flat at the first batch of hurdles and didn't get back on my fucking feet. Not with the hotel down the road threatening to eat us alive. Not with the stress of losing everything we'd given up our lives to pursue down here in the arse end of nowhere."

I turned my face back toward his, still bucking at his touch, even as my eyes met his with pain. "It was my fault," I admitted, finally. "I brought us here. I'm sorry."

I wasn't expecting him to smile. "You pretty much dragged us fucking down here, Grace. Wouldn't shut up about the place."

"You could have said no," I argued. "You should have said no."

He shook his head. "Fuck saying no to your dreams, Mrs Foster. Giving you your dreams is my whole fucking world. If we could go back, I'd do it all over again. Only this time I wouldn't let the shit knock me flying."

This was my Brett. The Brett I married. Strong and safe and bristling with fight, all for me. His eyes were as hungry as I'd ever seen them, his lips hungry to match as they landed on mine and took their fill.

"I've missed you," I whispered between kisses. "Please don't leave me again."

"I'll never fucking leave you," he whispered back. "I'll never leave my fucking self, either. Not for anything. Not for a poxy hotel down the road, nor a wanker that rolls up from London."

My breath hitched at the reference. "He's gone," I said. "It was always you I wanted. Not him. He was nothing."

His fingers dug lower in my knickers, curling just right to sink inside me to the knuckle.

"You wanted him," he hissed. "And I let him take you. I let him smash me to the ground and I took it like our team did with Hanley that night, too fucked up to fight him on an even playing field."

I gasped as his palm ground my clit, pushing back enough to shimmy my jeans down around my hips.

"He's gone," I said again. "It's all about us now."

All my needy thoughts of Thomas Heath scorched away to nothing. There was only my husband. Only his touch. His warmth. The hardness of his dick against my ass as he tugged down his own jeans and thrust his length between my cheeks.

I couldn't hold back the moan as he pinned me to the reception desk and teased the head of himself against my wet slit with his fingers still inside me.

I hadn't known want like it in weeks. Months even. Since before Thomas Heath ever darkened our door with his crazy offer, since before we'd found ourselves bogged down in the stench of final demand letters and paltry winter bookings.

"You still want him," he snarled, but I shook my head. It made him laugh a fresh low laugh. "I don't know if you're lying to me or to yourself this time, Grace Foster, but that sweet little cunt wants a fresh bout with Thomas Heath and there's no point fucking denying it."

I didn't know what to say, so I said nothing. My breath was a staccato string of gasps as I bucked like crazy to encourage his dick inside me, but he didn't take the bait, his sweeps of my wetness nothing short of torture.

"I don't even fucking blame you," he said under his breath. "The guy was on his fucking game from the moment he arrived until the moment he left. But next time he'll meet a different man when he steps through that doorway. Next time he'll meet a man who'll go up against him and win."

"There won't be a next time," I soothed, forcing down the way my belly lurched at the prospect. "I don't need to see him again. Not ever."

"No," he growled. "But I do, Grace. I fucking do."

I cried out when the head of his dick finally pushed in, thighs trembling at the stretch.

His fingers were still inside me, hooking the perfect spot. His cock strained for every little inch, throbbing hard as he stretched me wide.

"Tell me you want to see him again," Brett prompted, and I was so lost to the glorious pulse of my ragged pussy that I did nothing but groan. "Tell me you want it, Grace. Two of us at once, for fucking real. Tell me what you did to make sure it happens."

His mouth on my neck gave me shivers.

"What I did?"

"You know what you *did*, Grace."

I couldn't hide from him like this, not with his strength rippling hard at my back and demanding my all.

"I saved his business card," I admitted in a hiss, heart panging at the confession even as I spat it out. "I'm sorry… I don't know what came over me, I swear. I just grabbed it from the trash, and I didn't know… I didn't know what to do…"

I felt his smile. "Good girl," he whispered, and I didn't understand it. Not any of it. "Feels good to face the truth, doesn't it?"

I nodded, squirming like a wanton little whore as he circled his hips against my ass. "I wanted you there with him that night, I wanted you both."

"I know," he said. "I wanted it too. I've been wanting it ever since, nearly as much as I want to drive you as wild as he fucking did."

"You can," I told him. "I know you can."

"I will," he whispered, sinking his cock into me.

The wine was dulling my brain to slower than usual, rolling around my skull behind the haze of need between my legs. "Please," I whimpered. "Harder."

He gave me harder. So much harder. Taking a handful of my hair and pulling tight, slamming to the balls in a thrust that left me reeling.

"Next time he won't come out on top," my husband snarled. "Next time I'm gonna play him on an even field. I'm gonna watch his game and make mine better, show him a performance he'll never see coming." Another smile against my skin, and I could feel the fight right the way through him. "And then I'm gonna lift the fucking trophy."

Surely he couldn't… wouldn't… not seriously bring Heath back here.

I'd have sought out his eyes if his grip on my hair wasn't tight enough to pain my scalp.

I loved it. Craved it.

"Are you serious?" I whispered. "Brett, just tell me if you're serious. I can't take it…"

My head dropped forward as he loosened his grip, and when my eyes returned to focus they were staring right at his fingers.

And the business card he was holding there.

He slapped it on the counter, right by my face.

"I'm deadly fucking serious," he spat. "That cunt is due a rematch, and this time I'll be the challenger."

I came before he did, hard enough that he covered my open mouth with his free hand to stop me waking the kids in the rooms upstairs.

My pussy was a clenching little slut, eating up both the fingers and the dick he fucked me with so perfectly, his timing impeccable as he let himself follow me over the edge with a grunt.

We moved together, slammed together, breathing in frantic unison as our bodies thrummed in the madness.

He was still pulsing inside me when he picked up our reception handset and keyed in Thomas Heath's mobile number. I hadn't even caught my breath when he cleared his throat and prepared for the line to connect.

"It's really late," I said, eyes wide over my shoulder as I took in my husband with the office handset pressed to his ear. "He might not even hear it. Won't know it's us."

"Oh, he'll answer," Brett replied with a smirk that rivalled Heath's for confidence. "I fucking promise."

And he did answer.

Oh, fuck, he really did.

FORTY TWO

THOMAS

I was fresh from a shower with a towel low around my hips when my mobile vibrated on the bedside table.

I couldn't hold back the smirk. I knew it was her before I clocked the area code. Two days later than my estimate, so kudos to her self-restraint, but still well within my weekly prediction window.

"Grace," I said as I clicked to accept, my voice so sure of itself that I was certain I'd have her knickers wet before she was done with the niceties.

The response stopped me dead in my tracks.

"Wrong guess, asshole," Brett Foster told me, and his tone made my gut tighten. It wasn't the bitter growl of someone on the edge of a divorce, calling up to give me a mindless threat of violence from the other side of the country. There wasn't the slightest hint of insecurity, nor of a man struggling to stay on the rails of his own sorry life.

"Brett," I said. "This is a surprise. Not entirely pleasant."

It wasn't pleasant. My pulse was drumming, my composure straining as I fought the urge to hang up and bail on him and his shitty late-night call. I hated it, despised even the hint of my self-control reeling under pressure.

"Thanks for the business card," he continued. "So nice to know we could call on you."

"Purely good manners on my part," I lied, and I heard his arrogant smirk right across the miles.

"You don't know the meaning of good manners, Heath, but nice try."

I forced a sigh. "If you called me in the middle of the night purely to bid me thanks for leaving my contact details, I'll be saying goodnight."

But I didn't hang up, and the bastard knew I wouldn't. He hung on in silence just to prove the point, and it was all wrong. This whole ridiculous interaction was all wrong.

"What the fuck do you want?" I said, finally, and he laughed out loud before his voice calmed to a low rumble.

"You, me, and my beautiful wife," he told me. "No fucking sensors, no chairs set out at a safe distance, no pile of dirty cash to unbalance the equation."

It was my turn to laugh. "And why would I do that?"

"Because your ego won't let you turn down a rematch. You know it, and I know it, so cut the fucking crap."

My jaw tightened at his brashness. "You don't know anything about me. And you sure as fuck don't know anything about my ego."

"Oh, but I do," he said. "I watch, I learn. Watching from the substitute bench, you see fucking everything."

"This isn't one of your shitty high school sports games now. It's me taking what I want, when I want it." I let my strength gather itself in the pit of me, fighting every whisper of revolting nerves.

"Come back down here," he said. "Call it a challenge. Your game against mine. Grace's sweet pussy can be the referee."

"I've already claimed that prize," I goaded. "Many times over."

"You bought it, now it's time to earn it. Anyone can be a winner if they play dirty."

"Playing dirty is my favourite way to play," I hissed, expecting a rise from him that never came.

"Rematch next Tuesday," he said, with his voice too fucking even for belief. "The top suite is available, I'll make you a reservation right now, that's if you're up to the challenge."

"Look," I said, and my voice wasn't even at all. It was a hiss. A spit. Fuming with bile as the teenage memories came spewing back up. "I've no time for your sad fucking challenges. My time is in demand, and so is my dick. I've dipped it in your coastal honeypot to my satisfaction already, thank you."

I waited for the goading. The schoolyard taunts of how he'd kick my ass on the playing field. His primitive grunts about how I needed to get myself down there and show him what I'm made of.

But they didn't come.

"Fine," he said. "Have it your way. You know how to book online if you change your mind."

And then he was gone.

The line went dead. The dull bleep of the call-dead tone was enough to bring sweat to my forehead, my back blistering with the chill of hardball negotiations turned sour.

I tossed the phone on the bed, cursing Brett Foster for everything his life was worth. Cursing their sad determination to ignore the fact that they were ruined. That *I'd* fucking ruined them.

I poured myself a scotch and drank it down in one, savouring the vintage burn like it stood a chance of soothing the rancid pit in me.

And then I called up his fucking website, before my senses could catch up with the rest of me.

FORTY THREE

GRACE

I couldn't believe it when the ping of an online reservation hit Brett's phone before we were through to the bedroom, but he could.

His smile was triumphant, eyes glittering with glory as he turned the handset to face me. I didn't need to read the text, but I did anyway, taking the phone from his grip with shaking fingers.

Thomas Heath. Master suite.

A seven night booking.

Seven.

Seven nights.

My mouth dropped open.

"He can't be serious," I stammered, but Brett nodded.

"Oh, he can," he said. "He's fucking serious alright. But not as serious as I am."

"We should think about this," I flustered. "We don't know who he is, not really. We don't know what he's planning, what he's thinking, what he's capable of."

"Not yet we don't," he countered. "But we will. By the time that cunt checks out this time around we'll know everything we need to know and then some."

I nodded, flutters of rambling objections threatening to burst and break out loud, but they didn't. Couldn't.

This version of my husband was the one I'd walked up the aisle to and promised my all. The one I'd counted on to stand strong at my side for better or worse. The one who'd given me shivers in bed at night and hunger for skin on skin that drove me crazy through the day.

"He'll want to pay," he told me, and I believed him. "He uses cash like a shield. It's as much of a weakness as it is a strength. If not more so."

I raised my eyebrows. "I wouldn't mind a shield like that."

The tip of his head made me feel like a fool, despite the way he brushed my cheek with his thumb. "It's not about what's in your bank account," he said. "It's about what's in here." He dropped his hand to my chest, his palm warm against my breast and my beating heart. "It's about who you are. What you believe in. How much fight you've got in your bones."

I placed my hand over his and drew a breath, that beating heart racing like a train.

"Kiss me," I said, and he did. Fierce and fast, his mouth wide and his tongue violent as he walked me backwards to the bed. I'd barely recovered from the first orgasm when he tugged my jeans down for the second time. His tongue was as violent with my pussy as it was with my mouth when he dropped to his knees and ate me up, sucking and grunting like I was his greatest pleasure and my clit was his favourite dessert.

I was squirming with my fingers against his scalp when he reached out for our bottom dresser drawer, too wanton to question what he was diving for until the head of something solid pushed inside.

"You'll need to take two of us," he told me and my clit sparked wild. "We'd better start getting that pretty little cunt of yours up to the challenge."

Fuck, how he worked me. Fingers, mouth and every toy in that fucking drawer. I took it all and begged for more, begged for everything with a voice that didn't sound like me. And finally, when he presented my body with two toys at once, my ass clenching tight around a thick plastic shaft as my pussy strained to swallow up another, I didn't feel like me either.

I felt like the woman in cuffs on plastic sheeting. The dirty bitch who'd unravelled for a stranger and given him her all.

But this time it was my husband. This time my body thrummed with love as well as lust. And it was delicious. Delirious. Disgusting in all the right ways as he grunted at the stretch of my straining holes.

"I can't," I hissed, even as I bucked and squirmed. "I can't take it."

"You were born to fucking take it," he said back. "You'll take it in the flesh next week and it'll be every bit the filthy fantasy you've rubbed that clit off to every fucking day since he's been gone."

I came again right then.

And that night was the first night in bed that I didn't rub my clit to the fantasy.

I didn't need to.

It was also the first night in bed that I snuggled into my husband's side and let his steady breath soothe my fears away without so much as a flutter of backlash.

It was the first night since the rumour mill hit us almost a year ago that I slept like a woman without a care. Without a nightmare. Without a rush of palpitations in the morning at the thought of this place going away.

Sarah saw the change in me before I said a word about it. And when I'd finished telling her about the return of my old husband and his challenge, her smile across the breakfast table said it all.

She leaned in close for a hug once the kids were loaded in the car, her kiss on my cheek sweeping back to my ear for the final sisterly whisper before she went on her merry way.

"I'll solve the mystery," she told me. "By the time Thomas Heath from London comes back here you'll know everything from his shoe size to his favourite take out."

I hugged her so tight I lifted her from her feet, just like old times, me the big sister and her the little one.

"I'll miss you," I told her, and she laughed.

"I won't be a stranger," she said. "Your life is far too interesting to watch from afar."

FORTY FOUR

BRETT

Any half decent sportsman knows that commitment to training plays a big part in winning the game.

I was as committed as an athlete striving for world class fitness, pushing myself to the limits every night in my quest to master my wife's body.

I watched her through the eyes of a stranger in a brand new sport, observing all her quirks and quivers with absolute attention.

She had a whole host of whimpers I'd never fully appreciated. Shivers which blared out loud that she was teetering on the cliff of explosion, but they came in different flavours. I learned them all. Loved them all.

I loved all of *her*, and within a few days of this rediscovered me I knew without a single doubt in my body that she loved all of me too.

I could've cancelled Heath's reservation without breaking too much of a sweat, but I didn't want to. Not just because I had a point to prove, to myself as well as him, but because of Grace. Because of her dreams. Because of the way her eyes lit up at every filthy mention of us both stretching her full at once.

"One day to go," she told me as she stretched out her limbs in bed on Monday morning.

"One too many," I said, and flashed a smile.

Her confusion was delicious. Her smile was more fuel than I'd ever need to go through with such a crazy fucking rerun.

"You really want this?" she asked.

"Because you do," I answered. "Because I wake up hard every morning at the thought of you going wild between two men who'll be busting their nuts to be the best for you."

It was all the encouragement she needed to dive that pretty mouth beneath the bedcovers and check out my revelation for herself.

As much as I hated the sonofabitch Heath for his mission to fuck our shit up, I couldn't deny I owed the guy a grudging drink on me.

My wife was shining in ways I'd never seen before. Loving me in ways I'd never seen before. It was in the finer details, the way she responded so beautifully to the reacquired strength in me.

He'd seen it before I had, the little siren in my woman that craved a man strong enough in bed to drag her ashore and claim her as she thrashed on the sand. She was ripe to be exposed, loving the kind of growled out instructions which set her free from her well-ordered brain and her perfect manners.

Hell, I owed him more than a drink. I owed him a slap on the back as well, but he wouldn't be getting one. Not until it was the commiserating slap of a *well-played, loser*.

She fussed all day long getting his bedroom right for him. Polishing every surface to gleaming like it would make a damned bit of difference to a prick like him. He'd be there for the pussy and the pomp, not the fucking decor, but I smiled wide as she showed off her handiwork, kissing her cheek at a job well done.

We were busy for a Monday, springtime coming in fast and bringing the long weekenders with it. Our bar was surprisingly bustling as we busied ourselves behind the pumps, and that's when we first heard them — the tales of refunded bookings from the place down the road.

"They offered an alternative," the one guy told us. "But it was twenty miles north, nowhere near as nice as this place."

We checked out their website once we'd wrapped up for the night, Grace's bottom lip pinned between her teeth as she crossed her fingers and stared at the laptop screen.

"Postponed," I said, not quite believing it for myself. "New opening date July provisional, ready for the summer break."

"This is crazy," she said, clicking refresh obsessively just to see it reappear time and time again.

"Crazy good," I replied and closed the screen.

It was crazy good. Our bookings were on the up, the pings coming through steady and growing. Our reviews were glowing positive and our repeat bookings were coming in strong.

"All we need is a chef," she told me for the hundredth time, and I was coming to believe her. "If we can get a decent chef in place by the summer we'll smash their sorry asses."

And there we had it. Competitive Grace, blooming out from the shadows with enough fire to burn their shit hole to dust.

I held her close in bed when we finally got there, my arms tight around her as she breathed in my breath.

"Tomorrow," she said, and grazed her fingers up my back. "I hope he's ready for round two."

"We're saying no to the money," I told her. "No matter how much he puts on the table."

"No matter how much?" she asked with a giggle, and I nipped the squidgy tip of her nose.

"No matter how fucking much, Grace. The answer's no. No thanks, you smarmy cunt, we don't need your fucking money."

"I wouldn't put it in quite those words," she sighed. "But I'll toe the same line in sentiment."

"How about, no thanks, you smarmy cunt, we don't need your fucking money, just your dick?" I suggested.

I loved her laugh. "No, not those words either."

"Say it," I told her. "Just to me. Say it like you mean it."

Her eyes were dark in the pale moonlight, so clichéd but so true as they stared right at mine.

"No thanks, you smarmy cunt, wanker-face Heath, we don't need your fucking money, just your dick. Hard please. Make it good. And this time make sure you fucking come for me, asshole."

I'd almost forgotten about her own insecurities, losing sight of them under my own fight and fury.

"He'll come for you," I told her. "You've just got to believe it, Grace. Hell knows, *I* believe it."

FORTY FIVE

THOMAS

The drive was a bastard, my knuckles white on the steering wheel as I sped across country to my fight of a fucking lifetime.

I'd take him. Show him up for the useless piece of shit he really was under all the bullshit bluster he'd been carrying around his whole life. I'd show his pretty wife who the real man was in the room, leaving her with no uncertainty whatsoever that her quaint little life on the coast was nothing without the thrill of a real man's cock inside her.

I'd up the stakes this time, so huge they'd have to balk at the pressure or push themselves into an outcome that would fuck them up beyond all doubt and reason.

One hundred grand on the table for a week with Grace in London. At my place, doing my every bidding and feeding my every whim.

I pulled into their car park expecting the same pitiful straggle of cars I'd seen last time around, but the place was bustling, people hogging the front and chowing down on ice creams as they watched the sea, and a couple of kids dashing along the railings brandishing buckets and spades.

I held the door open for an elderly couple before I'd even stepped inside the place, finding the Fosters busy behind the bar serving lunchtime drinks, Brett's hand resting on the small of Grace's back every time he wasn't pulling a pint. My gut shrank at the sight.

I hung back in the doorway, watching. This wasn't the scene I'd imagined walking into. I expected thinly-veiled misery, her eyes scanning for mine every heartbeat, needing another helping of the filth I could deliver like she needed a gulp of sea breeze.

Brett noticed me first, eyes narrowing as his chin dipped in a barely courteous nod. A scotch was waiting when I stepped up to the bar and took a seat, shunted gruffly across the woodwork with a flick of his hand.

"Customers. What a novelty," I said with a smile. "I'd make the most of this trade. You'll be all on your lonesome when the beast down the road opens its doors for the summer."

"Glad to see we're interesting enough to keep tabs on," Brett commented. "You didn't strike me much as a hotelier, so I guess it's just our sterling personalities you find irresistible."

"Not your personalities," I countered with my voice low. "Just your wife's dirty little holes begging for my dick."

He leaned over the bar top. "I wouldn't call it begging," he told me. "She just fancies trying out a double helping of dessert. I'm sure she'll find yours is bland and tasteless when we're both side by side on the serving platter."

"I admire your optimism." I raised my glass to my lips. "I hope you're as optimistic when we set up the stakes."

Grace stepped up beside him in time to hear my statement, and I despised the look that passed between them, eyes laughing at some private joke.

A joke about me.

The feeling was both alien and uncomfortable, dredging up points in time when every joke I ever heard was about me. Worse than their shitty humour was the way Brett saw my discomfort before I'd had the chance to hide it.

"Oh, come on, Heath," he said. "You didn't seem the tetchy type. Life got you down these past few weeks? Another couple seen through your crappy little marriage-wrecking games and proved themselves immune to your meddling?"

"No," I told him. "No couple ever sees through my intentions. I'd go easy on the self-congratulations until they're truly warranted."

It was Grace who rolled her eyes and waved her hand between us. "Alright, guys, save it for later. We've got customers to take care of."

She handed me the key to my bedroom and I retreated into a marginally safe space while I got my thoughts together. The place was immaculate. Polished to perfection and neat enough to appease the very fussiest consumer standards in my soul.

It took me a moment to notice the chairs were missing, and that at least brought a smile to my face.

Three in a bed this evening, in the real sense of the word. I unpacked my case carefully, ensuring every item of clothing was hanging neatly before I ventured up to the window and stared out at the front.

I'd forgotten how pleasant this place really was, so snug in the sandy cove between rocky outcrops. For a split second I wished I was a genuine guest looking forward to kicking my feet back and appreciating a break from the city madness. Maybe one day.

But not today.

Not this week.

They were enjoying a chilled bottled water at an empty bar when I re-joined them downstairs, freshly suited in a finely pressed suit with gold cufflinks and a fresh sweep of my hair.

I refused another scotch, opting instead for a water of my own, and that's when I decided to begin the negotiations in earnest.

"One hundred grand," I told them, pausing for the unavoidable hunger to sweep behind their eyes. But it didn't come. I cleared my throat before I repeated the figure. "One hundred thousand pounds," I said, but Brett raised his asshole fingers and encouraged me on.

"Yeah, we heard you. One hundred grand. We don't want it."

I laughed my favourite bitter laugh. "Sure you don't."

"Believe it," he said. "We don't want it. There's not a sum in the world we'd take from you, so save your bargaining chips for someone who wants them."

I looked over at Grace, but her face was a picture of easy calmness, not even a flash of disagreement in her eyes.

"Money makes the world go round," I told them. "Don't be fools."

I'd forgotten just how beautiful that woman was until she stepped up to the bar top and stared right at me. Her curls were bouncy and her cheeks were healthy pink without being flushed. Her eyes were excited and her nervousness was well disguised, her stance all natural as she leaned in close.

"Money might make the world go round," she whispered. "But it doesn't make the man." I didn't flinch as she reached over the counter and pressed her fingers to my chest, cursing the prospect that she'd feel the speed of the beats under my shirt and find them racing. "What's in here makes the man," she finished.

It was so preposterous I laughed until my sides hurt, barely coming up for air until she'd stepped away.

"Did you two join some hippy love commune in my absence?" I smirked. "Or maybe it was all the therapy you needed in the aftermath."

"Sad," she said. "It's sad when people are so cynical of human truths. I think it's maybe you who needs the therapy."

"Sex therapy," I countered. "So, let's get back to business. One hundred grand on the table, up against one full week with Mrs Foster in London on my home turf."

They both laughed as they shook their heads.

"What part of *we don't want it* don't you understand?" he asked, and for the first time in the whole poxy exchange it occurred to me they might actually be serious.

"We just want you," Grace added, and that really did spark a rise of something uncomfortable in the depths of me. "No stakes, no bargains, no crazy cash offers. Just you, and us. No time restraints, no buzzing alarms, no silly red lines."

"Bar closes at ten tonight," Brett told me. "We'll be up at your door at ten thirty. Feel free to have a few drinks on the house in the interim."

"I'll think about it," I replied, acting as nonchalant as I could muster. "And in the meantime I'd suggest you consider your own sanity too. You'll be thankful of my generosity when summer comes calling and this place is dead around your ankles."

They were laughing between themselves again when I knocked back the rest of my drink and made for the exit.

FORTY SIX

BRETT

He didn't show his face back in the bar that evening. Grace kept looking, eyes flitting to the doorway at every sign of movement. Only a short time ago that would have grated me to my core, but not now.

I knew she was mine, heart and soul. I just needed to prove her body was mine too, and not just with the testament of the ring on her finger. I needed to prove it to that smarmy sack of shit upstairs.

Our customers were early-nighters in the main, the bar almost empty by the time we started wrapping up for the night and planning to make a move. The final couple finished up their drinks at shortly before ten and headed to their rooms semi-drunk smiles on their faces.

They were off to get some, it was beaming all the way through them. Just as it was beaming through my Grace.

She'd breathe out a puff of an exhale every time our eyes met, conveying nerves I knew were all genuine and no doubt strumming her body like a tight-bowed violin. There was more to it than that, though. The husky glint in her stare whenever it crashed into mine. The way she brushed against me every time she passed, hovering close for just a moment, the heat of her firing my skin up through my shirt.

She wanted it. Now more than ever.

Wanted us both. Wanted *him*.

She'd wanted that slimy prick from the very minute he'd first laid his sleazy deal on the table, but now it was deeper, darker, entwined with her own fractured ego crisis and her desire to do better next time.

That was the one remaining issue that vexed me deeper than the others. The others I could fight head to head, but this one, the way she held herself so responsible for his feigned indifference in bed with her, this one made me blister.

Tonight should have been purely about two men facing off in their quest to thrill my beautiful wife, not about my beautiful wife doubting her abilities to bring off a man who'd made it his mission to deny her.

He wouldn't be denying her this time around. Not when the head to head pushed him outside his comfort zone. He'd be vulnerable just as much as we were and I knew it. He'd have to be. Winning's done that way — pushing yourself outside your comfort zone and giving your all, and Thomas Heath fancied himself every bit a winner, just as I did.

Grace's nerves came right to the forefront as we got ready for the imminent replay. She was dithering between outfit choices as I stepped out of the shower, holding up her favourite lingerie sets to her naked body one after the other.

"Which one?" she asked, a deep scarlet lace bra and knickers set in one hand and a white satin basque and thong in the other.

I wouldn't be drawn into expressing an opinion, knowing full well that my stunning wife would look divine in whatever she went with. I wanted her to seek out her own truth, and gravitate toward the option that would feel most like her own skin.

"You already know the answer," I told her. "You just don't know you know it. Which one is it going to be?"

It was red. I could tell before she said it, guided purely by the way her eyes moved over her reflection in the mirror.

She fastened herself into the push up bra as I watched her, shifting those beautiful milky tits into perfect position in the lacy cups. It took everything I had not to rip her straight back out of it, my mouth already watering at the prospect of the feast.

She shimmied into her knickers, pulling them high enough on her hips that the pretty red fabric packaged that silky mound like a birthday gift. No stockings, no slutty crotchless invitation for a prick like Heath. This was all her. Beautiful and chic, while being naturally understated. I couldn't take my eyes off her as she slipped on a tight black minidress and tugged the skirt down around her thighs. It didn't come low, hugging the curves of her ass like it was sprayed right onto her body.

She teetered as she stepped into black gloss stilettos, arms held out for balance as she found her footing. She settled into her groove in a beat. Her shoulders pulled back and high, her tummy up and under, showcasing those perfect tits like a dream.

"Will I do?" she asked, with a hand on her hip, and I smiled. How I fucking smiled.

"You'll take his breath away," I told her. "Just like you've taken mine."

She waved my compliment aside like I was bigging her up for the sake of flattery, but I saw the glow of pride as she gave a final turn to the mirror.

I found I was dressing up for the occasion myself, picking out one of my finest black shirts from the wardrobe and pairing it with my best pair of dark jeans. I sprayed myself with quality scent — the stuff Grace bought me the Christmas before last.

She breathed me in as she joined me at my side, slipping her fingers into mine as she pressed up beside me. "You smell good enough to eat, Mr Foster."

"My mouth's the one watering," I told her. "Soon you'll have him slavering over a main course of Mrs Foster too."

"Shall we take anything?" she asked, nodding over to the now chaotic heap of sex toys on permanent display since I'd found my rhythm.

I shook my head. "No."

No props. Not tonight.

Just him, and me.

I could hear her every breath as we left our private turf and made the ascent. Her hand was trembling in mine, but I was solid, unmovable, jaw gritted firm at the prospect of what was to come. My rap of knuckles on his door was as fierce as I felt, thumping loud in the quiet of the corridor before I stepped back to face him square.

When he answered it was with the same fire, swinging the door open wide and seeking out my glare with his for a full, hard second before stepping aside.

"Punctual," he said. "Just as well, since I don't tolerate timewasters."

His eyes were eating my Grace up as she stepped on through. I wished she could see how much he wanted her, but her shyness kept her head down low, her smile so self-conscious that it panged my gut.

"Let's not waste any fucking time then," I told him, and he stopped in his tracks on the way to the minibar at the other side of the bed, smirking like the same callous sonofabitch as always when he gave a single nod.

"Have it your way."

"Always," I said.

Grace dropped to sit on the edge of the mattress closest to me, looking back and forth between us all the while we stared each other out. I didn't take my eyes from his, my hands without a hint of nerves as I went for my top button.

His were as composed in return as they went for his. Working his way down his shirt without a flash of fear as he exposed his chest.

I'd seen it all before, in so much fucking detail it was burned into my memory. His solid frame, toned without an excess of bulk. The ripple of abs so pronounced as he shrugged his shirt aside and went for his belt.

I had the upper hand as I shrugged off my own, knowing full well how much bigger my chest was than his. My own bulk was broader, my own abs more than fit enough to hold their own against his gym-toned physique. I was darker, hairier, every bit a caveman next to his smooth pampered skin. I felt like one too.

I dropped my pants comfortably, making no move to conceal the raging hard on I'd been sporting since arriving in his corridor. And there we were, naked, his own dick just as fucking proud as he kicked off his trousers and stepped to the side.

There was a surrealism to this competition, no reservations about sporting a throbbing dick in front of another man. If he was feeling any awkwardness, he didn't show it. We were strangely composed as we viewed our opposition across the bed, our pretty prize positioned between us, right where she needed to be.

"How's it fucking feel to have a rival on the pitch?" I asked the cunt. "No free runs this time, Heath. I'm in it to win it."

"You people always are," he replied. "I've seen off hundreds of your type."

You people.

Your type.

And there it was again, that deep-veined spite.

His laugh wasn't genuine as it sounded out. "How the fuck do you propose we call the winner? First to three? Every climax counts?" He shook his head. "This is a fool's game, ill thought out. Cash terms bring structure."

"Cash terms aren't worth shit," I told him. "It counts for nothing."

He shrugged, his dick still rising tall. "I'll say it again. How will we know who wins?"

My smirk was all genuine. "We'll know."

"Fine," he said. "Let's see how desperate your pretty wife's cunt is for another man's cock, shall we?"

He was on the bed in a flash, stealing the moment, and she was ready for him, in body if not in mind, shifting toward him so eagerly as he came for her, even though her eyes flashed back to mine.

I didn't stop her, not even breaking a sweat as his mouth claimed hers and guided her backwards. She fell willingly, dropping onto her back and letting her knees open wide. And there you had it, the impact he'd had on my woman, too great to have glossed over, even if we'd never seen him again.

He was running through her veins. Burned into her thoughts. Wants. Memories.

He'd claimed her deep enough in that one night that he summoned her like a ringmaster calls his acrobats, forcing her into tricks without so much as barking an order.

She lifted her hips as his knuckles swept her slit through her knickers, and she was wet for him, the lace damp enough to darken as he stretched it tight between her pussy lips and tugged hard against her clit.

Her moan was instant, fingers clutching at the sheets as she tensed.

"They always miss me," he said for my benefit, but he didn't need to. I could see it clearly enough for myself.

His mouth was rougher more quickly this time than last, nipping at her jaw before sweeping down her throat. She stretched to offer him more, her eyes on him as I dropped onto the mattress on her other side.

But not for long.

Soon they'd be all for me.

FORTY SEVEN

GRACE

My mini dress was up around my hips in moments, legs spreading wide for Heath's crazy skilled fingers. My belly was a mess of lust, fluttering with an ocean of tiny wings as his mouth found mine.

He nipped me, sucked me, swept his warm lips across my exposed throat and it was pointless to fight the sensations. Pointless to fight *him*.

I reached out for my husband as he joined us on the bed, his knees dipping the mattress at my side enough that my body moved towards his. His fingers brushed up the tender skin of my inner thigh, setting me alight with their close proximity to the other man's.

The fear was intoxicating, addictive, my thoughts tumbling as my heart thrummed wild.

Two men.

Two gorgeous men.

I prayed I was up to taking everything they had to give. But more than that, I prayed I was up to giving them everything in return. I wanted them grunting out of control, lost to the pleasure I was delivering. I wanted every hole filled with the proof of what I'd done to them, what I'd driven them to.

I wanted to taste him. Heath. I wanted to watch his expression shift from calm master of himself and the universe around him to a man swept up in me. Consumed by me. Pushed from his axis and reeling in the waves, desperate for everything I was giving.

Just as I was desperate for everything he'd shown me last time around and left me wanting.

I couldn't fight it. Didn't want to. My arms snaked naturally around both guys, pulling them closer as the tension blistered between them.

There was no chance for Brett to reel against the revulsion of another man's fresh-on-my-lips kiss as I sought out his mouth and slipped my tongue out to greet his. It was crazy, a different man's fingers grazing my clit through my knickers as my husband kissed me deep. The rhythm was mismatched in a way that was delicious, two hot bodies pressing tighter to mine as someone tugged my mini dress down at the neckline and freed my tits from my bra.

And then there were two hands. One on each, pinching and pulling at nipples that ached for it. My heels pressed to the mattress and shifted my ass into the air, my pussy craving the same attention.

It was easier than I expected to find my groove and ask for what I wanted. I didn't speak a word, just let my fingers do the talking. Thomas Heath's hair was soft in my grip as I guided his mouth to my nipple. He nipped sharp in what felt like a quick flash of punishment for my boldness, and then he swallowed me, sucking so hard I mewled into Brett's fierce kiss.

I knew right then that tonight would be rough.

Brutal.

Caught between the blows as two men fought for their pride.

I felt guilty for wanting it that way, but I did. I felt like a traitorous little slut as I slipped my leg between Heath's and angled my pussy in his direction.

Please.

I couldn't have spoken it any louder if I'd have screamed it from my lungs. Another nip at my breast and his fingers taunted me, sliding down the ruched fabric over my stomach to tease my clit.

I felt his hard on as he pressed his length to my hip, and there was no hint of reservation there about another man's nakedness. Brett's cock was throbbing just as proud when I sought it out with my sweaty palm, squeezing tight to feel the pulse in his shaft. There was no doubt about it, both guys were impressive in everything. From their dirty eyes to their firm abs, and lower. Their dicks were more than enough to reinforce their self-belief, swollen enough to deflate my confidence in taking them.

Brett had pushed me hard through long nights, straining me to the hilt to make me ready for this. I felt anything but ready as the reality of two huge meaty dicks throbbed so threateningly against me. It didn't matter though. I'd take them. Even if it broke me and left me an aching wreck for days. Even if they tore me open and left me sobbing, I'd still beg for more.

It was in me. The fantasy too deeply ingrained to step down from the challenge. It was every dirty night with my hand down my knickers, mind spinning like crazy at the thought of being eaten up by two at once. It was the forbidden thrill of taking more than one man, more than my fill, more than most women ever got to experience, even if that one man proved beyond all doubt to be one too many.

Brett broke the kiss with a hiss of breath, thrusting his hips and working his dick between my tight fingers, hand plunging between my thighs and tugging the wet lace of my panties to the side.

Please.

Another silent beg. This one with needy eyes staring up at the man who'd delivered me to my ultimate fantasy for the second time over. He gave me what I wanted, two thick fingers to the knuckle as Heath's fingers circled my squealing clit.

Please.

This time it was a whimper, coaxing my husband's face down toward my tit, daringly close to the other man's sucking mouth and the slurps he was making on my skin.

He fought it, hovering rigid for a long moment as he stared at Heath's mouth clasped so tight to my flesh. They must have both felt the pressure, because I watched Heath's eyes flick up toward my husband's, flashing with disgust before he responded with a bite on my flesh that took my breath. His teeth gripped tight and held, but it was the strength of the suck that had me whimpering.

He was marking me, and the bruises would last for days.

Brett must have realised it at the exact same moment, because his reluctance disappeared in a flash, his eyes wide on mine as he clamped his mouth to my bare skin and nipped with a strength of his own.

Fuck, it was the most incredible soreness. I craved more, wanting enough bruises from these two delicious mouths to last a lifetime.

My nipples cried out as they both broke the contact, and I surveyed the damage through hazy eyes, pink flesh blooming bright and glistening with fresh spit.

Dirty. It was so dirty. And so was I.

"Let me suck," I breathed, and I wasn't sure who I was talking to.

It was Brett who answered me, positioning himself in a straddling kneel above my face and slapping the head of his dick to my cheek.

I didn't need encouraging, mouth open wide for the swell of him as I tipped my head back and drank him in. My hand slipped between my legs, but no sooner had my fingers landed on my clit than Thomas pushed them aside. His thumb pressed hard, still but brutal, making me gurgle around a throatful of dick.

I knew this place from last time. The way he turned me into a slut with every touch and gesture. The way I couldn't resist squirming in my bid for more.

"Dirty little whores earn their pleasure," Heath grunted, and my soul winced. "Be a good girl and suck like you mean it."

I did mean it. I meant every lick around Brett's dick, sucking hard enough that my cheeks caved in, throat retching wet and head bobbing under him.

"Suck," Heath growled and I whimpered.

Brett took my hair and helped my head back and forth, fucking me like a ragdoll as his balls bounced on my chin.

"Let's hope your pussy sucks half as well as that slutty little throat," Heath added, and thrust three fingers all the way in.

I clenched with everything I had, muscles taut to aching as I gripped his fingers with every strain of strength in me. I coughed up spit all over Brett's cock and groaned for Heath to fuck me hard, a glutton for punishment as his wrist became a terrible piston, his fingers a punch to my womb in their bid to open me wide.

It was Brett who growled next time. "Suck me," he told me. "Suck my fucking dick like the filthy little slut that you are."

I could normally read my husband like a book, every tense and strain of his balls was a language I'd learned my whole adult life, but not tonight.

Oh fuck, not tonight.

I scrabbled at the sheets as Heath's thumb pressed to my clit and circled wide, and Brett seized the moment of my toppling excitement, digging his cock into the very depths of my throat to choke my cries.

It was mute but loud, their timing impeccable as they struck together to make my climax vicious in its intensity. My clit spasmed and spiralled, hips wriggling as Heath finger-fucked me out of my mind. It was all I could do to snatch long breaths through my nose, throat filled to bursting by my husband's pulsing dick.

But he didn't come. There wasn't even a salty taste of precum as Brett tugged free, my mouth gaping wide as I caught my breath.

I knew Heath saw it. He couldn't not. Brett shifted himself in a heartbeat to face his rival, cock still proud and dripping with my spit as I gasped and recovered from my first explosion.

"Round one to me," Heath said with a smirk and licked his fingers clean.

"Like fuck it was," Brett replied. "Now get in my wife's pretty throat and see how well you hold up to the same fucking pressure."

"My pleasure," Heath said, with his trademark smirk.

But he was wrong.

The pleasure was all fucking mine.

FORTY EIGHT

THOMAS

I was way out of my groove in this sorry situation, cursing myself for being dragged into silly games so far out of my comfort zone as I ploughed Grace's cunt with brutal fingers.

I shouldn't be here. Not with both of them, and most certainly not without a heap of my cash on the table to keep the sway firmly on my side. Brett was different this time around, barely recognisable as the buckling pile of *has been* I'd forced into a corner so easily.

He was worryingly back in *his* groove as he slammed his dick into his wife's retching throat, fucking her hard without a hint of a concern that I was up against him.

I hated how it twisted deep inside, provoking the reaction of that poor pathetic boy I'd been trying to keep at bay for weeks. The boy who hated everything the popular teenage Brett Foster stood for. Hated his bravado and bullish jibes, the confidence he carried in his shoulders like nothing in the world could tear him down.

The years I'd spent convincing myself I could be the one to throw him from his footing were shrivelling away to nothing. Drying up around me as I kept my walls up high.

I forced it down. Choked it tight. Keeping my focus on the woman writhing on the bed between us, playing her with every ounce of concentration I could muster as her pussy responded to my fingers.

Bringing her off was easy. Knowing the right words to send her body quivering was as natural as the breath in my lungs. Keeping my cocky front watertight under the scrutiny of her asshole husband was not.

I told him I'd won the first round, claiming her climax as my own, but even as I forced out the arrogance I knew he wasn't buying it. He was still in full control as he pulled away from her mouth and left her ragged, his cock barely twitching as her spit dribbled down his thighs.

I told him it was my pleasure to take his place, but it wasn't. I wasn't prepared for the full intensity of sharing a woman with another naked man, flesh on display so vulnerably next to his. I wasn't prepared for the equal footing of the battle between two men striving to give their best game.

Grace was already open wide as I took up position. She tipped her head back to stretch her eager throat, whimpering for more as I pushed into the sloppy wet tunnel he'd left behind.

She was hot. Tight. Noisy. Everything I'd dreamed of as a teenager watching her from across the street with his hand in hers.

And more.

She was so much more.

"Fuck her filthy mouth," he snapped as I paused to enjoy the sensation. "She's hungry for it."

I wanted to tell him to go fuck himself. The words were on my tongue, ready to be as much of a cunt as I could summon from the depths, but that sad fucking boy inside left me mute.

I thrust my hips hard enough that Grace's throat clenched hard. She coughed up a huge gob of drool as I pulled out all the way, letting out a groan as I charged all the way right back in. I was expecting a mirror image of our earlier arrangement, but the prick jumped right in and slammed his dick in her horny cunt, setting her so fucking wild that her throat hummed with stifled moans that made my balls tighten.

No.

I gritted my teeth against the pleasure, digging my fingers into my naked thighs in an attempt to regain my composure. It didn't work. Not with the slap of flesh on flesh as Brett Foster grunted and slammed.

It was her excitement, so fucking beautiful as she writhed and whimpered. Her stretched mouth was grinning around my cock, hands reaching for her husband and urging him on.

I wasn't going to come for her. Not yet. Not fucking ever if I could keep a fucking handle on it.

My eyes were closed as I paced myself, relief flooding through me as I regained my composure. And then I felt it there, the faintest hint of that sad little boy craving something that made my gut turn.

Camaraderie. The sad fucking thrill of Mr Popular slapping me on the back for a job well done. Mutual respect in a place I'd never wanted it, and certainly never earned it.

I'd never fucking wanted it. Not then and certainly not now. The teenage ghost in me was a sad little asshole, offsetting everything I'd battled to accomplish in all these years after high school.

I wanted to tear Brett Foster down and leave him destroyed, showing once and for all that I really was the better man. I wanted to claim his pretty wife as mine, leaving no illusion that she wanted anything but me.

These were the stakes, right here and now. This was the battle I'd been building up to my whole life.

"Fill the slut up," he grunted, laughing low like a jock on the sports field. "She's a cat wanting some filthy fucking cream from your balls. You'd best get giving it to her."

And she did want it. Her moan was all for my filthy seed as she struggled to take more.

No.

I pulled out before she could claim her prize, slapping my wet dick against her open lips as I shifted to face the guy fucking that sweet pussy. His eyes were dark, hips in a fiery rhythm as he gave her every inch in brutal torment. His thumb was on her clit, pressing hard in the way I'd been doing. He knew the moves. *My* moves. He knew what buttons I'd been pressing to get such a glorious reaction from his sweet bride.

He'd been practicing. Seemingly every fucking minute of every fucking day.

I'd been burying myself in shitty mountains of work to distract myself from the desire for round two with his wife, and he'd been learning from what he'd seen that night. Pushing himself forward. Bigger. Better. Ripped with composure I'd thought long dead in him.

"More," Grace whimpered, opening her mouth up like a needy fish, slippery wet and desperate.

I couldn't give it to her, especially not when that hungry mouth strained to take my balls, her tongue a tease of epic proportions as her body burned my eyes with its perfect glory.

Her tits were divine, my love bite already darkening alongside his. Her nerves were alight, limbs shivering and jerking as her husband fucked her hard.

"Fill her the fuck up," he barked again, and this time my eyes narrowed.

"I'll give her what she fucking earns," I countered, and he shrugged.

"Fuck her fucking throat and she'll show you what's earned," he goaded. "What's up with you? Too fucking shy to shoot your load? Grow some balls, Heath."

"It's not about the climax," I argued. "It's about the performance."

But he didn't care. His thrusts were hard enough that her face pressed tight to my dick and balls, mouth flapping wide as she reached her crest for the second time.

My cock wasn't even in her as she exploded with orgasm number two. It was all for him.

I cursed under my breath as the win struck his senses, well aware that no amount of bravado on my part would kill his victory.

The flicker of embarrassment was hard to subdue, Brett's eyes on me as he pulled from her pussy and presented his still raging hard on proud for my viewing.

"Yeah," he told me. "It's about the fucking performance. You'd better get with the game, Heath."

It was all the fire I needed.

His pretty wife was still gasping as I pulled her body out from under and dragged her up onto mine.

"Next fucking round," I said.

FORTY NINE

GRACE

My husband had set me on fire. I was burning up so hard I was shivering. Writhing in quicksand as the orgasm sucked me deep, but it was Thomas Heath with his fiery eyes who tugged me free.

I was still panting as he pulled me out from underneath my husband, lost to everything but the pulse of my pussy flooding all the way through me. My heart was secondary to my buzzing clit, my whole body governed by its new natural centre.

Dirty.

I was every bit as dirty as they were telling me, and I felt it. Knowing all too well that I would never be the same after this.

And neither would they. Not either of them.

In all my nights with my hand down my knickers, I'd never imagined this. The fantasy never came close to the reality of two hot bodies fighting silently over mine.

Brett was proud to bursting, regardless of the way his rival yanked me up onto him and encouraged me onto his solid dick. His smile was guarded but definite, his eyes eating us both up as I wriggled against another man's body.

Heath was more and less than I'd dreamed, all at once. His body was every bit as ripped as I remembered, muscles undulating his skin with every shift of his hips up toward mine. His moves were as well crafted, his knowledge of my sweet spots impeccable. His tone was dark and dirty, yet satin enough to set me scorching. But he was losing his calm and I knew it. Despite having virtually no concrete evidence I could use with hard reason to support my verdict, I knew it.

It was in his flashing eyes, his delayed hiss of breath, the strain of his cocky smirk as he urged me faster on top.

Once again, it felt so wrong to be riding another man, but I took on a life of my own under my surface level reluctance, finding my beat up on top as my pussy cried for more.

I shouldn't want more, not tonight, not even in a month from now. The fact I did was a revelation that spat through my veins, but that just goaded me onwards.

And there it was again, rocking underneath me with Heath's hips. The need to conquer him enough to make him climax. I daren't hope, daren't even dream he was as close as I'd hoped he was just a short while earlier with his dick in my mouth. I couldn't imagine the salty taste from his tip onto my tongue was anything more than wishful thinking as I'd swept my taste buds for more.

I pressed my palms to his chest, rolling my hips as I dropped down onto his full length. His knees came up to support my back, thighs tense behind me as my pussy slavered all over his crotch. I wasn't expecting him to shunt me high and forward, not even for a moment. I was in full flow with his dick in my pussy when he set me off balance enough that the head of his cock pressed to my clenching asshole.

I wasn't ready, but it didn't matter, not to Heath. He grabbed my hips and pulled me lower, gritting his teeth as I grunted out loud with the strain.

"Give me that dirty little asshole," he snarled up at me. "We all know you're an anal-loving whore."

I hated how his intimate knowledge made me bloom with self-consciousness, towering tall over him as I writhed to take him deep. It was so embarrassing, cutting me to my core that I was being such a slut for this filthy man.

But Brett didn't care.

He was smirking harder than his rival when I flashed him a look, nodding in encouragement as I inched down onto Heath's ramrod of a cock and let my ass loosen to take him.

"Do it," Brett hissed. "Do it, Grace. Ride his dick like you fucking mean it."

I did mean it. My groans were all real as I let my weight pull me down.

I'd expected this to be Brett in my ass. It made no sense in terms of logic, but it was him I pictured bucking up and under, his thumb on my clit to make me hiss louder. Having Brett watch me with Thomas was nothing like the last time around. There were no white knuckles and crappy red lines, no guilt at the strain my husband must be feeling to see me enjoying another man while he was rooted to the spot far beyond arm's reach. Brett's cock was hard and dark in his slow moving fingers, his gaze full of want as he watched me inching me down onto another man.

So I did it.

I took Thomas Heath in my ass like a wanton little bitch, far more desperate to see him unravel than I was to unravel myself.

I focused on his perfect features as I circled my hips and took him deep, forcing down my shyness and letting my natural instincts take over. I leaned forward with enough bravery that my fingers travelled up the fine ripples of his abs, dancing over his chest before coming to rest on his shoulders. And then I fucked him. Rode him slow and smooth. Rode him with everything I had as my pussy slicked up his skin. I closed my eyes and felt it all, every single tightening muscle underneath me, every move he made, every hiss of his breath as he pushed up to meet me.

My nerves were dithering deep, but my natural urges took over. I dropped to his chest without warning, my tits soft and sore against his firmness as I lay flat and raised my fingertips to his jaw. I didn't kiss him. Couldn't kiss him. His jaw was too firm, eyes too hard, but they didn't stop me meeting his fierce glare with a smile. It came from the heart, a crazy flash of affection amidst the filthiness, and it must have touched something equally crazy within him, because he swallowed hard as his dick twitched inside me, and his eyes softened to meet mine right back.

It was all the encouragement I needed.

When my lips pressed to his they were gentle. My kiss was real. Genuine. *Me.*

The kiss that came back was nothing like I'd felt from him before. The fingers that took my hair and held me to him weren't those of a man straining for supremacy, but straining for closeness. I'd have sworn blind that I was delusional if it wasn't right there, right in me, just as it was in him.

I didn't stop. Couldn't stop. I kept kissing him as my ass ate up his dick with hungry sucks, the pleasure rippling through me without a care for the pain of the stretch.

It was beautiful. And dirty. Disgusting.

Wrong, and right.

Deep and fucked up. Shallow and pretty, with glitter sparkles as my husband watched with his own dick throbbing in his fingers.

I moaned in Thomas Heath's mouth as the third climax threatened, my limbs aching at the thrill. I moaned again as his rasp of breath came right back at me, daring *please*, please fucking do it.

He fought losing control, but I didn't let him, not this time. There was no alarm clock to save him as my fingers touched to his cheeks and my kiss deepened. I was right there with him as his eyes opened and focused on mine, my own excitement cresting with him as he thrust up to meet my every movement.

And it happened.

Oh fuck, how it happened.

His hands on my hips driving me down, his tongue deep in my mouth as his fingers swept up my spine and held me tight to him.

In another world, in another place, this could have been something, meant something.

In another world, *we* could have been something.

But in this one we were only something for as long as it took him to explode inside my asshole.

He was cursing under his breath before he was done twitching deep, shunting me free quickly enough that his cum drooled from my ass all over his jerking dick.

I wanted to say something. Anything. Just to make him stay. Just to make him know it was alright. That I'd loved it too.

But I couldn't say a word as he rose to his feet with his dick in his hand and retreated to the bathroom.

I only wished my husband had the same restraint I did.

He didn't.

His voice rang loud and victorious, following Thomas into the bathroom as the door slammed behind him.

"Three fucking nil to me."

FIFTY

BRETT

I should've been smug as shit to see Heath shooting his load like a desperate cunt into Grace's needy asshole, and I was.

The victory was loud and proud, my own cock twitching in warped fucking excitement as I worked it slow and shallow in my palm. Seeing that sonofabitch lose his cool and come for my Grace was a joy beyond every sensibility I'd ever known. Seeing her wounded confidence repair itself in front of me appeased every scrap of concern I had about this fucked-up arrangement.

It was worth it.

Seeing that sweet little smile on her face as she collapsed onto the bed with his cum still dripping from her asshole was worth every scrap of misery the cunt had landed on our doorstep and then some.

The bathroom door was closed tight behind him, the sound of running water blocking out any words I could have chosen to speak to my wife, but I didn't need words.

My touch said it all, pulling her to my chest and wrapping her in warm arms, my cock pulsing against the small of her back as she struggled to regain her composure.

"This is crazy…" she whispered, and I kissed her damp hair.

My words were all from instinct, alien to me even as I said them.

"This is all about you from here on in. No point-scoring, no ego, just you and what you want. Whatever you want, Grace. I'm all in."

Her hands stroked my arms, her body so small against mine, and it was about her. Seeing her so content between me and that asshole was all the reward I needed.

"He came," she told me, her voice so small.

"How could he not?" I replied. "You were irresistible."

I was still holding her tight when the bathroom door swung open and Heath stepped back into the room. His belly was still glistening from washing himself down, his cock back to hardness even though his expression was foul. It took a real scrap of restraint not to goad him further into his cesspit of losing, but I held back, giving him a nod as he came closer.

"It's not game over yet," he said, but his smirk was nowhere to be seen.

I could have pushed his every fucking button to pound my win home even harder, but I didn't.

"It is game over," I told him. "It's all about Grace from here on in."

He paused, standing over the bed with his eyes fixed on mine, trying to work out just what the hell I was going on about, I'm sure. I answered with a shrug.

"All about Grace," I said again. "She has fantasies. We're going to live up to them."

"Just like that?" he asked, still seething hard. "You're really going to abandon your jock attitude to make sure your pretty wife gets her fill? I doubt that very much."

Another shrug came so naturally. "Doubt it all you like, it's the truth."

"And what do you get out of it?"

My smile was all for her, even though her eyes were on him. "The same thing you do, a beautiful woman taking her fill. Don't tell me you don't want her. I'll believe some of your posh boy bullshit, but not that."

He didn't look convinced as he dropped down onto the mattress. He looked at her for a long while, his cock hard against his thigh as that chess master brain of his ticked through his moves.

"This isn't over," he told me. "We'll take a rematch."

"Temporary truce," I said.

And there it was again, whatever festering resentment he held towards me burning bright in his eyes before he gave a nod. I pushed it aside as Grace squirmed in my arms.

"A truce sounds good," she told us, tipping her head back to greet me with a smile.

That smile settled everything. I'd call a truce for a thousand years if it brought even half of that smile to her lips.

I shifted away from her, leaving her exposed between us, and this time there wasn't so much as a hint of nerves in her posture, her limbs wide and welcoming as she beckoned him to close the distance. It perplexed him, his whole body tensing as he weighed her up.

"If this is some stupid conspiratorial game at my expense–" he began, and it made me sigh.

"Don't judge everyone else by your own fucked-up standards, Heath. Not everything is at someone else's expense. This isn't your London city bullshit here."

"Everything is always at someone else's expense," he told me, but moved all the same.

He looked different this time, his actions less aggressive as he closed the distance between him and my wife. His hands were solid but not as assured as they reached for her. She moulded into him perfectly. Effortless as her arms wrapped around his shoulders and urged him down onto her.

"I want you both," she whispered. "Both at once."

The idea of the close proximity to another man's nakedness brought a shiver down my spine, but my dick was still pulsing unperturbed. He slid into her pussy in one deep thrust, taking her leg and hoisting it high. I watched as an onlooker without the sheen of bitterness, absorbed fully by the sight of him balls deep inside the sweet little cunt I'd called mine for a lifetime, the surrealism addictive as she coaxed him for more.

It was late. The night gobbling us up with its quiet mystery. I let myself sink into it, thumbing my balls idly as I contemplated a potential week of this and everything it would bring.

Her hands were all over his back as he found his stride and fucked her hard. He buried his face in her neck and kissed her like he meant it, and she was right there, urging him on. It should've killed me, but it didn't. Didn't even come close.

I wondered on some fucked-up level if this would be enough to change the prick into someone less eager to fuck everyone else's life up around them. If this would mean something, anything. If Grace would be the calm to ease off the storm in whatever fucked-up part of him he'd dragged down here to our doorstep.

And then I wondered if I really cared. *Why* I really cared. If I'd ever known the cunt at all. If I'd ever deserved some of the hatred in his gut.

She told him it felt amazing. *He* felt amazing. She told him she wanted it *harder, faster, deeper. More.*

I held back and let him give it to her, watching through eager eyes as he took her where she wanted, his whole body thrusting as he claimed her. Until she reached for me. An outstretched arm begging for closeness.

I gave it to her, shifting up on my haunches and presenting myself close enough that I could taste the sweat on the air, my own limbs working as theirs did, bringing her up and onto him, his dick impaled all the way as she landed hard and leaned forward, offering up that pretty asshole to two at once in a bid that saw me desperate to dig in deep.

I cared nothing for the risk of balls against balls as I positioned myself behind her and brushed the head of my dick against her winking ass. She was still dribbling his filthy cum from her hole, and in any other circumstances it would have made me retch my fucking guts up, but not tonight.

I closed my eyes as I pressed in hard, adoring how she whimpered and tensed at the strain of two.

Her exclamation was feral, but not averse, rocking back against the intrusion as she whimpered with the stretch.

He groaned along with her as I pushed my way inside, and I was there too, grunting at the sensation of another man's dick filling her up to the brim along with mine. It was enough to offset any disgust, my balls aching to unload inside her as I took her hair in my fist and held her tight.

"Fuck us," I barked. "Both of us. Work our fucking dicks like you want it."

She gave it her all, gritting her teeth and shunting back like a dirty little angel as we stretched her wide. She took it like a trooper, murmuring like a slut as we ploughed into her, hedonistic in her desire to take us both in all the way.

Bottoming out was a thrill that zipped right through me. He must have felt it too, because he grunted like I'd never heard him, cursing as she squirmed.

"This is my dream..." she breathed, and it was obvious.

I let my weight pin her between us, two bodies sandwiching her tight as I thrust my own hips to take her hard.

The grunts were low and loud, both of us taking our fill without the need for bravado.

"Fuck my wife," I told him. "Give it to her."

He did. Shunting his hips to alternate with mine until she was squealing, and then he shifted, sinking into my rhythm. In and out together, both of us in unison, filling her to bursting, then leaving her hanging loose and winking for more, over and over and fucking over, until we were only flesh seeking more. Seeking her. Seeking the warmth of two tight fucking tunnels milking us dry.

My chest was heaving against her back, balls thrumming with the need to unload, and he was right there with me, I heard it in his voice, felt it in his thrusts, desperate as he raised his hips for deeper.

"Come for us," I growled in her ear. "Show us what a greedy slut you are."

Her clit must have been pressed tight to his flesh, her writhing taking on a new sense of urgency as she struggled against my grip.

"I've never felt like this…" she breathed, and I didn't doubt it.

I'd never fucking felt like this either, so lost in the moment as another guy's brimming balls mashed with mine. It was revolting, but fucking perfect. It was the most natural thing in the fucking world to tumble into the white abyss along with her, caring for nothing but the thrill as I shot my load fucking deep.

And I knew he was there right along with me, his breath as loud as mine amongst the thrust and slap of flesh on flesh.

She shuddered and wailed like a woman crying at sea, clinging on tight to him as her asshole swallowed my dirty gift and sucked for more.

I had nothing else to give her, my dick pulsing and spluttering as my thrusts stilled to nothing and his stilled under me.

And there we stayed. Breathing. Twitching.

Enjoying the flesh of the gorgeous woman between us as she whimpered out thanks in desperate, meaningless phrases.

I'd have stayed there forever, happily embedded in that moment of pure disconnected pleasure, but it was him that moved us, urging her off him and me along with her, only to pull free and head for the edge of the bed, dropping his legs over the side and digging for his clothes as Grace and I remained a tangled heap of heavy breathing.

"I'm getting some air," he told us, without even glancing in our direction as he stepped back into his pants. "I'll be wanting my bed to myself when I return."

He didn't wait for a response before he buttoned up his shirt and grabbed his jacket, barely fastening his shoes before heading for the door.

Grace waited in my arms before she spoke again, waited until he was well and truly gone before she flipped in my grip to stare up at me.

"What the hell was that?" she asked. "Why the hasty retreat?"

I didn't have a fucking clue, and neither did I care.

But she did.

As always, my Grace was storming after the mystery, desperate to unravel the threads.

"I'm going after him," she said.

FIFTY ONE

THOMAS

I was a stumbling mess as I took the rear stairs two at a time, my shirt barely fastened properly as I tumbled from the back door onto the terrace. I craved air, space, the cleansing chill of the sea breeze against my skin.

I craved Polly's sweet messages to help me make sense of my own fucked-up brain, lost in the spinning world of haunting memories and my own fractured ego.

The ego these people had destroyed in the face of all the preparations I'd made for their destruction.

They'd beaten me. *He'd* beaten me. That cunt Brett Foster had beaten me like the scrawny little school kid who couldn't stand up to a beefy piece of shit like him all over again.

I should hate him. *Them*. I should hate this place, hate what it was doing to me, hate everything it stood for here, and my own idiot bastard decision to come running when he called.

But I didn't. I didn't hate any of it.

Grace's touch was divine, filled with something I'd shied away from my whole fucking life.

Truth.

Her touch was true. Genuine. Filled with want and warmth enough to drive a man crazy with the need for more.

I'd never seen it, nor wanted to. My slut of a mother had put paid to that with her string of asshole fuckwit boyfriends right the way through my youth, throwing out the ones worth anything and climbing mountains for those who weren't, and all the while I cursed from the side-lines and shivered in bed at night — hoping, praying, that my real father would see the error of his ways and come running back to make it all better. That one day I'd be worth enough for him to acknowledge I was a part of him.

Only that day never came. No matter how hard I worked, or how much fucking money I made. No matter how high I climbed or how many people I stepped over, he was never there. Never even willing to reach out and make a call.

And now he was dead.

Dead and buried with only Brett fucking Foster listed as his offspring in his last will and testament.

I slammed my fists against the railings as I stared out to sea, my balls still aching empty and my dick still wet with Grace's juices. I stared out at the choppy waves and cursed myself for ever coming here in the first place, reaching into my pocket for a cigar as I choked back the ridiculous tears of that sad little boy inside and swore I'd leave in the morning, never to return.

I'd barely got a grip of myself when I felt her behind me. My back tingled at her closeness as she stepped right up, craving more of everything

I should despise.

A quick look around confirmed her jock asshole husband was nowhere to be seen.

"This is a private moment," I barked, but she didn't even flinch.

"That was a quick exit," she commented, her voice so even as she positioned herself at the railings to my left.

"What did you expect? A shared toast at a job well done? The three of us reminiscing over the shudders of your slutty little cunt as we ploughed you deep?"

I wasn't ready for her laugh. "Maybe, yeah. It was a job well done."

I bristled at her humour, taking a deep puff of smoke and blowing it out hard.

"It was a temporary truce," I told her. "It meant nothing."

"A temporary truce from what exactly?" she asked, and her humour was all gone. "Do you know us? Do we know you?" She paused. "Did we do something to you?"

I didn't say a word, and she kept on rolling.

"I've been thinking about it, and I don't know. It just doesn't... add up. And I don't get it. I've tried working it out, but the picture doesn't make sense."

"Stop trying to make sense of senseless things," I told her.

"That's the thing," she replied. "I don't think anything about this whole weird setup is senseless. You don't seem like a senseless man."

When her arm hooked into mine it was enough of a jolt that I almost dropped my cigar to the beach. I was torn. Rigid and reeling all at once as that idiot boy dared to wish for more. I hated him. *Myself*. Hated not being good enough, because that's what this was, ultimately. One big fucking failure. Two people being strong enough to tear down years of bitter planning. Two people daring to have something I'd convinced myself didn't exist.

Something that would last. A love that was stronger than the cash I'd thrown at them, or the physique I'd built up to compete with any other man.

I knew in that moment, right there on the seafront with that woman's gentle arm wrapped in mine, that it didn't matter what I did in this place, no matter how hard my body claimed hers, or how much cash I tempted them with, or how sharp my moves were to tear them down.

They'd still be standing.

Maybe not here, with a hotel struggling to stay afloat. Maybe not even with the contented smile of two people looking forward to their years to come. But they'd be standing together, even if it was up to their knees in rancid, festering shit, with nothing to their name.

They'd still be side by side.

"Love doesn't exist," I said to the sea, caring little for the fact she was hearing me. "It's nothing but the desperate quest of lonely people trying to find a missing piece of themselves. It's pitiful. Desperate. Nothing but a pathetic illusion."

"That's a very sad way of looking at the world," she said.

"Sad but true."

"And that's why you do this? With the money? To prove love doesn't exist?"

"Something like that," I snapped back, and took another mouthful of smoke.

"You split people up with money, don't you? How many before us?"

My smirk felt so welcome when it reappeared on my face. "Plenty."

Her arm didn't leave mine. "It won't work here. Sorry, but it won't. I guess we'll be the blip on your winning score sheet."

"So it seems," I said. "I'll leave first thing, case closed."

I despised how the defeat sounded even in the stillness.

"Or you could stay," she said, with a softness to her voice at odds with the situation. "Stay. Walk the beach. Eat breakfast. Talk. Drink whisky. Have a holiday."

"I'm sure your good husband would be very happy with that arrangement,"

I scoffed, but she shrugged.

"He isn't nearly so bad as you think he is. You asked for every bit of venom. He's just a guy trying to live his life and make me happy. You were the one who wanted to tear us apart."

"And are you happy?" I asked. "Has this little fantasy lived up to your expectations?"

Her giggle was divine. "You could say that." Her arm squeezed mine. "I'd be more than happy for a rerun, taking out the crappy point-scoring, that is."

"You don't know me," I told her. "You don't know what you're playing with."

"You're right. I don't." She sighed. "But this place is good for the soul, and I think yours is begging to be found."

I'd have laughed in her face if that sad little sonofabitch wasn't in my throat.

"Don't go," she said again. "Not before you've worked it out." One final squeeze of her arm in mine and she pulled away. "The room is on us, as long as you need it. So's the pussy and the ass, if you want those too. On the house. Just, please, no more plots of marital destruction."

I turned to face her as she backed off. "That's an invite for another three in a bed, is it? Despite knowing I'm all out to bring your marriage to its knees?"

"It's an invite for you to find what you're looking for. I'd love to prove you wrong. Love does exist. It's all around us, all the time."

"And what then? Shack up in a cosy little ménage, will we? That would make quite the pretty picture."

Her eyes twinkled in the darkness. "I think a cosy little ménage would most definitely be a case of one too many, Mr Heath. I only have enough heart for my husband, even if my body is keen to enjoy two. But there's someone out there for you, you just need to be willing to let them in when they come calling. Maybe this place will help."

Someone out there for you.

I felt empty enough to break in that moment. More isolated than I'd ever felt, even huddled in a corner of my old shitty bedroom while my mother entertained another of her disgusting suitors.

"You're sex drunk," I told her. "Go back to your husband."

Her smile was bright. Delicious.

"I'm on my way," she said. "Enjoy your quiet room. I'll see you at breakfast I hope." She turned away to retreat back to the hotel, but flashed me one final look over her shoulder. "Goodnight, Tom."

She was long back inside when I finished up my cigar and tossed the butt down onto the beach. I was in my car before I realised it, the key in the ignition before I had any idea where I was headed.

And then it dawned. The cold, hard reality that I had nowhere to head to, only back to London for an eternal string of the same nameless, mindless, soulless days.

A full English fry-up sounded as good a destination as any.

At least that's what I told myself when I headed back upstairs.

FIFTY TWO

BRETT

I watched them through the window, hanging far enough back that they stood no chance of seeing me there. The room was dark at my back, my eyes focused on their outlines at the railings illuminated by the dull orange glow of the porch light. I watched Grace take his arm in hers, and it surprised me how little threat I felt at their close proximity, given that I'd just watched her ride his dick like a dirty slut all night long.

I didn't feel any threat at all, in fact. Not tonight, and likely not ever again. Call me a dumbass optimist, but I was flying high, determined that if Heath was some fucked-up trial sent to test us, all he'd done was leave us stronger. Sure, the grinder may have dragged us through with gnarly teeth in those early days after his departure, but we'd healed stronger, better. Not least with the breathing space of a financial buffer in our account to ease the stress away.

Winning should have been everything. Beating that smug cocksucker in a way he couldn't dispute should have brought a grin to my face like no other. But the victory wasn't nearly as glorious as I'd imagined.

I found myself questioning if victory ever was really that glorious when it came at others' expense. My dad had claimed so, ready with a firm handshake and a clap on the back whenever I'd done him proud, but invariably I was always out to topple someone else right afterwards to earn more of his praise. Always more, more, more.

My happiest moments in my lifetime were undeniably with Grace, knowing she was there at my worst as well as my best. Knowing I didn't need to prove my worth to her every day of my life. Being able to breathe easily at night in her arms, knowing she was mine and I was hers.

But still, here we were. Heath in our midst, on some crazy mission to fuck me over, for reasons unknown.

He wouldn't manage it.

My heart did a joyous flip as she pulled away from him and headed back inside where she belonged. I was waiting in our bedroom with the lamp on low and the bedsheets folded back to welcome her, soaking her in with warm eyes when she crossed the threshold and headed my way with a wince and a smile. She tossed her fluffy cardigan aside and kicked off her pumps, coming for her side of the bed without so much as a bathroom detour.

My arms were ready and waiting as she sought them out, her skin cold to the touch as she pressed to my side.

"That was really something," she told me. "I'll be aching for a week."

"A good ache, I'm hoping."

Her giggle was intoxicating. "A good ache, yeah. I just hope my dainty parts go back to some semblance of normality."

I didn't broach the subject of him at the railings, and it took her a minute, breathing steadily against my shoulder as she warmed herself with my body heat.

"He's a lost soul under all that cash-rich swagger. I think he's searching for something he isn't even sure he's searching for."

"He's a cunt," I said, simply.

She slapped my arm playfully. "Brett Foster, don't be so dismissive of other people's shit. That could be us one day, searching for something."

"Searching or not, he's still a cunt," I repeated. "I suspect he'll always be a cunt. Ruining other people's happiness with his cunty ways."

She didn't have a response for that. It took me a while before I continued, enjoying the sensation of her skin against mine.

"So, what's the cunt searching for?"

"Love," she said, just like that, and it made me laugh out loud.

"Sure he is."

"He is," she insisted. "Whatever happened to him, he's so cynical he's a black hole. He doesn't think it exists."

"Maybe it doesn't for a selfish prick like him," I said, my smile still bright as my laughter eased off.

"Or maybe he's a selfish prick like him because he doesn't believe it exists."

"That's a chicken and egg situation I don't want a part of."

She pressed her lips to my shoulder. "I hope we're the ones who make him rethink."

"By you taking his dick at the same time as mine? Unlikely, sweetheart."

She stiffened at that, pulling away enough to flash me a look of disappointment.

"What?" I said. "It's the truth."

"There's more to this than me taking two dicks at once."

I shrugged. "I doubt he's thinking all that deeply about it, Grace. He wanted to fuck us over, and we proved he was full of bullshit ego. That's what he's smarting about."

It was when she rolled over and nestled down under the covers that I knew she was stewing on something bigger. She welcomed my arm as I wrapped it around her waist and held her tight.

"Talk to me," I whispered. "Tell me what you're thinking."

"You'll say I'm stupid."

I kissed her neck and she shivered. "I'd never say you were stupid."

I gave her breathing space, waiting in the quiet for her to formulate her words and wondering eventually if she was already lost to sleep. She wasn't. Her fingers squeezed mine before she started speaking.

"I think he's realising that what we have is real. I think he's struggling with it."

"Struggling to see us happy? Yeah, because he's a cunt."

I was ready for her to stiffen and she did. I was apologising before she squirmed away, sighing deep as I urged her to continue.

"We could show him," she said. "I mean, he'll see it, from being around us. Maybe it'll open his mind, make him think it's possible."

"And that's what you want, is it? To help the guy in his quest for love? He comes along wanting to destroy everything that matters to us, and you want to set him on his merry way with romance in mind?"

She shrugged in my arms. "I believe in helping people. Sometimes the people who need help the most aren't the people we think deserve it."

"He definitely doesn't," I insisted, but my resolve was weakening in the face of everything the asshole had brought on us.

"He saved our hotel," she added, but I sighed.

"By trying to destroy us."

"Doesn't matter, he saved the hotel and brought us back to life. Brought *you* back to life."

She was right on that front. I felt more of a man than I'd felt in months. It was me running through my veins, and the relief was welcome.

"So, what do you propose we do?" I asked her, and she shook her head.

"I don't know. Show him, I guess."

"Show him by inviting him for threesomes every night this week?"

The look she gave me over her shoulder was nothing short of wonder. "We're going to do this every night?"

"If that's what you want. It's your fantasy."

"And what about yours? What's your fantasy?"

My smile was all real and all for her. "To see you happy, no matter where we find it."

"I love you, Brett Foster," she said, and landed a kiss on my lips. "I'd marry you all over again if I could."

It was all the encouragement I needed to agree to the unbelievable.

"Alright," I told her. "We'll show the prick what love is. We'll see how much he can stomach. Be warned though, there's more to this than some asshole on a quest to break down marriages all over the country. He knows me. Knows us. Fuck knows how or why, but he does. This wasn't just a random seaside visit for him."

She held up her pinky finger and I linked it in a promise before I even knew what I was agreeing to.

"We'll show him who we are, no matter what," she said. "And I'll get hold of Sarah and see where's she's at with her mystery solving. We'll get to the bottom of his *hate the Fosters* attitude, if there really is one."

"Deal," I said. "But can I at least have a silent gloat when I kick his ass all over again in the rerun?"

She managed a laugh this time. "You really are your father's son. I wouldn't expect anything less."

But she was wrong.

For the first time in my life I felt like anything but.

And for the first time in my life, the prospect of change didn't feel so bad.

FIFTY THREE

GRACE

I could barely move when I woke up. My ass felt like I'd taken a train, my pussy aching so bad as I got out of bed.

Brett was sleeping soundly. It was earlier than the alarm, the light a dull silver through the window as I stepped on over.

I felt different. Alive and raw and perfectly sore. But most of all, I felt loved. Maybe now more than ever.

I'd been loved my whole life, from my incredible parents to my awesome sister, through my gaggle of school friends to the man who'd love me since my teens. The idea of never having experienced love that could stand the test of time was a tragedy I couldn't fathom, not for the life of me. The prospect of expecting nothing more than a life of self-serving coldness was enough to bring a shiver to my spine.

The toughest shells hide the softest creatures, and the smallest dogs often have the loudest barks.

The bark of Thomas Heath was pretty damn loud, especially with the boom of hard cash to back up its volume, but I couldn't help thinking this was maybe deceptive. An illusion I was only just beginning to glimpse beyond.

Maybe he was one of those delicate souls in a bitter barricade. Maybe fate had brought him here to find help in the most unlikely of places, just like he'd offered it to us. A silver lining under a very ominous cloud.

Of course, there was the possibility that I was overthinking things and he really was just a selfish cunt, as Brett would say, but I couldn't shake it off. I watched the sea crash along the shore outside, the life his dirty proposition had saved for us, and I couldn't deny the urge to help him right back.

Sometimes help comes from the strangest directions. Hell knows, we'd discovered that for ourselves. Maybe he'd discover it too.

My husband woke with the alarm and reached across my empty side of the bed in his quest for me. He raised his head once he discovered my absence, and I greeted him with a smile from my place at the window.

"Hey," I said.

"Morning, gorgeous," his sleepy voice welcomed. "How are you feeling?"

My walk must have said it all when I crossed the room back to him. He pulled a grimace on my behalf as I fell into his arms, but I didn't want his sympathy, I wanted his promise for more.

Just not today.

Today was about recovering. About a quiet hotel day with our happy guests and Thomas Heath.

I was humming all the way through my shower, soaping up Brett and giggling as he soaped me up right back with tickling fingers. My mood was light and easy, genuinely happy after months of tension, and so was his. It was in his eyes, his smile, his silly gestures. It was in the way he stared at me in the mirror while he brushed his teeth and I towelled down. It was in the way his hand took mine once we were dressed and heading through to the kitchen, his whistle bright as sunshine as he dug out the supplies for breakfast shift.

I liked all this. I liked it a lot.

And I especially liked Thomas Heath's appearance at the breakfast table shortly before nine. He took a newspaper from the rack and set himself down at a window seat, spreading it out over the lap I'd ridden so thoroughly the night previous, and I approached with a confidence I'd never known in his presence, my smile bright and easy as I asked him for his order.

"What's it going to be? You must have quite an appetite."

His smirk was back on his face but not convincing. "Several of us have quite an appetite around here it seems."

"Must be the sea air," I said, choking back a ridiculous giggle. I wasn't a giggler, not even in high school, not really, but the urge was intense, laughter threatening to spill loud and dumb through our breakfast room. I guess that's what true happiness does to you.

He leaned toward me, his beautiful face cocked just right to catch the morning sunlight. "The sea air and one horny little pussy, Mrs Foster. I'm now well aware why your husband has been so keen to keep hold of you all these years."

There it was again, the allusion to the past in his words. Nothing concrete, but still it was undeniable. My belly fluttered with a whole host of nervous vibes, but loudest amongst them all was that *knowing*, knowing that he *knew us*, just as Brett had said.

That's what had me reaching for my mobile phone just as soon as I'd scribbled down his order for a full English and retreated into reception.

I opted for a text message, seeing as my sister was rarely on social media.

Any news on Polly Piper? Thomas Heath is back here. I need to know ASAP please xx.

I hadn't so much as made it through to the kitchen with the order book for Brett when the buzz struck up in my jeans pocket.

He's back?? Wow. I'm on it. Kids have been crazy and she wasn't in the bakery last week. Sick or something. I'll head down there this lunch and put her on the spot.

I loved my sister. The string of hearts and kisses in my response must have made that clear enough to her, too.

Maybe Polly Piper would lead to nothing, especially now they were no longer friends on social media. Sarah may draw a blank and we'd be back to the drawing board, but the tickle up my back dared to hope for more.

I shared the news with Brett when I handed Heath's order over and he quirked a brow.

"Let's hope she strikes gold. Her digging skills better be good."

I nodded. "They run in the family."

He smiled at that. "You're in the wrong career. Fuck hotel management, you should retrain to be a detective."

It wasn't the first time he'd said that. I waved him off like always, wondering afresh whether this was really the right gig for us. We were still doing shit on our search for a chef, our bookings picking up to steady, but still on the rocks with that shitty hotel opening down the road.

I guess I was still wondering about the finer details when I headed out to Heath with his morning coffee. His eyes ate me up as I placed his mug on the table, this time without the crappy little sachets of sugar he despised.

"Penny for them?" he asked, and I met his gaze before deciding he sounded genuine.

"Just a penny?" I replied, a smile on my face as I dropped into the seat opposite. I was done with the cruddy barriers and suspicions between us. He was him and I was me, on home turf, struggling to keep this place on its feet and done with dancing around the fire of his crazy games.

I took a breath before I answered him, watching his well sculpted fingers as he took his mug and lifted it to his lips.

"Your money helped, but this place still needs work."

He swallowed his first sip of coffee, avoiding his grumble at the quality. "This place is doomed with the hotel opening down the coast," he told me, and my stomach tightened. "You'll waste money trying to save it. You'll waste time trying to hang on. Not just you, but everyone else in this village alongside you."

"You don't know–" I began, but he carried on talking.

"I do know," he said. "I've been dissembling other businesses for years. First that rival hotel will open and bring bargain seekers flooding in. The chain stores will follow, lapping up the new trade and choking out the established businesses. You'll have cheap arcades and ice cream vendors. Chain grocery stores and budget boozers. This place has numbered days ahead, I'd be making the most of them if I were you, with one eye on the exit."

"There is no exit," I told him, and my voice was much huskier than I intended. "We'll never sell this place for what we bought it for, even if we wanted to, which we don't."

He tipped his head. "Then get out as quickly as you can."

I shook my head. "Brett would never leave." I paused, deciding whether I should really spill this stuff to someone who seemingly wanted to destroy us. I opted to carry on, unsure what difference it could possibly make. "The inheritance from his dad paid for it. His dad was…" I tried to weigh up the words.

"Was what?" he asked, shifting forward in his seat with more interest than I'd have anticipated.

His eyes were wide and focused. His stance attentive in a way I'd never seen.

Maybe he wasn't all that bad. Not really.

Maybe I could tell him. Should tell him.

Maybe he'd be able to help me unravel all this sorry shit and wade through to safer turf.

"His dad was demanding," I finished. "That won't come as much of a surprise, I'm sure. I mean, you've seen Brett. He's competitive to the max. Always trying to be a winner, no matter what the odds."

"Competitive is one word for it," he said. "I have plenty of others."

"That's rich coming from the guy who offered us obscene money to destroy our life."

"Not your life," he replied. "Just your marriage."

My eyes were wide and focused right back on his. "That *is* our life."

Something moved in his eyes before he looked away. He stared through the window at the waves, and I stared at him. Something was happening, to the man who'd rocked up on our doorstep with a proposition of filthy insanity. Maybe to us too, but definitely to him. I couldn't put my finger on what that something was, or what it meant, but it was there, skirting at the edges of whatever messed-up connection we were developing here.

Moving figures took my attention. Two boys running along the railings with their buckets and spades swinging wide. I couldn't hold back the smile as their poor mother dashed along after them.

That should be me one day, chasing after our children, right here, in this place we loved so much.

"That's what you want, is it?" Thomas asked, clearly reading my thoughts. "A perfect little family in this perfect little cove?"

"No family is ever perfect," I told him, which was certainly true. "But I want my own little imperfect family in this perfect little cove, yes."

He didn't say a word, so I continued with mine.

"My sister has two girls, they love it here. Seeing the magic in their eyes as they shape their dreams out of sand down there is one of my greatest treasures. They're amazing. Their imaginations are amazing. I hope we get our own slice of the same incredible cake one day."

Still he said nothing. Again I continued, this time with a question.

"What about your family? What are they like?"

I waited for his answer, still smiling as the boys disappeared from view.

"I don't have a family," he said finally.

I felt it like a shard of glass in my chest, his words clipped and curt. Dead.

"Not anyone?"

He shook his head. "A mother who doesn't count for much."

"No father?" I asked, and he shot me a glare.

"A string of potentials. Nobody who gave a shit enough to stick around."

"I'm sorry," I said, and I meant it.

Our moment was disturbed by Brett's heavy footsteps. The full English in his grip was stacked high today. I couldn't help but notice the extra rashers of bacon and the double helping of toast.

"Thought you might be hungry," my husband announced as he placed it in front of our guest with a thump.

I could've hugged him so hard, thanking my lucky stars that I was blessed with such goodness in my world. Brett caught my expression and matched it with a smile of his own.

"You two dirty kids having fun plotting the rerun?"

I laughed, but Thomas didn't.

"No," I said. "We were talking about families."

"And you'd better leave our guest to enjoy his food," Brett told me, and held out his hand.

I glanced at the other man before I accepted, but his eyes were still on the front outside, staring into nothing. Distant.

He was still staring into nothing as we stepped away, and again as I poked my head around the kitchen doorway amidst loading the dishwasher with Brett.

It was only when I stepped out to fetch his breakfast plate that I registered he'd disappeared, no sight of him anywhere in the dining room or reception as I headed back to his table.

He was gone, but his breakfast wasn't.
His food had barely been touched.
Just like his black-hearted soul.

FIFTY FOUR

THOMAS

Family. The word made me retch. I fought back the heaves as I struggled for composure.

Seeing Grace's pretty smile as she pondered some beautiful imaginary future was enough to set me reeling, my appetite spoiled for the morning and then some. As I stared down from the wrought iron railings I was becoming so accustomed to, I considered it may well be spoiled for life.

The boys were down there, digging an ambitious pit of sand in their bid to build a fortress on a mountain. In the face of my pitiful unease, I felt the strangest desire to help them.

But no man does that. No man *can* do that. Not in times where everyone fears everyone, with good reason.

People's intentions are rarely for the good.

I could imagine them having children, the Fosters. I could imagine it here, in this quaint little haven on the coast, with their coats buttoned high and their wellington boots slapping along the front in bad weather. I could imagine Brett teaching them to kick a ball on the sand, and Grace spreading out a beach mat big enough for the whole family, dusting down their feet before heading back up for a warming Sunday dinner, should they ever get that nebulous chef vacancy filled by somebody half decent.

And then, in some fit of absolute idiocy, I imagined myself heading down here for a long weekend to spend time with the bunch of them. Some grotesque excuse for an uncle who'd always bring them generous gifts from the city and spoil them with more ice cream and donuts than would be in any way acceptable.

It pained. Stabbing like a dagger of broken fucking dreams. Of what I'd told myself was an impossible illusion worth nothing, and yet found here. A beacon of genuine possibility in this beautiful little piece of bliss in the middle of nowhere.

I pulled my coat collar higher and headed down onto the sand, daring to skirt close enough to those little boys' antics that I could hear their animated discussion. *Higher, higher, make a moat! A moat!*

I'd dug myself a moat so deep it was untraversable. I'd left Polly on the other side, her sad face calling through the years, begging for passage. And now she was gone.

I walked for hours, through the morning and then through lunch, heading beyond the outcrop at low tide and onto the wide open beach beyond. I stared at the sweet cottages on the clifftops, wondering who lived up there, so precariously high in this glorious space. I stared at the horizon, and the never-ending crashing of the waves. I stared into myself, and the pit of despair I'd compounded for a lifetime. For the quest I'd pursued without fruition, its ultimate goal already buried six foot deep.

And I wondered how the holy living fuck I was going to escape from this place and be able to breathe back in my old stagnant life.

I craved Grace's warm arms around my neck. Brett's ridiculously grudging smile as he delivered an extra helping of toast on my breakfast plate. I craved the laughter of the offspring the pair of them may be lucky enough to have one day. The sight of Christmas wrapping discarded across the dining room floor as their kids dug into their presents with Christmas carols playing on the TV.

And Polly.

I craved Polly.

I craved her with every drop of blood left in my cold, hard veins.

Resisting the urge to message her took every scrap of my restraint, my ugly core still bleating loud enough to shy away from the one constant light in my dark sky.

When my mobile phone buzzed in my hand I caught a breath, but it wasn't her. It was Grace. A superficial text that would have meant nothing to most men, but to me it meant everything.

We're having honeycomb ice cream sundaes after lunch. Do you want one?

I tipped my head to the clouds above, unable to hold back the smile.

And then I replied.

I want your sweet little cunt, Grace. Spread wide and pounded hard. I want to see you squirm as you struggle to take two. I want your gaping asshole weeping cum down your pretty thighs.

I waited. Puffing on yet another cigar as I contemplated what the fuck her response would be.

When it came it was every bit as beautiful as her.

Honeycomb ice cream first though, yes? I'm not sure my gaping asshole is up to another pounding without a sugary warm up. x

A kiss.

She ended with a kiss.

And that ended me.

I stubbed my cigar out on the rocks, and decided to face my future.

Fuck knows how hard a road lay ahead, but I'd never once shied away from a challenge in my life.

I wasn't about to start now.

FIFTY FIVE

BRETT

"He isn't going to want honeycomb ice cream, Grace. He barely touched his breakfast this morning." I was trying not to smile as I said it, but she was making it impossible.

Her efforts to please the sack of shit who'd come smashing through our life were sweet enough to tickle me deep, though they fucking shouldn't. They should've been enough to set my blood boiling and kick that sonofabitch out on his posh boy ass.

"He will," she insisted, digging in the fridge for the honey topping.

I folded my arms as I watched her, leaning in the doorway as my cock twitched at the sight. Her pretty ass tight in jeans, her thighs straining as she reached a high shelf.

"This is why we need a chef," she told me. "They'd make a much more impressive sundae than I ever will."

"We should run them through the task at the next interview. *Fuck lobster and crayfish, show us your ice cream skills.*"

"Joke all you like," she said. "Dessert is everything."

I shook my head and turned away, staring back out at the empty dining room and trying to imagine it filled to bursting one day. Ice cream wouldn't bring the crowds, but a decent menu really might. I was being convinced, slowly but surely. Enough to consider opening up our vacancy to potential live-in staff, should we need to.

But that wasn't for today.

Today was about Heath and ice cream and this naively cute little mission Grace was on to warm up his cold blood.

"Heard back from Sarah?" I called over my shoulder.

"Not yet. Soon, hopefully."

I checked my watch. Lunch had been and gone, and in theory so had the donut run back in Gloucestershire.

"You really think Polly Piper knows a man like Heath?"

She approached with an arm full of ridiculous ice cream toppings. "So social media claims."

"*Claimed.*"

"I hardly think it can have been that much of a mistake," she insisted. "It was bold as brass, you saw it too."

I still found it hard to imagine. I found it hard to imagine anyone being friends with that cunt, let alone some small town bakery girl from back at our school.

What I was able to imagine was watching him drive my Grace wild all over again. Teamwork came in the most unlikely of places sometimes, I'd learned that well enough on the sports field, but its results this time around were worth the uneasy truce. I'd shake his hand in a heartbeat for the sake of watching my wife lose her shit between us just once more this week.

The memories would last a lifetime.

She assembled the array of toppings on the breakfast counter and dug out some sundae bowls from underneath.

"Do you think he likes honeycomb?"

"I think he likes you," I told her, and the flash of a smile on her face told me she appreciated the compliment. "I'm sure you could feed him honeycomb sundae from your pussy if he refuses it with a spoon."

"Too cold." Her giggle was divine. "I'll consider it as a last resort. Maybe it will dull yesterday's ache as a side benefit."

She stepped back to view her display, nodding to herself that she was onto a good thing with the arrangement. It was sweet enough to burst.

My beautiful wife squeaked as I stormed up behind her and swept her off her feet. Her legs dangled loose, her laughter ringing out as I swayed her from side to side and landed a kiss on the first sliver of bare neck I could find under her hair.

"I'll eat your dessert," I said. "All night long, every night of the week, forever more."

She spun to face me as soon as I dropped her to her feet, and her eyes were warm enough to melt my guts to a puddle.

"Not when we have little Fosters running around the place, you won't," she said. "We'll be exhausted."

I couldn't hide the shock at her line of conversation, and she nodded silently as I tipped my head.

"Soon," she continued. "Here if we can save the place, or back home if we can't. I don't care, Brett, just as long as we're together."

Her easiness perplexed me. The idea of losing this place so alien I couldn't stomach it.

"We'll save it," I told her, but she shrugged.

"I hope so, but it's not everything. *We're* everything, you and me. Anything else on top is a bonus."

This wasn't her. Not the woman I'd seen destroying herself over the potential loss these past few months. Her stance was calm and easy, eyes twinkling as they stared up at mine.

It was me who felt the twist of failure. Me who shook my head and gritted my teeth and jabbed a finger toward reception.

"We'll do it," I insisted. "You and me. This is our place. Our legacy."

"Or your dad's," she whispered, softening the blow with a brush of her fingertips down my cheek. "This place was my choice, Brett, but it was his money. I wonder sometimes whether your drive to save this place is more about us or him."

"That's absurd," I snapped, but it was with too much venom.

Her eyes said it all. Her words didn't need to.

"Heath brought more into our lives than fifty grand in the bank," she whispered. "He brought a whole pile of shitty insight along with him. I've been wondering if that's actually been worth more than the money."

"Insight into how not to be a total cunt all your life."

Her smirk was the opposite of the one he wore on his face every fucking opportunity, it was humble and kind. Everything I'd fallen in love with all those years ago.

"Insight into the important things," she countered. "Insight into how lucky we are to have the essentials. I'd never swap our love for his lifestyle. I don't think he'd be able to say the same."

"So, what now? You want to friend the guy? Get him coming down here for weekend breaks and ice cream sundaes? Maybe he can watch the kids while I slam the hell out of your sweet pussy in the room next door?"

She laughed, and so did I.

"Maybe."

"You're crazy," I told her, and I meant it in the very best of ways. "Last week he wanted to destroy us. This week you want him to turn into a childminder."

"My horizons are broadening," she whispered. "Like the other parts of me."

"And how about this evening? Do you think you'll be up to broadening them all over again?"

A wink and another smirk, and if she'd have asked for my heart on a steel platter right then I'd have carved it out gladly.

"Ice cream first," she said. "And then we'll see."

FIFTY SIX

GRACE

He could have ignored my stupid text messages, far away on the sand somewhere. He could have put it down to an idiot hostess attempt and shrugged it off as nothing.

But he didn't.

I couldn't hold back the grin as Thomas Heath appeared in reception with his coat collar high, shrugging off his outer layers without a word as I fought the urge to leap up and down on the spot.

I didn't know what was coming over me. It was bizarre. A seemingly mindless attempt to forge a human relationship with someone inhuman. Yet still, I couldn't stop.

"You couldn't resist the honeycomb temptation," I goaded with a laugh. He didn't laugh back, but he did manage a flash of a smile.

"I couldn't resist the lure of a pretty little pussy, regardless of whether its owner insists on spooning ice cream down my throat."

His words zipped right through me, my pride blooming bright, even though it was little more than a joke.

It didn't feel like a joke.

He couldn't resist. Couldn't resist *me*.

I was still grinning like a fool when Brett stepped on through with a pile of receipts in his hand. He started when he saw our returning guest, raising an eyebrow but offering a nod without any outward sign of bristling.

"You came back for sprinkles, then? Just as well, or she'd have sent a search party down the beach."

"I'll bear that in mind next time I get an invitation," Thomas said back, and it kept my grin at full throttle.

Next time.

I couldn't stop myself wondering how many next times there would be. This week, or maybe another. If there *was* another.

If we'd ever see him once he checked out this second time round.

If he'd run back to the city and never come back.

If he knew us at all. If he ever had.

"I'm not much of a fan of desserts," he told me. "But for you, I'll make an exception."

I didn't recognise my own filthy mouth as it took on a life of its own. "I'm not much of a fan of taking two dicks in an already wrecked body, but for you, I'll make an exception."

Brett was silent for a long moment, and so was Thomas. Both of them staring like I was an alien minx beamed down from the stars.

It was me who laughed first, long and loud, with tears pricking my eyes at the absurdity of this whole situation and how it had changed us all.

"She's quite the siren, your wife," Thomas said, and it set me off all the more.

"She is this week," he replied, and I caught sight of the glint in his eyes.

Their low laughter was the world. Their lust for me was the moon in my sky, pushing and pulling my tides, my whole body reeling with crazy sensations.

Confidence.

It was confidence.

Relief.

Priorities reordered.

Love.

Life.

The excitement of two hot bodies pressed to mine.

It was everything.

And nothing.

The whole universe laughing at itself in my belly.

"I'm sorry," I wheezed, but they didn't make a move to stop me. They were steady, smiling back at me with a hint of puzzlement that tickled me that little bit harder.

And then there were more people there. Guests returning from the beach and finding us hovering there in reception, me lost to words as Brett stepped behind the counter and handled their enquiries about a dinner venue.

I met Thomas Heath's eyes as I swallowed my laughter, and his were bright. Hard. Burning.

His were enough to set me spinning, wanting more of him along with my gorgeous husband.

Not later, but then.

Right then and there.

I forced myself to look away from him and wave away our guests to the pub in the village with a decent semblance of a professional smile. One day I wouldn't be doing that, sending them away to eat elsewhere. They'd be staying right here, no matter if I had to scour the whole world to find someone for our kitchen.

I couldn't risk looking back at Heath, so I didn't. I slipped out from behind the counter and led the way into the dining room, gesturing to my array of pudding supplies with a flourish.

"You really did go all out, didn't you?" our blonde guest said, and I nodded. "Always."

A look passed between the two men that set my heart on fire. It wasn't bitter, nor competitive, simply two men sharing their humour at the zany woman in front of them.

It was perfect.

My fingers were shaking as I dug the honeycomb ice cream from the freezer and attempted the three desserts. I felt like a fool, a total idiot as I slavered on the honey topping, but it didn't matter. All that mattered was keeping the mood right between the three of us as I handed over my creations and pointed to the window seat Thomas chose every morning.

I watched him eat, my knee pressed to my husband's under the table, foot tapping as I weighed up the potential of him casting this off as nothing. Saying my ice cream was shit. Provoking an argument out of nowhere.

He didn't. Neither of them did.

"You can keep the ice cream duties for yourself once you finally manage to snare a decent chef," Thomas said when he was halfway through.

"I can?"

It was Brett who nodded his agreement. "Very nice."

It was preposterous. A couple of scoops of ice cream and a dusting of stupid sprinkles. Just something from a kid's party no matter what kind of mid-afternoon adult treat spin I wanted to put on it.

If only it were the only mid-afternoon treat I had in mind.

I looked at the clock on the far wall. Approaching four p.m., which left a few quiet hours before guests returned and made themselves ready for the bar after dinner. It left a few hours I wanted to fill, and parts of me I wanted to fill with them.

I really was officially crazy, thrumming with desire for something I shouldn't want in a million years, especially not with a man we'd despised in those early days, and who Brett still thought was a blast from the past come back to tear us down.

Still, I couldn't stop. Didn't want to stop.

Getting to my feet was dithery, my sundae spoon clanking against the glass as I gathered up the other empty bowls and retreated to the kitchen to put them ready for the dishwasher.

It was when I pushed back through the kitchen door that I found them shoulder to shoulder in silence, both of them with eyes on mine as I pulled myself up sharp.

We couldn't.

Shouldn't.

My ass was still sore as I clenched it, but my pussy was fluttering through the ache, begging for more.

I really was a slut this week.

"It's afternoon..." I began, risking speaking empty thoughts to nothing if they weren't on my wavelength.

My mind may have been dubious, but my flesh was reading the broadsheet. I knew they were with me, down deep where it mattered.

My feet took an instinctive step backward as my husband made his move. "The reception door buzzes our suite," he said. "It's our most sensible venue."

Most sensible, but most dirty, having Thomas Heath in our own private space. I nodded regardless.

"You mean now? Right now?"

"We ate your ice cream," Thomas rasped, taking a step forward of his own. "I'm with your husband, I think it's about time your pretty mouth returned the gesture."

With your husband.

It was the only hint of camaraderie I'd ever heard uttered between the two of them, and it was more than enough to keep me moving, keep me retreating to my usual space.

I just hoped we wouldn't regret opening our personal doors to someone so determined to break them down.

Our living room was more of a mess than I'd have liked. Clothes draped over the sofa as I retreated through to the bedroom. Luckily, Thomas Heath didn't seem to mind my untidiness, his gaze all on me as he followed me through.

Maybe I shouldn't have taken him through to our most intimate area. Maybe the living room itself would have done. But as I crossed the threshold into our deepest private territory, I knew it was a good call.

It sizzled here.

Burned here.

His presence felt dirty and bursting with life in here.

I was shivering all over as I dropped to my knees on the mattress and both men stepped up to join me.

And my mouth was already open wide for cream number two when they dropped their pants.

FIFTY SEVEN

THOMAS

This was ludicrous.

The Fosters' bedroom should have been a tomb of everything I hated, but instead what I found in there was an intimacy I'd been shielding myself from my whole fucking life.

Their bedsheets were still crumpled from their sleep, bunched under Grace's ass as she stared up at us with eyes starving for cock. Just as well she had two to greet her.

Brett's was out before mine, but only by a heartbeat. It was thick in his hand as he presented it to his wife's open mouth, and mine followed soon after, slapping against her cheek as she sucked him in.

We alternated, feeding her deep as she retched up her ice cream, and it was addictive. She was addictive.

I took her hair in a rough grip, loving the way she mewled at the roughness against her scalp, but instead of forcing her onto my pulsing cock, it was his I guided her to.

"Take it," I grunted. "Take it like a good girl. Show us how much you fucking want it."

She fucking wanted it. Her eyes were wide and needy, flitting between us as she struggled to swallow him down. I couldn't hold back the smirk as her dainty little fingers dipped between her legs, brushing her clit through the denim of her jeans as she wriggled on that tight little butt of hers.

I was going to fuck her hard. So fucking hard. Knowing full well how her ass would protest after the pounding she'd taken just hours earlier. But I didn't care, and neither would she, not when we'd worked her up to desperation, coaxing that screaming little whore right out from inside her and driving her wild.

I'd never felt the need for another man at my side, not by any stretch of my twisted imagination. The potential of Brett fucking Foster adding something positive to my performance would have brought me out in boils just a few days earlier, but then and there it made sense.

He made fucking sense.

His competitive drive, just like mine. His reluctance to give in to his own weakness, no matter what the cost.

The only difference between us was her. More specifically, everything she represented to assholes like us who needed to rule the world.

Love and life. Warm arms. Loyalty.

Trust.

Something greater than we were. Something worth more than all the triumphant battles we'd forced our way into over the years combined.

"Your wife is a dirty little bitch," I commented, and he smirked right back at me, taking the compliment in the way it was intended.

"My wife is greedy for two dicks in her," he said, and she whimpered around his meat.

"Screw your pretty honeycomb sundae," I told her with a smile. "We're going to fill your belly with something much better."

It was Brett who took her chin in his grip and angled her off him. I shifted my stance alongside him as he guided her flapping mouth onto my dick instead.

"Show our fucking guest how fucking welcoming our resort is, Grace," he grunted, and wrapped his fingers around the back of her neck tight enough to shunt her deep. Her throat spasmed around the head of my cock, her wet lips tight to my balls as she spluttered on me.

Her eyes were brimming as she stared up, her fingers a needy flurry between her legs as she rubbed herself.

"Your husband is going to fuck that sore little ass hard enough to make you cry," I snarled, and his palm worked his dick that little bit harder. "But not until you've swallowed us both down like the desperate bitch we know you are."

She sucked in breath as we freed her from my cock, spit dribbling down her chin as she nodded her pretty head.

"Open wide," Brett grunted, and she did, stretching those lips like a beautiful slut and pushing her tongue out all the way. His dick slapped it, hard. Bouncing and thrusting, bouncing and thrusting. He'd learned that from me, but this time the recognition didn't fire me up with spite.

I wasn't expecting him to shoot me a look bordering on conspiracy.

"Think that dirty little mouth can take two?"

It should have shrivelled my dick to nothing, but my balls tightened so hard I thought they'd burst.

"At a stretch," I said, and stuck my fingers in her mouth, tugging her cheek out to the side until she grunted. He followed my moves, taking her lips at the other side and pulling until she was a filthy open hole for a mouth, gummy and disfigured, beautifully grotesque as she fumbled with the zipper on her jeans.

I gritted my teeth as we moved together, blanking my mind out from all reservations as I pushed my cock in that wide open mouth alongside his. She could barely take it, eyes flaring as we shunted in. His dick was a throbbing piece of meat next to mine, but it didn't matter. Her lashing tongue was all that mattered, struggling for room as she gagged and slavered around us.

"Look at your wife," I grunted. "How fucking pretty."

"The prettiest," he said.

It was the messiest fucking blowjob I'd ever encountered. Brutal in its throes, but bizarrely fulfilling. I loved the ridges of dick straining out through her hamster cheeks, the wildness in her eyes as she fought for breath through flaring nostrils.

I'd never have pictured her like this back at high school, not in my craziest dreams, but then again I'd never have pictured any of this.

The surprise was all welcome, my hips thrusting to claim more of her, right along with his.

Dirty little Grace Foster was a delightful vessel for our pleasure seeking. Possibly too delightful. My excitement didn't adhere to my bidding, spiking through me so much quicker than I'd grown used to. But that didn't matter a shit, either. He was right there alongside me, losing his cool at a similar pace, eyes closed as he tried to fight it, his dick twitching the full length next to mine.

"Fill her up," I grunted. "Let's give her a fresh round of dessert before we tear her open."

He didn't need asking twice. His jerks in her mouth said everything and were enough to send me over the edge right alongside him. That sweet dirty mouth took it all without protest, throat bobbing as she struggled to swallow.

She failed.

Thick streamers of cum spewed up as we pulled out of her, splattering her face and chin before she had the barest chance to get herself under control.

Her fingers were in her knickers, twiddling hard, her tongue working to lick up her spilt cream as we stared down at her with twitching cocks in hand.

It was my thumb that gathered up the thick slimy cum trails and pushed them into her mouth.

"Swallow," I said, and she did, showing her empty mouth when she'd smacked her lips.

The girl had watched a lot of porn in her time, that was certain.

"We don't have all night," Brett grunted and pushed her onto her back. "Guests will be heading in for drinks soon enough. You're gonna have to fucking take it."

Her nod was nervous, but it came. Her hands did little to help as he tugged her jeans off from the ankles and tugged her knickers down her thighs with them. I took up position at her other end, freeing her shoulders from her neat blouse and pulling it free. Her cami was easy, up and over her head, her lacy bra along with it. She was naked in a breath, squirming out of her sodden knickers herself and kicking them off onto the carpet.

I loved seeing her like this, naked against our fully dressed composure. I pre-empted Brett's movements and he did the same with mine, working as a passable duo to spread her legs wide open and wrench them high.

Her clit was already dabbling in a pool of its own excitement, her battered cunt clenching her slit into pretty pouty lips that demanded slamming hard. She cried out when I dipped in two fingers, but Brett held her firm.

"Take it," he grunted. "Let him use that slut of a pussy, Grace."

She'd settled in position by the time he retreated from the bed. I barely had the chance to stare after him when he dropped down onto the carpet and pulled their bottom drawer open. I laughed low when I caught sight of the collection in there. Toys on toys. So many it was like a fucking toy shop.

He pulled out an impressive looking vibrator and a chunky dildo to match. I admired his logic, taking the dildo from him with a firm hand and pressing its swollen plastic head tight to her fluttering slit.

I waited until he pressed the vibrator to her clit, her legs thrashing for a moment while he got a grip of her. He held her tight, firm in his arms, countering her wriggling with a strength that suited him.

And then I fucked her. Rammed that plastic fucking dick all the way home inside that slurping wet pussy, and watched her roll with the motions.

She wailed, bucking all the while she adjusted to the stretch, but her clit did its dirty little job and set her alight, her whimpers all hungry as I worked up into a rhythm.

It was when he gripped her harder still, his eyes burning with the undeniable flame of domination, that I realised he'd come to the same conclusions about his sweet wife as I had.

He knew her submissive tendencies with the same certainty I'd come to know them, his hard grip every bit as calculated as he spread her wide for me to fuck her rough.

"Take it," he growled. "Fucking take it, Grace."

She did take it. She took it with whimpers but no protests, not even when he spat on his fingers and reached them round to her battered asshole.

I would have tipped my hat to him if I'd been wearing one, irrevocably impressed by the determination with which he squirmed those digits deep in that raw little hole.

"You're gonna take us both," he hissed to her. "Hard. Fucking hard, Grace, do you understand me?"

He'd seen it in her, just as I'd seen it, slumbering meekly behind the shy smile she'd been wearing a lifetime. And now she was unlocked.

She trembled as she yielded to his will, nodding her head as she let her body move in tune with ours. This sandwich of male flesh would be so much more than the last, I could feel it, *we* could feel us, all of us simmering to the same fucking tune as we rocked and rumbled, and ploughed her sore little holes open anew.

She'd take us both, and when it strained enough to bring tears to her eyes, she'd be begging for more of the same.

I knew it.

He knew it.

And his pretty wife knew it as she gazed up at us with those shimmering whore eyes of hers.

She came like a banshee with that thick fat plug in her cunt and Brett's fingers in her ass. She squealed loud enough that he clamped her mouth closed with his palm, stifling every whimper as her body thrashed like a fish under ours.

And then she squirted.

The little whore fucking squirted all over my hand when I pulled that dong out of her.

She bucked like a bronco, the ripples racing through her as her gaze flicked between us, and I laughed, I couldn't help myself.

The woman had no idea what was happening to her. Nothing that really made sense in that cute little brain of hers.

"Is that–" she began, and my laughter picked up a notch.

"No," I said. "It's not piss."

Her relief was palpable, her giggle rippling through her as she shook her head.

But she wasn't giggling for long.

The stare that passed between Brett Foster and I was counter to every other we'd ever shared. A nod was all it took, from him to me and mirrored back, and I could read him, just the way that he could read me.

And then we grabbed her.

FIFTY EIGHT

GRACE

I had no idea what was happening with my body. Wetness, shivers of excitement bordering on convulsions, my chin sticky with cum and drool, even now after swallowing most of it down like a dirty bitch.

This shouldn't be me. I shouldn't be this woman.

But I was.

And I loved her. Just like they did.

I could see it in them. Both of them. Lust and want and something else. Love from Brett, blazing right through his features, but from Thomas something more than desire. Care. Pride. Affection, even. Stuff that made my heart shudder.

I was too fucked to protest when two sets of strong arms grabbed me up and tossed me like a doll between them. This was new, this shared *thing* they had going on. An unspoken camaraderie which suited them much better than the festering simmer of competition.

I could get used to this, I thought, managing a grin as Thomas raised me high enough to wrap my bandy legs around his waist. That changed in a beat when I slammed down on the cock he'd positioned just right for my still-pulsing pussy.

No, I'd never get used to this. Not in a million years.

I was still burning up, squirming against the sensation as I bucked for more, my arms wrapped so tightly around the neck of this man who'd flipped our world on its head that I'd have sworn I'd never be able to let him go.

And then there was Brett, the man I loved more than the whole universe, pressing tight behind me, breathing into my ear as he pressed his cock to my poor clenching ass.

"Fuck," I whimpered. "Oh, fuck."

I knew it was coming, throwing my head back onto his shoulder as he pushed his way inside.

It hurt. Fuck, how it hurt. But I couldn't stop, didn't want it to stop, craving it more than reason as my heart pounded loud in my ears.

There was nothing like it. Nothing in all the years that could have prepared me for this. Caged between two firm grunting bodies, limp as they pounded me with long, deep thrusts.

Two at once.

I was taking two big dicks at once, without the stability of anything other than the two of them suspending me between them.

I barely knew who I was kissing, one of them, then the other, all my focus on how it felt to be stretched so wide, filled to bursting. Brett's hot mouth was on my neck as Thomas plunged his tongue deep into my mouth, and I loved it, loved both of them.

This wasn't a game for me, not anymore. This wasn't a passing fantasy in the night with my hand down my knickers. This was real. All-consuming in my desire to please them both.

"That's a good little slut," Thomas breathed, and my heart bloomed.

"Fucking take it," Brett snarled, and I did. I took everything they had.

My eyes were springing with tears from the strain, my lungs ragged as I fought the urge to wail out loud, but I was moving with them all the same, sweating cold and hot, mashed against rippling muscle both in front and behind.

"Come for me, please," I cried. "Please come for me."

Thomas licked my open lips before his answered, and his smirk set me on fire.

"Not until you do," he said, and I felt it in them both, the same crazy need to feel me fall apart between them.

It came so much easier than I expected. *I* came so much easier than I expected. My stomach muscles were clenched so tight I feared I'd never stand straight again, every nerve in me spiralling as those two fat cocks slammed in hard. My pussy throbbed raw before the ache of climax found me, that sweet spot deep inside unravelling with a string of sparks that had me convulsing.

My ears were ringing as I heard them grunt along with me, the expletives hissing loud enough to grit my teeth as I cursed like a whore.

I didn't care that my cheeks were wet with tears and likely blooming pink. I didn't care that they'd claimed all of me, likely to leave me a ruined limp mess for all time.

All I cared about was the way they thrusted into me, both of them reaching their peak as I screamed out with mine.

I couldn't think.

Couldn't do anything but hold on tight.

Couldn't stop my body burning up and screaming for more.

Until it was done.

We were done.

They held me so tight, still suspended between them as I strained for breath, and this was the most fucked-up moment of all, feeling so right between two men who'd felt so wrong.

I'm sure I was smiling. I'm sure my words made no sense as they tumbled breathless from my lips.

And I'm sure they were smiling too as they moved together onto the bed and kept me tight between them.

We stayed for an eternity in the cold afternoon light, three bodies breathing and holding, three bodies coming down from a crazy high I'd never known.

It was Thomas who pulled away first, stroking my cheek with a tenderness in his fingertips I'd never felt from him.

Brett folded me further into his arms, nuzzling my neck as I watched the other man get to his feet and retreat to the bathroom.

I wondered if this was it, a beginning of another retreat as he bailed and ditched us high. But no, he came back with a smile on his face and his dick still proud, giving Brett a playful slap on his arm as he passed by on his quest for his clothes.

That playful slap meant everything.

I couldn't hold back the grin at the shift in the room. Coaxing Brett away from me with an urgency from deep. He got it, kissing my neck once more before dragging himself away from me in search of clothes of his own.

It was when he slapped the other man back, right between his shoulder blades, that I knew the page was turning.

"Fuck," he said. "They were some moves."

"Didn't move too fucking bad yourself," Thomas said back, and I sighed happy onto the mattress, well aware that my holes were still weeping all over the sheets.

It was disgusting.

Beautiful and disgusting.

Hot and beautiful and disgusting.

But as I moved afresh, I knew I wouldn't be repeating the experience in a hurry.

Everything hurt. Every single thing.

I laughed as the guys caught my discomfort, clearly visible through my smile. Their arms were right there waiting, lifting me to my feet and keeping me tall until I found my balance, two smirks at full volume as I dithered my way to the bathroom to splash my face with cold water.

My reflection was different in the mirror. My hair slick and messy all at once, my eyes wild and watery, my lips puffy from dicks and kisses.

I couldn't hold back the laughter as I splashed myself cool.

The guys were pretty much dressed when I stepped back in to join them, absorbed in a low grunt of a conversation like two old friends. And that, right there, that was the greatest outcome of all, zinging right through me as I dared to reach for a fresh pair of knickers from the drawer.

Brett dropped to his knees to help me dress, and I watched Thomas all the while my husband guided my body in every which direction.

Thomas looked as different as I felt, his smirk at odds with the asshole I'd come to know these past few weeks. I didn't know what to say, so I didn't, just kept my smile easy on his as he fastened up his shirt cuffs.

"Whisky," Brett announced, when he finished pulling my cami top down over my head. "I think we need a decent shot of whisky."

"Whisky would most certainly be welcome," Thomas agreed, leaning back for a stretch before landing a palm on his stomach. "But first food. I'm ravenous."

That was hardly a surprise and I told him so with a giggle. One honeycomb sundae does not a meal make.

"Help yourself from the kitchen," Brett told him. "Grab whatever you want."

Thomas tipped his head before his exit. "I'm thinking steak. Rare. Fries on the side."

"Go for it," my husband said. "You'll find the butcher's finest in the fridge."

It was only with his hand on the door handle that Thomas glanced back to face us. "How about you filthy pair? Hungry enough to join me?"

My nod was instant, and so was Brett's.

"Steak for three sounds really good," I told him. "We'll be out to join you as soon as I've managed to get myself buttoned up straight."

We watched him leave, saying not a word as the door swung closed behind him. Brett's raised eyebrow was the only communication but it summed up far more than a mouthful of words.

He liked it.

Fuck knows, I think he even liked Heath.

And so did I.

I grabbed my blouse and buttoned it up with still dithery fingers, reaching into my jeans pocket to check my phone was still in place before attempting to clasp up the button.

It was only when I pulled the handset from my pocket that I saw the flash of the message icon. I unlocked the screen with a thumb swipe, not surprised that I'd missed the bleeping in all the double dick action.

My sister. Sarah's name flashed up before the message text. There was more than one. A whole string from the looks of it.

I stopped dead, swearing my heart would pass out on me as I struggled to comprehend the words.

Thomas Heath IS Thomas Browning. My fucking God, Grace. We KNOW him. x

No.

It couldn't be.

We couldn't possibly.

My fingers were shaking to a whole new tune as I called up the next.

Polly Piper knows him. I caught her before she left the bakery for the day and she cried like a baby before she told me the truth.

He's Thomas Browning. No fucking shit. Tina Hadley is his mother.

I felt sick as I clicked for more.

Jesus Christ, Grace, call me. Please call me. x

But I hadn't. Of course I hadn't.

I could barely bring myself to click on the final message. I had tunnel vision as I stared, unable to face so much as glancing at my husband as he adjusted his collar in our full-length mirror.

Thomas Heath's dad was George Foster! Fuck! Tina was with George Foster at Alvington Plastics before he hooked up with Brett's mum. Shit, Grace. Thomas Heath is Brett's stepbrother. His actual stepbrother. I can't even…WTF?! CALL ME! x

I couldn't call her.

I couldn't do anything.

My mouth was open as Brett headed back in my direction, my desire to throw my phone out the window overriding every urge to show him the messages.

But I couldn't not. I daren't not.

I didn't even have the beginnings of reason as he landed a kiss on my cheek and raised an eyebrow.

"What's up with you, Mrs Foster? Two at once left you a little pale?"

The shake of my head was slow. The way I handed over my handset was slower.

His brows knitted as he scanned my screen, and then they loosened, every one of his features going slack with shock as he scrolled up and down.

"This can't be right… my dad wasn't…"

That's when it hit me. What this would mean for Brett's pedestal memory of his dad if this were true.

Brett's dad was a hero beyond fault in his eyes. Beyond the tiniest hint of criticism, no matter what the situation.

"Dad wouldn't have… no fucking way…" His laughter didn't come close to convincing. "There's no way, Grace. If Thomas Browning was my dad's boy he'd have…"

It broke my heart to see the way his eyes darkened as he swallowed.

"I'm calling my mother. She'll set this straight."

His fingers were shaking as they fumbled with my phone keypad, unwilling to even seek out his own mobile before keying in his mum's number.

I reached for him as he put the phone to his ear, but he stepped away, pacing through to the bathroom as his *hello* barked out.

It was when the bathroom door closed that I knew this was really real.

Really, really real.

And it was when I heard him scream out loud that I knew Polly Piper wasn't lying.

FIFTY NINE

BRETT

Thomas Heath wasn't my dad's boy. No fucking chance.

It made no fucking sense, not any of it. Not that Thomas Heath was Thomas Browning from high school. Not that he knew my dad at fucking all.

My dad had been a perfect father, ever since he'd rocked up at our dining table when I was five years old going on six. I remembered it, even now, all these years later. Just like it was yesterday. His smile. The way he ruffled my hair and helped my mum with the dinner plates. The way he patted me on the back when I got top marks for my homework.

The way he was always fucking there. Always. Always urging me to do better, do my best, be a winner.

How could he urge me to be a fucking winner if he had another boy cast aside somewhere else in our fucking town? How could he walk away from his own fucking kid to shack up with someone he barely knew?

I knew he loved my mum. He loved her until the day he died. They were good together. Perfect together.

Yet I knew from way back when that I had to keep away from Tina Hadley. Knew she was trouble. Remembered how my dad's eyes darkened at the mention of her name, Mum's lips pursing as she told me to *stay away from those people*. And by *those people* she'd meant him too.

Thomas Browning.

A kid I only vaguely remembered. Scrawny and pale, blonde hair and thick glasses. Weak and pathetic.

"Brett," Mum's voice sounded out. "What a nice surprise."

But it wouldn't be. It wouldn't be a nice surprise at all.

"Tina Hadley," I barked. "Tell me about Tina Hadley. Who was she?"

The pause was too pronounced. "Why do you want to know about Tina Hadley? Who's been talking about her?"

"Her fucking son is right fucking here, in our fucking hotel!" My voice was too loud and I knew it. Beyond all reason.

And that's how come I knew the truth of it. The truth festering in my gut.

Mum was quiet. Silent as I tried to get myself together.

"Tell me Thomas Browning isn't Dad's boy," I told her, and my voice had a weakness to it I hated.

"Brett–" she began, but I cut her off with a bellow.

"TELL ME!"

She couldn't tell me. Of course she fucking couldn't.

"WHY?!" I boomed. "Why would he fucking do that? Why would he have another kid and never fucking mention it? Never see him? Never say anything?!"

"It's complicated," she said, and I couldn't hold back the bitter laugh that pulsed right through me.

Complicated.

Isn't it always?

"Try me," I snapped, holding my breath until she spoke again.

"Tina was… difficult. Your father's relationship with her was… strained."

"Not strained enough that he didn't knock her up and have a fucking kid with her."

"He didn't know that…" she blustered. "Not at the time… not for years. Tina was… easy… she liked men. Lots of men."

"Is Thomas Browning my dad's fucking son or not?" I demanded.

"He thought so…" she breathed. "By the end, anyway. But not at the beginning, Brett, I promise you. He'd have never left if he'd known…"

It didn't matter.

My head was shaking as I weighed it up, and no matter which fucking way I looked at it, it didn't matter.

Dad had a kid with another woman. He moved in with us and left him behind. Didn't call. Didn't venture fucking near the whole time we were growing up in the same fucking town.

"Why would he do that?" I asked her, hating how weak I sounded. "How could he do that?"

Her sigh was enough to choke me up. "People aren't perfect, Brett. Relationships are complicated. Emotions are complicated. People don't always make the right choices in life."

But *he* did.

My *dad* did.

He was always right. Always strong. Always pushing me to follow in his footsteps. And I'd failed. So many times I'd failed. Never scoring enough goals. Never getting high enough marks. Always nearly. Always well done but better luck next time.

And the whole fucking time he'd slapped my back and told me to *dig deep, son* he'd been nursing the biggest fucking blip of all. Walking out on his own boy without so much as a glance back over his shoulder.

I'd gone to the same school as the son he'd walked out on and I didn't even know it. Didn't question the instructions to steer clear of *those people* because why the fuck would I?

I always did what he said. Always believed in what he believed in.

He was my fucking dad. My. Fucking. Dad.

But he wasn't.

He was Thomas Browning's fucking dad.

And Thomas Browning was in my fucking kitchen cooking steak with my wife's fucking pussy juice still on his fucking dick.

"I'm sorry," Mum said, too little too late. "He was sorry too. He thought about contacting Thomas, weighed it up for years, but Thomas was…"

"Was what?" I snapped. "What was Thomas?"

"Successful," she breathed. "Thomas was very successful. He's very wealthy now. Your father was worried he'd think he was after his money. He wasn't after his money, Brett. He wasn't like that, he just wanted to apologise…"

Fuck, how it hurt.

I was crippled in that bathroom, doubled over, fighting the urge to sick up my bowels through my fucking ribcage.

"There was a letter with the lawyer, part of the will," she went on, like she hadn't said enough already. "We couldn't locate Thomas when the will was read. He'd changed his name several times and his contact details were unavailable. It's still filed at the office downtown. If he's there we should get it couriered."

"A letter?" I wheezed. "A letter for Thomas? From Dad?"

Her sigh said everything. So fucking defeated I wished I could knock myself out and never wake up to this shit again. "Yes, Brett. A letter. I didn't see the point in telling you… not then…"

"We're not done with this," I snarled. "We'll never be done with this, do you understand me? WE'LL NEVER BE DONE WITH THIS!"

I jabbed the screen hard enough with my thumb that the screen turned black, then tossed the handset onto the tiles without two shits for the way it skittered against the shower tray.

I sat on the toilet seat with my palms against my sweaty temples as I struggled to make sense of this whirlwind of shit.

Grace's tap at the door was light when it came. Her voice edged with the same desperation I was feeling.

"Brett, sweetheart, can I come in?"

"No," I said. "Give me a minute."

She didn't.

The handle turned and the door inched open, her fingers curling around the frame before her face peeked around the side.

"I'm sorry," she said. "I just…"

I'd never been so grateful for my Grace as I was when she saw my despair and sprang into life. Her arms were everything I needed, holding me tight as she pulled my face to her chest and smothered me in all the love I'd need to breathe a single breath.

"You didn't know," she whispered. "This isn't your fault, Brett. Not any of this."

Getting to my feet was the hardest thing I'd ever done in my life, but it was just the tip of the fucking iceberg.

Facing Thomas Browning was still to come.

SIXTY

THOMAS

I'd never cooked for other people before. It was a surreal realisation as I fired one of the Foster's big griddle pans up in their kitchen and prepared to slap on three steaks.

It'd been a long fucking time since I'd done something with the genuine desire to please people rather than tear them down. It felt strangely good. Alien in its attraction.

So did the pride at Brett's slap on my back and the knowledge that for once in this sorry lifetime we'd worked together instead of at odds.

I tried to keep a hold of my thoughts, reminding myself with that same bitter chill as always that we were still enemies for all intents and purposes, but I didn't believe it. Not with the same gut-wrenching spite I'd been carrying on my shoulders through living memory.

There was an easiness at the prospect of an evening in the bar with a whisky in my hand. An appeal to flowing conversation that I'd never experienced.

The steaks were cooking nicely when I heard the creak of a door to my right, my smile brighter than I'd have imagined when the bulk of him stepped into view.

It disappeared in a pulse of shock, shrivelling up the moment I saw the expression of dread on his face.

I fought it anyway, gesturing to the griddle pan with my spatula as he stepped on into the room. Grace was at his rear, her face wracked with the same gaunt horror as they stopped a few paces from my side.

"I hope you're hungry," I bleated regardless.

"I'll never be fucking hungry again," Brett said, and I cursed the fucking world for my ridiculous sliver of optimism.

It was instinct that saw me turn the hob flame to nothing and brace myself for the carnage. I didn't fully appreciate what was coming until his words knocked me sideways.

"Browning," he said. "Why didn't you fucking tell us?"

My teeth were gritted long before I met his eyes with mine. "Because it's not my fucking name anymore." My pause was long enough for the spite to choke back up. "And because it's none of your fucking business."

I wasn't expecting the way he shunted me, knocked off balance by his sheer bulk as he charged me back through their kitchen and slammed me into the wall. "My fucking dad's every bit of my fucking business," he snarled.

My hands rose up between us in a breath, shunting him back with as much strength as I could summon from the weaker position. It was enough to push him off me, and there we stood, stare burning stare.

"He wasn't your fucking dad," I spat, hating myself for the way his shoulders sagged at my words. "He was *my* fucking father, you were just his chosen fucking son. I bet that fills you with fucking pride, doesn't it? Knowing you were the better boy. The better son. The better fucking man."

"He *was* my dad," he spat back. "I didn't know you fucking existed.

There's no fucking pride here. None. Not one fucking bit."

Grace was at his arm before he spoke another word, her touch solid as she reached for his hand and clenched it in hers.

"What the fuck are you doing here?" he said, and there was a desperate twinge to his voice.

It made me feel like fucking death.

"I didn't manage to prove to the old man that I was worth a shit jot more than being his substandard cast off. Proving it to you was the next best thing."

His fist slammed the wall at the side of my head. I didn't flinch, my eyes firm on his as he choked on his disgust.

"This is bullshit," he hissed. "You thought it would make you a big man to come down here and rip me and Grace apart? You thought that would make you feel so much fucking better, did you? Like that makes you a fucking man?"

I despised how ridiculous my logic sounded from his mouth. Not least because it *was* fucking ridiculous. The whole concept of proving one-upmanship after a lifetime of inferiority by fucking someone's wife in front of them seemed a pitiful initiative when it was under such a vile spotlight, my insides shrivelling all over again to realise I was still the sad, bitter little cunt who'd festered his way through high school.

"I should leave," I muttered, heading for the door without a care for how pathetic a weasel the retreat would make me.

It was Grace who reached out for me and wrapped her arm in mine. "No," she said, surprisingly firm for such a delicate little creature. "Not now. Not this time. Nobody's going anywhere."

I couldn't watch as Brett Foster lost his shit and threw the griddle pan from the hob. It crashed into the sink with a clatter, the meat still spitting as it landed.

I had no words as he bellowed aimlessly, his hands in his hair as he stumbled along the worktop.

"Go through to the bar," Grace whispered. "Please."

I should've made a run for it, straight out to my waiting car before they'd got the chance to come after me, but I didn't.

I pressed my back to the wall in the dining room, breathing deep as the world caved down around me. Their voices were loud in the other room, but I couldn't keep a track of them. There was only my own crazy train of thoughts, hate and spite, regret, fear. The curled up wreck of the boy deep inside.

My move to the bar was slow and laboured, the world spinning all around me as I dropped myself down on a stool and waited for whatever was coming my way.

I didn't even look behind me as the minutes ticked by, praying to a God I didn't believe in that the bar would stay empty long enough for the Fosters to take whatever action they deemed necessary.

I heard Brett's footsteps loud when they came, bracing myself for a blow that didn't land on me. He threw himself through the hatch to the other side, grabbing hold of a whisky bottle and taking a swig right from the neck before reaching for a pair of shot glasses and shunting one in my direction. The amber nectar splashed all over the bar top as he poured us full glasses.

My fingers were shaking as I raised mine to my lips, knocking it back in one as he did, only to have him refill it straight after with another.

I held back on downing this one, but he didn't.

"My mum said yours was a slut," he barked, and if he expected argument he wasn't getting any.

"Yes, she was."

"Dad didn't think you were his."

My smirk was bitter as fuck at that. "I'm sure the truth would have occurred to him as the years passed by. I look very little like my mother."

"You look very little like my fucking dad, either," he snapped, but he was lying on that front. It wasn't blatant, but it was there. Our narrow shoulders, our high cheekbones, colouring. I'd seen enough of it, even growing up, to know the truth.

"I thought he'd acknowledge my existence if I could only be good enough," I admitted, even though it twisted in my gut. "You didn't exactly make it easy for me. Every corner I turned you were always ahead, always winning, always loud and brash and proud as a pig in shit."

"Because he pushed me to be," he snarled, flashing Grace a desperate glare as she dropped herself onto a stool at my side. "Because he believed in me. Because he was always there, always asking for my best, always demanding." It hurt as he said it, me as well as him. "I'd be nothing without him. I'm everything I am because he made me this way."

"And so am I," I spat. "I'm everything I am because he made me this way."

The truth was an irony that rocked me to my core. Both of us sitting here, ruined by a dead man, both in such different ways it was laughable.

"He can't have known," Brett hissed, still fighting the obvious. "There's no fucking way he could have known."

"I was always right there," I told him. "We were in the same fucking town. I saw you every fucking day. Saw him at every fucking school sports game, hoping that would be the one he met my eyes."

He tossed another whisky back and I managed a sip of mine.

"You wanted to destroy me," he said, and I didn't deny it.

"I wanted to destroy everything."

"That would have made you feel better, would it? Taking everything away from me?"

I shrugged. "I don't know anymore. I don't think I ever really did."

My honesty seemed to do something to him, his eyes widened just a fraction, his jaw giving an almost imperceptible nod. "I don't think either of us knew shit."

I didn't argue with that.

There was no fire in me spitting to compound his pain to match my own. No fight left inside to prove some ridiculous point that I was worth something.

I felt worthless sitting there, not because I was a kid who struggled to amount to anything back before it meant anything, but because I'd lived a life meaning nothing through all the years following.

The money meant nothing. The businesses meant nothing. The marriages I'd ruined meant nothing.

I'd learned it here, in the place I'd come to claim my ultimate crown. I'd learned it in Grace Foster's warm arms and in the slap on the back her husband had finally blessed me with. In this quiet cove and the quiet love of the two people building their dreams.

I wasn't prepared for the pain of his next statement. It hit so hard my shoulders buckled over the bar top, my fingers white around the whisky glass as I fought the undulations.

"We could've been brothers."

"Brett," Grace started with a voice dripping with pain.

I dragged my eyes to the man across the counter, reeling with every cell in my fucking body to find him as ruined as I felt. He was barely standing, doubled over with his arms braced on his thighs.

"You could've fucking told me," he continued. "Am I really such a cunt that you'd rather ruin my fucking life than tell me the fucking truth?"

I shrugged at that. "You weren't exactly approachable when I knew you first time around."

His spite was fully justified. "I was just a fucking kid when you knew me first time around."

"And so was I."

I was barely aware of Grace's fingers coming to rest on my arm. "You're really Thomas Browning," she whispered. "I remember you. I remember you in the school corridors with Polly Piper."

I wouldn't have believed the despair could have reached a higher level, but the mention of Polly's name took it there.

"I'm surprised you remember anything of me, Grace. You barely had a glance for me back then, much less a cognisant memory."

"When were you going to tell me?" Brett grunted, and I opted for the truth for once.

"I wasn't. I was going to take your wife and leave you on your knees, trusting that would prove for once and for all that I was the better man."

His laugh was empty. "You think stealing someone's wife makes you a better man?"

"I did."

"That's an asshole move," Grace said, her fingers still resting on my sleeve. "And I'd never have left Brett. Not in a million years. No matter how many times you made me come with your fancy finger work."

My smile was all real as I looked at her. "That's what I've grown to realise, yes."

"So why did you come back this time around? Why did you stay?" Brett questioned, and I shrugged all over again.

"I wish I knew."

"That's bullshit," he snapped. "You're the kind of guy who knows what shape his shit's gonna be before he squeezes it out. Don't fucking tell me you don't know what the fuck you're doing here."

And it was bullshit.

The whole fucking thing was bullshit, and I was done.

"Because I found something," I admitted. "Here. I found something here. Something real. Something that made me believe in something." I waved my stupid words away with my hand, but Grace reached out and took it in hers.

"Don't do that," she whispered. "Don't toss it away like it's nothing. It's not nothing."

I closed my eyes but still I could feel his burning into me as he spoke. "We could've been fucking brothers."

"Please," I hissed. "Please don't say that."

"But it's true," he said. "We could've been fucking brothers. We could've been drinking here as two men who gave a shit about each other. Two men from the same fucking stock, even if it was fucked up in the first fucking place."

"We're not from the same stock," I told him, but it was his turn to shrug.

"Not genetically, no. We're nothing alike. Not one fucking bit. But I'm my dad's boy, raised by a man who pushed me to be the best. And you're his actual blood, born with the urge to be the best, just like he fucking was. You're from blood, I'm from the man. Makes no fucking odds, we could still be fucking brothers."

I didn't have a response for that, so I knocked back my whisky.

"This is crazy," Grace sighed, and she wasn't lying.

"I should go," I said, despite having no urge to go anywhere, no matter what the shit storm.

That was the cold, hard reality outside of this one. I had nowhere to go. Nowhere worth anything.

Brett's finger jabbed through the air in my direction. "You're not fucking going anywhere."

"Please don't," Grace added, and I could have died right there in front of them.

"I don't understand," I managed, my words coming out like bursts of pain. "Why don't you want me gone?"

Brett was pouring me another shot before he answered, and his voice was bursting with pain when he responded, just like mine.

"Because you may be a cunt," he said. "But you're still my fucking brother."

I heard Grace suck in breath as I swallowed the burning lump in my throat.

"I mean it," he added. "I lost my fucking dad, I'm not losing his fucking son, too. Not when I'm just growing to like the sonofabitch."

I'd never cried in front of another soul. Not since Polly Piper all those years ago when she glimpsed me at my worst.

But I cried now.

SIXTY ONE

GRACE

I put a *do not disturb* sign on the bar door, and luckily we didn't get any guests knocking that night.

Both men were hunched over the bar top for the early part of the evening, the man I'd known as Thomas Heath looking nothing like Thomas Heath as he cried big sobbing heaves that took his breath.

Brett wasn't far behind him, I'm sure, but he held his composure remarkably well, every inch the elder of the pair as he reached out a firm hand to grip the younger man's shoulder. I struggled to piece together what any of this really meant, so I kept my distance, there but not there, making my presence known without pushing in too hard on their working things out time. I hoped they could work things out. Even though the whole mess was a result of one man's desire to ruin the pair of us in the name of pride,

I still clung on to the hope that the bones of something half decent could be salvaged from the carnage.

My body was still aching hard from taking them both as I finally accepted a glass of white from my husband. I was close enough to Thomas that I could hear his shallow breathing as I sat beside him. I took his fingers in mine, daring to squeeze hard enough that he looked across at me.

"Please stay," I said, "at least for tonight."

"I'm not used to this," he replied, a ghost of a smile on his mouth. "People normally want me gone, unless they want my dick in them."

My own smile was a lot brighter than his. "I've been very happy to have your dick in me, but that isn't why I want you to stay. I think I'm done with two dicks for a while."

"Grace," Brett said with a grimace, and I cursed myself for too much too soon.

I was still adjusting to the idea that Thomas was George Foster's biological son, and therefore, in some fucked-up way, Brett's stepbrother. I guess that made the whole threesome situation utterly gross on some level, but I'd be lying if I said I felt it.

The only thing I'd come to feel was delight between the two of them, fucked-up or not.

Tom's eyes on mine conveyed that he was feeling on my wavelength, and that made sense to me. He'd never had a family, not one that meant anything. His relationship with his mother was clearly strained at best, and the string of stepfathers after his dad left had obviously amounted to nothing decent.

Brother, stepbrother... none of it meant much to him.

But it meant everything to Brett. I could see it in his eyes as he weighed up the other man with this revelation in mind. Hurt and confused and hopeful all compounded into one strange expression.

I knew Brett missed his father. I knew he was struggling every day of his life to live up to his legacy. To be confronted by a biological relation to the man he'd loved so dearly was more than enough to set his senses reeling. I found myself wondering if they ever stood a chance to find steady footing again.

"Why the name change?" I said aloud to Thomas, eager to keep the communication flowing.

"Why *not* the name change?" he replied. "None of my mother's surnames meant anything to me. Hadley, Browning, Smith, Jones, Weston. Who gave two shits? They never lasted."

"What about Heath?" I asked. "Why Heath?"

I felt his smile in my belly. "He was the only one I cared for, Gareth Heath. He tried hard with me, told me I could call him dad one day when I was ready."

"What happened to him?"

His smile dried up in a beat. "Mother fucked someone else, of course. Some piece of shit from the local pub. Gareth wanted to give it another go even then, but she told him to get his stuff together and leave. I heard her talking to one of her whore friends about him later, saying he had a tiny dick and didn't know what to do with it. I made the decision from that point that I'd make it my mission in life to prove to slutty women there was more to a man than his sexual prowess, or destroy them in the process."

I couldn't deny his logic. His brain was one of reason, his methods devoid of all emotion but laced heavily with the strategy of some deranged genius.

I was very glad to have been the slutty woman to have proved him wrong. Though I wasn't a slutty woman really. Not even passable as one. There was only Brett for me in heart and soul, and always had been.

Brett and the fifty grand needed to save our life together.

The men were drunk on whisky when we finally said our goodnights, and I wasn't far behind them.

There was an awkward moment as we got the lights and headed to the doorway, all of us hovering between the route to our private quarters and the staircase upstairs.

It was Thomas who made the call for us, and I was glad of it.

"I'll see you for breakfast," he said. "Not too early."

"Breakfast," Brett confirmed, his expression strong and constant as Tom reached out a hand for a handshake.

Tears sprang up in my eyes as my husband used the grip to pull Thomas forward into a man hug, his palm firm on the other man's back as he bid him a good night.

I could only nod and smile so as not to cry, wrapping him in a hug of my own that found him rigid against me.

Time. It would take time to unravel all of this.

I tried to choke my emotions back for the sake of Brett's as we washed up for bed together.

We were lying in bed in the darkness when he sighed and hugged me tighter.

"He's my brother, Grace."

"Stepbrother," I said. "That you're only just getting to know."

"But still, he's my brother. My dad's boy."

My fingers stroked his forearm. "And we'll take it one day at a time," I offered. "We need to see how this falls together, Brett. It's still so early."

I knew what was brewing before he said it.

"This thing with the three of us. We can't…" He took a breath. "How can we…"

I shook my head against his shoulder. "Don't think about that now," I told him. "It doesn't matter. None of that matters now."

But it did matter. I could still feel them both inside me, aching both at the thought of doing it again, and at the thought of never feeling Tom's naked body next to mine from this point on.

I was grateful when sleep found Brett, swallowing him up with the same easy breathing I'd come to depend on for my own.

I was less grateful when the hours ticked on ahead and I was still staring at the ceiling, still reeling from the heartache of finding out the man I'd fucked for money was my husband's stepbrother.

It was the most natural thing in the world to slip out of bed and step up to the window, even if I ached every step.

It was also becoming the most natural thing in the world to find the man I'd known as Thomas Heath standing out on the front smoking a cigar.

I guess it made it a triple whammy that it was becoming the most natural thing in the world to step out and join him, too.

SIXTY TWO

THOMAS

I didn't want to leave. I didn't want to get in my car and drive away from this place, not even now, as the Fosters' world churned raw around me.

I felt her there before I heard her, the touch of her fingers becoming too familiar as they slipped in the crook of my elbow.

"I'm sorry you had a rough start," she told me, and although the words were nothing more than a dab of sherbet on something thoroughly grotesque, I had no doubt she meant them.

"I watched you for years," I admitted. "You and him, hand in hand like you owned the world."

If she was taken aback she didn't show it. "You seem to think we had it all. It really wasn't as glamorous as all that. We were just two people loving each other. We still are."

I breathed in cigar smoke as I weighed up the truth in her words, feeling like a fool all over again for my idiot goal to tear them down.

"I didn't believe it existed," I admitted. "Love, I mean. It seemed a desperate concept for lonely people too weak to stand alone."

"And like I told you before," she said. "That's a very sad way of looking at the world."

"You'll note I used past tense," I pointed out, and couldn't hold back a smirk amidst the crazy.

"Noted," she said, and her grin in the moonlight was enough to take my breath. "I'm glad we gave you that insight."

We stared at the sea with her arm through mine. I felt rooted to the spot, unable to tug her closer despite the intimacy we'd shared, but unwilling to let her go, holding off the point I'd have to face my own isolation all over again.

"Do you want to be his brother?" she asked, and I admired her bluntness.

"I'm not sure what I want," I admitted. "I wasn't expecting to enjoy what we've shared nearly as much as I have."

"I think we could all say the same."

I didn't doubt it. The connection between all of us was alive, even if somewhat deranged.

"It'll be hard for him," she continued. "He loved his dad so much. The guy was on a pedestal, could do no wrong."

"It'll be hard for all of us," I said, then took a breath. "But especially him, yes. He has a concept of family vulnerable to breaking, as do you. I wasn't blessed with the same luxury."

"But you could be," she whispered as a wave crashed below. "You could be blessed with the same luxury, if you'll hang around, let him find his family in you."

My laugh was barely more than a rasp as I tossed my cigar over the railings. "We've shared your pussy, Grace. I'm not sure that's the best precursor to sharing a brotherly bond."

She didn't argue with me.

"About that," I continued. "I'm not sure we'll be able to forget it ever happened, no matter what family bridges we try to construct from nothing."

She didn't argue with that either.

"I'm tired," she said, and squeezed my arm. "You must be too. Please walk me back up to the porch, I'm aching like stink and at least fifty percent of that is your fault."

The little minx in her was still burning bright, no matter the oil slick we were drowning in.

It was my pleasure to walk her up to the porch, and my pleasure to land my lips on hers with a whisper of goodnight.

As I turned away from her and retreated to my own bedroom, I wondered whether that would be the last time I'd ever taste her.

And as I slipped between the sheets into a cold, empty bed, it worried me that – in spite of everything past and every potential future on offer – I hoped it wouldn't be.

I'd grown to enjoy the touch of a woman like Grace Foster far too much to let her go.

Which made it likely we were all fucked. All three of us and our dirty pleasures, not least if Brett Foster was my new brother.

Because I had more than an inkling I was falling in love with his wife.

SIXTY THREE

BRETT

Mum tried to call me ten times over that next morning. I didn't pick up. I had nothing to say. Not then and likely not for a long while to come, having more than enough shit to sift through on my own without her adding a fresh pile on top.

My wife and I were picking at a late breakfast with my new blonde brother just about as merrily as possible when the courier stepped through the reception doorway and pinged the bell.

My heart dropped through the floor as I signed for the package, knowing full well what the fuck was likely to be waiting inside.

I wasn't prepared for my dad's handwriting on the letter when it dropped free of the document wallet. I was also unprepared for the way Heath's eyes widened as he clocked the scene.

"Mum said it was left for you," I explained as I handed it to him with uncharacteristically shaky fingers. "In the will, I mean. They couldn't find you, with the name change."

"I doubt they tried particularly hard," he said, and I'm sure that was the truth of it.

All three of us stared at the envelope in his hands as he turned it over and over.

The writing was a familiar scrawl, close enough to home that it choked my breath.

Tom.

Not even Thomas. Just Tom.

"I'm not entirely sure I'm ready for this," he said, and I offered up my hands.

"It's your gig," I told him. "Between you and him, whenever you're ready."

I felt a godawful mix of sadness and relief as he slipped the unopened letter into his inside pocket.

"I'm going to head out for a walk," he said. "I must at least attempt to clear my head a little. Care to join me?"

Grace slipped her hand over mine before I could consider my answer. "Elaine's here for the laundry," she told me. "We could go for a few hours. Catch some sea air."

I shrugged, resigning myself to continue bobbing along on these crazy waves we were riding.

"Sure," I said. "Let's do it."

We did do it. Wrapped up tight against the morning chill with Grace's hand in mine as we made our way slowly down the beachfront and around the craggy outcrop. Thomas was surprisingly relaxed given everything he must be feeling with that envelope burning through his pocket. He kept his eyes high on the cliffs and his smile as easy as I'm sure he could muster.

I choked everything back in my bid to keep putting one foot in front of the other, and eventually, after what felt like miles of steady rhythm on sand, I finally began to feel it.

Calm.

The permanence of the sea, crashing on a constant loop against the shore. Grace's fingers warm in mine, her steps falling into sync with every move I made, on instinct from years at my side.

And now there was him too. Right by us. His steps in tune with ours along the coast. Here with us, from nowhere, a stranger with enough money to tempt us into the craziest decision of our goddamn lives. A stranger who wasn't a stranger.

He was my brother.

My fucking brother.

I couldn't stop looking at Grace looking at him. Her eyes were on him as often as they were on me, her expression muted but optimistic, eyes bright with the prospect of what lay ahead – of what *could* lay ahead – even though it made my gut lurch.

We'd developed a vague measure of boyish respect, him and me. Like a rival turned good on the sports field, only it wasn't a sports field, it was my wife's pretty pussy and he'd been scoring along with me.

And it was different now.

It should be different now.

No more. Not ever again. A line so red in the fucking sand it should blow away his dickish sensor and everything it stood for a million times over. This one was firmer, deeper. Red from blood and pain, and a relationship that should never cross that sordid line ever a fucking gain.

So, why did I still want it so fucking bad?

He pointed up to a little white pub on the clifftop and I gave a nod. The walk up was brisk enough that it pumped my blood hard through my veins, and through my dick with it. Realising I was thinking about him on her as we stepped over the threshold of the place was enough to turn my stomach. It wobbled and lurched, bacon and eggs mashing into a vile soupy mess in my gut.

I retreated to the gents with a clipped smile on my face, barging into the cubicle before retching my breakfast straight up into the bowl.

My balls were aching, wanting to share my beautiful wife's holes with him all over again, my face burning as I retched up so hard there was nothing left to spew. This was fucked. *We* were fucked.

I flushed the cistern when I heard the creak of a door beyond the flimsy little box partition I was in, praying he wouldn't hear my discomfort, if it was indeed Heath coming calling.

"That walk upset your stomach?" he called out as the stream of his piss sounded out in the cubicle next to mine.

"Something like that," I grunted, and he sighed before he flushed.

I met him at the basins, both of us staring at the mirrored wall tiles and not each other.

"Your wife still makes me hard," he told me, and I visibly fucking flinched.

"I can't deal with that," I blurted. "Not today, Heath, not today."

"She does," he said. "And that isn't going to change, not today, not tomorrow, nor the day after."

"We'll figure it out," I insisted, but his smirk spoke volumes.

"I should go. For definite, before this shit really does rear its head," he said, but I shook mine.

"Don't start that same old shit up," I told him. "You're not going anywhere until we know where we're fucking at."

"Where we're at, is a pub a few miles from your place, with your pretty wife walking between us and thinking about taking us both in her wet little cunt. Where we're at, is you vomiting your breakfast up because your balls are tense for another round and you're picturing me as your brother. Your brother fucking your wife."

"Where we're at, is a brand new fucking page," I insisted. "And we'll figure out what's fucking written on it, alright?"

I slapped his arm and he groaned as he shook his hands in the basin. "If you insist."

I did insist, not least because I didn't know what else to do.

Grace was waiting by the open fire in the main seating area when we headed back through, a large glass of white in front of her and a smile on her face. Two pints were waiting on the bar top for us, the place deserted aside from the three of us in our high-buttoned jackets and the barman reading the morning paper on the counter.

I placed my hand on Grace's knee as I joined her on her comfy bench, and Thomas sat down the other side from her, his own knee so close to hers they were virtually touching as he leaned forward. He drank half of his beer down with a sigh of relief, and I did the same, thanking my blessings for alcohol and the distraction it offered in this space.

We could do the same at our place, hang out in the bar over a mountain of whisky, but it wouldn't last forever. Wouldn't even last the full week out before Grace was flashing the eye and wanting more all over again, even if she didn't realise she was doing it.

"Tom," she said out loud. "Can we call you that?"

He tipped his head. "I guess you can call me whatever seems fitting, given that the goalposts have moved."

The goalposts weren't even on the same fucking field.

"Tom," I said. "Cheers."

He raised his glass to mine, as did Grace.

It was the most awkward toast of my life, my gut unsettled for a second round before I'd even downed the rest of it.

But this time I couldn't call another bathroom retreat, not with two pairs of eyes right on mine. I was forced to deal with it, brush it off with a smile I didn't feel and get to my feet at the earliest opportunity.

"Let's go," I said, and the new dynamic was set, so much fucking different from the old one.

Both of them sprang into action, following my lead. Heath without so much as an empty sneer in opposition to my leadership.

That's when I knew it, for sure. I really was the older brother. The one who would take the lead in decision making. In us. In her. In governing every fucking mess we'd likely land ourselves up in while trying to make it out of this sorry state.

It was the most natural thing on earth to sling my arm around my wife's shoulder as we dropped back down to the beach. And the most natural thing on earth for her to reach out for the man she'd grown accustomed to taking along with me.

I fought the urge to retch all over again as she took his hand. And he saw it. He must have fucking seen it.

His smile was bright but false as he dropped her grip and held back his footsteps to lag behind.

Digging the envelope from his pocket was the perfect illusion. Pretending he needed space was the only way we'd have walked on by without protest.

"Give me a few minutes," he told me, and I nodded, tugging Grace along right after me.

"Take all the time you need," I said.

SIXTY FOUR

THOMAS

I watched them walk away, hand in hand. Both of them glancing back over their shoulders until they were out of view.

The letter was burning, and so was the thought of them. The thought of where this was going. The man I could be, with them at my side.

And her.

Polly.

The thought of her was enough to burn me alive from the inside out.

I'd always been a man of strategy, of surveying the whole board before I contemplated my next move. And so I did, seeking out the nearest piece of rock on the beach and taking a seat, staring out to sea. I turned that letter over and over, my heart in my throat as I wondered what words would be in there to greet me after so many years of silence.

Maybe the angry ramblings of a man as lost to me as he'd ever been. Maybe the rant of a father who'd never wanted to know the boy he'd turned away from all those years ago.

Or maybe something else.

Something I daren't even hope for.

I finally plucked up the courage to tear into the seal with a vicious thumb, my jaw gritted as my heart pounded hard.

It was handwritten, the scrawl dancing before my eyes before I focused on the greeting.

Dear Tom

And so I read it. Page to page in a blur of heartache and tears, my breath barely rasping as I struggled to comprehend the meaning in those words.

It was nothing like I'd ever imagined. More than enough to bring me to my knees on that quiet beach with the Fosters heading into the distance.

My whole life spun before my eyes, every bitter decision I'd ever made crumbling to pieces and freeing the boy and his weakness and his tears to wail at the sky. The wind was a sting against my face, the spray from the waves dampening my cheeks along with the wetness from my eyes.

I knew it then and there, in that desolate heart of mine still reeling, that my life should have been so much more and so much less all at once.

No amount of money would cushion the blow of love denied. No amount of businesses fractured to shards would have healed the shards inside.

And no amount of marriages ruined would have been enough to convince me that I'd missed nothing but broken promises.

The afternoon was dulling as I ventured back up that beach, the light from the Fosters' porch a beacon in the fading day. They were waiting with edgy smiles as I stepped into the bar to join them, a whisky waiting on the bar top before I'd even taken a pew.

They didn't ask, not either of them. No questions and no prying, just the well-meaning stares of two people I'd hated more than all reason just a few short weeks ago.

I drank my whisky and passed the time of day with nothing but small talk, which they ate up gladly.

Talk of movies, and old holidays and their life back home back when they lived it in parallel to mine. Laughter about old teachers and recounting of Brett on the sports field, none of it filling me with spite as it had done for as long as I'd known.

And then, finally, as those other few residents around us drifted upstairs for the night, our own goodnight loomed loud in the air between us.

Only tonight I didn't want to wave them off at the stairs. I wanted to be with Grace. Sharing the same closeness I'd come to rely on like air these past few days. Now possibly more than ever.

She saw it in me, I know she did, those eyes so similar in colouring to mine seeking out my gaze with a delicate smile on her pretty lips.

I watched her squeeze Brett's fingers once he'd got the lights and dipped under the bar hatch, her grip conveying so much unspoken as his stare mashed with hers.

"I think we all need a port in the storm tonight," she told him, and I felt his reluctance, every cell wavering at the prospect of closeness with a man whose relationship to him he was still trying to decipher.

I felt it too.

And Brett knew it.

But more than that I felt the need for another human body pressed to mine. The warmth of someone's arms.

Of Grace.

And of him alongside her. Loving her as hard as I could. Harder than I ever could.

"No dicks," he grunted, and it brought a grin to my face and a laugh alongside it.

"Fine by me," I said. "We'll keep it PG13."

It was the strangest bliss in the world to follow them through to their room, pulling off my clothes so easily as they got ready for bed with their bathroom door wide open. I daren't venture upstairs for my own supplies, choosing instead to throw myself into the moment when Grace appeared back in front of me with her pretty tits still in her lace push up bra.

My cock was hard in my boxers, my balls tight enough to blow at a simple touch, but she was careful, wrapping me in arms that gave me what I needed without tipping me over the edge.

Brett was already between the sheets when she led me around to her side, sliding in ahead of me and coaxing me in after her.

"This isn't sex," she breathed, for his benefit, I'm sure.

It wasn't sex. It was a tangle of limbs and her body heat at my side, her fingers against my shoulder as they stroked my skin along with her breath.

I'd never done this. Not once.

Never shared a bed with another body for anything other than cold, hard fucking.

I thought sleep would be impossible, nothing like the wave that washed right over me. His breath was steady before mine, deep as the mattress shifted under all three of us and he rolled into his wife, his arm landing across the full breadth of her tiny ribs and landing right on mine.

He didn't pull away, and neither did I.

"Sleep," she whispered, and I nodded in the darkness.

For once I did what I was told. Without question, without deeper motives.

The sleep that found me there was the best sleep I'd ever had.

But the dreams, of words and memories and that letter I'd read so desperately on the empty beach that afternoon.

They were the best of all.

SIXTY FIVE

BRETT

I knew what she was doing. I knew her logic was selfless, splitting herself between two men who'd come to crave her. Offering herself without restraint, between them both and her bid to make them whole.

But it wouldn't work.

Not here and now, not anymore.

It didn't stop me wanting it. Didn't stop me thinking about it. Didn't stop me waking with my heart in my throat at the realisation all over again that I had a brother. A real fucking brother. Made of the same flesh and bone as the man I'd looked up to more than anyone in my whole fucking life.

My dick was hard at the memories of that same flesh and blood boner fucking my beautiful wife until she screamed, but my gut was reeling afresh as I kicked my feet out of the covers and left them a tangle of sleepy limbs as I retreated to the bathroom and pushed that squeaky fucking bolt closed.

And there I stayed. For way too long. Contemplating moves that made no sense, doomed every which way I looked at them.

I wouldn't ask him about the letter, not now and not ever. He could tell me when he was ready, or never at all, and that was his call to make. His secret to keep.

But it pained. It fucking pained that the last words ever heard from my dad – our dad – were for his ears and not mine.

I choked back the bitterness as soon as it came up.

I'd had plenty of words from my fucking dad. The least Tom deserved was a couple of scrappy pages almost three years after I said my goodbyes at his deathbed.

Grace slammed her palm against the door as I was wiping my ass.

"Brett? Are you coming out?"

I forced a laugh. "Jeez, sweetheart, give me a second, will you? I doubt that brother of mine wants to smell my crap first thing in the morning."

I hoped it was convincing, but I doubted it. I blew my nose loudly enough that they'd hear it, shuffling about the place like this was a regular morning ritual, even though she'd know it wasn't.

"Brett?" she called again, and I pressed my mouth to the door.

"Go ahead to breakfast," I told her. "I'll be a few."

"Fine," she said. "I'll get Tom to help me. Take your time."

It hurt as much as everything else of late, the idea of them laughing over a fry-up together, an idea that was both beautiful and disgusting all at the same time.

That about summed up this whole sorry affair – both beautiful and disgusting.

Disgusting were the thoughts still tumbling in as I jerked my hard cock in my fingers and screwed my eyes shut in search of a mental blankness which wouldn't come.

I wondered if he was feeling it too, that same disgust. But I doubted it. He'd known the truth all along. The truth about a brother he'd been missing since we were kids. A brother who didn't so much as glance at his scrawny ass through our school years.

Too late. It was much too late for that.

I came with a hiss of breath, spurting cum all over my hairy belly and wiping it down with a tissue and a groan.

This couldn't go on. Not in this halfway land of shadow and torment.

We were either all in, or we weren't.

Brothers or pussy-sharers.

And today would be the day we made the call, before it sent all three of us fucking crazy.

Scrap that.

More fucking crazy.

SIXTY SIX

GRACE

Brett tried, I know he did. Thomas did too – finding a groove alongside me at breakfast while Brett busied himself in the kitchen.

I wanted to tell him to settle down into his seat like the guest he should be, but I didn't. I could feel it from him with every gesture, how much he wanted to help. How much he wanted to find his sense of self at our side.

I wanted to believe he could find it here. That on some fucked-up planet he belonged here alongside us. With us. The three of us forging some crazy three-way *thing* that defied all social conventions but worked all the same.

My sister's texts kept buzzing in my pocket, demanding an update. But I held back right through the morning. That's the first reality check I really got – the prospect of telling Sarah that Thomas was indeed Brett's stepbrother but I was loving him all the same. That in future his cock would be deep alongside my husband's every day from here on in.

But was that any future? Really? Was that the road laid out ahead for us? With kids, in this little slice of paradise we were so desperately trying to carve out a future in?

I'd have managed to convince myself a whole lot better if Brett's face didn't look like death when he joined us in the dining room after the final guests had finished up their fry-ups.

The dawning reality that two in a bed alongside me was doomed to be one too many was enough to hitch my breath in my throat, the pain at losing something I'd enjoyed so much bubbling up to tear me open from the inside out.

"What today?" Thomas asked as Brett slid into the seat at the table next to me, and I saw something so clearly brewing there between them. The younger brother looking to his elder for guidance in a place where there had only been hate and confusion.

Brett's shrug was casual enough to dismiss his own warring emotions.

"I dunno," he said. "We talk about being brothers. We act like brothers. We try to forge some fucking route through this crazy shit fest. I dunno, Tom, we'll work it out."

Tom.

He called him Tom.

And so did I when I spoke again.

"So, Tom," I said with a smile. "Did you sleep alright?"

A nod was all that was forthcoming until he finished up his coffee and shot Brett a stare.

"I slept just fine," he said eventually. "Better than fine."

"Good," I said, and I meant it, despite the compulsive tap of my foot under the table.

Brett felt it. His hand on my knee said it all.

"When do you need to get back to London?" he asked his brother, and Tom's shoulders stiffened.

"Any time," he replied. "No time. It doesn't matter. I've got all I need right here."

Both of us hitched our breaths in unison, but he broke out a grin.

"I meant my laptop," he said. "I have my laptop with me. The world at my fingertips."

And so it was.

Brett made preparations in the bar and I dug into the usual room changes while Thomas grabbed his laptop and busied himself at the same window seat in the dining room he was coming to be a regular presence in. I said hello every time I ferried past him, my own heart warring over the potential outcomes of this crazy dynamic and which way it would likely swing.

I sought out my husband when I heard him in the kitchen, assembling pans on the rack with his face still etched with his own rioting emotions.

"Hey," I said as I wrapped my arms around his neck. "We'll work this out."

"How?" he asked, and I took a taste of his lips before I answered.

"We'll find a way," I told him, hoping I sounded more convincing than I felt inside.

"He's my brother," he hissed, and I nodded, feeling it every bit as much as he did.

Only I didn't. Couldn't. I had no idea how it would feel to discover my father had been lying to me through all living memory.

"Stepbrother," I tossed his way on instinct, but his whole body tensed in my arms.

"*Brother*," he said. "The more I look at him, the more I see Dad."

And there we had it. The verdict of doom in the silence of the room.

It was my turn to tense, and his eyes crashed into mine with a whole world more pain.

"Talk to me," he said. "Tell me what you're thinking."

But how could I? I didn't even know myself. My pussy thought one thing, my brain another, and my heart was living in her own little flurry, wanting more than she could ever have.

"I don't know what I'm thinking," I told him, figuring he'd taken enough lies for the next ten years already.

"I guess that's something we've all got in common," he groaned, and held me tight.

Guests came and went, streaming in and out oblivious to the carnage all around us. I checked in a family with four young kids, and waved off a heavily pregnant woman with her nice young husband in tow. I scrolled through our upcoming bookings and the few chef CVs waiting in my inbox. I tried to function, tried to breathe, tried to convince myself this would all have a happy ending.

Maybe it would.

But I doubted it would be for all three of us, not right here and now.

Maybe not ever.

It was Brett who cooked for us, summoning us both to our own private living space while he laid out freshly caught cod in batter at our modest dining table. The buzzer was on call to ring right through from reception, and it did. Three times running, each time setting *him* running before I had the chance to get to my feet.

"He's finding it tough," Thomas commented when the door closed behind him for the latest mad dash.

"We all are," I told him, and he gave me a nod.

"Some of us have had longer to accept the situation than others."

I shook my head. "None of us have had time to accept this situation," I argued. "There are just different aspects we're having to sift through. None of them are easy. None of them make sense."

But he didn't agree with me. His gaze was firm on mine when I dared to meet his eyes.

"It makes sense to me," he said. "More than the rest of my life ever has."

That was the first real moment I felt it, the danger of loving another man alongside the one I'd given my life to. It was his twinkling eyes. The smirk I'd come to know was hiding a whole tumble of nerves behind his perfect features.

It was in the tension of his shoulders I knew was rife under his shirt. In the way my pussy clenched and fluttered.

And my heart.

It was in my heart.

Strong enough to make me feel sick as the spring of emotion bloomed behind my eyes.

"I'm not sure he'll be able to deal with all of this," I whispered. "Not like this."

He dropped his gaze but his smile didn't falter.

"Maybe none of us will."

I wished more than anything I could argue, my heart finding a route through this that made sense for all of us.

"I need to go back to the city," he said, and I felt my soul cry. "We all need some space to adjust. All of us, Grace. Not just Brett."

I nodded, my fingers reaching out for his and gripping at the most inopportune moment.

Brett barged right through as I squeezed his hand in mine, standing mute for too long before coming back to his half-finished meal. I didn't let go of Thomas, not until it was clear this wasn't some secret gesture he'd uncovered from the shadows.

I was spread wide on a platter, my heart real and true, my motives as pure as they could be with two men flanking me in bed last night.

Thomas cleared his throat before he repeated his statement for the benefit of my husband.

"I'm leaving in the morning," he said. "Work calling."

Brett cleared his throat right back. "I thought you said you had the world at your fingertips."

The other man didn't miss a beat. "The world, yes. My project managers, no. There's something about face to face you can't substitute."

"You can say that again," my husband said, and I prayed he'd argue for more time, for more closeness, for more everything.

He didn't.

"Brothers can use the telephone, right?" he continued. "Email, too. Fuck, even carrier pigeon. The city means nothing, we can still…"

"I'll be back," Tom said, forcing a grin at the iconic phrase.

I wished I could smile right back, but my lips wouldn't move that way.

I wanted to beg them for one more night between them, no matter how desperate it sounded. I wanted to coax them for one more chance to feel the both of them inside me, but I never would. No matter how my slutty little clit begged me to sell out my mind.

We tucked into our dinners in silence, and I kept my tongue at bay, hating myself for even the hint of selfishness threatening to run riot.

I hoped neither of them would see it. That neither of them would ever stand a chance of seeing me the way I was coming to know myself.

But he did see it. Brett.

I saw it in his eyes as he placed his cutlery down on his empty plate and stared right at me.

"One more night," he said. "I guess we should all work out what we need from it. It's worth speaking up in this shit storm, no matter how fucking crazy it sounds."

I never would.

Not now, not ever.

I'd never voice the urges pulsing deep, but it didn't matter.

Because if my husband knew one thing in this hell hole of emotion, it was me. His wife. The woman who'd been at his side since we were old enough to count for something.

His smirk was every bit as confident as his blonde brother's had been when he first rolled up on our doorstep, and it told me, beyond all doubt, that my silence wasn't worth anything, not anymore.

They may have split me open already, but it was Brett who was unravelling my insides without a sound. It felt intrusive.

Addictive.

Strangely horny to feel him digging deep without a word.

"Let's drink," he said. "Let's see if whisky can't set the scene for our final evening, shall we?"

I was burning up before I'd even nodded my agreement.

SIXTY SEVEN

THOMAS

The air was different between us that evening. Tense and tight and laced with the unspoken web of crazy flitting through all of us.

I wanted Grace. He wanted Grace.

Grace wanted us.

I held back from all action, opting for a cold glass of water instead when the whisky bottle came out. The bar was relatively packed for a hotel that was doomed in a few months, people laughing easily at tables nearby while I struggled to keep myself in check.

I didn't trust myself drunk, not tonight.

I didn't trust myself at all, in fact, not with that beautiful woman so close at my side and the words of her husband's father still scorching my inside pocket. As much as I'd have liked a clear route glimmering ahead of us, the reality was a whole world more messy. It was the antithesis of how I chose to structure my life, always looking before leaping, always being certain of the outcome of every move.

I guess that's how come I finally knew I couldn't stay in this place. Not with such emotional chaos running rife through my veins.

My ultimate problem was that I had nothing left to race home to. The wind of bitterness had well and truly left my sails, leaving me cast aimless on a sea of nothing more than chaos.

I needed to find myself, now more than ever. I needed to discover the potential of the boy I'd dismissed as a nobody and finally let him breathe.

I needed to dream. To plan. To let myself feel the ground under my feet for the very first time without charging ahead to some glorified excuse for victory at others' expense.

I needed to say my goodbyes.

Brett didn't employ the same self-restraint as I mustered. The whisky flowed easily through his shot glass, and his words flowed easily along with it. Talk of sports and which ones we could watch together. Talk of barbeques in the summer where I could meet Grace's sister and her two little girls. I grinned along with him, nodding my head at every one of his ideas, not having the sliver of spite left within me required to tear down his optimism.

Grace was quiet. Simmering with the same bursting tension I'd revelled in over my very first visit. Her foot was tapping its crazy rhythm, her smile plastered on wide, even though she wasn't feeling it.

It was only when the final guests left for upstairs that Brett finished up his final shot and slammed his empty glass on the counter.

I stood up from my stool prepared to retreat to my own room for my final evening, just to make the tension more bearable, but his slap was solid on my back when we reached the fork in the road, pressing hard to my spine and guiding me past the staircase with his eyes firmly ahead.

"Last night," he said. "Let's do this."

We held back for Grace to head on by, her eyes glinting with life as she dared a glance back at us.

Fuck me, she was more beautiful in that moment than I'd ever seen her, her hair curled so perfectly from the nape of her neck, her lips dusky pink and begging for the kind of brutal kisses that would leave them swollen.

I wished they'd be mine.

Brett shot me one more blistering stare before his wife dropped to the bed and kicked her shoes off. He was rough with his shirt buttons, drunk fingers more savage than cautious as he tore the clothes from his body.

I took my cufflinks, placing them carefully on the nightstand before taking more concrete action.

"Show me how much you want your husband's cock," I barked at Grace, and she ate him up with the hungry eyes I'd been missing so much since the last time.

She didn't need telling twice.

His dick was hard when she pulled it from his pants, his jaw gritted hard as she sucked it in with her greedy mouth.

I pulled up a chair, a mirror image of the first crazy night I'd spent with their nakedness, my legs crossed at the knee as I reclined back for a decent viewing.

"I don't have fifty fucking grand for you," Brett grunted, and his smile was drunk but real.

"Draw a red line in lipstick if you want it even," I said back with a smirk.

"No sensors," he told me. "You don't need a barrier, Tom. I think my Grace wants us both to pitch in all night long."

He wasn't wrong.

Her eyes were on mine even as she sucked him deep, spluttering around the length of him like the dirty little slut we'd trained her to be.

I hoped I'd remember this for a long fucking time, breathing long and slow as he fucked her pretty throat and she slavered all over him.

"Show her what you've got for her," I told him, and he gave me a nod.

"I'll show her what I've got for her," he responded, and gripped her throat with the same brutality I'd shown him all those nights ago.

He was learning. Every skill I'd learned by heart blooming deep in him through his sportsman's vision. It was a joy to watch him slam his gorgeous wife to the bed and tug her dress down around her perky tits.

My mouth watered at the sight of them. Hungry to clamp down and mark her skin just as he was doing.

I ignored the twitch of the dick in my pants, shifting in my seat as the two people in the room with me found their groove.

They were different. *He* was different. Enough for the both of us combined as he sank into the authority he'd seized with both hands since the recent tornado of shit revelations rocked his world. He'd find himself in himself without question, exploring his own natural dominance through a whole different lens without the flawless illusion of his father to live for himself.

And fail for himself.

Risk himself in ways he'd never dared. Express himself in ways he'd never considered.

I was feeling it too. A whole world waiting out there, calling the whole new person I was becoming through this pain. Pain and hope.

Grace wrapped her legs around her husband's waist, grinding against his naked cock as his mouth ravaged her and his hands pinned her wrists overhead. He was rough enough that she shied away from him, whimpering for more as her body betrayed her. And there she was, the Grace we'd coaxed from the demure woman who'd smiled out through her eyes all these years. The little vixen who tumbled over herself for more. Deeper.

Everything.

Brett didn't look at me as he tugged her knickers to the side and slammed in hard.

I didn't expect him to. Didn't want him to. Didn't even contemplate the possibility of an invite as her body squirmed under his and he ate her up.

His eyes were brutal on hers, his face just an inch away as he whispered obscenities I couldn't make out and didn't need to. She was transfixed, all her focus on the man who was claiming her, balls deep in the cunt that had grown so needy for its fill.

I waited until he pinched her nipples so hard she squealed, rolling her head back against the pressure as his power came to the fore.

I was quiet when I edged the chair backwards and made for the bathroom, waiting until their cursory glance had checked out my destination well enough for them to cast it aside as nothing and return to their pending climax.

I knew there would be another to follow it, and another after that. Their rapture couldn't be contained in one single fuck session, not by a long way. It was raw and ripe. And ready.

Ready for me to say my goodbye.

I flicked on the switch in the bathroom to flood it with light, making sure I let out the noise of the door closing before retreating with backward steps into the shadow of their living room doorway.

And then I ran.

Quickly enough that I couldn't change my mind, taking the stairs to my room three at a time and scooping up just my basic belongings before taking the rear stairs and tossing the essentials in my passenger seat and striking up the ignition.

There was no sign of them when I'd finished scrawling a handwritten note of my own and posted it through the main porch letterbox. The door was firmly closed on the world for the evening when I reversed from my parking space and headed along the coast with a smile on my face.

This time, like the last, I had no idea where I was headed.

Only this time, I didn't care.

SIXTY EIGHT

GRACE

I knew it long before I summoned the ability to call a break.

We both knew it.

The hum of the bathroom extractor fan was still going strong as my husband slammed his cock into my asshole and I ate him up with whimpers too pained to hold back.

I didn't want to hold back. Or him, either.

I wanted everything he had to give. Everything he would always give.

But still my eyes filled up as Brett called a temporary time out with a kiss on my lips. He went to that bathroom door with his breath still ragged, and I watched him there, my heart thumping with more than an easing climax.

"He's gone," he said, and I nodded.

We got ourselves together without another word, slipping into clothes than would count as passable should a guest be wandering. His room was unlocked and empty, the toiletries still piled in the shower room the only real remainder of his presence.

I knew it was done for us, my heart tickling with the undeniable truth that he'd made that call permanently and not just on a whim in the night.

Brett was deep in thought when we trudged down to the reception desk and flicked the light on.

The letter on the doormat spoke more words with its existence than it could possibly contain inside.

To my brother and his dearest wife, it said on the envelope in scrawled writing, not dissimilar to George Foster's

Brett held it close enough so that I could read it too as he tore the envelope open to reveal nothing more than a compliment slip with Thomas Heath's letterhead on the top.

I struggled to hold back tears before my eyes had even focused.

Dearest Brett and his most beautiful Grace,

For all the times I made the wrong call at other people's expense, here is my chance to make the right one. Finally.

Thank you for your hospitality, but this time, as with all others that would exist from this point forward, I really am just one cock too many in your sweet little slice of paradise.

This isn't goodbye, but rather, goodbye for now.

Yours, with love and heartfelt thanks from the heart I swore I would never feel,

Tom.

There was no point holding back tears any longer, not when I read his sign off.

Because my poor husband was already lost to them by then, his chest heaving as he struggled to choke them back.

But I wouldn't let him. I pulled him into arms that were all for him. And as Brett held me tight and sobbed into my shoulder, I loved Thomas Heath more than I ever thought possible for caring enough to drive away.

I just hoped his goodbye really would be for now and not forever.

Luckily for us we had belief where Tom was just finding it.

Belief in love.

Believe in commitment.

Belief in family.

And belief in the man who'd threatened it all, just to set us free.

EPILOGUE

THOMAS
TWELVE MONTHS LATER

Tom,

    My son.

    It's taken me a long time to put that in words. Far longer than I'll ever be able to live with.

One day soon, when these lungs of mine breathe their last and I cross over into whatever fate awaits me in the great beyond, I hope there is at least one angel there to greet me with open ears, just so I can tell them how proud I am of the son I don't deserve.

I don't deserve you, Thomas, nor your forgiveness.

I'm just asking you, please, son. Please give an old man the chance to express how sorry he is for his biggest mistake in his life.

I've been hard on my other son, Brett. Too hard at many times, hoping to instil in him the urge to live his life to the fullest and not make the same mistakes a fool like me made through his own weaknesses.

I could tell you about your mother. About the heartache I felt when she was loving other men, but I won't. There is no excuse that would come close to defending my absence from your world when it mattered.

You see, son, it doesn't make a difference. Blaming other people never does. People can be shit-bags and assholes, but our failures are always our own. Own them, change them, demand more from yourself than a pat on the back and a better luck next time.

I should have owned mine long ago.

I'm sorry I haven't owned them sooner. Believe me, I've wanted to. I just wanted to make sure my Brett found his feet in life before unleashing his disappointment in me. He looks up to me more than he should do, and that's a mantle I carry heavily. I hope you can understand me for striving to father at least one of you boys in the way you deserve.

He's a good lad. A good husband. His wife, Grace, is a gem of a woman too. You'd love her, I'm sure, if only they had the chance to be a family at your side, the way I should've been.

I've followed you eagerly from afar, biting my tongue until the point I dared risk facing my failures. Only, you didn't make any of your own.

I'm proud of you, Tom. Proud of all you've achieved. Proud that you work so hard, push so hard. Aim so high in this world and conquer everything set to topple you.

I'd have loved to reach out before now, but I know how it would look. I know the suspicion you'd hold in your heart about my true motives for breaking that barrier and calling you my own while you are flying so high.

It's not about the money, Thomas. I don't want any money from you. I know I could never reach out now, I've lost my window of ever of holding you close, the way I should have done when you needed me, but I can write this message to you, and hope that you read it when I'm gone.

I don't want anything but your knowledge that there was a man and he loved you, even though he was too weak a fool to say it when he had the chance.

If you read this, please consider building bridges with my Brett.

He should've been your brother, and he would have done you proud. I'm sure you'd love him, just the way I do, and he'd love you right back, the way I do.

Goodbye, son.

Yours with a love you'll never know, and a heart that wishes for nothing more than your awareness of the truth,

Your dad, George.

I know it by heart already, my father's letter. I've kept it in my inside pocket every step of the way around this beautiful globe of ours. Through the sprawling states of the USA while speeding in a growling Mustang, to the sedate canals of a freezing Venice in the heart of winter.

I've seen it all, done it all, and his words have been there every step of the way. Reminding me what it's like to carry regret with you until you die.

I won't be making that mistake myself.

"Hello, Dad," I speak aloud, staring at the sky on this sunny spring morning as the cemetery chirps with life. "I'm pleased today is under more pleasant circumstances than the last."

I drop the white rose onto the green bank of earth and drop my letter down with it.

"It's taken me a while to come back to this place. I needed to find my feet first. Not in a world of handshakes and stocks and shares, but in people. In life. I have you to thank for my awakening." I can't hold back the smile. "Well, you and my brother, of course."

I pull out my latest postcard from my pocket. I've yet to send this one to their sweet slice of heaven. The final one I posted from overseas was from Paris, just a week ago from now. I trusted they were still getting them, a new destination every week with the same short text I'd been sending since driving into the night and out of their life all those months ago.

Thinking of you. Goodbye is not farewell.

Tom x

And a kiss. I always ended it with a honeycomb ice cream kiss.

I hope they are ready for my reappearance one day in the not so distant future. I hope they've missed me even a fraction as much as I've missed them as I've forged my first genuine path in this world, with the boy inside me taking greater gulps of air with every step.

I'm not scared of him now. Not scared of heartbreak or disappointment or putting my newly-discovered heart on the line.

Not scared of love.

Of life.

"They're still down there, Brett and Grace," I tell the dead man under my feet. "An anonymous businessman snapped up the hotel down the coast from them. He got it at a bargain price as well, I hear, since they couldn't get their staffing crisis under control. Rumour has it he's going to turn it into a training centre for disadvantaged youths, but I've heard he's generally quite a cunt, so those rumours aren't running too rife through the city."

I light up a cigar, my first in weeks.

"I'm sorry we never met. I guess we've both got plenty of mistakes we'll carry to our grave. Maybe you'll be waiting for me on the other side and we can shake hands like grown-ups looking to start again." I chance a smile. "Or maybe we'll hate each other for our similarities. Either way, I look forward to it."

I tip my head at a passing couple, my heart pounding at the clench of her fingers in his.

"In the meantime," I continue. "I have some mistakes of my own to rectify. I just hope she's been reading my postcards before she bins them."

I reach out to touch the headstone, no longer hating the name Foster and everything it stands for.

"Goodbye, Dad. I hope Brett and Grace are up the duff by now. I'm hoping there's a little niece or nephew to greet me when I head back down to the coast with my new bride on my arm." I pause to take a final drag on my cigar, only this time I don't drop it onto his grave. "Wish me luck, of course, she might not say yes to me yet. I know I wouldn't."

I laugh at that.

But that doesn't matter, not today.

Winning isn't everything, not anymore.

It's the taking part that counts.

And I'm hoping to take every part of Polly Piper she'll give me.

THE END

ACKNOWLEDGEMENTS

Ok, so, this book turned out to be quite a tale. Considerably longer than I anticipated. I hope you have enjoyed it to this point!

As always, I have some people to thank. *Clears throat*

John Hudspith, my amazing editor. You came through for me all the way. Thank you. Couldn't do this without you. I know I say this time and time again, but it's true.

Letitia Hasser from RBA Designs, for so much more than just the cover this time. This design is all on you, this title is all on you. The initial spark of this story is all on you. Thank you!

To Jon at Read Owl Book Trailers (who also happens to be my other half) – thank you for the amazing trailer, I love it.

Nadège Richards for the beautiful paperback formatting – thank you so much!

My PAs Tracy and Marci – thank you, ladies, always.

Gel, for the amazing teasers – thank you so much for all your hard work.

My author buddies, who have been super amazing on this project – Isabella Starling, Leigh Shen, Willow Winters, Jana Aston, Louise Bay, Sierra Simone, SC Daiko, and especially the enthusiasm and beta reading of my amazing friend, Jo Raven. I love you all!!

Isabella, as always I'm shouting you out for living at ours so much of the time. We love you here. Always. And you sort out my files and make them functional. In short, you are awesome, please keep it up. :D

To all my other author buddies, who make me smile every day. You know who you are by now.

To my beta readers – your enthusiasm means everything. Of course, of note – as always – is the incredible Louise Ramsay, who I always count on so much for early feedback, plus this time the amazing Maxine McCormick – thank you so much!

To my friends, who barely saw me throughout the creation of this book, and who put up with my incessant book talk so patiently. This applies *every* book. Constantly. Lisa and Maria especially. Thank you!

Andy – thanks so much for the hotel conversation. You helped loads. Your insight was really appreciated.

To the bloggers, reviewers, my book group members and all of you amazing people who support my work. I couldn't do this without any of you. I am, and will forever be grateful to all that you do for me.

And to my family – Mum, Dad, Brad and Nan – thank you for being on my side, always.

You are my everything. You too, Misha. Thanks for being my fellow ENFP at the weekends. You rock. :D

ABOUT JADE WEST

Jade has increasingly little to say about herself as time goes on, other than that she is an author, but she's plenty happy with that fact. Living in imaginary realities and having a legitimate excuse is really all she's ever wanted. Jade is as dirty as you'd expect from her novels, and talking smut makes her smile. She lives in the Welsh countryside with a couple of hounds and a guy who's able to cope with her inherent weirdness.

FIND JADE (OR STALK HER – SHE LOVES IT) AT:
www.facebook.com/jadewestauthor
www.twitter.com/jadewestauthor
www.jadewestauthor.com

SIGN UP TO HER NEWSLETTER HERE,
SHE WON'T SPAM YOU AND YOU MAY WIN SOME GOODIES. :)
www.subscribepage.com/jadewest

Printed in Great Britain
by Amazon